PRACTICE MAKES PERFECT

CLODAGH MURPHY

First published in 2014 as *Some Girls Do*. This edition published in Great Britain in 2026 by Boldwood Books Ltd.

Copyright © Clodagh Murphy, 2014

Cover Design by Head Design Ltd.

Cover Images: Shutterstock

The moral right of Clodagh Murphy to be identified as the author of this work has been asserted in accordance with the Copyright, Designs and Patents Act 1988.

All rights reserved. No part of this book may be reproduced in any form or by any electronic or mechanical means, including information storage and retrieval systems, without written permission from the author, except for the use of brief quotations in a book review. This book is a work of fiction and, except in the case of historical fact, any resemblance to actual persons, living or dead, is purely coincidental.

Every effort has been made to obtain the necessary permissions with reference to copyright material, both illustrative and quoted. We apologise for any omissions in this respect and will be pleased to make the appropriate acknowledgements in any future edition.

A CIP catalogue record for this book is available from the British Library.

Paperback ISBN 978-1-80557-802-4

Large Print ISBN 978-1-80557-801-7

Hardback ISBN 978-1-80557-800-0

Trade Paperback ISBN 978-1-80635-069-8

Ebook ISBN 978-1-80557-803-1

Kindle ISBN 978-1-80557-804-8

Audio CD ISBN 978-1-80557-795-9

MP3 CD ISBN 978-1-80557-796-6

Digital audio download ISBN 978-1-80557-799-7

This book is printed on certified sustainable paper. Boldwood Books is dedicated to putting sustainability at the heart of our business. For more information please visit https://www.boldwoodbooks.com/about-us/sustainability/

Boldwood Books Ltd, 23 Bowerdean Street, London, SW6 3TN

www.boldwoodbooks.com

For Jordan and Will, same as it ever was

1

I'll Try Anything Once (but I won't try that)

You never know what's going to end a relationship, do you? People break up for all sorts of reasons: money; infidelity; simply falling out of love; irreconcilable differences, like one of you wanting children when the other doesn't. With me and Mr Handy, it was a disagreement over poo. I wonder if that's a first.

If you'd asked me at the start what would make me end it with Mr Handy, I might have said it would be his cultural snobbery, the annoying habit he had of putting empty containers back in the fridge or that he was very stingy with his kisses during sex. In the beginning, I could see any number of reasons why I might break up with him. Poo was not one of them.

He was a slow burn for me. When we began dating, I didn't think he was a keeper. He was too neat, too serious, too intense. He could be a bit tight with money. But he kept showing up, and eventually he made it into my regular rotation by dint of his persistence and his mad oral skills. He grew on me, and I started to consider going exclusive with him. He was perfect boyfriend material – nice house, good job, lovely chubby cock. And his hands! I've written whole blog posts about his hands. His incredible sense of touch more than made up for the lack of kissing.

But this week I broke up with him over coffee and cake at Starbucks. There were no tears, no recriminations, no bitterness. No one's heart got broken – we weren't in love. But it was sad. We cared deeply about each other and we always had fun times together, both in bed and out of it. We were sad that it was over.

In the end there were irreconcilable differences: he wanted to take a dump on me and I didn't want him to. It may not seem like enough of a reason to finish things. We could probably have compromised, worked around it. But I saw how disappointed he was by my refusal. I could tell that he saw me as his best shot for making this happen. I'm the most adventurous girl he knows – he's told me so many times – and I wondered if that was the reason he'd stuck around. Had he been building up to this all along? When I realised how much the idea excited him, I knew it was time to let him go. Because the point is, we don't have to compromise – either of us. That's the beauty of not being in love.

I'll miss his tongue, the way he would go down on me for hours on end, his snarky commentaries on movies, and most of all, his amazing hands. I hope he can find another girl who will be everything he wants. Someone who can deal with his shit – literally.

As for me, I'm an open-minded person, and I'll try most things. But I won't try that. It's not a turn-on for me, and I don't want to bear the brunt just because some guy failed his—

'Toilet training!'

'Sorry?' Claire's head snapped up as she simultaneously clicked out of her blog. A woman was standing in front of the cash desk, agitated, a toddler grizzling in a buggy beside her.

'I'm looking for a book on toilet training,' the woman said breathlessly, almost hopping from foot to foot, as if she was desperate for the loo herself, while she jiggled the buggy.

'Okay, follow me,' Claire said, jumping up from her seat. 'I'll show you where they are.' As she stepped away from the desk, she glanced back at her computer screen to make sure that her blog was definitely closed. She led the customer across the shop floor to the 'Babies and Parenting' shelves, and pointed out the section devoted to books on toilet training.

'Oh, there are so many.' The woman sighed. 'Which one is the best?'

'Why don't you have a look through them and decide which you think would—'

'I don't have time for browsing. Can't you recommend one?'

'Well, this is very popular,' Claire said, pulling out a book and handing it to her. 'It's got lots of great reader feedback online, and it's recommended by Unholy Mother – you know, the blogger?'

'I don't do mummy blogs,' the woman said, flicking through the pages impatiently and far too rapidly to take anything in.

'Oh, you should read Unholy Mother.' Claire smiled. 'She's hilarious. I don't even have children and I love it. She's done this really funny series of posts recently about toilet training her son that I think you'd find—'

'Yes, well, I *do* have a child and I'm far too busy actually *being* a mother to have time to read about some bint's hilarious escapades with her special little snowflake.'

'Oh... right.' It was on the tip of Claire's tongue to say that Unholy Mother wasn't like the typical mummy blogger, but she thought better of it.

'I'll take it,' the woman said, shoving the book at Claire. Her child had kept up a low-level wail throughout the exchange and cranked it up a notch as they all trooped back to the cash desk.

When she had paid, Claire put the book into a bag and handed it to her customer with a smile.

'Thank you.' The woman tucked it under her arm. 'Do you have a bathroom?' she shouted, over her child, who had now graduated to piercing screams.

'Er... no, sorry. Not for public use, I'm afraid.'

The woman tutted, rolling her eyes. She stuffed the book into the bottom of the buggy and turned towards the door, the child's howls fading as they exited the shop. Yvonne was restocking shelves near the door and held it open for them.

'Another satisfied customer, I see,' Yvonne said, as she joined Claire at the desk. 'What was her problem?'

'She bought a book on toilet training, then asked if we had a loo she could use. I think she wanted to get stuck in right away.'

Yvonne laughed. 'Pity she didn't buy the latest Jamie Oliver. She might have made us lunch if we'd let her use the kitchen.'

'At least she'll bump up my weird-customer score,' Claire said. 'Put it on the chart.'

'It's a tough field this week.' Yvonne pulled a chart from one of the desk drawers. 'You're going to have to up your game if you want to topple the supreme champion,' she said, gesturing to herself with a smug smile. 'I've been top of the league every week since I started here.'

'You have an unfair advantage,' Claire said.

'I do seem to be a bit of a magnet for the unhinged.'

'It's not that you're a magnet for them. You encourage them, so you get all the loony repeat business.'

'I just try to be helpful.'

'Right, like the time that customer was looking for signed copies of Jane Austen's books and you said you could get them for him.' Jane Austen was his wife's favourite author, he had explained, and he wanted them as a gift for her birthday.

'And I did!'

'Yes, signed by *you*. It's fraudulent.'

'No, it's not. I signed them "on behalf of", so it's not like it was forgery.'

Claire rolled her eyes. 'And every time someone comes in trying to find a book they can't remember the title of, you always sell them something.'

'You say that like it's a bad thing. I'm giving them what they want – that's good service.'

'You're a charlatan.'

'You'll miss me when I'm gone.'

It was still a few months away, but she *would* miss Yvonne when she left, Claire thought, as they giggled their way through a quiet morning in the shop. She was only working part-time at Bookends while she was at college, and would leave at the end of the summer, when she was taking a year out to go travelling. Tom, the owner of the shop, would miss her too, much to his own bemusement. Yvonne had never ceased to surprise him since the first day she'd turned up for work, looking like she'd got lost on her way to a *Vogue* fashion shoot. She'd been a vision in cashmere and silk, and the bag clutched under her shoulder would have cost most of Claire's monthly salary. With her smooth blonde hair and flawless skin, she looked like she lived on Evian water and alpine air. Claire and Tom had watched with wary skepticism as she'd taken up her position behind the cash desk, clapped her hands and said, with kindergarten-teacher enthusiasm, 'Right. Let's sell books.' But then she had proceeded to do just that, with breathtaking capability.

Claire had never met an actual trust-fund baby before, but Yvonne was the real deal. Her father, a multi-millionaire who had made his fortune in plastics manufacturing, gave her everything his money could buy – from the pony she'd got when she was ten to the car she'd picked out for her upcoming twenty-first birthday. At first Claire couldn't understand why she was working at all. She certainly didn't need to pay her way through college, and her meagre salary wouldn't cover so much as the tips of her Hobbs shoes or the taxis she regularly got to work when she was running late, which was most days. But she soon came to realise that what Yvonne craved most was her father's attention, and this job was one way of making him sit up and take notice. Yvonne had father issues up the wazoo.

But she was unfailingly good-natured, a cheerful, willing worker and a good laugh, and Claire had grown very fond of her.

'You're still coming on Friday, right?' Yvonne asked.

'Oh yes. Definitely.' Claire made an effort to sound excited about the party. One of Yvonne's friends was opening a new upmarket bar, and Yvonne had asked her to the launch. Claire wasn't really a party person and she wouldn't know anyone else there. For once she wished she had the excuse of needing to keep her mother company, which was her usual fall-back. Yvonne was constantly inviting Claire out, but Claire usually had to turn her down. This Friday, for once, there was nothing stopping her.

'Yay!' Yvonne clapped her hands. 'It's great that your mum's in hospital and you can go out and have a bit of fun.'

'Yeah, brilliant.'

Yvonne gasped, clapping a hand over her mouth. 'Oh God! Sorry. I didn't mean it's great that your mum's in hospital—'

'It's okay,' Claire said, with a reassuring grin. 'I know what you meant. And it *is* nice to be able to go out on a Friday night for a change – even if I do feel a bit guilty that I'm enjoying myself because Mum's in hospital.' Her mother was undergoing hip-replacement surgery.

'Oh, you shouldn't feel guilty. That's not fair. You should be able to go out at the weekend anyway. Why should you always be the one staying home with her?'

'Well, I live with her...'

'Even so, you shouldn't have to give up your social life completely. What about your brothers? Why don't they take a turn sometimes and let you go out?'

'Well, they have kids, so I suppose it's difficult,' she said, without conviction, parroting the excuses her brothers and their wives would make for themselves. It was okay for her to criticise them, but if anyone outside the family did, she automatically leapt to their defense. But neither of them was much help, and Claire sometimes felt she might as well have been an only child. Neil and Ronan were both considerably older than her so she had often felt like one growing up. There were only a couple of years between her brothers, but Claire was what their mother, Espie, termed 'the shakings of the bag', arriving ten years after Neil, the eldest, when Espie was forty and her marriage to their feckless father was stuttering to its end.

'All the more reason,' Yvonne said. 'Your need is greater. You're single – you should be out there having fun and meeting people. They're married. They have kids. Their lives are already over. They'll only be sitting at home watching TV or talking about gardening and... kitchen islands and stuff,' she said, wrinkling her nose. 'They can do that just as easily at your mum's house and give you a break.'

It was nothing Claire hadn't frequently thought, but she didn't want to dwell on it now. 'Anyway, I doubt I'll be meeting anyone on Friday. They'll all be too young for me.'

'Oh, come on, you're not that much older than me.'

Though there were only seven years between them, Claire felt positively ancient next to Yvonne. That was the effect living with a sixty-eight-year-old woman had on her.

'Anyway, there'll be lots of people there. They won't all be my age. Luca's coming,' Yvonne said. 'He's around your age.' Her eyes lit up. 'He might do for you,' she said thoughtfully.

'Please! I don't want your sloppy seconds.'

'Oh, he's not! We went out a couple of times, but I never got jiggy with him in the end.'

'But I thought you told me he had a huge willy?'

'Oh, I've never actually seen it, but you can tell he's got a huge one the minute he walks into a room.'

'Why? Does he pull it after him on a trolley?'

Yvonne laughed. 'No. But no one has that much swagger unless it's backed up by a very large package.'

'So, too much man for you, was he?'

'I think he was. He kind of scares me a bit.'

'But you think he'd be all right for me?'

'Oh, he's not creepy or anything,' Yvonne said hastily. 'But he can be a bit... dark. I suppose he has the artistic temperament. He can be a proper moody bastard.'

'Sounds charming!'

'And he's such a player. I just like them a bit more on the tame side.'

'That's true.' Yvonne usually went for rather fey, borderline effeminate pretty boys, and would spend hours fretting about which side of the metrosexual/gay border they occupied. She was always asking Claire's opinion about whether a straight man would have facials, watch *Strictly Come Dancing* or own a Kylie Minogue CD.

'I think you were right – I only went out with him to piss off Dad.'

'I never said that!'

'But it's what you were thinking.'

Claire smiled guiltily. She had indeed suspected that Yvonne had only ever been interested in Luca for his shock value. She could guess Yvonne's uptight, stuck-up father would consider him wildly unsuitable boyfriend material for his precious only daughter. An unemployed, permanently broke artist, he apparently lived in squalor in a notoriously rough area of the inner city.

'And you were right,' Yvonne said. 'See? You're so wise. That's the advantage of age.'

'Hey, a minute ago you were saying I wasn't much older than you.'

'Well, you're older in wisdom.'

'Anyway, if you couldn't handle Luca, what makes you think I could?' Claire might have been older in years – and even in wisdom – but she knew that Yvonne had far more experience than her when it came to men.

'I have complete faith in you,' Yvonne said airily.

'Seriously, Yvonne, you know I'm out of practice. Don't you think I should start off with someone a bit easier?'

Claire's social life had taken a nosedive three years ago when she'd moved home to look after her mother, and somehow she'd never managed to kick-start it again. She still couldn't understand how she had let herself get into such a rut, but time had gone by so quickly. Suddenly she'd realised she hadn't been on a single date since she'd returned to Ireland. And the longer it went on, the harder it was to change anything. She felt like such a fuddy-duddy, compared to Yvonne, her life so circumscribed. When she had been Yvonne's age life had seemed full of possibilities. Studying in Edinburgh, she'd had a nice circle of friends, gone on dates… It all seemed like a lifetime ago now.

'Luca might be just what you need,' Yvonne said, her eyes bright. 'Dive in at the deep end. I mean, you don't have much time, do you? Your mother isn't going to be laid up for ever.'

'No, that's true. All good things must come to an end,' Claire said drily.

'Oh, you know what I mean.'

'Well, I'll do my best.'

'Still, maybe you're right – from nought to Luca might be a bit too much. But there'll be lots of cute guys to choose from. Don't worry, you won't go home empty-handed.'

It sounded more like a threat than a promise. Claire was dreading this party more by the minute. She was relieved when Tom emerged from the back room where he had been doing the ordering and paperwork.

'How's your mother, Claire?' he asked, as he joined them.

'She's fine. I called the hospital and she's over the operation, back on the ward.'

'Glad to hear it. She'll be there for a few more days, I suppose?'

'Yeah, they're keeping her in for two or three days, and then she has four weeks in a convalescent home.'

'Oh, that's great. It'll be a nice break for you,' Tom said. 'Why don't you go early today? You can visit her and still get home at a decent hour.'

'Are you sure?'

'Positive. Yvonne and I can cope with the hordes,' he said, indicating the lone customer he had passed earlier, who was browsing the travel shelves. 'Can't we, Yvonne?'

'Absolutely!'

'Okay, thanks.' Claire smiled gratefully at him.

'Oh, look! He's getting away!' Yvonne wailed as the customer headed for the door.

'He was looking for guides to Bolivia,' Tom said. 'We don't have any.'

'But we've got Chile!' Yvonne said, already moving from behind the desk to chase after the man. 'I hear that's *much* nicer.'

'She's amazing, isn't she?' Tom said admiringly, as Yvonne accosted the man at the door and led him gently back towards the travel section. 'Born to sell.'

'No one goes home empty-handed...'

2

Claire breathed a contented sigh as she let herself into the house that evening having paid a visit to the hospital on the way home. Her mother was still groggy after the anaesthetic so she hadn't stayed long, but now that she knew the operation had gone well, she could relax and enjoy the rare luxury of having the house to herself. She didn't like to admit it to Yvonne or Tom – she felt guilty acknowledging it to herself – but it was nice to have the freedom to be spontaneous and to please herself, with no one else to answer to or worry about.

Her mother's health had been so bad over the past year – hardly a month had gone by without some incident. Claire had come to dread getting a phone call at work to tell her that Espie had been rushed to hospital, and as she turned the corner into their road each evening after work, she would find herself automatically checking for an ambulance outside their door. It was a relief to know that her mother would be surrounded by medical staff for the next few weeks, and if anything happened, she was in the right place.

Claire had enjoyed living alone when she was at university, and it was nice to have the freedom and independence of her single life again, if only for a short while. Of course, things were different now. When she was a student, all her friends had been footloose, and there was always someone to ring up on the spur of the moment to go for a drink or see a movie. But she had left her university friends behind when she moved home, and she had lost touch with most of her old schoolmates. Though she had loved Edinburgh, she sometimes wished she had gone to university in Dublin: now she would have had college friends living nearby. Lisa, her best friend since childhood, had moved to Canada at the start of the year, and though they emailed and Skyped regularly, Claire missed having her around. Other friends were pairing up, so she saw them less and less, and over the last few years her circle had shrunk to the point where it was almost non-existent.

Nowadays she did most of her socialising online. She chatted to people on Twitter and Facebook, most of whom she'd never met, and the closest thing she had to a sex life was writing her blog, 'Scenes of a Sexual Nature', in which she lived vicariously through the erotic adventures of her alter ego. It was a quiet, almost nun-like existence for a girl of her age, and from time to time she worried that she was becoming a freakish loner. Even her mother occasionally suggested that she should be out enjoying herself with people her own age, meeting men, falling in love and having adventures. But Claire had never been the type for adventures. She hated nightclubs and was content to spend quiet nights in reading, chatting to her online friends or watching television with her mother. Besides, her dismal social life gave her more time to devote to writing and blogging. Sometimes when she thought about the future, she feared that life had left her behind and she would never catch up. The idea scared her, but she tried not to dwell on it too much, and mostly she was happy with things as they were.

But it was very different from the life she had envisaged for herself – a life that had seemed to be rolling out in front of her just three years ago. After studying English literature, followed by an MA in creative writing, she had been planning to move to London and get an entry-level job in publishing. She had been looking forward to finding work and a boyfriend, starting a career... and then she had got the call that changed everything. Her heart still leapt into her mouth whenever she remembered the night Ronan had rung to tell her their mother had been rushed to hospital with heart failure. Claire had dashed home, not knowing what she would find. Espie had pulled through, but tests revealed a heart condition that needed constant monitoring and care. Despite her mother's protests that she was fine living alone, Claire would never have felt easy about it and, besides, she wanted to be on hand in case her mother had another crisis.

At first she had tried to find a job in publishing, but if they were hard to come by in London, they were even scarcer in Dublin. So, determined to make the most of her circumstances, she had decided to shelve the idea for a while, get a relatively undemanding job, and concentrate instead on her writing. All her life she had dreamt of being a writer, so it looked like a satisfactory Plan B. She had taken the job at Bookends, intending to devote all her free time to her novel.

It hadn't worked out like that, though. Between her job and her mother, she had found she didn't have as much time to herself as she'd hoped, and progress on the novel was slow and patchy. Then, a couple of years ago, she had written an erotic piece as an exercise for a creative writing class. She had enjoyed it so much that she had set up the blog to practice sustaining a voice convincingly – as well as to give herself an outlet for her creativity that didn't demand as much of her time.

She hadn't expected it to be so successful, but the feedback had been gratifyingly enthusiastic from the start and spurred her on to continue. Now it was one of the most widely read and popular sex blogs on the net. It was fun to write, and its success was a great source of pride and satisfaction. She loved getting an instant response to something she had written, and the way her followers engaged with her was a tribute to how completely she had been able to inhabit her character, the anonymous NiceGirl. Her 'About Me' set out her mission statement:

> I'm not a slut or a skank, just a nice girl who likes sex. Because nice girls do.

NiceGirl had her own Twitter and Facebook accounts, with thousands of friends and followers. Claire often wondered what they would think if they discovered the reality – a twenty-eight-year-old woman who lived at home with her mother and had had sex only a few times in her life. Even then she hadn't been sure what she was doing.

They would probably think she had all the hallmarks of a serial killer, she thought wryly, as she settled on the sofa with a glass of wine and opened up her laptop. There was a long, newsy email from Lisa, who was having a ball in Toronto. Claire enjoyed reading about her friend's adventures. If things had been different, they would have gone to Canada together. Instead, she was in the same old rut, and when she tried to dredge up some news to put in a reply, she couldn't think of a single thing.

She put the email aside to reply to later, and settled down to finish the blog post she had started at work today. When she had published it, she logged onto Twitter as @NiceGirl and posted the link to it with the message:

In which I talk about shitty break-ups… literally.

Scrolling down her timeline, reading through recent tweets, she saw that Mark Bell was around. A well-known London publisher, he was young, handsome and hugely influential, and Claire knew she wasn't alone in having a massive crush on him. He was the pin-up of London publishing, and had caused quite a flurry of excitement among the female members of her class when he had given a seminar on her MA course. As @NiceGirl, she had struck up an online friendship with him, and she loved their flirty, sparky relationship. He was a big fan of her blog, which was enormously flattering coming from someone of his stature in the publishing world, whose opinion she rated highly. She flicked back and forth between her blog and Twitter as the comments started rolling in on both, and it wasn't long before Mark tweeted her.

PublisherMark @NiceGirl Hello you! So, what are you wearing?

This had been a running joke between them since she had done a couple of posts on phone sex.

NiceGirl @PublisherMark Isn't this a bit public for that sort of thing?
PublisherMark @NiceGirl Thought we could combine phone sex & exhibitionism by doing it in public on Twitter.
NiceGirl @PublisherMark Two of my favourite things! What are *you* wearing?
PublisherMark @NiceGirl Necktie.
NiceGirl @PublisherMark Nothing else?
PublisherMark @NiceGirl It's dress-down Tuesday here.
NiceGirl @PublisherMark I bet your staff appreciate that.

PublisherMark @NiceGirl My rod and staff are delighted. They enjoy the freedom.

Claire giggled and took a sip of her wine.

PublisherMark @NiceGirl Actually, I was working at home today. But the cat likes it.
NiceGirl @PublisherMark How is the cat?
PublisherMark @NiceGirl She's great. Very feline.
NiceGirl @PublisherMark Huh! Typical cat.
PublisherMark @NiceGirl You never told me what you're wearing.
NiceGirl @PublisherMark A big smile.
PublisherMark @NiceGirl Did you wear that for me?
NiceGirl @PublisherMark Of course. I know it's your favourite.
Locksie @PublisherMark @NiceGirl Oh, get a room, you two!

Emma Locke, a colleague of Mark's and a mutual Twitter friend was @Locksie.

PublisherMark @NiceGirl @Locksie Don't pay any attention to her. Just jealous because we're burning up Twitter with our smokin' hot chemistry.
NiceGirl @PublisherMark We'll have to get a smoking room, then.
PublisherMark @NiceGirl Or we could get steamy in a steam room. Sorry about Mr Handy, by the way.
NiceGirl @PublisherMark Oh well, better to be the dumper than the dumped on.
PublisherMark @NiceGirl I never thought he was right for you anyway. Seemed like a bit of a shit.
NiceGirl @PublisherMark He was full of it all right. Very anal.
PublisherMark @NiceGirl So, about that room…
NiceGirl @PublisherMark I don't know. How would your cat feel about that?
PublisherMark @NiceGirl She's not the jealous type. We have a very open relationship.
NiceGirl @PublisherMark Really?

PublisherMark @NiceGirl Yeah. I suspect she already has someone else on the go.
NiceGirl @PublisherMark Comes home smelling of another cat?
PublisherMark @NiceGirl Doesn't come home at all some nights. Always out catting around. *Sniff*
NiceGirl @PublisherMark She doesn't deserve you.
PublisherMark @NiceGirl Well, I'm open to offers. You sound like a nice girl…
NiceGirl @PublisherMark Hey, 'nice' is my middle name. Actually, it's my first name.

Claire had another sip of wine and relaxed back against the sofa, feeling warm and tingly from their flirting. This was so much more fun than spending the night in a packed, noisy bar, random guys hitting on her with cheesy lines. Okay, there wasn't even the chance of a snog but the upside of that was that she didn't have to endure the tedium of standing around for hours in uncomfortable shoes, bored to death, shouting herself hoarse to be heard over pounding music. Chatting to Mark, she felt she was experiencing a little bit of the London literary life she had always dreamt of. She was grateful that the internet gave her access to it in some small way, but it also made her yearn for the real thing – socialising with people who cared about the same things as she did and shared the same interests, finding a boyfriend who belonged to that world, maybe meeting Mark himself…

She drifted away from Twitter to reply to some comments on her blog, and she was in the middle of typing a reply to one when a direct message popped up on Twitter. Her heart skipped a beat when she saw it was from Mark and she felt a little spark of pleasure, almost as if he had touched her.

PublisherMark Hi! Could we meet up IRL? I have a proposition for you.

Claire's heart was pounding as she read the message. She felt excited and a little nervous. She had never expected their flirting to carry through into real life. Had he really meant it about getting that room, she wondered, simultaneously thrilled and appalled. It took her a while to decide on a noncommittal response.

NiceGirl What sort of proposition?

PublisherMark It's about your blog. Would like to discuss doing a book. DM me your email address if you're interested.

Claire experienced a fleeting twinge of disappointment, but it was quickly replaced by elation. Mark was interested in turning her blog into a book. This could be huge! It was her dream to be a published author. Maybe Mark was about to make her dream come true.

She sent him the anonymous email address she used for blog purposes, and then she waited. She had expected him to email her immediately, but the minutes ticked by and nothing appeared in her inbox. He seemed to have disappeared from Twitter. She scrolled back through her timeline and found that his last tweet had been when he was chatting to her. She would just have to be patient, she thought, trying to busy herself with replying to comments on her blog and chatting to other people on Twitter and Facebook. Finally, she decided to step away from the computer for a while, and went to the kitchen to make dinner: a watched inbox never delivered.

She had just made sauce and put pasta on to cook when she heard the email alert on her laptop and raced back to the sofa. It was from Mark with the subject:

Proposition

She was almost afraid to read it, hesitating for a few seconds before clicking it open.

Hi, NiceGirl,

It was good to chat this evening, and thanks for the email address. Sorry for the delay in getting back to you. I was meeting some friends on the Heath for a run.

So, here's the thing. As you know, I'm a big fan of your blog, and I'd love to publish a book based on it, if you'd be interested in doing that. I think we could sell a lot of copies. Perhaps we could meet up to discuss it, if you're willing to reveal your true identity. It would be great to meet you in person.

Hoping to hear from you,

Mark x

Claire scanned the email rapidly, barely able to take in what it said. Then she read it again, analysing every word and nuance. The tone was less chummy and a little more formal than when they were chatting on Twitter, which was only to be expected when he was contacting her in a professional capacity. But he had signed off with a kiss, and there was nothing proper or professional about that. She was going to meet him *in the flesh* – and he was interested in offering her a book deal! She squealed with delight, hugging herself as she read the message again. Then she jumped up and did a little dance around the living room, glad her mother wasn't there to witness it. There was no way she'd have been able to explain her behaviour, and it was nice to celebrate a little, even if she was alone. She poured herself some more wine and raised the glass to her laptop in a toast, then sat back down and composed herself to type a reply.

Hi Mark,
 I would love to do a book based on the blog. It would be a dream come true for me! It would be great to meet you in person. I'm in Dublin (Ireland, not Ohio). But I would be happy to come to London to meet you, if that suits.
 Thank you! You've made my day/week/year!
 All the best,
 NiceGirl x

She agonised for ages about how to sign off – should she use her real name, or sign off with a kiss like he had. In the end, she decided to hold off revealing her true identity, at least until they had hammered out the details a bit more. But she didn't want to seem stand-offish, so she went for the kiss. A couple of minutes later, a reply came back.

Great! Would like to meet up sooner rather than later. I'll be in Dublin in the next couple of weeks. Not sure of the exact date yet, but I'll let you know as soon as I have it and we can arrange where and when to meet. Aren't you going to tell me your real name? And how will I recognise you? Or are you really a cartoon?

Claire smiled. Her avatar was a sexy cartoon woman. She replied:

I'll tell you my real name when we meet. And I know what you look like – I'll find you.

When they had emailed their goodbyes back and forth, Claire flopped back on the sofa, unable to settle to anything. She was so keyed up, longing to tell someone and go out to celebrate. But there was no one she could tell – at least, not yet. Catherine, the only person who knew about her blog, was on holiday. She would just have to keep it to herself for the moment. She went into the kitchen, found a bottle of cava in the fridge and opened it. When she had poured herself a glass, she finished making her dinner and sat down at the table. She would usually have turned on the television or read a book if she was eating alone, but tonight she did neither, enjoying the peace and quiet so she could absorb her news.

It was only later, after she had drunk half the bottle of cava, that worry set in. She was going to have to come out from behind her avatar and meet Mark face-to-face. She was nothing like the sassy sex bomb he would be expecting, and he'd probably be seriously disillusioned when he discovered she was just an ordinary girl with zero seduction skills. Maybe he wouldn't even want to publish the book when he met her.

She needed a makeover, and fast. She didn't have anything in her wardrobe remotely suitable for impersonating her alter ego. And she was meeting Mark in the next couple of weeks. She hadn't much time.

3

As she got ready to go out on Friday, Claire found herself wishing she could stay at home, open a bottle of wine, get a takeaway and spend the evening curled up on the sofa. The weather wasn't helping her resolve. It had started raining heavily on her way home from work, and since then it had turned into a newsworthy downpour that was already causing traffic chaos, making the sofa more appealing than ever.

But it was kind of Yvonne to ask her, and she felt she should make the effort – not just for Yvonne's sake but for her own too. She needed to push herself out of her comfort zone. And you couldn't let a bit of rain stop you going out – not when you lived in Ireland.

Her mother had been moved to the nursing home that morning, so she should take the opportunity to go out and spend a night with people her own age – or at least in the same ballpark.

As a concession to her comfort, she decided to take the car. That way she could escape whenever she wanted to, and wouldn't have to depend on public transport or wait for a lift from someone else. So, before she could talk herself out of it, she pulled on her wellingtons, put her shoes into a bag and splashed outside.

The Zone Bar was heaving when she arrived, and her heart sank. How could she have forgotten how much she hated this sort of thing? She searched the crowd for Yvonne and saw her surrounded by a group of solid, ruddy-faced young guys and tanned, waif-like girls in spindly heels and tiny dresses.

Even though she had made an effort, she felt dowdy and out of place among this glitzy throng with their sheen of wealth and privilege. They had the glow that money bestowed, from their subtly highlighted hair to their expertly manicured fingers. She felt as if she had wandered onto the set of *Made in Chelsea* by mistake. Her eyes darted to the door. Was it too late to make her escape? She could tell Yvonne that something had come up at the last minute – some crisis with her mother or a problem with the car. But even as she thought it, Yvonne spotted her, waving at her from across the bar. She sighed, pulling off her coat. She would just have to grin and bear it, she thought, forcing a smile onto her face. Maybe it wouldn't be so bad.

'Hi!' Yvonne beamed, enveloping her in a hug. She was towering over Claire in a pair of vertiginous heels, and wearing a spangly micro mini that seemed to make her legs go on for ever. 'I'm so glad you could make it! Lots of people have got stuck because of the rain.'

Damn! Why hadn't she thought of that?

'This is Ivan,' Yvonne said, putting her arm around the guy beside her – a thin, cool-looking boy with streaky blond hair. He wore wire-rimmed glasses, and a little silver cross dangled from one ear. 'It's his bar.'

'Oh, congratulations!' Claire smiled at him. 'Great place!'

'Thanks,' he said, shaking her hand. 'Thanks for coming. Have a cocktail.' He waved over a waiter with a tray of turquoise drinks. 'It's the house specialty.'

'They're totally yum,' Yvonne enthused, swapping her empty glass for another.

'Oh, I can't, thanks,' Claire said. 'I'm driving.'

'Oh. Well, have a mineral water, then.' He beckoned another waiter with a tray of glasses and Claire grabbed one.

'Thanks. Well, here's to your new venture!' she said, saluting him, then gulping some water. Ugh! She could have done with a cocktail. It was nice to have the freedom of her car, but the downside was that she couldn't have a drink to take the edge off her nerves.

Yvonne introduced her to the rest of the group – Fionn, Leah, Philip and Chloë.

'What do you do?' Philip, the guy beside her, asked.

'I work in the same bookshop as Yvonne,' Claire said. 'That's how I know her.'

'Ah, right. Are you studying?'

'No.'

Philip looked at her expectantly.

'I work full-time in the bookshop,' she explained.

'Oh, okay.' Philip nodded. 'You own it?'

'No, I just work there.'

'Oh, right.' Philip seemed perplexed by this.

'But she wants to be a writer,' Yvonne piped up. 'Don't you?'

'Well, yes.' Claire blushed. 'But that might never happen.' Clearly, having an ordinary job wasn't the done thing with this crowd.

'What sort of stuff do you write?'

'I'm working on a novel for teenagers.'

'Ah! So you're going to be the next J. K. Rowling?' Philip smiled knowingly.

'Um, yeah... fingers crossed,' Claire said weakly.

'Come and sit down for a minute,' Yvonne said, grabbing Claire's arm and leading her to a shell-shaped turquoise sofa. 'What do you think of Ivan?' she asked, plonking her drink on a low, chocolate-coloured table in front of them.

'He seems... nice,' Claire said warily, hoping Yvonne wasn't going to try to set them up.

'What about the earring? Is it on the side that means you're gay? I can never remember.'

Claire looked across the bar at him. 'No, I'm pretty sure it's the other one,' she said, realising with relief that Yvonne herself was interested in Ivan.

'The bar is nice, isn't it?'

'It's lovely.'

'He designed it all himself,' Yvonne said. 'He did the décor and everything. Do you think that's a bit girly?'

Claire laughed. 'No. He's got great taste,' she said, stroking the plush fabric of the sofa. 'But that doesn't mean he's gay. Anyway, why don't you just go for it? You'll find out soon enough if he is.'

'He might be in denial.' Yvonne poked her straw around in her drink.

'Then I don't think he'd go with the earring and play up his interior-decorating skills.'

'True!' Yvonne brightened. 'You talk sense, O Wise One. Thank you.'

Yvonne's friends soon gravitated towards the sofa, and they were joined by everyone except Ivan, who was working the room. Claire found herself having to explain her position as a bookshop assistant to each of them in turn, meeting with blank incomprehension every time.

'But... how *old* are you?' Leah asked her pointedly.

They all seemed to own chic shops or were hatching little start-up companies, playing entrepreneur on Daddy's money. Claire sipped her water as the inane chatter went on around her, wishing once again she had something stronger.

'Why did you have to invite that fucking pikey, Yvonne?' Philip said suddenly, glowering across the bar.

'Luca is not a pikey,' Yvonne said, as Claire followed Philip's gaze to another turquoise sofa on the far side of the bar where a dark-haired man was just visible between two very pretty blondes. One sat on his lap, her crotch-length mini riding up while his hand rested casually on her tanned skinny thigh. Claire was relieved to see that she was wearing underwear. The other was trying to get his attention with a frantic combination of hair-flicking and boob-shimmying.

'How do you know?' Fionn said. 'Christ knows who his parents are. He could be 100 per cent pure-bred gypsy for all you know.'

'Anyway, we know he's Romanian,' Philip said.

'Luca's no more Romanian than I am,' Yvonne said. 'He grew up here. He went to the same school as you, Fionn. He's as Irish as the rest of us.'

'You can take the boy out of Romania...' Philip said sulkily. 'What's Aisling doing with him, anyway?'

'Trying to get into his jocks, by the look of it.' Fionn smirked, turning to him. 'Are they the same lips she kisses you with?'

'Never again.'

'Don't pay any attention,' Leah said soothingly, putting a hand on Philip's knee. 'Aisling's just doing it to make you jealous. Don't let her get to you.'

'Round one to Aisling, I think,' Fionn said, watching as the hair-flicker gave up and stalked off. Seconds later the girl on Luca's lap peeled herself off and headed for the bar.

'Now's our chance,' Yvonne said, grabbing Claire's hand and pulling her up. 'Come on and I'll introduce you.'

Claire had no desire to be introduced to Luca, but she jumped at the chance to escape from Philip and the rest of them. Another minute with that lot and her head would explode.

'Sorry about Philip,' Yvonne said. 'He's not usually that bad. He's just pissed off because Aisling's sort of his girlfriend – she's the one who was sitting on Luca's lap.'

'Yeah, I gathered.'

'Luca!' Yvonne beamed, stopping in front of the sofa. 'Hi. This is my friend, Claire. She works at the bookshop with me.'

'Hi, Claire.'

Claire had never felt so thoroughly checked out as Luca's eyes raked over her. They were nice eyes, dark brown and wide apart, and there was something pleasingly feline about the shape of his face, framed by a mop of dark brown curls. He was very handsome in a rugged sort of way, but he lacked the polished, robust look of most of Yvonne's friends. His eyes were weary, and there was an unhealthy sheen to his skin. Still, he seemed interesting and real, like someone with stories to tell, and he made the other guys here look bland and insipid. He was wearing a threadbare black jumper, faded black jeans and a pair of battered black boots.

'Claire, this is Luca,' Yvonne said, flopping onto the sofa beside him and waving Claire to the seat at his other side. Claire perched on the edge not wanting to look like one of his groupies.

'What are you doing with Aisling Wilson?' Yvonne asked him. 'She's such a tart.'

'You say that like it's a bad thing.' Luca smiled wickedly.

'Honestly, I don't know what you see in her.'

'Well, she can do the splits. So there's that.'

'Oh, you're disgusting.' Yvonne punched him playfully in the arm.

He grinned. 'I like girls with low standards. So sue me.'

'Ooh, food!' Yvonne squealed, as a waiter appeared with a large tray of canapés. 'Great! I'm starving.'

'Me too,' Claire said, loading a napkin with a prawn on a cocktail stick and a little filo tart before the waiter whisked the tray away. She ate them each in one bite and was still starving.

'These prawns are great,' Yvonne enthused.

'They're very small,' Luca said, popping one into his mouth.

'Oh, Ivan wants me!' Yvonne exclaimed. He was beckoning to her from across the bar. 'Mind if I leave you two on your own for a bit?' she asked, jumping up.

'No,' Claire said, though she really didn't want to be alone with Luca. She found his raw sexuality intimidating.

'Knock him dead,' Luca said, lying against the arm of the sofa, pulling one leg up on the cushions and stretching the other out in front of him so that he was sprawled across Yvonne's space. Claire clutched her drink with both hands, leaning forward on her knees, horribly aware of Luca's scrutiny.

He had man-whore written all over him, she thought crossly. He was obviously the type of guy who couldn't meet a female without contemplating sex. Even though the bar was full of glamorous, sexy girls, he still couldn't resist giving her the once-over. Self-conscious, she racked her brain for something to say to distract him.

'Yvonne tells me you're an artist.'

'Yeah.'

'What kind of art do you do?'

'Painting,' he said, in a bored voice.

'Oh. What kind of paintings?' God, listen to yourself, Claire thought. You sound like the Queen trying to chat to one of her subjects. Next you'll be asking him if he had far to come.

'Big ones,' he said.

'Oh, that's...' She tailed off, nodding miserably.

'Yeah, really big. Oil paintings mostly. The kind no one wants to buy.'

'Right,' she said, feeling rebuked. Okay, so she wasn't good at small talk, but he didn't have to be so rude. Did he have to make it so obvious that he couldn't be arsed even talking to her for a few minutes? She didn't imagine that blonde's conversation had been scintillating either, but she'd seen the indulgent way he'd been gazing at her.

'And, no, I'm not the next Damien Hirst, or whatever other living artist you happen to have heard of. I don't own a gallery, and I'm not really a graphic designer or advertising creative who paints in his spare time.'

'Well, at least you've cleared that up,' she said stiffly, brushing imaginary crumbs from her dress. 'Because they were definitely going to be my next three questions.'

He raised an eyebrow. 'Well, if they weren't, it'd be a first for this evening. I'm not minted either, by the way.'

'I can tell,' she said, casting a scathing glance at him. *Don't sink to his level of rudeness.*

'Hey,' he said, with a laugh. 'How do you know I'm not just an eccentric millionaire who dresses like a bum for shits and giggles?'

She shook her head. 'I don't think Yvonne would have gone out with you if you were a millionaire. You're not her type.'

'No, Yvonne likes the pretty boys,' he said, looking across the room at Yvonne and Ivan. 'Not that I'm saying *I'm* not pretty.'

'Of course not.'

'So you think Yvonne was with me for my lack of money? She was using me to get at Daddy?'

Claire got the impression the idea wasn't new to him. 'Sorry.'

He shrugged. 'No biggie. We both got what we wanted out of it.'

Claire raised an eyebrow. He was implying that he had got sex, and she knew for a fact that wasn't true. 'Yvonne's not a bad person,' she said. 'She just has Daddy issues.'

'Yeah, I got that. Yvonne's all right. She's the best of *this* bunch, that's for sure,' he said, looking around.

Claire struggled to come up with something else to say, but drew a blank. She was relieved when she saw the leggy blonde returning from the bar with a couple of drinks. 'Oh, your, um... friend is coming back,' she said, getting up.

'Hey, you don't have to go.' Luca shifted so he only took up one corner of the sofa and there was room for three again.

'I'm in her seat.'

'Hardly. She was sitting on me.'

'Well, three's a crowd so...' Claire picked up her empty glass. 'I need another drink anyway,' she said, wiggling it around. 'It was nice to meet you.'

She turned on her heel, relieved to get away from him. Forcing what she hoped was a natural-looking smile onto her face, she marched up to the bar and asked for another glass of mineral water, trying to appear confident and nonchalant. She shouldn't have been so quick to ditch Luca, she thought, her eyes straying back to the sofa, where the blonde was making strenuous efforts to get back onto his lap. Just then, his eyes met Claire's. He gave her a little smile that was almost sympathetic. Claire looked away again quickly. She stood at the bar for a while, sipping her water. God, this was her idea of hell.

How much longer before she could reasonably call it a night? Maybe she could fill in some time in the loo...

'Claire!' Yvonne rushed up to her, Philip and Fionn in tow. 'We're all going on to a club after this. Will you come?'

'Oh, not tonight. I really have to go soon,' Claire said, glancing at her watch. 'I've got work in the morning, remember?'

'Oh, pooh.' Yvonne pouted. She looked over Claire's shoulder. 'Luca. You're not leaving already?'

Claire turned to see Luca behind her. He was on his own.

'We're going to a club later. Come with us,' Yvonne pleaded.

'No, I'm off home.'

'Alone?' Yvonne raised her eyebrows.

'Yeah, I'm beat. And broke.'

'How are you going to get home?' Yvonne glanced towards the large windows. Rain was still thundering down outside.

Luca shrugged. 'I'll walk.'

'You can't! You'll drown. And public transport has pretty much broken down. Get a cab.'

'Fine, I'll get a cab.'

Yvonne leant closer to him and whispered, 'Do you need some money?' Not quietly enough, though, because everyone heard.

'For fuck's sake!' Philip huffed, staring disdainfully at Luca. 'See what I mean?' he mumbled to Fionn. 'Fucking beggar, like the rest of them.'

Luca gave him a hard look. 'What did you say?'

'Nothing,' Philip mumbled sullenly.

'I'm fine, thanks,' Luca said to Yvonne. 'I can manage cab fare.' He leant in and kissed Yvonne, nodded to Claire, and left.

'Why do you have to be such an arsehole, Philip?' Yvonne fumed.

'Everything okay?' Ivan asked, coming over and frowning at Yvonne in concern.

'Philip's being a complete dick,' Yvonne said.

'What's he doing?' Ivan looked sternly at Philip.

'He was being racist and saying horrible things about Luca.'

'That's not cool, bro,' Ivan told him.

'I know.'

'Come on, man. I know you're upset about Aisling, but don't be a prick and take it out on everyone else. You should apologise to Yvonne and Claire.'

Philip sighed heavily. 'I'm sorry,' he said. 'I was out of order.' He seemed genuinely contrite and ashamed.

'That's okay,' Yvonne said.

He looked at Claire hopefully. She wasn't entirely convinced. That stuff hadn't come out of nowhere. But she never had to see Philip again, so she nodded acceptance.

'We're going on to a club later, if you want to come?' Fionn said to Ivan.

'Really?' Ivan turned to Yvonne. 'Are you going too?'

She nodded.

'Will you wait until I'm finished up here and I'll go with you? I have to stay to the end.'

'Of course.' Yvonne's face lit up.

'I'll see you guys later, then,' Ivan said, as Philip and Fionn drifted off.

'I should go,' Claire said. 'Traffic's going to be a nightmare, and God knows how long it'll take me to get home.'

'Okay,' Yvonne said, pulling Claire into a hug. 'See you on Monday.'

'Ivan's lovely. You should go for it,' Claire murmured in Yvonne's ear, then made for the exit.

Well, at least it was over, she thought, as she got into her car. She glanced at the clock on the dash. It was only ten. If the traffic wasn't too bad, she would have still have time to eat and watch some TV before bed.

4

The rain was coming down in sheets, gushing from overflow pipes and pouring onto the pavements, forming huge puddles and filling Luca's leaky boots as he trudged along. He had been up until four in the morning, working on a piece, and he was so fucking tired he could barely lift his feet. The hard concrete of the pavement even started to look inviting, and he was almost tempted to lie down on it, curl up and close his eyes. He couldn't get any wetter than he was already. If he'd been heading towards warmth and comfort, he might have had the energy to keep going, but the prospect of his cold, dismal flat didn't offer much incentive.

He shouldn't have bothered coming out tonight, he thought, as he squelched through puddles. It had been a complete waste of time. He'd thought he would at least get something to eat, but those pathetic canapés wouldn't have fed a bird and he was starving. His stomach was hollow and his saturated clothes clung to him. He was so miserable, he wanted to cry. He should have ignored that stupid wanker Philip and let Yvonne give him the money for a cab.

Out of the corner of his eye, he became aware of a car slowing beside him, keeping pace with him as it drove along by the edge of the pavement. Great. Now he'd picked up some pervy curb-crawler. That was all he needed. He heard the peep of a horn, but kept his eyes fixed straight ahead, forcing himself to put one foot in front of the other. The horn honked again and he turned this time, dredging up the energy to tell whoever it was to fuck off. But then he saw that girl from the bar – Claire – peering at him through the window and beckoning him towards the car.

Christ, had she *followed* him? Why couldn't they all just leave him alone? Sighing heavily, he waded across to the car and bent to the window.

'Get in,' she called, waving at him through the steamed-up glass. She leant across and opened the door. 'I'll give you a lift.'

'No, thanks, I'm fine.' He made to close the door again, but she put her hand against it, holding it open.

'Don't be silly. Get in. You'll be soaked.'

'I'm already as wet as I can get. Besides, I'll ruin your seat.'

'It's just a bit of water. The seats are leather. It'll wipe off.'

Of course the seats were leather, he thought wearily. He wanted to tell her to get lost, embarrassment at her catching him out in his lie about taking a cab making him prickly. Besides, he'd had enough of that lot tonight to last him a lifetime, and he really didn't fancy spending another five minutes with any of them. He was in no mood to be patronised by her. But the desire to sit down was overwhelming, and he could already feel the warmth seeping from inside the car. It was too much to resist.

'Okay, thanks.' He shut her door and walked around to the passenger side.

'So, where to?' she asked, as he slid in beside her.

'Where are you going?'

'I live in Ranelagh but—'

'Well, don't go out of your way. I live just off Mountjoy Square, so drop me wherever's convenient.'

'No, I'll drive you home,' she said, as she pulled back into the traffic, with a little frown of concentration. 'I thought you were going to get a cab.'

'I couldn't find one,' he said tersely. 'I decided it'd be quicker to walk.'

Thankfully she nodded and didn't call him out on the taxis that were all around them, their yellow lights glowing into the dark, signalling that they were free. At least she had the decency to let him keep a little of his dignity.

'You don't have any money, do you?' she asked.

So much for letting him keep his dignity. He leant his head back wearily and said nothing.

'For a cab, I mean?' she persisted, glancing across at him. 'You didn't have any money for a cab, did you?'

Jesus, couldn't she let it go? 'No, I didn't have any money for a cab,' he admitted.

'Why didn't you say? One of us would have lent it to you.'

'Because I couldn't pay it back.'

'That wouldn't matter.'

'It wouldn't be a loan, would it, if I didn't pay it back?'

'Well, one of us would have given it to you, then. Whatever.'

'I don't want handouts.'

'It's nothing to be ashamed of, you know – not having money.'

'I know that,' he said snappily. So why did he feel so fucking mortified? Still, it was easy to say that when you *had* money.

'Damn,' she muttered. 'This traffic is awful.' It inched along, bumper to bumper, the rain pounding the roof. It made the atmosphere inside the car claustrophobic. 'How do you know Yvonne?' she asked.

'We grew up near each other, hung out with the same crowd.'

Just then her mobile rang and she answered it on speaker. It was Yvonne, checking if she'd got home safe.

'I'm still stuck in traffic, but I'll get there,' Claire said. 'Have fun. And thanks again for tonight. I had a lovely time.'

He noticed she didn't mention having picked him up. 'Why do you do that?' he asked as she hung up and tossed the phone back into the centre console.

'Do what?'

'Why did you tell Yvonne you enjoyed yourself? You were miserable.'

'Was it that obvious?'

'Don't worry. Most people don't really pay attention to anyone else.'

'It wasn't really my scene.'

'So why say you had a great time?'

'It's called manners,' she said tightly.

They drove in silence for another few yards. She seemed nervous, drumming her fingers on the steering wheel when they weren't moving.

'How long have you been living in town?' she asked eventually, and he got the impression she had spent the entire silence coming up with something to say.

'You don't have to do that, you know.'

'Do what?'

'Make small talk the whole way.'

'Oh. Okay.'

They lapsed into silence, and she seemed to relax a bit. She spoke again only to ask directions when they got to Mountjoy Square.

'This is it,' he said, as they pulled up outside his building. He was relieved to see it wasn't too bad tonight. There was just one skanky couple across the street ripping ten shades of shite out of each other, and a lone drunk swaying in the doorway. It could have been worse. It usually was.

'You live here?' she said, peering up at the tall Georgian house.

'Yeah,' he said, opening the door for a quick getaway, one foot already on the pavement. 'Thanks for the lift,' he said, over his shoulder, as he got out. 'Bye!'

'Um, hang on.' She leant across and spoke to him through the open door. 'Do you think I could come in and use your loo? I'm desperate, and you see what the traffic's like. It'll be ages before I get home.'

'Oh well...' He huffed. Sweet Jesus, could this night get any worse? He'd told her not to go out of her way, but she wouldn't listen. He'd known he'd regret taking the lift. But he couldn't very well say no, could he? He'd have to let her come in, and then she'd see how he lived. He wanted to curl up and die at the thought.

'Please?' she said, grimacing painfully for emphasis. 'I'm about to have an accident.'

'If you don't mind leaving your car here,' he said, hoping the dodgy neighbourhood would scare her off. 'There may not be much left of it when you get back.'

'I'll have to take my chances,' she said, turning off the ignition.

'Okay,' he said. Play it casual, he told himself. This was where he lived and, as she had said herself, being poor was nothing to be ashamed of. If she insisted on coming in, she would just have to take him as she found him. Besides, she wouldn't be there long. She wouldn't have time for a good look around. Once she'd used the loo, she'd probably leg it out of there as fast as her lovely long legs could carry her. It wasn't as if he had to make her tea or anything. Wait... *did* he have to make her tea?

He opened the front door, studiously ignoring the drunk, who was belting out what sounded like a mash-up of 'The Fields of Athenry' and 'Poker Face' at the top of his lungs. Once inside, he rolled his eyes at Claire to make a joke of it. He wanted to rush her upstairs so she wouldn't have time to take in the mangy hall with its noxious smells and hair-raising noises. But he decided to give her a break and knocked on the door of his neighbour, Joseph, a Nigerian, who lived in the first flat with his wife and baby daughter. Joseph stuck his head out in answer to his knock, opening the door fully when he saw who it was.

'Luca!' He beamed.

'Hi, Joseph. Sorry to bother you. Could you do me a favour?'

'Of course. What can I do for you?'

'My friend's just coming upstairs for a minute,' he said, indicating Claire, who waved hello. 'She's left her car out front. Could you watch it for me?'

'Sure, no problem.' He smiled at Claire, ducked inside for a moment, then stepped into the hall carrying a huge colourful umbrella and closed the door behind him.

'Thanks. We won't be long,' Luca said, as he led Claire to the stairs.

'That's not something to boast about, Luca,' Joseph said, laughing as he went to the door.

'Thanks,' she said, as she followed him up the stairs. 'For getting him to watch my car. I really can't afford to lose it.'

Luca shrugged. He wasn't being entirely altruistic. If anything happened to her car, he'd be stuck with her until she got a taxi.

He lived on the third floor at the top of the house. He took a deep breath outside his door, bracing himself to play it cool. Then he opened it and ushered her in ahead of him, flicking on the light switch as he followed her. Nothing. *Oh, shit.* His heart sank. He flicked the switch on and off idiotically a few times, as if it was suddenly going to spring back to life, just because he wanted it to. But he knew that wasn't going to happen. Claire stood in the centre of the room gazing at him quizzically in the light coming through the window from the street.

'No electricity. Sorry.'

'Are you having a blackout or something?'

Lights glowed in the building opposite, and the streetlamps poured yellow rays through the window. Clearly there was no blackout. It was just him – his own personal blackout arranged especially for him by the electricity company. Well, he had been warned – several times. Still, on the bright side, it meant she wouldn't get a good look at the place – and there was no question of offering her tea. He would get her out quickly, then put on some dry clothes and get under the blankets with the remains of the bottle of whiskey he still had in the cupboard.

'The lights were on downstairs,' she said.

'Sorry, it's just... It's been cut off.'

'Oh.'

'Well, I have a torch somewhere for just such emergencies,' he said, going to the kitchen area and rooting through a drawer. He found it quickly and switched it on, relieved to find that it was working.

'There you go,' he said, handing it to her. 'The loo is just in here.' He guided her to the bathroom with a hand at her back. 'Hope you're not afraid of the dark,' he said, smiling as he closed the door on her startled face.

He went back to the living room, threw himself down wearily in the big soft armchair facing the street and closed his eyes.

* * *

Claire was appalled by what she had seen of Luca's flat. Granted, she hadn't seen much, but as she washed her hands, she looked around the little bathroom in the dim light of the torch. The poverty of it was heartbreaking. She frowned at herself in the cracked mirror over the washbasin. She felt bad now for asking to come in. He obviously hadn't wanted her to see where he lived, and now she knew why. It was a complete shithole. And he was soaked to the skin, with no electricity. She would have to get him to come home with her. But he was so touchy. How could she do it without making him feel even more humiliated and patronised? She sighed. Well, she had to try. There was no way she could let him stay here.

'Thanks,' she called, as she made her way back to the living room. She was greeted with silence. She shone the beam of the torch around, but she couldn't see Luca anywhere. Maybe he had gone back downstairs ahead of her. She stood for a while, taking in her surroundings. It was a large room, with high, wood-panelled sash windows. There was a little table in one corner and a small kitchen area separated off by an open archway. Most of the room was given over to painting equipment and materials. A large easel stood near the window, and the shelves were crammed with brushes, bottles and tubes of paint. Canvases of various sizes were stacked against the walls and propped up on chairs. She couldn't see the subjects, but Luca hadn't been kidding about their size – some were enormous. There was a threadbare sofa against one wall, and a large armchair facing the window. She went to the window and peered out, to see if Luca was on the street. But Joseph was alone, leaning against the bonnet of her car under his multi-coloured umbrella.

Turning away from the window, she gasped: Luca was in the armchair, his eyes closed, his chest rising and falling softly. She hesitated, not sure what to do. She couldn't leave him there in soaking wet clothes. He didn't look very comfortable, his head at an awkward angle.

'Luca,' she said softly, hoping it would be enough to wake him. But it wasn't. 'Luca!' She shook his shoulder gently.

To her relief, he stirred and opened his eyes. 'Oh, sorry. I fell asleep.'

'Sorry, but you wouldn't be very comfortable if you slept there for the night.'

'You done?' he asked, standing up.

'Yeah. Thanks.' She took a deep breath. 'You really need to get out of those wet clothes. You'll catch your death.' *You'll catch your death!* Had she really just said that? She'd definitely been living with her mother for too long.

He nodded. 'I'll change.' When she made no move to leave, he said, 'But I'll wait until you're gone, if it's all the same to you.'

'Oh.' She realised she was staring at him stupidly. 'Look, why don't you come home with me?' she said in a rush.

'What?'

'Well, you can't stay here. You have no electricity – no heat or hot water. You'll freeze.'

'You want me to go home with you?' he asked, a smile curling his mouth.

'Um... well, you have to stay somewhere. Do you have a friend you'd like to stay with? Or your family? I'll drive you wherever you want.'

He blinked at her for a moment, apparently bemused. 'No, I'll go home with you,' he said finally.

'Right. Good.' Somehow he made it sound like *he* was doing *her* a favour. 'Bring some dry clothes.'

'Okay. I'll just throw some things into a bag.'

* * *

In his bedroom, Luca pulled open drawers and stuffed a pair of jeans, a long-sleeved top and a sweatshirt into a duffel bag, along with a couple of pairs of boxers and some socks. He didn't have any other shoes, but hopefully his boots would dry out overnight. Then he opened the drawer of his nightstand and took out a packet of condoms, stuffing them into his jacket pocket. It wasn't like him to be so obtuse, but Claire had surprised him by being so forthright about wanting him to go home with her. He was usually good at picking up the signals, but it hadn't even occurred to him that needing the loo was a pretext to come up here with him. She hadn't seemed such a ballsy type at the bar. Well, still waters run deep, he thought, smiling to himself. Tonight wasn't turning out so bad after all.

5

It was after eleven when Claire pulled up outside a red-brick semi-detached house on a tree-lined road in Ranelagh. Luca took off his boots in the porch and she led him inside, dropping her keys on a table in the hall. He followed her into a small, cosy sitting room.

'Nice house,' he said, horribly aware that he was dripping onto the cream carpet.

'Thanks.' She bit her lip. She seemed nervous, as if she wasn't sure what to do with him now that she had got him here. 'I was going to make something to eat. Are you hungry?'

'Well, I had that prawn. So, yeah. I'm starving.'

'Let me take your jacket. I'll hang it up in the airing cupboard to dry.'

'Thanks.' He peeled it off and handed it to her.

'Um, sit down.' She waved to a sofa. 'Or would you like to have a shower? It'd warm you up. And I could put your clothes in the tumble dryer.'

'Thanks. A shower would be great.'

'Okay, this way.'

She led him up the carpeted stairs, and he wondered if she was aware of him perving on her arse as he followed her. It was a very nice arse. She had great legs too. He was tempted to slide his hand up between them, under her dress. Still, that could wait until after they'd eaten. If she had plans to feed him, he certainly wasn't going to do anything to stop her. Besides, she obviously wanted to get him clean first before having her wicked way with him. Maybe she was one of those uptight girls who always insisted on showering before sex.

'It's in here.' She opened a door off the landing and showed him into a bright, modern bathroom with a stand-alone shower in one corner and a large, claw-footed bath. Luca dropped his bag on the floor, while Claire opened a cupboard and pulled out a couple of towels. 'I'll put these here to warm up for you,' she said, draping them on a chrome towel rail on the wall. 'There's shampoo and stuff in the shower. Do you need anything else?'

'No, I don't think so.'

'Okay, well… I'll leave you to it.' She smiled shakily. 'Come down whenever you're ready.'

'Thanks.'

As soon as she left, he scrambled out of his clothes, throwing them in a pile on the tiled floor. Then he cranked the shower up as hot as it would go and stepped in. It was bliss standing under the scalding spray, clouds of scented steam billowing around him. He could have stayed there for ever, letting the heat seep through to his bones.

Eventually he turned off the water and grabbed a towel, warm from the heated rail and instantly comforting. When he was dressed in the dry jeans and sweatshirt he'd brought, he picked up his wet clothes from the floor and made his way downstairs. Following the noise of clattering pans, he found his way to a large kitchen. Claire was standing at the hob, watching over a steaming pot. She had swapped her shoes for a pair of fluffy slipper boots and had pulled a big woolly jumper over her dress. He was amazed to see that she was actually cooking. It was almost midnight. The most he had hoped for was a toasted sandwich.

'Perfect timing,' she said, as he came in. 'This is just ready. Did you find everything okay?'

'Yeah, it was great. Thanks.'

'Give me those.' She reached out for the bundle of wet clothes and he handed them to her. 'They'll be ready for the morning.' She crossed the kitchen and bent to open a cupboard door that concealed the tumble dryer. She tossed the clothes in and switched it on.

'Sit down,' she said, as she straightened, gesturing to a large wooden table in the centre of the room, set for two.

Clearly she was the sort of girl who thought there should be some sort of date before sex, he thought, as he pulled out a chair. He sat and she put heated dishes in both their places.

'I made carbonara,' she said, as she placed a steaming bowl of pasta in the middle of the table. 'I hope that's okay.'

'It's fantastic. I can't believe you cooked at this hour.'

'Pasta's quick. Help yourself. Would you like some wine?' she asked, going to the fridge.

'Yes, please.' The pasta made a satisfying squelching sound as Luca dug in the serving tongs and took a generous helping.

Claire poured white wine for them both, then sat down opposite him and served herself. 'I hope it's all right.'

'Mm.' Luca swallowed a mouthful. It was divine – salty, creamy, unctuous, and incredibly soothing. 'It's amazing,' he told her.

'Good.' She smiled.

'So how come I've never seen you around before?' he asked her.

'Oh, I don't know those people – just Yvonne. I work with her.'

'Right, at the bookshop.' He nodded. 'Do you like it?'

'It's just a job. But the people are nice. And I love books, so I'd rather work in a bookshop than any other kind of shop.'

She took a gulp of her wine. She was so nervous. For some reason he found that really sexy. He wanted to soothe and calm her, to put her at her ease, but he wasn't doing a very good job of it so far. He needed to get her into bed. He was good at making women relax there.

'Do you work?' she asked. 'I mean apart from painting. Do you have a regular job?'

'No, I'm just a starving artist – a living cliché. Hence no electricity.'

'Right.'

'But not so starving tonight.' He grinned as he wound another forkful of pasta. 'This really is fantastic. Thank you.'

'You're welcome.' She ducked her head shyly.

'Where do you usually hang out?' he asked her.

'Nowhere really. I mean, I don't go to bars and clubs much. It's not my thing.'

'So what do you do for fun?'

'Well, I...' She fell silent, thinking. 'I read, watch TV, go to the movies, meet up with friends,' she said finally. 'The usual, I suppose. Nothing very exciting.'

'Do you live here alone?' he asked.

'No.' She dropped her fork, took a sip of wine. 'I live with my mother.'

'Really? Your mother?'

'Yes,' she said. Her tone was defensive, as if she was sensitive about it, expecting him to mock.

Luca glanced towards the door. He hadn't seen any evidence of someone else in the house. She must be in bed. 'Well, that explains the house,' he said.

'What do you mean?'

'It just seems a bit... old-fashioned, I suppose. I mean, correct me if I'm wrong, but I'd swear there was a doily in the bathroom. At least I think it was a doily. I don't think I've ever seen one before.'

'It's just a doily – nothing to get your knickers in a twist about.'

'Sorry, it wasn't a criticism. I don't mean to be unkind.'

'It just comes naturally to you?'

He sighed. 'It seems to. I just meant this house doesn't feel like you.'

'And how do you know what I feel like?' She blushed as soon as she said it.

'I don't.' Yet.

'This is my home, okay? I'm sorry it doesn't have the edgy cool of your place.'

'Sorry. Don't mind me, I'm just jealous. I love this house.'

'You secretly long for doilies and net curtains?'

'I do. I go doily-hunting every weekend, but the old ladies always beat me to the best ones.' He was relieved that she smiled slightly at that and relaxed a little.

Still, a mother in the house was problematic. That meant they would have to be quiet, and he'd like to see Claire let rip. She was so tense – a good shouty fuck would do her the world of good. He hoped her headboard wasn't too close to the wall of her mother's room.

'I hope we don't wake her up,' he said tentatively, glancing at the ceiling.

'She's not here. She's... away at the moment,' Claire said.

'So, we're all alone,' he said, grinning and wiggling his eyebrows suggestively.

'Um... yeah.' She grabbed her wine and drained the glass.

God, poor thing. No wonder she was so out of practice. Living with her mother must really cramp her style. It might also explain why she was so desperate to make something happen tonight, while she had the place to herself. Maybe it was the only chance she'd had for a long time and she was determined to grab it, even if the effort was killing her. She obviously wasn't used to bringing guys home, and she was very shy. He wished he could make it easier for her. If only she knew she was already way ahead of the game. She didn't need to go to all this trouble – setting a table, cooking food, making conversation. He was used to girls dragging him home to fuck them in unmade beds with barely a hello. Well, he'd give her his A game tonight. If this was her once-a-year day, he'd make sure it was one she'd never forget.

'Well, it's late,' she said, when they were finished, standing and starting to clear the table. He could feel her tension as she scraped plates and fussed with the dishwasher. He was about to go over and take her in his arms when she turned around.

'I'll show you the spare room,' she said. 'I mean, you don't have to go to bed now. You can stay up as long as you like. If you want to watch TV or anything...'

She was suggesting he watch TV? Jesus! She had obviously used up all her nerve getting him here, and she had no idea how to make the next move.

'I don't.'

'Okay. Well, I'll just show you where you'll be sleeping and then you can do whatever you want.'

Whatever I want? It was on the tip of his tongue to make some suggestive remark, but he thought better of it. It might give her a heart attack.

He followed her upstairs again and she showed him into a small, neat room, the walls painted duck-egg blue. A high bed took up most of the space. It looked soft and billowy and welcoming, with four plump pillows and a thick white duvet. He was ready to crawl into that bed right now. He wanted it so badly it hurt, his eyelids drooping at the very sight of it. But he had some chores to do before he could climb under the duvet. He didn't mind. They were very pleasant chores.

Claire had moved into the room ahead of him and pulled the curtains. 'There's an electric blanket on the bed, if you want to use it,' she said, turning to face him, her hands clasped together tightly.

Luca dropped his bag inside the door and moved towards her stealthily, determined to make this easy for her.

'And there are extra blankets in the wardrobe, if you're cold—'

'Oh, I don't think I'm going to need those,' he said, smiling into her eyes. 'Am I?' Then he bent his head and kissed her, one hand cupping her face, his thumb stroking her jaw encouragingly, while he slid his other arm around her to pull her close. He felt her body go rigid, but he kept kissing her softly, coaxingly, trying to relax her. He slid a hand up under her jumper and cupped her breast gently over the material of her dress.

She yelped and jerked away from him. 'What— what are you doing?' she gasped, an outraged look on her face.

'Singing for my supper.' He bent to kiss her again, but she turned her face away. 'Come on, isn't that what we're here for?'

'Wh-*what*? You think I—'

'Hey, it's cool,' he said. 'It's okay to ask for what you want.' He put a hand on the side of her face to make her look at him. 'And it's okay to want this.' He leant in again.

'No!' She stepped back, putting distance between them, one hand raised. She looked as if she wanted to hit him but couldn't bring herself to do it.

Oh, Christ! Luca froze. One look at her shocked face, the panic and upset in her eyes, and he knew he had read the situation all wrong. She really was just being kind when she'd brought him home with her. She had taken pity on him, fed him and offered him a bed for the night, and he had repaid her by groping her and insinuating that she had only brought him there because she wanted a fuck. He wished she *would* hit him. He deserved it, and it might make him feel better.

'Sorry,' he said, trying to catch her eye, but she wouldn't look at him. Fuck! Now she'd throw him out and he'd have to spend another night being cold, wet and miserable, when he could have slept in that soft, warm bed if only he wasn't such a monumental fuck-up. Maybe at least his boots would have dried out a bit by now. Hopefully she would let him retrieve them before throwing him out on the street.

'Hey, I'm really sorry,' he said, instinctively moving towards her, but she cringed away from him. He stopped in his tracks, sighing helplessly and holding up his hands to show he meant no harm. It was a bit late for that. The damage was already done.

'I'm so sorry. I would never have – I thought you—' He gave a defeated sigh. He couldn't think of anything to say that wouldn't make things worse.

Claire surreptitiously brushed away a tear and sidled past him to the door. 'I'm going to bed now,' she mumbled. 'I have to get up early for work in the morning.'

She darted away before he could say anything more, leaving him standing dumbfounded in the middle of the room. He heard the door across the hall slam. He couldn't believe she hadn't kicked him out. She *should* have kicked him out, he thought, indignant on her behalf. He had abused her hospitality, insulted and offended her, and made her uncomfortable in her own home. And he had made her cry. She was probably sobbing herself to sleep across the landing right now, thanks to him – all because he couldn't recognise a simple act of unselfish kindness. He wished he could go back and replay the whole night, do it differently this time. He could see she was lonely and a bit sad, and he could have been company for her, maybe lightened her load a little. Instead he had made her feel lonelier and sadder. If he had any decency he would leave. He could stay with Joseph and his wife – he knew they wouldn't mind. It wouldn't be the first time.

But he clearly didn't have any decency because, even as he thought it, he was sitting on the bed, automatically pulling off his socks. The lure of the soft mattress and those downy pillows overcame his guilt. He got under the covers, and his conscience had only a few seconds to bother him before he fell into a deep sleep.

* * *

Claire was not so lucky. She tossed and turned, her mind spinning. She should have slapped him. She should have told him to get out of her house. It was so unfair. Why could she only think of the right thing to say when the moment had passed? She replayed the scene over and over in her head, only this time she didn't cry. She didn't cower and cringe as if *she* had done something wrong. This time she kicked him out into the rain, and she didn't even let him collect his boots first.

She hadn't wanted to bring him home, she thought, tears of rage burning her eyes. The last thing she'd wanted after the bar was a stranger in the house. But she'd felt sorry for him, so she had sacrificed a night of her precious solitude. And he'd thought she had brought him here for sex! He'd actually thought she expected it in return for dinner and a bed. Jesus! What an arsehole. She punched her pillow in fury.

Still, as her rage calmed, she couldn't help remembering how nice his lips had felt. How he had smelt of her shower gel as he pulled her closer. How hard and warm his body had been in the instant before she'd pulled away. It was such a long time since anyone had kissed her. Then the tears started again.

6

When Luca woke the next morning, he was momentarily baffled by the unfamiliar cosiness of his bed. Then he remembered where he was, as the events of the previous night came back to haunt him. Still, he couldn't help smiling to himself as he took in his surroundings. He was toasty warm under the duvet in the little box room, the rain drumming heavily on the windows making him feel even snugger. He grabbed his watch from the nightstand and checked the time, surprised to see that it was just after ten. He didn't usually sleep so late – but, then, he didn't usually have such a comfortable bed.

At least Claire would have gone to work by now and he wouldn't have to face her again. He threw back the covers and sat on the edge of the bed, rubbing his face. Then he pulled on a sweatshirt and went out onto the landing. He called Claire's name, just to be on the safe side, but there was no reply. The house was silent as he made his way downstairs, feeling like an intruder but glad to have the place to himself.

He felt a fresh stab of guilt about his behaviour last night when he found his clothes folded neatly on the kitchen table, his boots, stuffed with newspaper, underneath. There was a yellow Post-it note on top of the clothes. It read:

Help yourself to anything you want from the kitchen. No need to lock anything when you leave. Claire

He looked towards the window and sighed, not looking forward to going back out there. The rain was still bucketing down, and he didn't want to undo all the benefit of last night by getting soaked again. Surely it had to stop some time. He would hang out here for a while, and hopefully it would let up eventually. Then he would leave. Anyway, he reasoned, Claire wouldn't be back until the evening, and it would make no difference to her if he left now or just before she came home. He figured that her bookshop would be open until at least six on a Saturday so there was plenty of time before he needed to clear out. In the meantime, he could enjoy the warmth and comfort of the house.

He opened the fridge, pleased to see how well stocked it was. He would make himself a proper cooked breakfast – bacon and eggs, lots of toast with lashings of butter. Then he would stand under the scalding shower for another half-hour or so. If it still hadn't stopped raining he might watch a bit of television, have some lunch and maybe even take an afternoon nap. He would leave around five – rain or no rain – and would be gone well before she got home. It would be like a little holiday.

* * *

At work Claire was struggling to keep her eyes open.

'You look rough,' Tom had said, when she'd arrived. She had done her best with makeup and had bathed her eyes in lots of cold water, but she still looked like something out of *Night of the Living Dead*.

'Thanks. I went to that party with Yvonne last night,' she had told him, by way of explanation.

Thankfully, Tom was satisfied with that, had smiled sympathetically and spent the rest of the morning plying her with tea and digestive biscuits. It was a good thing Yvonne wasn't in today. She knew Claire hadn't had a late night at the party, and wouldn't have been fobbed off so easily.

She felt worn out and frazzled, having had hardly a wink of sleep. Thanks to that bastard Luca, she had been awake most of the night, crying and fuming. That was what she got for trying to be nice to someone! She should have thrown him out instead of cowering in her room as if she was afraid of him. But she hadn't had the heart – or, if she was honest with herself, the nerve. And that only infuriated her more. Why was she such a bloody wimp? Why couldn't she be more like her alter ego? NiceGirl wouldn't have had any problem kicking him out. But then NiceGirl probably wouldn't have wanted to. She would have met him halfway, and she would have given as good as she got. Claire was no NiceGirl and she knew it.

Maybe Luca knew it, too, she thought, horrified at the idea that perhaps he could sense her loneliness and inexperience. Did it cling to her like some kind of aura? Maybe he had felt sorry for her, she thought, with a mixture of shame and indignation.

What was worse, she couldn't help wondering what it would have been like if she had let it happen. Pitiable as it was, it was the best offer she'd had in a long time – the *only* offer she'd had in a long time. She wasn't likely ever to see him again, so what did it matter what he thought of her? It would have been good to get in a bit of practice, too, in case anything happened with Mark. She felt a little tingle of excitement at the thought that soon she would be meeting him for real. But she was nervous about it, too, because she really wanted him to like her – the real her, not the person he knew online. She wondered if there would still be the same spark between them...

But she mustn't let her imagination run away with her. Mark probably had a girlfriend, and even if he didn't, their online flirtation possibly wouldn't translate into real life. She spent far too much time living in a fantasy world. She needed to wise up and get real, literally. It probably would have been disastrous with Luca. He would be used to much more experienced, savvy girls. It would have been awkward and embarrassing, and she'd have felt hopelessly inadequate. Besides, her own self-respect meant there was no way she could have let anything happen with him – not when he saw it as some sort of *transaction*.

She should just put the whole sorry episode behind her. Maybe she could turn it into a sexy story for her blog. Luca would be gone tonight when she got home and she would have the house to herself again. She was looking forward to getting into her pyjamas and vegging out on the sofa with a takeaway. It was definitely a night for staying in by the fire, she thought, looking out of the window. The rain was still pouring down, rushing in rivers along the pavement. It was forecast to continue for the rest of day, and there was already flooding in some parts of the city. She felt a pang of guilt as she thought of Luca going out into the downpour and returning to his cold, bleak flat. She couldn't help thinking of the sad state of his boots when she had put them in the airing cupboard to dry last night. They were full of holes, the soles worn thin and completely separated from the upper on one of them. Still, he wasn't her problem.

The day dragged on. It was quiet, the rain keeping most people away, and those customers who did turn up were narky and difficult. Claire dragged herself through until six in a haze of caffeine.

'Any plans for tonight?' Tom asked, as they closed up.

'No, just bath and bed,' she said wearily. 'On second thoughts, maybe just bed. I don't think I have the energy for a bath.'

'Well, enjoy!'

'Thanks. You too.' Almost there, she told herself as she made her way to the car, thinking longingly of her sofa and TV. But first she had to visit her mother.

* * *

'Hello!' Espie beamed when Claire walked into her private room at the nursing home in Blackrock. It was large and bright, pleasant enough as these places went. Great efforts had gone into making it cheery and welcoming, more resembling a room in a hotel than a hospital. But there was no disguising the pall of sickness and infirmity that hung over the place.

Her mother was sitting up in bed, and Claire felt fleetingly reassured by how well she looked. But she knew her mother's robust appearance was just a cruel illusion. Even now it was sometimes hard to remember how ill she was when she seemed so unchanged in every way. Illness was supposed to alter people beyond recognition, but Espie Kennedy was as plump and rosy-cheeked as ever – except that now her complexion owed more to steroid flush than good health. She still had a mischievous glint in her eye, though, and a curve to her lips, which seemed always on the brink of laughter.

'So how are you feeling?'

'Fine. Bored, but fine. I missed you yesterday.'

'I went to that party with Yvonne from work, remember?' Claire said, as she took off her coat and sat in the chair by her mother's bed. 'I told you about it.'

'Did you? I think that bloody anaesthetic's knocked everything out of my head.'

'Oh, sorry. I thought you knew. You must have been expecting me,' Claire said, immediately feeling guilty.

'It's fine. I'd much rather you were out enjoying yourself. You don't have to come every day. I know you're tired after work.'

'Did you have any other visitors yesterday?'

'No.' Espie sighed, putting on a childish pout. 'I was bored out of my gigantic incontinence pants. No inner resources, that's my problem.'

God, Claire thought. Couldn't one of her brothers have made an effort, just *once*? She had purposely told them that she wouldn't be able to make it yesterday in the hope that one of them would visit. Why did everything always fall to her?

'I thought maybe Ronan or Neil would come in.'

'Oh, they're far too busy on weekdays. They have jobs, you know.'

'True,' Claire said. 'Unlike the rest of us.'

Neil was a senior executive in a major insurance company and behaved as if he were the only person in the family who had to work, which let him out of all social and family obligations. Ronan, who was a solicitor, was well-meaning but scatty, relying on his wife, Liz, to organise his life. Claire sighed. She should have known they wouldn't come.

'And let's not forget they're very busy with the children,' her mother said, a mischievous glint in her eye.

'Like Michelle would ever let us forget.' Claire rolled her eyes. Neil's wife was just as self-important as her husband and acted like she was the only woman in the world who had ever given birth.

'Anyway, don't worry about me,' Espie said. 'At least I'll be home in a couple of weeks. It's the lifers in here I feel sorry for. Poor bastards. They treat them like children. They can't make any decisions for themselves, and they have no privacy. Today someone brought in a dog for them to pet as a treat. If I ever get to that stage, just shoot me.'

'Okay.' Claire smiled. 'I'll put a gun on the shopping list.'

'So, tell me about the party last night. Was it fun?'

Claire shrugged. 'It was okay.' Her mother would probably have enjoyed it more than Claire had. Espie loved company, and had an insatiable appetite for meeting new people.

'Come on, I want details. Entertain me. Did you meet any nice men?'

'*Mum.*'

'You can't be mean to me when I'm laid up in hospital. You have to indulge me. You've a lot to learn about visiting the sick, young lady.'

'I'm not being mean to you. There's nothing much to tell, that's all.'
'Make something up, then.'
'Well, let's see... There were turquoise cocktails to match the furniture.'
'Did you make that up?'
'No, that's true.'
'Ooh, very glamorous. What did they taste like?'
'I don't know. I was driving, so I just had water.'
'Honestly! You're hopeless.' Espie shook her head ruefully.
'I know I'm a sad disappointment to you,' Claire said, on a yawn.
'You're knackered,' her mother said. 'You should get on home.'

Claire was shattered, but she felt sorry for her mother cooped up all day with no one to talk to. 'No, I'm fine,' she said. 'I can stay a bit longer. Do you want to play cards or something?'

Her mother hoisted herself up a bit in the bed, wincing. 'Well, maybe just a quick game to keep our hands in. We don't want to get rusty. There's a deck in the locker.'

Several rounds of gin rummy later, Claire got up to go.

'Claire,' her mother said, as she put on her coat, 'you know I was just kidding, don't you – about shooting me?'

'Of course! But I wouldn't mention it in front of Michelle, if I were you. She doesn't have our sense of humor.'

'God, no! She'd take me up on it, wouldn't she?'

'In a heartbeat.'

Claire was almost crying with exhaustion as she walked up the path to her house later that evening. She would just go straight to bed and draw the curtains on this wearisome day. She'd feel brighter in the morning after a good night's sleep. And tomorrow was Sunday so she could have a nice long lie-in.

She went straight to the kitchen and flicked the switch on the kettle. She was pleased to see that her impromptu guest had at least cleaned up after himself. Feeling a little more energised now that she was at home, she made tea and took it through to the living room, thinking she might unwind in front of the TV before bed. She flicked on the light and stopped in her tracks – because there on the sofa lay Luca, fast asleep, emitting a low rhythmic growl as he snored.

'Oh, shit.' Was there no end to the bloodiness of this day? Why was he still here? Maybe she'd just go straight to bed after all. She could pretend she hadn't seen him. She was too tired to deal with him right now. With any luck he'd be gone in the morning when she came down. But even as she started to back out of the door, he stirred.

* * *

Luca woke to find a dark-haired girl with hazel eyes staring down at him. She was vaguely familiar, but he couldn't quite place her. He glanced around the room, but he couldn't place that either. Presumably he'd shagged her last night and this was her place. It was the only explanation he could come up with, though he had no recollection of kissing her wide, beautiful mouth. But why was he on the sofa, and why were they both fully dressed? And why was she looking at him with such... horror? Then he remembered: food; warmth; a kiss she hadn't wanted; a soft bed. Claire – that was her name and this was her house. She was looking at him like that because he wasn't supposed to be here. He had been meant to leave while she was at work, but he'd just lain down on the sofa to shut his eyes for a few minutes... Fuck!

He sat up quickly, rubbing his eyes. 'Hi. Sorry – I must have fallen asleep. I didn't mean to...'

She watched him in silence and he could see she was trying to hide how upset she was at finding him still there. But it was clear she wanted him gone. He didn't blame her.

He sprang off the sofa. 'Look, I'll get out of your way,' he said, moving to the door. 'Sorry – and thanks for the bed last night. And the dinner.'

'That's okay.' She followed him into the hall. He found his jacket on the coat stand and she stood watching him as he pulled it on. 'Will your electricity be back on?' she asked, her eyes darting from him to the door, which was being rattled by wind and rain.

'No, but it's fine. I'll get it sorted.'

She chewed her lip, and he could tell she was tussling with herself, longing to be rid of him and trying to tamp down the better part of her nature that wouldn't allow her to kick him out into the rain. He wasn't sure which side he wanted to win.

'You'll get soaked again,' she said, with a resigned little sigh. He reckoned the better part of her nature probably won out every time.

'Look, it's not your problem,' he said, buttoning up his jacket determinedly. He had to let her off the hook. She had been kind to him last night and she didn't deserve to be lumbered with him any longer. She looked exhausted and he could tell she just wanted to be alone.

She followed him to the door. 'It's late, and... you're welcome to stay again if you want to. I mean, unless you have somewhere else to go.'

He opened the door and looked out at the rain. He couldn't bring himself to go out into it when he had a better offer. 'Are you sure?' he asked her.

She nodded.

'Thank you,' he said, closing the door. 'I promise I'll be out of your hair tomorrow. I'll leave first thing in the morning.'

'Well, you know where everything is. Help yourself to anything you want,' she said, as he removed his jacket and hung it back on the coat stand. 'I was going straight to bed anyway.'

Shit! Why couldn't he have had the decency to brave a bit of rain and leave her alone? Now she was going to spend the night hiding in her room because of his stupidity last night.

As she turned to the stairs, he stopped her with a hand on her elbow. 'Look,' he said, 'I'm sorry about last night, about trying to—'

'It's okay,' she said, not turning to look at him.

'No, it's not okay,' he said, more sharply than he'd meant to. But she shouldn't let him off so easily. 'I behaved like a total dick, and I'm really sorry.' He needed her to know that his apology was genuine.

She looked at him and nodded.

'Please don't feel you have to go and hide in your room to avoid me. I'm not a complete savage. I know I didn't show much evidence of it last night, but I can behave like a civilised human being if I have to. If you really can't stand to be around me, *I'll* go to my— er, to the guest room.'

She shook her head. 'It's not that. I was planning to go straight to bed because I'm knackered.'

She did look exhausted – not just washed-out physically but emotionally too. She was clearly on the verge of tears.

'Bad day?' he asked gently.

'Pretty shitty.'

'Not helped by coming home and finding me still here,' he said, smiling wryly. He noticed she didn't deny it. 'Have you eaten?'

'I'm too tired to even think about getting anything. But you help yourself to whatever you want.'

'Why don't I make us both something? You cooked for me last night, so it's the least I can do. That is, if you'd like…'

'Okay,' she said. 'I don't know what I have in, though.'

'How does scrambled eggs on toast sound? Not very exciting, but I happen to know you have the ingredients.'

'It sounds perfect.' She smiled.

'Cool. You were drinking tea when you found me. Why don't you go and finish it, and I'll bring the food in when it's ready?'

'Okay. Thanks.'

* * *

'This is really nice,' Claire said later, as they sat side by side on the sofa with plates of scrambled eggs and toast, and big mugs of tea. 'Thank you.'

'Are you usually this late getting home from work?'

'No. I went to visit my mother on the way home. She's in a nursing home at the moment.'

'Oh. When you said she was away, I assumed holidays.'

'She had a hip replacement last week, and she's in convalescent care now.'

'But she's okay?'

'As okay as she ever is.'

He looked at her questioningly.

'The operation went well. But she has a lot of ongoing health problems. She has a very dodgy heart so we constantly lurch from one crisis to the next.' Her eyes filled with tears as she spoke, and her jaw tightened as if she was trying hard not to cry.

'Is that why you still live with her?'

She nodded. 'She's quite incapacitated with arthritis, and between that and her heart condition, it's not really safe for her to live alone.'

'What about your dad?'

'He died when I was four. But he hadn't been on the scene for ages before that. Mum raised us on her own, really.'

'Us?'

'I have two older brothers. They're both married with children.'

'No sisters?'

'No.' She sighed wistfully. 'I'd love to have a sister. So, how about you? You said you grew up near Yvonne so you're from Dalkey originally?'

'Yeah. Well, not originally. I was adopted.'

'From Romania.' She nodded.

'Yeah.' He could see the questions in her eyes, and could tell she was struggling with herself not to ask them. He was glad. He didn't really want to talk about it. Then it occurred to him that maybe she didn't need to ask because she already knew the whole story. He hated the thought that she might know all about him. 'Who told you I was from Romania?'

'That guy, Philip, mentioned it.'

'I bet he did.'

'So what will you do about your electricity?' she asked.

'I'll figure something out.'

'Wouldn't your parents help?'

'I wouldn't ask them to.'

'Oh. Well, why don't you get a job?'

'Doing what?'

'I don't know. Anything. Just to pay the bills.'

'I'm an artist. It's not a very transferable skill.'

'Well, I'm sure there are plenty of other things you could do. I mean, if you can't make a living as an artist...'

Oh Christ, not this again. He'd had enough of being harangued over the years – by his parents; by random girls, who decided they would like to be with him if only he were different; by well-meaning friends who wanted to make him their pet project and sort out his life. This was why he didn't want a girlfriend. They were always trying to change you, to mould you into the person they wanted you to be.

'I mean, I write but—'

'You do?'

'Yes, but that doesn't mean I can just say, "I'm a writer," and give up work to sit around writing all day.'

'Why not?'

'Because I have bills to pay. I have my mother depending on me.'

'Well, I don't have anyone depending on me. If I'm broke, it doesn't affect anyone but me. Besides, I don't "sit around all day". I work hard. Do you work at your writing?'

'Yes,' she said, bristling. 'But it doesn't pay the bills, and I don't think it makes me too special to have an ordinary meaningless job.'

'Neither do I!' he protested. She obviously thought he was really up himself. 'I don't think working's beneath me, or any crap like that – though I've been told I'm unemployable, on numerous occasions, and at this stage I'm inclined to believe it.' He smiled ruefully. 'I do bits and pieces when I can – casual work that won't interfere with my painting.'

'Like what?'

'I do some framing occasionally for a friend who owns a gallery. And there are a couple of Polish girls in my building who work as cleaners. They pass on jobs to me sometimes when they have an overload.'

'Cleaning?' She raised a skeptical eyebrow, no doubt remembering his flat.

'Yeah, I'm not very good at it,' he said, with a soft chuckle. 'The only things I'm really good at are painting and shagging, and I haven't figured out how to make money from either of those yet.'

* * *

When Claire got up the next morning, Luca had gone. On the kitchen table he had left an A4 sheet of paper, with a pencil sketch of a bunch of flowers and a message:

Thanks for last night – and the night before. Sorry they're not real. Luca

Claire smiled at the drawing, touched by the sweetness of the gesture. Then she stuck it to the fridge with a magnet, as if to mark the end of her acquaintance with Luca. At least it had finished on a good note.

7
———

Let's Get the Party Started

Regular readers of the blog will know I'm not into threesomes. I might consider it with the right person, in the right circumstances, so it's not quite what the BDSM crowd would call a hard limit – but almost. So it might surprise you to know that I attended my first orgy last weekend.

If I wouldn't contemplate sex with just one extra person, how could I think about doing it with a whole group of people, most of them strangers? But here's the thing: people can do all sorts of things in a group that they wouldn't contemplate doing on their own. Psychologists have studied this. A sort of herd mentality takes over. It's partly the safety-in-numbers thing – no one feels responsible individually for what's going down. Guilt is shared and thus dissipated. So: the more, the merrier.

It all started at a swingers' event I attended with Mr Curious. You probably have ideas about swingers, right? I know I did. Even the word 'swingers' seems so old-fashioned, kind of sad and saggy, with a nasty tang of the seventies about it. It conjures up images of ghastly parties where a bunch of sad-sack suburbanite couples throw their keys into a bowl after a nice dinner, and some leering fat guy in bell bottoms wins the right to fuck you.

That's what I expected to find at the hotel when we rolled up for our swinging evening – sad, desperate men whose wives were no longer interested; bored housewives longing for the excitement of flashing their cellulite at someone new. But I went because Mr Curious was… well, he's not called Mr Curious for nothing and he wanted to try it. He'd heard about these parties from a colleague. Apparently the swinging scene is on the rise at the moment in our little part of the world. He'd read an article. He said he thought it wasn't like that any more. And, like I say, I wasn't averse – I wasn't particularly looking forward to it, but I was willing to give it a try.

And some of the people were just like I expected. There were a few women who clearly didn't want to be there and had been dragged along by their partners. They were always on the edge of the action, with a sort of desperate rictus smile on their faces, trying to look like they were being a good sport about it all but were just 'sitting this one out' while they watched their partner pounding into some tight-skinned girl half their age. Pretty grim. I felt sorry for them – and a bit cross that they wouldn't stand up for themselves.

But most of the people weren't like that at all. They were attractive, well-dressed, successful, and they appeared respectable – or as respectable as you can appear when you're sucking some stranger's cock while another fucks you up the arse and your husband cheers you on from the sidelines.

We fell in with a nice crowd, Mr Curious and I. We hooked up with a bunch of other couples. It got a little crazy and, without going into too much detail, I think we all had a very nice time. I got fucked seven ways from Sunday, I sucked a world of cock, I watched Mr Curious having the time of his life getting his curiosity well and truly satisfied, and everyone went home happy.

I still think three's a crowd. But eight? Eight's a party.

On Tuesday morning Claire sat in a café near Bookends, anxiously watching the door as she waited for Catherine to join her. She had been bursting to tell someone about her potential book deal since Mark had first emailed her. He had emailed again on Sunday and told her he would be in Dublin next weekend, and they had arranged to meet for dinner on the Saturday night. That had thrown her into even more of a tizzy. She was so nervous about meeting Mark in the flesh. She kept telling herself it was just a business meeting, not a date, and she felt a lot calmer when she thought of it like that. But it wasn't easy when Mark was being more flirtatious than ever. They were communicating now by text and email, and the fact that they were flirting in private made it seem more real. She was desperate to talk to someone about it. But Catherine, the only person who knew she was the author of 'Scenes of a Sexual Nature', had been on holiday in Spain with her girlfriend, and had just got back last night. Hating to seem needy, Claire had nevertheless begged her to meet up this morning – she'd explode if she had to keep her news to herself for one more second. She had taken the morning off when Catherine had agreed to come.

Catherine was a fellow blogger and a freelance journalist. She wrote the hugely popular 'Unholy Mother' blog, a funny, frank and (as the title suggested) irreverent account of first-time motherhood. They had initially met through the blogosphere, eventually moving on to emailing and finally meeting up in person, and they had become good friends over the past year. Claire knew she could trust Catherine, and it was a relief to have someone she could be completely honest with about her blog.

She looked up as the door opened and saw Catherine struggling through it with a buggy. She spotted Claire and waved, then manoeuvred herself awkwardly down the narrow aisle towards her, bashing chairs and customers' legs.

'Watch where you're going with that thing!' a man shouted at her, when she rammed his ankles.

Catherine rolled her eyes as she parked the buggy beside Claire's table. 'I brought Paddy, hope you don't mind,' she puffed, unwinding her scarf and flopping onto the banquette opposite.

'Not at all. It's nice to see him.'

'What's the big emergency?' Catherine asked, as she struggled out of her jacket.

Before Claire had a chance to answer, a waitress came to take their order.

'Could I ask you to fold that up?' she asked, frowning crossly at the buggy. 'It's in the way there.'

Catherine looked at her blankly. 'Do you have any high chairs?'

'Sorry?'

'I'd like a high chair, please. If you want me to collapse the buggy, obviously I'll need a child seat.'

The waitress's eyes darted between the buggy and Catherine. 'You want a high chair?' she asked, incredulous.

'Yes. If it wouldn't be too much trouble.'

The girl sighed. 'Fine. I'll see if I can find you one that's not in use. What can I get you?' Her pen hovered over her notepad.

'God, they're not very child-friendly here, are they?' Catherine remarked, when they had ordered coffee and the waitress had bustled off. She sank back against the banquette. 'I might have to negative-review them on my blog.'

'Well, I hate to mention it, but maybe they'd be more child-friendly if you had an actual, you know... child,' Claire said, nodding to the buggy. They both turned to look at it. A large Paddington Bear was strapped securely into the seat.

'Hmm, you may have a point,' Catherine said.

That was why Claire knew her secret would always be safe with Catherine, even if she hadn't already found her to be a completely trustworthy person. Claire knew secrets about her, too, and as Catherine was fond of joking, mutually assured destruction was the best collateral. In fact, Catherine had the most to lose if it ever got out that the happily married young mother who wrote so entertainingly about life with her firstborn was, in fact, a childless lesbian. Her popular mummy-oriented blog had attracted a lot of advertising, and she made a good living from that and her journalism. She was always in demand for features on parenting issues, valued for her quirky insights into child-rearing as well as her solid, practical advice.

They had 'come out' to each other slowly, Claire being the first to admit, during a drunken conversation in a Mexican bar, with her guard lowered by too many tequila slammers, that she made up all the stuff on her blog. Catherine had been delighted and countered with her own confession that she had never given birth, wasn't married to a computer programmer called James, and her baby son, Paddy, was a fictitious creation, a cobbled-together combination of Paddington Bear and the Grouch from *Sesame Street*. (He looked more like the Grouch, she explained, but he had Paddington's sweet nature.)

'Is that for review?' Claire asked, waving at the buggy.

'Yeah, I was sent it to road-test. That's why I brought Paddy today – thought I'd kill two birds with one stone. So far it's performed pretty well. The straps are easy to do, and it's excellent for ramming wankers in the shins,' she said, scowling at the man who had shouted at her. 'But I suppose I should try it out on an actual child. Paddy doesn't wriggle around so much when you're strapping him in. Maybe we should borrow one of your nephews and come back for another visit, in the interest of fairness.'

'I don't know how Michelle would feel about her children being in the service of the enemy.' Claire laughed.

'How is your beloved sister-in-law? Still writing "Diary of a Smug Mummy" or whatever she calls it?'

Just then, the waitress returned with a high chair. 'You're in luck,' she said sullenly, shoving it at Catherine.

'Thanks.' Catherine took it from her.

'But if anyone else needs it, I'm going to have to ask for it back,' the girl warned, then stomped off towards the kitchen.

'They're not very adult-friendly either,' Catherine mumbled to Claire.

'Well, she probably thinks you're a victim of care in the community.'

'You'd think she'd be more sympathetic, then,' Catherine said, as she got up to assemble the high chair. 'At least this will give me a chance to see how easy the buggy is to collapse.' She grunted and huffed as she wrestled with the chair, but she finally got it open and positioned it at the side of their table. Then she lifted Paddington into it ('I won't bother strapping him in') and began to collapse the buggy.

'God, I'm ready for a lie-down now,' she said, when she'd finally got it flat. She rested it against the side of the banquette and sat down again.

'A mother's work is never done.' Claire smiled.

'Tell me about it!'

When the waitress returned with their coffee, she eyed Paddington sitting up in the high chair, but said nothing.

'So,' Catherine said, leaning across the table, 'what's up?'

Claire took a deep breath. 'Mark Bell contacted me – about the blog.'

'Mark Bell! Wow!'

Claire smiled. She'd known Catherine would get how big this was immediately. She took a sip of her coffee. 'He wants me to do a book based on it.'

Catherine gasped. She straightened in her seat, eyes wide. 'What? Oh my God! This is huge!'

'I know!' Claire grinned.

'We should be having champagne. Anyway, congratulations!' She bumped her mug against Claire's.

'Thanks. But let's not get ahead of ourselves. Nothing's been finalised yet.'

'Still – Mark Bell! I'm sure it's only a matter of time. I'm so pleased for you.' She gave Claire's arm a squeeze. 'You totally deserve it.'

'Thanks.'

'So, what's the story? What happens next?'

'Well, he's coming to Dublin at the weekend. I'm meeting him for dinner on Saturday.'

'Wow, he's keen. Mind you, I can't say I'm surprised. He's totally got the hots for you.'

'He hasn't, though – not really.'

'Oh, come on. You two have some serious chemistry going whenever you're on Twitter. You can tell he's gagging to be one of your Mr Men.'

'Oh God, don't say that!'

'Why not?' Catherine frowned. 'You like him, too, don't you?'

'Yes, but—'

'Of course you do. He's clever, friendly – he seems really nice. And he's very attractive, if you like that whole male penis thing.'

'Which I do.' Claire giggled.

'Which you do. So what's the problem?'

'Me,' Claire said, spreading her arms. 'I'm going to be meeting him in real life. And I'm not exactly the person in that blog, as you well know.'

Catherine considered this, then shrugged. 'You've obviously managed to convince him so far – not to mention your thousands of followers. And he's hardly going to give you a practical, is he?'

'No, but...' Claire chewed her lip. 'He's going to expect me to be this really sassy, confident person that I'm not.'

'Yikes, yes – I see what you mean. So, basically you need to learn how to act like a ho?'

'NiceGirl is not a ho!' Claire protested indignantly.

'I know, I know. She's just a nice girl who likes sex. Still, you can't go wrong being a bit slutty with men, can you?'

'You think?'

'Don't ask me. I have no idea what men like. I'm just going by what I see on TV and in movies.'

'What do you think I should do?'

'Whatever you have to. This is Mark Bell we're talking about. Come on – it's your dream. You can act sassy for one night, can't you?'

'God, I don't know. I'm not much of an actress. Besides, if he decides to go ahead with a book, it won't just be one night, will it? And if it does get published, there'll be publicity and everyone will see that NiceGirl and I don't match up.'

'Okay, slow down. Let's take this one step at a time. Just worry about Saturday for now.'

'You're right.' Claire nodded, trying to calm down. 'But that only gives me a week to catch up on years of experience,' she said, starting to panic again at the enormity of the task ahead of her.

'But you don't need actual experience. You can just bluff it.'

'I suppose.'

'Besides, he probably doesn't even expect you to be as ballsy as your blog. He knows you're a writer – that's why he's interested in you. He's probably factored a certain amount of fiction into what you write.'

'I doubt he's factored in that I'm a total fantasist.'

'Look on the bright side. It's a breeze compared to what I'd have to do to impersonate my alter ego.'

'True,' Claire said, glancing at Paddington. 'At least I don't have to produce a fully-fledged toddler before Saturday. How's Paddy been anyway?'

'He's great,' Catherine said, smiling fondly at the bear. 'Completely potty-trained.'

'How old is he now?'

'He turned two last week. Did I tell you I'm thinking of having another?' Catherine said.

'Really? Isn't it a bit soon?'

'Well, all the other mums who started out with me seem to be going onto their second now. I need to stay ahead of the curve.'

'How would Paddy react to that, do you think?'

Catherine cocked her head to the side thoughtfully. 'I haven't decided yet. He might be madly jealous – there'd be a lot of mileage in that. Or he could fall totally in love with the baby, which would be adorable.' She shrugged. 'I'll see what the other babies are doing, I guess.'

'Maybe it's a good thing you're not ahead of the curve on this one.'

'I wish I could have been more help,' Catherine said apologetically, as they finished their coffee, 'but I know all I want to know about seducing men, and that's bugger-all.'

'It's okay,' Claire said. 'It's great just to be able to talk it out with someone.'

'Oh, I know!' Catherine perked up. 'Why don't you ask that girl you work with? She's a bit of a slapper, isn't she?'

'Yvonne? She's not a slapper. She's just—'

'A nice girl who likes sex, right?'

'Yes.'

'She's the perfect person to help you, then. She's exactly who you're pretending to be.'

8

Claire waited for the afternoon lull before she broached the subject with Yvonne. When there was just a lone customer, desultorily thumbing through a selection of health and fitness books, she decided it was time.

'Yvonne, there's something I want to ask you – a favour, really.'

'Sure!' Yvonne answered. 'What is it?'

Claire was touched that Yvonne was so ready to help even before she'd asked what she was getting into. 'I have this, um... date and—'

'Ooooh!' Yvonne squealed, beaming from ear to ear. 'A date? Really?'

'Yes—'

'Tell me everything. Who is he? Where did you meet him? Is he seriously hot?'

'Well, that's just it. I haven't met him exactly – not yet.'

'Oh.' Yvonne frowned in confusion.

'I met him on the internet.'

'You didn't tell me you were internet dating!' she said, her smile returning.

'I'm not really. I just... I joined a site one night a while back when I was fed up – for a laugh, you know? I didn't think anything would come of it. Anyway, I had to write a profile to be able to look around. But I wasn't taking it seriously, so I wasn't exactly honest in what I wrote.'

'Are you "Thai"?' Yvonne asked knowingly.

'What? No! Of course not.'

'Well, I'm sure it's nothing you can't pull off, then. Go on.'

'Well, I got a message from this guy on the site, and he seemed really nice, and... well, I was genuinely interested. We've been emailing and stuff. But now I'm going to meet him for the first time in real life.'

'So you're going to have to be whatever you said you were in your profile.'

'Yeah.'

'And you want my help?' she said. 'I'm flattered. So, tell me.'

'Well... I gave the impression that I was really sort of... sexy.' Claire blushed, feeling ridiculous.

'Sexy? Is that all?' Yvonne looked aghast.

'Um... yeah. But I mean *really* sexy, you know – really experienced and stuff.'

'You mean a bit of a slapper?'

'Not that. Just a nice girl who likes sex.'

'Huh! Like the girl on that blog you're obsessed with.'

'Yes, exactly like her.' Yvonne had often caught Claire reading 'Scenes of a Sexual Nature', but she had assumed she was just a devoted fan, not realising she was proofing her own posts.

'Well, I don't see why you need my help with that.'

'Because... I need to seem sexy and sassy and sophisticated, and, well, I'm not.'

'You are sexy! You just choose not to show it.'

Claire looked down at her drab, nondescript clothes. There was nothing remotely sexy or appealing about the way she dressed. She'd lost her way style-wise in recent years, and had pretty much given up bothering. 'Well, anyway, I thought you might be able to help me.'

'Because I'm a bit of a slapper?'

'Of course not!'

'Let's face it,' Yvonne said cheerfully. 'I *am* a bit of a slapper.'

'No, you're not. You like men, that's all. And sex. There's nothing wrong with that.'

'Well, this is going to be easy-peasy. I thought we were going to have to make you six foot tall or something. You just need a bit of a makeover.'

'What would you have done if I did need to be six foot tall?' Claire wondered.

'I'd have thought of something. Anyway, don't worry, we'll sort you out. I take it this means we get to go shopping.'

Claire sighed. 'Yes, it does. But I don't have a huge amount to spend,' she warned.

'I can do sexy on a budget. I could do your makeup for you, if you like. When are you meeting this guy?'

'Saturday night.'

'Well, I could come round to yours – help you get ready.'

Claire could tell from the gleam in Yvonne's eyes that she was already excited at the prospect of having her own life-size dress-up doll to play with. She didn't know if she liked the idea of being Yvonne's plaything, but she was being so kind, Claire didn't have the heart to say no. Besides, she needed all the help she could get. 'That would be great – if you really don't mind. I mean, you probably have better things to do on a Saturday night.'

'I'd love to help. And I can get ready to go out myself at the same time.'

'It's not just about clothes and makeup, though. I need to learn how to act the part too – you know, be flirty.'

'I can totally help with that. I'll give you a crash course in seduction techniques.'

'And dating protocol. I don't know what guys expect these days – how far you should go on a first date, things like that.'

'As far as that goes, it's the same as always,' Yvonne said. 'We have all the power.'

'*Really?*'

'You just have to own it.'

Claire sighed. She obviously had a hell of a lot to learn.

'Do you have a rule?' Yvonne asked.

'A rule? What do you mean?'

'Like, a three-date rule. You don't sleep with a guy until you've been on three dates.'

'Oh! No. Should I?'

Yvonne shrugged. 'It's up to you. My friend Judy has one and she swears by it. She says you have to give the guy time to get attached first, so he's not as likely to run off the minute you have sex.'

'Right.' Claire was feeling clueless again. When had dating become so scientific and organised? 'Do you have a three-date rule?'

'Me? No. I'm always telling myself I'll hold out, but two is as far as I've ever got. I have no willpower.'

'I can't remember if I have any willpower,' Claire joked. 'It's been a long time since it was put to the test.'

'So, what are you doing for this date?'

'We're going to dinner.'

'Okay, dinner is good for a first meeting, especially with someone you've met on the internet. You want to go somewhere public. But make sure to tell someone else where you're going, just in case.'

'Yes, Mummy.'

'And if he invites you back to his place—'

'Oh, he won't. He's coming over from London.'

'London? He's keen.' Yvonne gave her a grin that said, 'Go you!' 'But he could still invite you back to his hotel room.'

'I'll say no.'

'Well, you can play it by ear,' Yvonne said. 'He might be too hot to resist.'

'You're giving me permission to go to his hotel room?'

'Absolutely – you deserve some fun. And I'm sure you have good instincts.'

'What about the three-date rule, though?'

'I think you've held out long enough. Judy wouldn't approve of me saying this, but if you want to go for it, do. Anyway, if he's the sort of guy to run off once you've had sex, you might as well find that out on the first date before you waste any more time.'

Claire was relieved this wasn't a real date she was going on, just a business meeting. It all seemed so complicated.

'So, when are we going on this shopping trip?' Yvonne asked.

'We're both off on Thursday morning?'

'Thursday it is, then.'

'Thanks, Yvonne. I really appreciate it. I don't expect miracles—'

Yvonne stopped her with a raised hand. 'Is "Sales" my middle name, or is it not?'

'It is.'

'Well, this is just another sales pitch,' she said, 'only with you as the product.'

Claire smiled weakly.

'Speaking of sales,' Yvonne said, sliding out from behind the desk, 'that guy doesn't know it yet, but he's just about to buy the yoga manual he's been thumbing for the last half-hour.'

Claire watched her go, not at all sure what she had let herself in for.

* * *

'What do you think?' Claire asked, on Thursday, as she stood in front of Yvonne, tugging at the hem of a silky red slip dress, very conscious that it barely covered her crotch. She couldn't possibly appear in public in it. It would be like going out in her underwear.

'It's great! Very sexy,' Yvonne enthused, eyeing Claire from her position on a velvet sofa.

'It's very expensive,' Claire hedged, glancing again at the price tag. Yvonne had brought her to this upmarket boutique, saying it was *the* place to go if you wanted to do sexy on a shoestring. But clearly Yvonne's shoestrings were made of ritzier stuff than Claire was used to. Still, at least she could make the excuse that she couldn't afford it. She didn't want to hurt Yvonne's feelings when she was being so helpful.

'It's perfect,' Yvonne continued. 'That colour looks really good on you. But you need to wear some seriously high shoes,' she said, glancing at Claire's bare feet. 'And definitely no knickers.'

'What—?' Claire paled. 'I don't want to look like a hooker.'

'You won't. But you can't wear knickers in a dress like that. Apart from the fact that there's no way of avoiding VPL, it sends the wrong message.'

'I'm not trying to tell him I'm rentable by the hour.'

Yvonne rolled her eyes impatiently. 'There is nothing tarty about that dress, okay? Besides, you couldn't look slutty if you tried.'

Claire bit her lip. 'I'll take that as a compliment,' she mumbled.

'Good, because it was meant as one.'

Claire stared at herself in the mirror and tugged at the hem again. The colour was nice, and she did like the dress as far as it went – it just didn't go far enough. 'Maybe if I wore it with leggings…'

'*Leggings*?' Yvonne shrieked in disgust. 'No way! If you can't wear knickers with it, you certainly won't get away with leggings.'

'I think it could work as a top,' Claire said. What she needed, she thought, was a second opinion.

'What we need,' Yvonne said, as if reading Claire's mind, 'is a second opinion.' She grabbed her mobile from her bag and punched buttons as she spoke. 'Preferably male.'

'What are you—'

Yvonne held up a finger, silencing her. 'Luca,' she said, into the phone, and Claire froze in horror. She shook her head frantically at Yvonne, who ignored her and turned away, continuing to talk. 'I'm over at Threads with a friend and we need some advice. I was wondering if you could pop over and help us.'

Oh God, this was turning into a nightmare. She was desperate to get out of this dress, if there was even the remotest chance that Luca would turn up. She tried to dive for the changing room but Yvonne stuck a leg out, blocking her way.

'Well, you'd get to ogle my friend in a very skimpy dress – and she has really nice legs,' she was saying now, smiling into the phone. 'And I suppose I could buy you lunch.'

'Claire,' Yvonne said after a pause. 'You met her. She was at Ivan's party the other night. I don't know if you – oh! You do?'

Jeez, she was being sold to him like a prize heifer!

'We're in luck,' Yvonne said, snapping her phone closed. 'I remembered that Luca's helping to hang an exhibition at the gallery just across the road. He's going to call over.'

'Well, there's nothing for him to see here,' Claire said, making another lunge for the changing room.

Yvonne shot up off the sofa and stood in front of Claire with her arms folded. 'Come on, I know he seems a bit of a sleaze, but Luca has a great eye. He's an artist. Plus, he's a man.'

'But I don't need another opinion. I already know—'

'He actually remembered you from the party!' Yvonne told her. 'That's not like Luca. You must have made a big impression on him.'

Claire cringed inwardly. She knew exactly the sort of impression she'd made on Luca. At least he'd had the decency not to fill Yvonne in on what had happened between them. But she'd thought she'd seen the last of him. 'Please call him back and tell him not to bother,' she begged.

'Too late. Here he comes now,' Yvonne said. A bell rang as the door swung open, and Yvonne beckoned him over.

He strode across the shop and threw himself onto one of the sofas in front of the changing area. 'Hi, Claire. I hadn't expected to see you again so soon.'

'So, what do you think?' Yvonne waved at Claire with a flourish.

Luca folded his arms and looked her up and down slowly. Claire kept her eyes on the floor, squirming under his scrutiny. Her skin prickled as his eyes ran over the length of her body, as though they were physically touching her.

'Obviously she'd be wearing heels,' Yvonne told him. 'You have to use your imagination.'

'It's a very sexy dress,' he said finally.

'Yes!' Yvonne punched the air with a triumphant smile. 'That's what I said.'

'But it doesn't suit you,' Luca said, ignoring Yvonne and talking to Claire. Her eyes shot to his before she could stop them.

Yvonne gasped. 'That's a horrible thing to say.' She frowned at him.

Claire felt her cheeks burning. Damn him – had he come here to humiliate her?

'Hey, I didn't mean it like that,' he said, his eyes widening in horror.

'It's fine,' Claire said. 'I *told* you,' she said to Yvonne, wishing she could hide in the changing room and not come out until both of them had gone.

'You said it's a sexy dress, and then you said it doesn't suit her. What exactly *did* you mean?' Yvonne demanded.

Oh God, please just drop it, Claire begged silently.

'It *is* a sexy dress. And she's a sexy girl. You were right about the legs.'

'Well, then…'

'But you don't *feel* sexy, do you?' Luca said, eyeballing Claire.

She certainly didn't feel sexy now. She felt silly and pathetic, as if she was trying to be something she wasn't – like a child tricked out in her mother's cocktail dress.

'Well, she will when she's got her makeup and heels on,' Yvonne said. 'And no underwear, of course. No one could feel sexy in bare feet and M&S knickers.'

Sweet Jesus, could this get any worse? Now Yvonne was sharing with Luca what kind of knickers she had on.

'I will *not* be wearing no underwear.' She fidgeted, tucking her hair behind her ears.

'Back me up on this, Luca,' Yvonne said.

'Jesus, do you want to give the poor girl a coronary?' He shot Claire a sympathetic look. 'No.' He shook his head. 'No way.'

Maybe Luca wasn't so bad after all, Claire thought.

'The key to being sexy is feeling sexy,' he said. 'How do you feel in that dress?' he asked her.

'Exposed,' she said. 'Self-conscious. Ridiculous.'

'Right. And that's how you look—'

'Luca!' Yvonne gasped in outrage, while Claire wished she could evaporate.

'Shit! I didn't mean you look ridiculous. I meant you look embarrassed, self-conscious, like you're trying to make yourself invisible. Your shoulders are up around your ears and you haven't stopped fidgeting for one second.'

'Well, that's because you're both staring at me.'

'Exactly. You can't go out in a dress like that if you don't want people looking at you. That's a dress for a woman who wants to be noticed.'

'Well, what would *you* suggest?' Yvonne asked him, speaking as if Claire wasn't there. 'This is what she was thinking of wearing,' she said, picking up the dress Claire had first chosen and waving it at him. Claire thought it was very nice – a classic LBD, simple, understated… a bit boring maybe, but she had felt good in it: comfortable, safe.

'Okay.' Luca eyed the dress with distaste. 'So what we need is a compromise – something in between hooker and nun.'

'That is not a hooker dress,' Yvonne fumed, pointing at Claire.

'And that's not a nun dress,' Claire mumbled sulkily.

'What's the occasion anyway?' Luca asked.

'Dinner. She's got a date!' Yvonne told him, sounding more like a pushy mother by the second. Claire prayed she wouldn't go into details.

'Good for you,' Luca said softly. 'And you're letting Yvonne dress you? Seriously?'

'I thought you were going to help, Luca. If you're just going to criticise—'

'Okay.' He jumped off the sofa, holding up his hands in a conciliatory gesture. 'Leave it to me. Take that thing off,' he told Claire, snatching the black dress from Yvonne and marching away.

Claire went back to the changing room, hung the red dress on its hanger and waited. She was beginning to think Luca was never coming back when his arm appeared through the curtain.

'Here, try this,' he said, thrusting a hanger at her.

Claire examined the dress before unzipping it to try it on. It was the palest shade of green, the bodice a soft velour, while the neckline and long sleeves were sheer chiffon. She pulled it on, loving the feel of it. She had wanted a dress with sleeves like this ever since she had first seen Grace Kelly in that blue dress in *High Society*. She wondered why she hadn't noticed it – but then she remembered she'd been zeroing in on black. She felt like hugging Luca when she looked in the mirror. It was perfect – sexy but classy. The bodice was fitted, clinging to her curves, but the skirt was full, layers of chiffon that swished when she moved, and fell to just above the knee. And the colour really suited her.

'Well?' Yvonne asked, from the other side of the curtain.

'Yeah, it's, um...' Claire pulled the curtain back and stepped into the shop, where Yvonne and Luca were waiting expectantly. She stood in front of them for inspection, not minding their scrutiny now. She even did a little twirl.

'Wow!' Yvonne said, grinning with delight.

'Perfect.' Luca smiled. 'My work here is done.'

'Thanks, Luca,' Claire said. 'I really love it.'

'You've earned yourself a big lunch, mister,' Yvonne said.

'I can't make lunch,' he said, with a grimace. 'I'm meeting someone.'

'Well, I'll owe you.'

'I'll hold you to it. Enjoy your date, Claire,' he called, as he left.

9

Luca sat up in bed munching an apple as the afternoon sun slanted in through the blinds, warming him and creating strips of honey-coloured light on the polished wooden floor of Aisling's bedroom.

'Well, that was a long time coming,' she said, with a triumphant smile.

He looked at her stretched out naked beside him on the rumpled sheet, her long blonde hair tousled. Damp tendrils clung to her forehead and the sides of her face. '*You* were a long time coming,' he said.

She made a sleepy, satisfied noise and nestled deeper into the pillow.

'Give me a bite.' She nodded at the apple.

Luca nipped her shoulder lightly. 'There you go.'

Aisling laughed and grabbed the apple from him.

'Hey!'

'Bite me!' she said, and bit into it with a juicy crunch before handing it back to him.

Luca finished it and lobbed the core into the basket in the far corner of the room. Then he checked his watch. It was almost three. 'I'm going to head off,' he said, swinging out of the bed.

'Don't go.' Aisling groaned pettishly, reaching for him, but he was already sitting on the edge of the bed with his back to her. 'Why don't you stay?' Her fingers stroked his spine.

Luca sighed. 'I told you. I'm meeting my father for dinner later, and I want to get some work done before that.'

'You mean painting?' She didn't try to hide the sneer in her voice.

'Yes, painting.'

'But that's the beauty of being your own boss. No one can stop you skiving off for an afternoon whenever you want. I just told Nicola I wouldn't be back for the rest of the day. I could tell she was livid, but there's nothing she can do about it.' Aisling owned a very chic and expensive bag shop in the Powerscourt Centre where, like her stock, she was more decorative than useful.

'Well, unlike you, no one else can do my work for me.'

'So take a day off,' she drawled, in a bored voice. 'Who cares?'

'I care,' he said, standing up and turning to her.

'You could paint me.' She spread her arms wide and looked up at him appealingly.

He studied her, his eyes slowly raking the length of her body. She was a beautiful girl, there was no denying that – she had a fit, toned body, soft, well-tended skin, great tits, regular features. But there was something vacuous and bland about her prettiness that held no aesthetic interest for him. There was no character in her face, no little quirk or irregularity to make it interesting. It was flawless, doll-like... *boring.*

'Is this new?' he asked, bending and reaching out with one finger to touch the tattoo at her hip – a cluster of small, coloured stars. He hadn't seen it before, but it was a long time since they'd last slept together.

'I got it a couple of weeks ago. What do you think?'

'It's cool,' he said, sitting down beside her, his finger tracing lazily over the tattoo.

'You're the first person to see it.'

'Really? Not even Philip?'

'No.' Aisling raised herself up on her elbow. 'Philip and I are on a break.'

'Yeah?'

'You didn't know?' She sounded surprised.

'Why would I?'

'Well, I'd have thought it was obvious. I mean, do you honestly think I'd be here with you if I was still with Philip?' she asked indignantly.

'Honestly? I think you would, yeah,' he said, with a smirk.

'Fuck you!' she said softly, but she wasn't even trying to hold back her smile. Aisling liked her reputation as a ballsy man-eater. 'Well, I wouldn't,' she said archly. 'I may play around, but when I'm with someone, I don't cheat.'

'Very admirable. You're almost up there with the Virgin Mary. Lucky for me, then, that I caught you when you were between gigs with Philip.'

'What makes you think I'm getting back with him?'

'Because it's what you and Philip *do*. You'll probably still be breaking up and getting back together when you're both ninety.'

'Not this time. I'm going to tell him it's over for good. He's really pissing me off. He can be such a knob.'

'You'll get no argument from me there.'

'So you think I should?' She looked up at him coquettishly from beneath her lashes. 'Break up with him?'

'If you want to.'

'What kind of answer is that?' she said, her smile swiftly replaced by a scowl.

'What do you want me to say? If you want to break up with him, you should break up with him.'

'I want to know what you think. I mean, how would you feel about it?'

Luca shrugged. 'Dump Philip, or marry him and have his babies – what difference does it make to me?'

'How can you say that? I just told you I wouldn't be here with you now if I was with Philip.'

'Look, I'm not saying it hasn't been fun, but that'd hardly be the end of the world, would it?'

'Charming!' she said petulantly.

'Anyway,' he grinned, 'I could catch you next time around.'

'I told you, there isn't going to be a next time. If we split up this time, it's over for good. Then you and I could have lots more afternoons like this,' she said seductively, playing with the hair on his chest.

'Well, don't break up with him on my account—'

'Jesus!' she huffed, pulling away abruptly. 'Why are you being like this?'

'Like what?'

'You act like you don't even care.'

'I'm not acting. I *don't* care. And neither do you, remember?'

'Maybe I've changed my mind.'

'Well, I haven't changed mine.' He stood. 'I'm going for a shower.'

'You're such a shit, Luca,' she hissed to his back.

Yeah, whatever, Luca thought wearily, as he stalked into the vast open-plan living room. Aisling lived in a spacious loft-style apartment at Grand Canal Dock. On his way to the bathroom he stopped by the floor-to-ceiling windows overlooking the water to take in the view, leaning his forehead against the glass. He was so fed up with girls telling him he was a shit because he didn't want what they wanted – especially when he'd made it perfectly clear what he didn't want from the start. He wasn't the one changing his mind, and it wasn't his fault that Aisling had been lying, pretending she was cool with casual sex because she wanted him to stick around long enough for her to change him.

'For fuck's sake, Luca, get away from the window,' Aisling said behind him. 'People will see you.'

'So? I've got nothing to be ashamed of.'

Her eyes flew to his dick. 'No.' She smiled saucily as she walked towards him, completely naked. She stood beside him at the window, looking down at the people passing on the walkway below.

'Aren't you worried people will see *you*?' Luca asked.

'You're not the only one who has nothing to be ashamed of.' She touched his hand, stepping closer so her breasts were brushing against his chest. 'Why don't we really give them something to look at?'

His body was already starting to respond to her. 'I told you, I have to go,' he said, pulling away from her and starting to gather up his clothes, which were scattered around the living room. He could shower at home. Now he just wanted to get out of there.

Aisling's smile disappeared and she folded her arms, her face like thunder as she watched him hastily getting dressed. Thank Christ they hadn't gone to his place, he thought, as he zipped up his jeans and pulled on his T-shirt – he'd never have got rid of her. But Aisling had refused to go there on the grounds that it was 'minging'. Sometimes living in a shithole had its advantages.

'I'll see you around, yeah?' he said, as he pulled on his jacket. He leaned in to kiss her, but she reared away from him.

'Just piss off!'

Outside the apartment, Luca didn't bother waiting for the lift, running down the stairs as if he was being chased.

Where the fuck had that come from? Aisling was the last person he would have expected to turn clingy and demanding. Quite apart from the fact that she was a notorious player, she had this ongoing thing with Philip, and they always ended up back together, no matter who else she amused herself with in the meantime. In fact, their friends often said she was using Luca to make Philip jealous – which was fine by him. He was happy to help.

And now she'd suddenly decided to glom onto him. He'd obviously made a mistake, taking her at her word that she wasn't interested in anything serious. But what the fuck was she thinking? They didn't even like each other – not really. He was always clear about what he wanted – and didn't want – right from the start. So why did it inevitably end up with him being told what a shit he was, some girl shouting and throwing stuff at him, or acting hurt and accusing him of having misled her?

They always thought they'd be the one to transform him into their idea of the perfect boyfriend if they could just fuck him enough times. Well, screw that!

* * *

The gallery that represented him was giving him his first solo show in September, and even though it was now only the beginning of May, he didn't feel he had a lot of time. So he spent the rest of the day working furiously on a couple of pieces, swapping between them so that he could get on with one while he left the other to dry. The frustrating thing about working in oils was how long it took the paint to dry between layers, so he usually had two or more canvases on the go simultaneously. He quickly became engrossed, completely absorbed in what he was creating, and regretted wasting so much time with Aisling. Still, it wouldn't be happening again anytime soon – he'd burnt his bridges there. That had been happening a lot lately. If he kept it up, he'd run out of girls to sleep with in Dublin, he thought wryly. He'd have to become celibate or move somewhere else. Maybe it wouldn't be such a bad thing to give that a rest for a while anyway. If nothing else, he'd have more time to focus on his painting.

At six, he downed tools, cleaned up and got ready to go out. He had arranged to meet his father at an Indian restaurant close to the private hospital where he worked. It was a favourite haunt of Jonathan's for their occasional father-son get-togethers because it gave him a rare opportunity to eat Indian food, which his wife didn't like.

Luca walked the short distance from the bus stop to the restaurant, which was on a quiet, tree-lined road, with a little courtyard in front. He automatically scanned the parking space to the side, checking for Jonathan's BMW. He was alarmed to recognise his mother's Mercedes there instead, unmistakable with the stuffed dolphin in the back window – it had been a permanent fixture for almost as long as he could remember.

Fuck! He stopped in his tracks. Was this some sort of ambush? He really wasn't in the mood for a showdown with Jacqueline. He'd had enough aggro for one day. He hesitated outside, contemplating turning around and leaving. He could ring Jonathan and make some excuse, say something had come up unexpectedly. But he'd feel like a shit if he did that. He knew Jonathan meant well and just wanted everyone to get along. He might as well get it over with. Squaring his shoulders, he opened the door and went inside.

He was about to give his name to the maître d' when Jonathan spotted him, waving at him from a table across the room. Luca was surprised to see that he was alone and seated at a table for two. He still approached the table warily.

'Hi, Luca.' Jonathan greeted him with a smile and stood to give him a quick hug.

'Hi,' Luca said, clapping him on the shoulder. 'Where's Jacqueline?' he asked, as he pulled out the chair and sat opposite.

'Jacqueline?' Jonathan frowned. 'I think she's at her book club tonight,' he said vaguely.

'Oh. I saw her car outside…'

'Ah, right. Mine's in the garage, so I've been driving hers this week.'

Luca relaxed, relieved that his mother wasn't going to be joining them.

'I would have told you if she was coming,' Jonathan said, a little sadly.

'I know. Sorry.' He should have known his father wouldn't spring something on him like that. It wasn't his style.

A waiter came to take their drinks order – Cobra for Luca and non-alcoholic beer for Jonathan. They studied their menus in silence.

Luca's eyes were drawn to Jonathan's hands where they rested on the table in front of him. They were surgeon's hands – cared for, immaculately manicured, skilful. They looked safe, assured, capable. Luca suddenly thought he would like to paint them.

'Have you decided what you're having?' Jonathan asked him.

'Oh!' Luca snapped out of his reverie. 'Sorry, I was just looking at your hands.'

Jonathan raised his eyebrows quizzically.

'I was thinking I'd like to paint them.'

'These?' Jonathan held up his hands in front of him as if he'd never noticed them before. 'Really?' he said, with a little self-deprecating laugh. But he looked flattered.

Luca smiled back, glad to have pleased him, even in such an insignificant way. It felt good to make someone else happy. He wished he could do it more often, but he didn't seem to have the knack. 'Could I?'

'Of course. I'd be delighted.'

The waiter returned with their drinks and took their food order.

'Cheers!' Jonathan said, raising his glass to Luca's when the waiter had gone. 'It's good to see you, Luca. We don't do this often enough.'

'Cheers!' Luca clinked his glass against Jonathan's. 'How's the butchery business?'

'The butchery business is thriving. How's the daubing business?'

'Dismal.' Luca took a sip of ice-cold Cobra. 'I haven't sold anything in ages.'

'Are you okay for money?'

'Fine,' Luca answered hastily. He didn't want Jonathan to think he was looking for a handout.

'Are you sure?'

'Yes, absolutely. I did some work for the gallery this week.' At least he'd managed to scrape together the money to get his electricity switched back on.

'Well, you have your show coming up in September. Hopefully that will be your big breakthrough. We're looking forward to it.'

'You're all coming?'

'To your first solo show? Of course! We're very proud of you, Luca.'

Luca was pretty sure Jacqueline wasn't proud of him. He wouldn't blame her. He had given her little enough reason to be.

'How's it coming along? Does it have a title? A theme?'

'It doesn't have a title yet, but it's all about the way the model or subject is used, how the artist imposes meaning on the subject and controls the story, so the subject is silenced and possibly misrepresented. They have their story taken off them—' He broke off. 'Sorry,' he said, running a hand through his hair. 'It's hard to talk about it without sounding really wanky.'

'It doesn't sound, er... wanky at all.' He frowned thoughtfully. 'It sounds quite... personal.'

'Anyway, the painting's going really well at the moment.'

'Glad to hear it. I'm sure big things will happen for you soon, Luca. You deserve it.'

They were interrupted by the arrival of the waiter with their food, silent while he unloaded dishes onto the table.

'You haven't been to the house in ages,' Jonathan said, as he spooned curry onto his plate. 'We hardly see you any more.'

Luca felt bad that Jonathan got shut out of his life by default because he couldn't get on with Jacqueline. He liked Jonathan a lot. He was a good man – kind, caring and scrupulously fair. He had always tried to make it up to Luca for Jacqueline's coldness towards him, intervening on his behalf if he felt she was being too harsh, trying to spend 'quality time' with him at weekends, making a special effort to play with him or take him on outings, just the two of them. But he worked long hours and he wasn't around enough to make a real difference.

He wasn't really Luca's father – Jacqueline had adopted him and his sister, Alina, on her own – but he had been around from their first days in Ireland; he and Jacqueline had married six months later. Far from putting him off, the ready-made family had seemed to appeal to Jonathan, and he had thrown himself into the role of father enthusiastically and wholeheartedly.

'I just think it's probably better for everyone if I stay away.'

'Nonsense,' Jonathan said briskly. 'We miss you.'

Luca occupied himself with scooping rice onto his plate and tearing naan bread, not knowing what to say to that.

'You'll be coming for Ali's birthday, at least?' Jonathan asked.

'Yes, definitely.'

'She'd be so disappointed if you didn't.'

'I know. I wouldn't miss it.' He couldn't bear to let Ali down.

'Good. Do you think you'll be bringing anyone?' Jonathan asked, clearly trying to sound casual, but Luca could hear the caginess in his voice, saw the effort he was making to appear offhand, as if he was unconcerned about the answer.

'No,' Luca said, with a crooked smile. He almost added 'don't worry', because he knew exactly what had prompted the question and the wariness behind it. The last time he had gone to a party at his parents' house – a New Year's Eve party five or six years ago – he had brought with him a girl he had met in rehab. He hadn't been seeing her, they weren't even particular friends, and he had only brought her because he knew he could count on her to behave appallingly. She hadn't let him down. In fact, she had far exceeded his expectations, projectile vomiting all over the bathroom and stealing cash from his mother's dressing table before disappearing into the night in search of the nearest dealer. Luca still felt burning shame when he remembered it. He had wanted to upset Jacqueline and had succeeded spectacularly, but it had been the very definition of a hollow victory.

'No, I'll be coming on my own,' he reiterated.

Jonathan simply nodded in acknowledgement, but the relief rolled off him in waves.

The time passed quickly as they chatted, and it was after eleven as they left the restaurant.

'Just drop me to the bus,' Luca said, as they walked back to the car. But Jonathan insisted on driving him home.

'I need to go to a supermarket on the way,' he said. 'Jacqueline asked me to pick up a few things.' He stopped outside a convenience store a little way from the restaurant. 'Do you want to come in?' he asked Luca.

'No, I'll wait here.'

'Okay,' he said, opening his door. 'I won't be long.'

Left alone in the car, Luca's eye caught the photograph attached to the dashboard on the driver's side with a magnet. He hadn't seen it in a long time, and he was surprised his mother kept it there where she would see it every day, a constant reminder of her disappointment. He picked it up to examine it more closely. An old colour photograph, it was creased with age and curling up at the edges. He only vaguely remembered the day it had been taken. He wasn't even sure if it was a true memory or if he had been told about it so often that he thought he remembered it. It had been taken outside the orphanage in Negru Vodă. His mother had her arms around her new children, him on one side and Ali on the other, both squinting into the sun and looking suitably bewildered at the start of their new life. Jacqueline beamed at the camera – a smile that said she couldn't believe her luck. It was an establishing shot: the beginning of their family.

He smiled as he looked at Ali, so shy and cute, her eyes sliding to him for reassurance. He hardly recognised himself in the little boy who stood staring straight ahead, his expression fierce. She should have known, he thought. She should have taken one look at that face and thrown him back. Ali would have forgotten him soon enough and they could all have been happy. They would have been a perfect family without him.

He remembered the mixture of terror and excitement with which he had made the journey to Ireland, and wondered if it had been the same for Jacqueline, bringing two little strangers to live with her. It was his first time on a plane. There had been a lot of firsts – the taste of chocolate, the kindness of his new mother's hands in his hair, the softness of the bed he had lain down in that night, the quiet of a night not filled with the nightmares of frightened children; hot water, clean clothes, plenty of food. It was a strange new world in which everything was warm and soft, and no one ever hit you.

Maybe Jacqueline kept it there as a reminder of happier times, he thought. Whatever else had happened since, they had been happy that day, full of hope. He had let her down, he knew that. She had only wanted to give him a life worth living. He had hurt her with his aloofness, and she took his self-reliance as a rebuke. But he didn't know any other way to be – he had been fighting too long to stop.

As Jonathan emerged from the shop carrying two plastic bags, Luca replaced the photograph and fixed it with the magnet hastily, almost guiltily, as if he shouldn't have been looking at it. He felt almost as if he had been prying into someone else's life.

'Thanks for dinner,' he said, when Jonathan dropped him off outside his building.

'I enjoyed it. We'll do it again soon, yes?'

'Yeah,' Luca said, as he opened the car door.

'And come out to the house,' Jonathan called after him, as he got out. 'Don't be a stranger.'

Luca waved as Jonathan drove off. *Don't be a stranger.* He wasn't sure he knew how to be anything else.

10

'Okay, you can do this,' Claire told herself, taking a deep breath and pulling open the door of the restaurant. She tossed her head back and strode confidently up to the maître d'. Half of her had been hoping Mark would already be there waiting, so she wouldn't have to sit at the table on her own, and the other half wanted to get there first so she would be seated when he arrived and wouldn't have to walk towards him while he watched. But when she gave her name to the man and told him she was joining Mark Bell, he informed her that Mark had already arrived. When he had taken her coat, he led her to the table. Claire made a determined effort to keep her head up and appear confident as she followed him. The dress helped. She knew she looked good, and the sheer material swishing around her legs sensually as she walked boosted her confidence. Yvonne had worked her magic on her makeup and hair, and she felt sophisticated, glamorous... and, yes, *sexy*.

She saw Mark first, recognising him instantly. Just as they reached the table, he smiled at her and, to her surprise, her nerves melted away because he seemed so friendly and familiar. It was like meeting an old friend. She knew this person and was happy to see him.

He stood as the maître d' walked away. 'NiceGirl, I presume?' he said, holding out a hand to her.

She nodded as they shook hands. 'Claire,' she said. 'Claire Kennedy.' He was taller than she'd remembered, but just as handsome.

'It's very nice to meet you.' He leaned in, kissing her cheek, and she felt a little shiver of excitement as his stubble brushed against her face and she breathed in the warm sandalwood tone of his aftershave. He waved her to the seat opposite him.

'What would you like to drink?' he asked. 'I thought maybe we should start with some champagne. We have something to celebrate, after all – at least, I hope we do.'

'Champagne would be lovely, thank you.'

She was aware of his eyes on her as the waiter fussed around with an ice bucket and a bottle of champagne, but she didn't feel self-conscious or want to squirm. Far from making her uncomfortable, the frank appreciation in his eyes gave her a warm glow. Maybe this was a magic dress, she thought whimsically. It was certainly helping her to get into character, like an actor's costume. She jumped when the champagne opened with a loud pop.

'Well, here's to the beginning of a successful partnership,' Mark said, as he raised his glass.

'Cheers,' she said, clinking her glass with his.

'So, I love the blog,' he said. 'Obviously.'

'Thanks.' *Now* she was uncomfortable, her nervousness returning as she thought of all the things he thought he knew about her. She was proud that he liked her writing, but she'd written some pretty filthy stuff on her blog, and he thought it was true. He thought she was completely upfront about laying bare the most intimate details of her sex life for all the world to see – and it was a pretty lurid sex life. She took a slug of champagne to cover her embarrassment. She had to try not to think about that too much.

'It's nice to meet you in the flesh. I have to admit I'm quite relieved,' Mark said, with a cheeky smile.

'Relieved? Why?'

'Well, you hide behind that avatar on Twitter and you write your blog anonymously. I had no idea what you looked like or who you really were. You could have been a ninety-year-old man for all I knew. You could have looked like a sumo wrestler.'

'Oh, I never thought of that.' She had been so caught up in her own anxiety about the meeting that it hadn't occurred to her he might be nervous too.

'Mm. I was quite tempted to run away before you turned up. I didn't want my illusions shattered.'

'Well, I may not look like a sumo wrestler, but I don't look anything like my Twitter avatar either.'

'No, you're much prettier.'

Claire raised her eyebrows. 'I think my avatar is hot.'

'She's okay,' Mark said, 'if you like that whole overblown, cartoonish thing. Me, I'm a sucker for a woman in three-D.'

Claire laughed. 'Anyway, you've read the blog,' she said. 'Surely you could tell from that that I wasn't an old man. Or a sumo wrestler.'

'It could have been made up. Lots of people pretend to be something they're not on the internet. It's easy.'

'I suppose so.' She frowned, feeling guilty. He was talking about her, only he didn't know it. Now was her chance to tell him that she wasn't really the person in her blog. He probably wouldn't mind – it would still be better than finding out she was a ninety-year-old sumo wrestler or whatever.

But then she felt needled by the implication of his words. 'Would it make any difference if I was a ninety-year-old man? Or if I looked like a sumo wrestler? Would you have changed your mind about wanting the book? I mean, I'd still be the same writer.'

'Of course the writing would be the same, but I don't know that I'd be interested if it turned out to be the sordid fantasies of some decrepit old pervert.'

She laughed. She had to admit he had a point. She could imagine the shocked reaction of her followers if it turned out she was a dirty old man.

'As for how you look,' he said, giving her an admiring glance, 'it's not just about the writing. It's the whole package, and it's a lot easier to sell an attractive young woman than an old man.'

Claire blushed, and was glad that the waiter appeared just then to run through the specials. When he had gone she buried her face in the menu to regain her composure. The food sounded wonderful.

'Are you ready to order?' Mark asked her, as the waiter returned.

'I'll have the crab cakes, and then the duck, please,' she told the waiter.

Mark ordered smoked salmon followed by beef in Guinness. 'When in Ireland…' he said to Claire, after the waiter had gone. 'So,' he began in a more business-like tone, 'how do you feel about going public?'

'Nervous,' Claire admitted. 'Kind of terrified, actually.'

'Are you sure you want to do it?'

'Yes,' she said cautiously. 'I think so. I mean, I really want to do the book. I've always wanted to be published. But the rest... I'm not so sure.'

'Well, you don't necessarily have to "come out" as the author. We could publish the book anonymously. It would have its own advantages. We could use the mystery around your identity as a publicity angle – build up the intrigue about who you really are.'

'I never thought of that. Is this a plan you came up with when you thought I might be some old codger?'

He grinned sheepishly. 'Well, you have to be prepared for all contingencies.'

'Do you think it would work equally well if I published anonymously?'

'Your blog is very popular, so you've got a good platform to start off from. And sex always sells. I think we can make the book a big success either way.'

'But...?' She heard the reservation in his tone.

'But the fact that you're an attractive woman is a bonus. It really helps with the media.'

'I don't know how good I'd be at the publicity stuff,' Claire said. 'I'm a bit shy.'

'Is that what motivated you to write your blog anonymously?'

'Well, that and the subject matter. I mean, it wouldn't be great for work, for instance, if everyone knew I was writing that stuff. It's not the sort of thing you'd want your boss to know about. I also thought it would be best if people couldn't trace me. You come across some very strange people on the internet, especially with the sort of stuff I write about.'

'Yeah, I can imagine.' He nodded. 'You probably get some real weirdos.'

She laughed. 'Half of them think I should be consigned to Hell, and the other half want a bunk-up.'

Mark frowned. 'Well, I suppose that would be a consideration, too, in deciding if you want to be identified as the author.'

They were interrupted by the arrival of their starters.

'You must've told some people about the blog,' Mark said, as they began eating.

'Only one – a friend. None of my family know about it.'

'They don't know about your blog or about your, er... personal life?'

'They don't know any of it. I'm not sure how I'd feel about them finding out.'

'Do you think they'd be shocked?'

'Well... yes, probably.' She was actually less worried that they'd be horrified than that they'd die laughing and call her on it. They could even expose her as a fraud if they wanted to. Her mother would probably love the whole thing, and be enormously proud. But Michelle would be livid – and jealous. Like Claire, she was a writer who dreamt of being a published author, and she always had something snide to say when someone else got a book deal. She would hate Claire getting there before her, and Claire wouldn't put it past her to blow the whistle out of spite. She could be pretty poisonous. Of course, none of the family could know for sure that she wasn't living a double life as a sex bomb with a string of secret lovers. It wasn't as if she would share it with them if it were true. But somehow she thought they'd have a damn good idea that she'd made it all up. And how pathetic would she look then?

'Do you think it would be possible to keep it a secret?' she asked.

'Well, obviously some people would have to know. But we could keep the circle as small as possible, and get everyone to sign non-disclosure agreements. What about the men?' he asked.

'The men?'

'The men you write about – Mr Bump and Grind, Mr Curious, Mr Fussy, all that lot.'

'Oh, them.'

'I know you use fake names, but is there a chance that any of them would recognise themselves?'

'I really don't think they'd cause problems.' Mainly because they don't exist.

'Still, if you go public and you're on television or in the newspapers, it wouldn't be hard for someone you'd been with to put two and two together.'

'True,' she said, deciding it would be as good an excuse as any if she decided she wanted to remain anonymous.

'It's something to think about anyway. You don't have to decide anything right now. And if we do publish anonymously, you can always decide to go public further down the line, if you want. It could even give the book a second bite of the cherry when the initial publicity has died down.'

By the time their starters were cleared, the champagne bottle was empty, and they ordered some red wine.

'So, tell me a bit about yourself, Claire,' Mark said, when their main courses had been served.

'Like what?'

'Anything. I know absolutely nothing about you – except for the explicit details of your sex life, of course.' He grinned.

She smiled ruefully, the champagne buzz overriding her shyness. 'Well, let's see. I'm twenty-eight, the youngest in my family. I have two older brothers, both married with kids. I have a degree in English literature. I work in a bookshop – an independent.'

'But you'd like to write full-time?'

'I'd love to.'

'Well, hopefully we can make that happen.' He smiled. 'Do you write other stuff?'

'Yes, I write fiction. I'm working on a young adult novel at the moment.'

'I'd be happy to take a look at if you'd like.'

'You would?'

'Sure.'

'That would be great. I mean, it's not ready to show to anyone yet, but when it is, I'd love you to read it.'

'I'd be glad to.'

'Anything else you'd like to know?'

'Well... I know you don't have a boyfriend as such – you're still auditioning for the role, yes?'

'Sort of.'

'How many candidates are there, now that Mr Handy's out of the picture?'

'Actually... I may exaggerate a bit on the blog,' she admitted.

'Really? How much?'

She took a deep breath. 'At the moment there are...' she looked up at the ceiling as if counting '...none.'

'None?' His eyebrows shot up, but she couldn't help thinking he seemed rather pleased.

'Do you think I'm an awful fraud?'

'I'm just surprised. I did allow for a certain amount of artistic license –

several of my female friends who read your blog tell me that no single young woman could be getting that much action.'

'Well, they're right.'

'You're not going to tell me you make it all up, are you?'

'Oh no!' she gasped, in mock horror. 'It's sort of a blend – part reality, part fiction. Like *Made in Chelsea*.'

'Some scenes have been created for our entertainment?'

'Exactly. Some of the men I describe are actually a mash-up of a couple of guys I've dated. Or I write about stuff that's happened in the past. Some of the guys I made up completely, for my own amusement,' she admitted, with a guilty smile.

'Mr Bossy?' he guessed.

'Mr Bossy's real, but he was a long time ago,' she heard herself saying. She had no idea where that had come from. Surely it would have been simpler to make him fictional, and the more straightforward guys real. Well, it was said now – too late to take it back.

'So there's no one in your life at the moment?'

'It's my guilty secret.'

'Would it be very cheesy to say I find that hard to believe?'

'Very cheesy. But I happen to love cheese,' she smiled, 'so I'll let you get away with it.'

'So, seriously – how did that happen?'

'Well, your friend is right. Good men aren't that thick on the ground. And I'm quite fussy. There's also the fact that I live with my mother now.'

'You live with your mother?'

'She's been ill. She has a dodgy heart and she's quite incapacitated, so I moved back home to look after her,' she said.

'Well, I can see how that would curtail your social life.'

'It's fine. I think it came at a good time, actually – gave me a chance to take stock. I was getting tired of playing the field anyway. I think I'm ready for something more serious.' Wow, she had no idea where all this material was coming from, but she liked it. Turned out improvisation was her thing! Who knew?

'Well, at the risk of sounding even cheesier, may I say I'm glad to hear that?' he said, with a slow smile.

Claire smiled back. 'So, what about you?'

'Well, I'm a publisher, as you know. Thirty-two. I run. I live in Highgate with Millie and we have a pretty volatile relationship—'

'Millie?' Claire was surprised by how disappointed she felt.

'My cat. I told you about her.'

'Oh yes! The feline one.' She smiled in relief. 'How is she?'

'I'd like to say she was jealous about me coming to meet you, but she's not arsed, as usual. Sometimes I think she's just using me for my money. She has very expensive tastes.'

'You should ditch her. She doesn't deserve you.'

'I know, but I'm a besotted fool,' Mark said, putting his hand on his heart and pulling a pathetic face.

'What about your family?'

'I'm an only child. But don't believe the propaganda,' he said, with a grin. 'We're a much-maligned group.'

'So you *weren't* a spoilt brat who thought the world revolved around you and didn't know how to share?'

'Well, I have to admit I'm not good at sharing. I was a nightmare at playschool.'

'What about your parents? Do they live in London?'

'They moved to Cornwall when my father retired. I visit as often as I can, which isn't often enough.'

'So… girlfriend?'

'No. I've been dating a bit, but nothing serious. I broke up with my last girlfriend about six months ago. Sophie,' he added, with a faraway look in his eyes. 'She was even more high maintenance than Millie.'

'Had you been together long?'

'About five years, off and on. Mostly on.'

'That's a long time. What happened?'

'We were fighting all the time. We made each other miserable. So we decided to call it a day.'

'Well, at the risk of sounding cheesy, may *I* say I'm very glad you did,' she said. She couldn't believe how easy she was finding it to flirt with him. She hardly recognised herself. She didn't know what had got into her, but whatever it was, she liked it. It was fun, dressing up, flirting her socks off with Mark, seeing the admiration in his eyes when he looked at her. She was really enjoying being this person, and she was delighted that the spark between them was still there in real life. She liked Mark, and she felt they already had a connection that went way beyond a superficial Twitter flirtation.

When the mains were cleared away, Mark became more business-like again.

'Do you have an agent?' he asked her.

'No. Do I need one?'

He shrugged. 'It's up to you, but it would probably be advisable. It shouldn't be hard to get one when you already have a deal on the table.'

'And do I?'

'If you want one.'

'Yes! I do.'

'I'll get a formal offer in the post and have a contract drawn up. But, in the meantime, can we shake on it?' he asked, holding out his hand.

'Definitely!' Claire grasped and shook it heartily.

'Great! I look forward to working with you.' Mark beamed at her. 'Now, do you want dessert?' he asked, looking at the menus the waiter had just handed them.

'I'm absolutely stuffed,' Claire said, 'but they do have sticky toffee pudding...'

'Want to go halves?' Mark asked.

'I thought you didn't like sharing?'

'I need the practice.'

'In that case, yes, please,' Claire said eagerly, thinking he might well be the perfect man.

'So what made you decide to work in the bookshop?' Mark asked.

'It wasn't really a decision. It was more a case of what I could get. My original plan was to move to London and try to start a career in publishing.' She wondered if their paths would have crossed. 'I tried to find something in that field when I moved home, but... it didn't happen.'

'Well, I'm glad about that.'

'You are?' She frowned.

'Yes. Instead of joining the hordes of writers *manqué* working in publishing, you've skipped that bit and actually become a writer.'

'Well, it wasn't part of any grand plan.'

'Still, that's the way it's worked out.'

'I suppose it is.' She smiled. Maybe he was right and everything had happened for a reason. 'Are you a writer *manqué*?'

'Not really. I've written some short stories, but I don't have any ambitions to write full-time. I enjoy what I do. I get a real buzz out of discovering and nurturing talent. Like yours.'

When the bill came, Mark paid. 'Don't even think about it,' he said, when Claire reached for her purse. 'It's on expenses.'

'That was lovely, thank you,' Claire said, as they stood. She hadn't noticed the restaurant emptying, but as they walked to the exit, she realised that they were the last to leave. She had enjoyed Mark's company so much that the time had flown. They made their way outside, where a line of taxis was waiting. 'It was really good to meet you,' Claire said. She was sorry that the evening was over so soon.

Mark must have felt the same because he said, 'Do you fancy going for a drink?'

Claire looked at her watch. 'I don't think there'll be anywhere open.'

'We could go to my hotel and have a drink in the bar.'

'Where are you staying?'

'The Merrion.'

'Okay, yes.' She was happy to spend a bit more time with him and get to know him better. He was only in Dublin for a short time so she wanted to make the most of it.

It was a short drive to the Merrion Hotel. Mark paid the taxi driver and took her hand as they walked up the steps to the entrance.

'I love this place,' Claire said, as they went into the gracious marble lobby with its classical columns and ornate plasterwork.

Instead of heading straight for the bar, Mark came to a halt in the lobby, taking both her hands in his. 'So, we could go to the bar,' he said, gazing meaningfully into her eyes, 'or we could have a drink in my room.'

'Oh!' Claire suddenly felt gauche, her thin veneer of sophistication evaporating, like Cinderella's finery, to expose her as the naïve, clueless girl she really was. She had no idea what the signals were, what the etiquette was.

'Um... the bar?' she said in a small voice.

He nodded, and led her across the lobby to the comfortable lounge. She tried to gauge his expression, but she couldn't tell if he was disappointed. They sat side by side on a sofa in front of a real turf fire and a waitress appeared to take their order. Claire had felt mellow and relaxed as they left the restaurant, but now she was tense and on edge. Mark didn't seem put out, but there was still that heat in his eyes when he looked at her.

She didn't want any awkwardness between them, so she had to say something to clear the air. She waited until their drinks were served.

'Well, cheers – again!' Mark said, clinking glasses with her.

She clutched her glass of Bailey's in both hands, trying to come up with something to say. She couldn't just blurt out that she wasn't going to sleep with him, could she? What if that wasn't even what he'd meant? Then she'd look really stupid – and presumptuous.

'Mark,' she began tentatively, 'I know my blog is kind of... out there, and I come across as this really forthright person – promiscuous, even.' She felt her face flame. 'But the truth is... well, I don't usually move that fast. I mean, despite the impression you might have of me, I don't sleep with someone on the first date. In fact, I have a five-date rule... not that this is a date, but—'

'No,' Mark interrupted, leaning forward urgently. *'I'm* sorry. Believe it or not, I don't usually come on that strong so quickly either.'

Come on strong. Huh! So he *had* been asking her up to his room for sex. At least she had learnt something tonight. She made a mental note: 'Come back to my hotel for a drink', translation: 'Come back to my hotel and have sex with me.'

'I guess I just feel like we've known each other longer than we really have,' he said.

'I know what you mean.' She felt the same. She'd had a crush on him even before they'd met.

'Forgive me?' he asked, seeming genuinely remorseful. 'Please don't blame a guy for trying.'

'I don't,' she said, and meant it. If she was really the girl she was pretending to be, she would probably have taken him up on the invitation to go to his room. The combination of the food, the wine and her beautiful dress had left her feeling languid and sensual. She felt desirable and desired, a heady sensation.

'You don't forgive me?' he asked, alarmed.

'No.' She smiled. 'I mean I don't blame you for trying. I just didn't want you to think—'

'I don't think anything, honestly. And I don't presume you're promiscuous. I'm really sorry if I offended you.'

'No, it's fine. Really.' She relaxed back on the sofa, able to enjoy her drink now.

'Could you just forget I said that and meet me tomorrow? Maybe show me around a bit?' He looked at her pleadingly.

'Would that be like a date?'

He smiled. 'Only if you want it to be. It could just be two people hanging out. My flight isn't until the evening. Maybe you could join me for brunch here. Unless you're busy with your mum, of course.'

'No, she's convalescing in a nursing home at the moment, so I'm all yours.'

'Good. I like the sound of that.'

Shortly after that, Claire got a taxi home. Mark walked her out to see her off, and gave her a kiss on the cheek as they said goodbye. He smelt so good, and his skin was so warm and firm as his cheek brushed hers, that Claire was tempted to throw herself into his arms and say she'd changed her mind and would go up to his room, after all. But she knew that, once she got there, she'd have no clue how to handle herself. So instead she skipped down the steps into the waiting cab and floated all the way home. She felt dizzy with excitement. Mark, her book deal... Suddenly it seemed that the life she'd always wanted could really be hers. She was dying to tell someone about it, only sorry that there was no one to tell. Instead she hugged it to herself like a lovely secret.

* * *

She felt keyed up the following day as she made her way to Mark's hotel. She got off the tram at St Stephen's Green and walked to Merrion Street. It was a beautiful day, cold, but bright and sunny. She had dressed casually in black skinny jeans with calf-length suede boots and a green V-neck sweater. After all, she figured her alter ego would have dress-down days – even NiceGirl couldn't go around looking like a siren twenty-four/seven. The sweater was one she hadn't worn in years, but she had chosen it with Yvonne's tips for sexy dressing in mind, because it was figure-hugging, and the deep V of the neckline would draw the eye to her cleavage. She had also followed Yvonne's advice and worn a pendant, which she was supposed to play with to draw attention to her breasts. There was nothing sexy about her red duffel coat, or her woolly scarf and gloves, but she reasoned that surely even sexy girls would feel the cold.

Mark was waiting for her in the lobby. He leapt up to greet her when she arrived and they kissed each other on the cheek. Then they went down to the cellar restaurant, where they ordered smoked salmon and creamy scrambled egg. Claire felt there was something deliciously intimate about eating together the morning after they had been out, as if they'd spent the night together.

'So, what should we do for the rest of my time here? I've got about...' Mark glanced at his watch '...three hours before I need to go to the airport.'

'Well, there's all the usual tourist stuff – Trinity College, Book of Kells, Guinness, Christchurch Cathedral, galleries...' Claire reeled off the standard itinerary. 'We could go on the hop-on, hop-off bus,' she suggested. 'Or there's the Viking Splash. That's basically a bus tour, too, but you wear horned helmets and do lots of roaring, and then you go into the Grand Canal Basin at the end.'

'I don't really fancy anything touristy.' Mark wrinkled his nose. 'Something more laid back, maybe.'

'We could go for a walk? It's a lovely day.'

'A walk would be good.'

'Great. I know just the place,' Claire told him.

They lingered over brunch for at least an hour, chatting easily. Then they headed off in the direction of Merrion Square, Claire leading the way.

'This isn't where we're going,' she told Mark, 'but I thought we should pay our respects to Oscar since we're in the neighbourhood.' She brought him to visit the colourful statue of Oscar Wilde in the park, pointing out the house opposite where he had grown up.

When they had spent some time reading the quotes on the pillars that formed part of the memorial, she led him towards St Stephen's Green, heading in the direction of Earlsfort Terrace. She had a blissful sense of well-being as they walked slowly along the side of the park. The trees were covered in young, bright green leaves and cherry blossom, and tulips were visible through the green railings. It was officially the beginning of summer, the first Sunday in May. There was a sense of newness and possibility, of the world coming to life again, and she was part of it.

'Is this where we're going?' Mark asked, as she led him through the gates of the National Concert Hall with its imposing façade, the billboards outside advertising symphonies and performances by world-famous soloists.

'No.' Claire led him through the car park to the back of the building, then through an arched gateway into the hidden grandeur of the Iveagh Gardens. 'This is one of my favourite places in Dublin,' she said, as they passed the statue of Count John McCormack, the famous Irish tenor, near the entrance. It was her least favourite feature in the gardens – it was too new and pristine, she thought, too prosaic and at odds with the romantic decay of the older, lichen-covered statues with their classical lines and missing limbs.

She was disappointed to hear the squeals of children as they crunched along the wide gravel path, flanked by two large ornamental fountains. She found a bench and they sat down – a couple of children were playing nearby while their father watched. Claire tried not to resent them, but she loved the gardens best when she had them to herself, when they felt like her own secret place. As if on cue, the father rounded up his children, and they headed to the exit.

'Alone at last,' Mark said.

'I thought they'd never go.'

He cocked his head to the side, regarding her consideringly. 'You're very sweet.'

'You sound surprised.'

He smiled. 'You're different from how I imagined.'

'Oh?' Claire wasn't sure she liked where this was going. 'Different how?' Did she really want to know?

'I thought you'd be more...' He hesitated.

'What?' She thought of all the ways the sentence could end – more sexy, more ballsy, more confident, more fun, more interesting...

'Can I be honest?'

She nodded. 'Of course.' *Please don't say 'sexy'. Or 'interesting'.*

'Well, to be honest, I thought you'd be a bit... intimidating,' he admitted finally.

'Oh!'

'More strident. You're nicer than I was expecting.'

'Really?' She felt a warm glow from the way he was looking at her.

'Much nicer.'

'I did tell you I was a nice girl.'

'The name should have been a giveaway.'

'So, is "nice" a good thing?'

He nodded, smiling at her. 'Nice is good.'

'Not *too* nice?'

'No. Just right.'

'Come on, let's explore some more,' she said, getting up.

They wandered in companionable silence through all the hidden nooks and crannies of the garden, down stone steps leading to dark verdant paths, past the statues of girls in flowing robes that stood on plinths, their lichen covering blending with the bark of the trees so they seemed almost to merge with the landscape. They came across some broken pieces of large statues lying on the grass, half buried in the bushes and wondered what their story was. The gardens were empty, the only sound the crunch of their feet on the gravel.

They were walking along one of the smaller paths when Claire stopped in front of a statue. 'She's my favourite,' she told Mark, shielding her eyes from the light that filtered through the trees as she looked up. 'There's something so... noble about her. She's so elegant and poised.'

'Even though she's only got one arm,' Mark said.

'It's not an easy look to pull off.' Claire laughed. 'But there's something about her. I think she's a warrior.'

'I think she's completely charming,' Mark said. But when Claire looked around, he was looking at her, not the statue.

'Sorry,' he said, laughing ruefully at being caught. 'That was *really* cheesy.'

Claire giggled. 'It was a bit.' But she didn't mind.

'Oh well, since we already know I'm the cheesemeister general, I might as well ask – can I kiss you?' He was gazing intently into her eyes now, moving closer.

Claire nodded breathlessly.

'I have to warn you – if I kiss you, this is definitely a date.'

'Still, yes,' Claire whispered, and he bent his head slowly, tentatively to hers. His lips were soft and warm and he kissed her slowly, gently, pulling away too soon. Claire instinctively reached out, clutching his sleeve.

'Again?' he whispered, his breath clouding between them.

'Again,' she breathed. And he kissed her again, right there among the ruined statuary.

Claire felt dazed and giddy as they walked back to the hotel, hand in hand. She wondered what Mark was feeling. She doubted that this was what he had expected to happen when he'd met her – chaste kisses and hand-holding, like teenagers. But he seemed happy. In fact, she was pretty sure his goofy grin matched hers whenever they caught each other's eye. She waited in the lobby while he collected his bags, already bereft at the thought of him leaving.

'Will you come and stay with me in London?' he asked, as they stood at the top of the steps. 'I have a spare bedroom,' he added, when she hesitated. 'We could discuss the book, spend some more time together.'

'I'd love to.'

He beamed. 'Soon?'

'I might be able to get over next weekend or the one after – my mother's in a nursing home for the next few weeks. Once she comes home, I'll need to be around for a while.'

'Well, see what you can arrange. I'll be in touch.' He kissed her goodbye, then jumped into the waiting taxi.

11

'How was your date?' Yvonne asked, the next day, as they opened boxes of books in the store room.

'It was lovely,' Claire said, smiling broadly. 'Best date ever.'

'Ooh, tell me all,' Yvonne said. 'Did my flirting tips help?'

'Yes, they were great,' Claire lied, so as not to hurt Yvonne's feelings. In fact, she had forgotten to do any of the things Yvonne had taught her – fiddling with her hair, mirroring his movements, sucking food off her finger, 'spontaneously' touching him. It turned out she hadn't needed any tricks at all.

'We just really clicked. He's smart and funny and *seriously* cute. And he was so easy to talk to, I felt like we'd known each other for ages.'

'Well, look at you, all loved up.' Yvonne grinned. 'So, did you go back to his hotel?'

'No. I mean yes, but just for a drink. I didn't stay.'

'You're making him wait. Nice move.' She nodded. 'As your dating coach, I approve.'

'I told him I have a five-date rule.'

'Good for you! Even Judy'd be impressed by that. Five is harsh!'

'Do you think it's too many?'

'No. If five is what you want, then it's just right.'

'And we met up again yesterday for brunch, and hung out together until he had to go to the airport.'

'Excellent. You really like him, don't you?'

'Yeah, I do – a lot.'

'Are you seeing him again?'

'He wants me to go to London, so I'm going to try to get over while Mum's in the nursing home.'

'It's a pity he's so far away.'

'Yeah,' Claire agreed. But in many ways it was a blessing. If she wanted things to progress with him – and she did – she was going to have to wise up fast. He would be expecting some serious skills and she had no moves whatsoever. She needed a far more advanced form of teaching than Yvonne could provide. She had been mulling it over all night and had finally come up with an idea as to how she could get it. But the very thought of it made her stomach churn with anxiety.

In the meantime, she was glad she had bought herself some time with the five-date rule so she could visit Mark in London without pressure. 'How did your date go with Ivan?' she asked Yvonne, to take her mind off her plan. There would be time enough to think about it tonight.

That evening, Claire sat at the kitchen table with her laptop and a glass of wine, scrolling through the escorts' websites and trying very hard not to tear her hair out. This was proving a lot harder than she'd thought – and she hadn't thought it would be easy when she'd come up with the plan in the first place. The guys looked so scary in their pictures, all ripped and muscle-bound and striking ridiculous poses. And then there were the close-ups of their junk in tight underwear! She couldn't see herself with any of them. But how else could she get some quick sexual experience with no strings attached? She just had to knuckle down and pick someone.

This one looked quite friendly, she thought, clicking on a photo of a skinny, fairly ordinary-looking boy. But as she read through his profile, she just felt sad. He was only nineteen – just a kid, for Christ's sake! There was no way she could go with someone that young. Ruling out gay men and the under-twenties narrowed the field considerably, but didn't make her task any easier. Reading their profiles was depressing. They were mostly foreigners and very young, and there was something heartbreakingly desperate about their constant availability, their willingness to service men, women or couples anytime, anywhere, their eagerness to fulfill the fantasies of random strangers.

Still, they wanted the work, she told herself. She would be just another job to them, and they would be doing it whether she hired them or not. What would Carlos from Brazil think, she wondered, if she wanted to pay him to teach her the art of the blowjob? He had probably had worse gigs. He had a sweet face and sounded kind. He guaranteed to give you the time of your life and make all your fantasies come true, and he seemed sensitive towards first-timers or those who were new to escorts. He said he could go at your pace and would take time to chat – though at a hundred euro for a half-hour, she didn't think she'd have much time to waste on chat. In fact, she should make a detailed plan of how she wanted to use the time when she met up with Carlos.

'Oh, who am I kidding?' she said aloud, closing the site. 'I can't do this.' But how the hell else was she going to learn? This was one situation where books and Googling weren't going to be enough. She needed some real-life, hands-on experience. She shouldn't have passed up the opportunity to have sex with Luca that night, she thought. At least she'd have got back into the game.

And then she thought of what he'd said that night – 'singing for my supper'. He'd been willing to sleep with her in return for a bed for the night. Maybe she could take him up on that, after all – not in exchange for a bed, but she could pay him. And later he'd said the only things he was good at were painting and shagging, but he hadn't figured out how to make money from either. He needed money. She needed no-strings sex. Maybe they could help each other. It might be the perfect solution.

* * *

The next evening she raced home from work and spent ages getting ready to go over to Luca's. It was difficult to know what note to strike. She'd never propositioned anyone before, and she wasn't sure about the dress code. It felt like somewhere between a date and a job interview.

'You're overthinking this,' she told herself, as she tossed another dress on the bed to join the growing pile. Half of her wardrobe was lying there now and she groaned in frustration. She finally opted for a pair of black trousers and a fitted white shirt. She had to get out of the house quickly before she lost her nerve.

She had no trouble remembering where Luca lived, but she wasn't sure of the number of his flat. She knew he was at the top of the house, though, so she took a chance and pressed the bell for ten, the highest number. She held her breath as she waited for a reply, forcing herself to resist the urge to flee.

Chances are he's not even home, she thought, the idea bringing instant relief. If he wasn't in, she'd take it as a sign. But then there was a crackling from the speaker beside the bells.

'Hello!' she shouted. 'Is that Luca?'

There was more crackling from the speaker and then it went dead. She stood waiting. Should she press the bell again? She didn't even know for sure that it was Luca's flat. But then she heard movement inside, the door opened and Luca stuck his head out. 'Oh, hello!' He looked surprised to see her.

'Hi. Um... can I come in?' Oh God, maybe he wasn't alone. Maybe he'd run downstairs to get rid of whoever was at the door because he had a naked girl to get back to.

'Sure.' He stood back and waved her into the hall. 'The buzzer doesn't work,' he said, as he led her to the stairs.

'Oh. Sorry.'

He waved her ahead of him on the stairs and she felt self-conscious as they climbed, aware of his eyes on her back. She hoped he wasn't checking out her bum. She shouldn't have worn tight trousers.

He led her into the living room and she was struck once again by the poverty of the place. The air was thick with the heavy smell of oil paint and turpentine, and a large canvas stood on an easel by the window.

'Were you working?' she asked, noticing the streaks of blue and red on his hands and arms as he ran his fingers through his hair. 'Sorry, I hope I'm not interrupting.'

'No, it's fine. Have a seat.' He nodded to the couch and she threw herself onto it gratefully. 'Do you want a drink or anything?'

'No, thanks,' she said, her voice sounding breathy and nervous.

He frowned down at her, his hands on his hips. 'So – you wanted to see me?'

'Yeah. I wanted to, um... talk to you about something.'

'Okay. Shoot.'

She swallowed hard, running her sweaty palms along her legs. 'It's hard to — I'm not sure where to start,' she stammered. 'I wanted to ask you to do me a favour— well, not exactly a favour because I would pay you,' she amended hastily. He just stood there, looking at her, and she felt very flustered.

'So what's the favour?' he asked.

She took a deep breath to steady herself. 'Well, remember that night when you were at my house and you, um, you... you said you were singing for your supper...' She felt her face burning and kept her eyes trained on her hands, unable to look at him.

'Yeah, and I'm really sorry about that. It was a stupid, crass thing to say. But I thought we'd got past it. I thought you'd forgiven me.'

'Oh, I have.' She looked up at him. 'It's just... I was wondering if I could, um, change my mind.'

'Change your mind?' He frowned. Then his eyes widened. 'Oh.'

'I don't mean in exchange for staying that night,' she rushed on. 'I'd pay you.'

He sat down beside her on the couch and she felt his warm hand cover her fidgeting fingers. 'Calm down,' he said.

'Sorry, it was a stupid idea. I shouldn't have— I should go.' She moved to stand up, but he stopped her with a firm grasp on her hand.

'Let me get this straight,' he said. 'You want to pay me to have sex with you?'

She forced herself to look him in the eye. 'Yes,' she said, relieved that he understood and the worst part was over.

'I'd fuck you for free, in case I didn't make that clear the other night.'

She blushed. 'But that wasn't for free, was it? You were "singing for your supper".'

'Look, I was talking shite. I thought that was what you wanted. But, despite the impression I may have given, I'm not in the habit of trading sex.'

She sighed. 'No, of course not. Sorry. I didn't mean to insult you.'

'It's okay. So, what do you say?' He jerked his head in the direction of the bedroom. 'On the house.'

She gulped. Damn, he hadn't understood at all. 'Um, no, that's not what I meant. I don't just want you to fu— I mean, I don't want to just have a one-night stand. I want you to teach me stuff.'

'Stuff?' He narrowed his eyes.

'Sex stuff. It's kind of a long story.'

'I've got plenty of time.'

'Do you think I could have that drink after all?'

'Beer okay?'

'Fine.'

He disappeared into the kitchen and came back with two bottles of Corona and handed her one. It was ice-cold and wet with condensation.

'Cheers!' He clicked his bottle against hers and sat beside her on the sofa. 'So – what's the long story?'

Claire took a sip of beer, trying to decide how to start. 'I write this blog,' she said. 'It's a sex blog.'

'A sex blog?' Luca raised his eyebrows.

'Yes. I write about my, um… experiences – the men I go out with, the things we do. It's quite raunchy.'

'Good for you!'

'I've been writing it for a couple of years now, and it's very popular. I have over 20,000 hits each month, and I'm the number-one sex blogger in the search engines.' God, she was babbling. Why was she telling him her stats? 'Anyway, the point is I've written about a lot of different experiences, a lot of different men. It's very explicit.'

'Okay,' he said, scratching his head. He looked bewildered.

She bit her lip. 'But the thing is, I haven't done any of it. There aren't any men. None of it's real.'

'So you make up these stories? You write down your fantasies? That's kind of hot,' he said, with a wicked grin. 'But I don't see the problem. There's no law against it, is there? Everything you write on your blog doesn't have to be true.'

'The problem is, a publisher's interested in it. He wants me to turn it into a book.'

'So? Just make it up, like on the blog.'

Claire chewed her lip. 'But he'll expect me to be all sexy and sassy, like the girl in the blog, and I'm not.'

'You seem to have done a good job of winging it so far.'

'Okay,' Claire said. 'If you don't want to help me, that's fine.' She took a swig from her bottle to cover her embarrassment, aware she was blushing furiously.

'There's more to it, isn't there?' Luca scrutinised her closely, and then a slow smile spread across his face. 'Is that who you went on a date with the other night – this publisher dude?'

'Well... yes.'

'You like him, don't you?' he asked.

'Yes, okay, I like him.' Claire blushed. 'But he thinks I'm this total sexpot, when in fact I have hardly any experience in... that area. So, you see, it's not just about having a – a fuck,' she forced herself to say it, almost choking on the word. 'It's a more long-term project.'

'Okay. Anyway, I'm not saying no.'

'You're not?'

'I'm not saying yes either,' he warned. 'I'm not exactly sure what you want me to do. What would you want me to teach you?'

'Well... everything, I suppose. How to... you know, be good at it. And blowjobs and stuff.'

'Blowjobs?' Luca was sitting so close, his dark eyes twinkling with amusement. 'So basically you want to pay me to let you suck my dick?'

She couldn't meet his frank, open expression, her eyes darting away. 'Well...'

'Sounds like my kind of job,' he said. 'When do we start?'

'So you'll do it?'

'I don't know. What does it pay?'

'Oh, I've researched the going rate for this sort of thing—'

'You have?'

'Um, yeah. I was going to hire an escort, but I couldn't get up the nerve. Anyway, I didn't like the idea of being with a professional, um...'

'Hooker,' he finished. 'So you thought you'd go for a talented amateur. Look, I'll fuck you, if you want. You don't have to pay me.'

She flinched at his bluntness. 'But I told you, I don't want you to just fu— do that. Why should you do it for nothing anyway? I'm not someone you'd choose to, um... do that with.'

'You've got all the usual girl bits, haven't you?' he said, his eyes raking over her body. 'I'd say you're plenty my type.'

She cringed, but stood her ground. 'I want you to *teach* me. You'd have to put up with me being useless and be patient with me. Why shouldn't you get something out of it? It's only fair. Besides—' She stopped abruptly. She didn't want to offend him.

'Besides?' He raised his eyebrows questioningly.

'Well, we'd have to do it here. I mean, I can't do it at home in front of my mum.'

'You could always close your bedroom door.' He grinned mischievously.

'You know what I mean.'

'Yeah. So you want to come here?'

'Yes, so I'd have a vested interest in you not getting your electricity cut off and stuff,' she mumbled, her eyes roving around the living room.

'Right. Gotcha.'

'Only if that was okay with you, of course,' she added, suddenly realising he might not want her there.

'Not having my electricity cut off? That'd be fine with me.'

'No. I mean, me coming here. We could go to a hotel if you'd prefer.'

'No need for that. It's fine for you to come here.'

'So… you'll do it?' Claire asked hopefully.

He sighed. 'Yes, okay,' he said, sounding reluctant. 'I'll do it.'

'Thank you.' She sagged with relief. At least all that excruciating humiliation hadn't been for nothing. 'We can work out a schedule. I'll be very respectful and I won't intrude on your personal life. I mean, I wouldn't want to complicate things with your girlfriend or anything.'

'I don't have a girlfriend.'

'Oh – well, that could change.'

'It won't. I don't really do girlfriends. And that's another thing.'

'What?'

'This is going to sound unbelievably arrogant, but if we're going to do this, we need to sort out some ground rules.'

'Okay.'

'And number-one rule is you don't get hung up on me.'

'You're right!' she said, with a harsh laugh. 'That does sound unbelievably arrogant.'

'Sorry, but I just want us both to be clear what this is,' he said, waving his hand between them. 'Women tend to be more emotional about sex, and if you're as inexperienced as you say you are… We're going to be doing things, intimate things, and it might make you feel – well, I just don't want you to confuse sex with love or to start thinking about me like a boyfriend.'

'Don't worry. The fact that I'm paying you will take care of that.'

'Yeah,' he nodded, 'maybe it's a good thing you'll be paying me. It'll be a reminder that this is a business relationship.'

'Maybe we should draw up a contract,' she said stiffly, needled.

'No need for that. I just don't want you accusing me of misleading you. I don't want you to have false expectations.'

'I won't. Anyway, I'm doing this because I want to be with Mark, remember?'

'Okay. So what's the going rate for this sort of thing, then? What were you going to pay the escort?'

'They mostly seem to charge a hundred euro for half an hour.'

Luca gave a low whistle.

'I know!' She rolled her eyes. 'So I wouldn't be able to afford that many lessons anyway.'

'How much have you budgeted for this little project?' he asked, an amused smile playing around his lips.

'I haven't exactly. I was just going to play it by ear. But I have five hundred, and after that I couldn't afford to spend more than a hundred euro a week.'

'Well, you can do a lot in half an hour,' he said, edging closer to her on the sofa. 'And maybe we could work something out.' He reached out with one finger and began tracing her collarbone where it was exposed by the open neck of her shirt.

Claire gulped. 'Like what?'

Luca looked into her eyes for a long time before answering, his finger lightly stroking her skin. 'I could take part payment in kind, maybe.' He leant forward and pressed his lips to the hollow at the base of her throat, his finger tugging at the neck of her shirt.

'You mean – sex?'

Luca lifted his head. 'Yeah. Why not? I like sex. I don't have a regular girlfriend. Maybe apart from your lessons, you could—'

'Service you?'

'You make it sound so cold.'

'I thought cold was what you wanted.' Paying him in sex – she wasn't sure how she felt about that. What did that make her? But it was no worse than what she had suggested to him.

'Well, think about it anyway.' He kissed her, one hand stroking down her arm, then coming up to open the top button of her shirt.

Claire pulled away. 'What are you doing?'

'Obviously we're going to have to start with the basics. This is called kissing. I'm kissing you. It's part of what's known as foreplay. Do you want to take notes?'

'Oh! I don't – I wasn't planning to start right away. I'm not... prepared.'

'I don't mind a bit of undergrowth if that's what you're worried about.'

'It's not,' she yelped. But it so was. She had lots of prep work to do before she'd be ready to let Luca see her naked. She didn't even have any decent underwear. 'I— I don't have any cash on me right now,' she said.

'You can owe me,' he said, leaning in again.

'No.' She pushed him away. 'I'd rather pay upfront.'

'Well, why don't I give you a free sample? Try before you buy.' He was nuzzling her neck, his breath warm on her skin.

'No, that really won't be necessary.'

'Suit yourself,' he said, finally giving up and sitting back.

'We need to go over the rest of the ground rules first anyway. For instance, how much time will you be able to give me? When would be the best time for me to come here?'

'I tell you what, give me the five hundred and I'll give you all the time you need.'

'Really? That would only allow me two and a half hours with an escort.'

'Well, I believe in giving value for money. Think of it as a special offer – buy one, get one free.'

'I have work in the daytime, so I'd have to come in the evenings.'

'That's fine.'

Claire fished in her bag and pulled out a diary. 'Would Thursday evening be convenient for you to start?' she asked.

Luca smirked and she knew he was mocking her formal demeanor. 'Thursday evening is perfect. I'll pencil it into my diary.'

'Now, another thing. I'll be going on the pill, but I want you to wear condoms as well. I'll pay for them – and any other expenses involved.'

'Okay.'

'Do you have any questions? Any rules you'd like to add – apart from not getting hung up on you?'

'Just one question – what's the name of your blog?'

'My blog? Why?'

'I think I should have a look at it, don't you? So that I have an idea of what we need to cover.'

'Are you going to make a lesson plan?' she asked, giggling.

'Maybe I will. I'm a conscientious worker.'

'I'm glad to hear it. It's called "Scenes of a Sexual Nature".' She stood up, brushing the creases in her trousers. 'Well, I'll see you on Thursday,' she said, holding her hand out to him in a formal gesture.

He stood, taking it. 'I still think we should do it now,' he said softly, his index finger stroking her palm. 'Just a quickie – to get it out of the way.'

'Why do you think we should do that?'

'Because you'll build it up into a big thing in your head, and then you'll be nervous on Thursday. If we did it now, you wouldn't have time to get all worked up about it.'

'I couldn't be much more worked up than I already am,' she said, with a panicky laugh.

'Relax, Claire,' he said, as he saw her to the door. 'There's nothing to worry about. Learning can be fun – you'll see.'

* * *

Well, that was weird, Luca thought, as he closed the door behind Claire. He wasn't sure how he felt about her bizarre proposal, and he still couldn't quite believe he'd agreed to it. But she'd been kind to him the other night when she didn't have to be and he felt he owed her. Besides, he needed the money. And it would be no hardship to him, having regular no-strings-attached sex with her.

He just hoped he could rely on Claire not to start wanting more – because that never ended well. If he'd learnt one thing in life it was that you couldn't rely on other people for your happiness, and he certainly didn't want anyone relying on him – he would only let them down.

He and Ali had been to enough therapists and shrinks throughout their childhood for him to know he had attachment issues. But he was sick of girls who thought they could be the one to cure him of them. He knew he was a bit fucked up, but he was fucked up in a way that worked for him. It was a survival mechanism and it kept everyone safe. Because bad things happened when you started wanting more.

12

The following day was mild and sunny, and Claire met Catherine for lunch in the park. The shop was quiet, so Tom had told her she could take her time.

'How did it go with Mark?' Catherine asked, pulling a foil-wrapped roll and a bottle of mineral water from her bag. They were sitting on plastic chairs at the edge of a group of mothers and wriggling, squealing toddlers, who were watching the end of a puppet show. It was part of an all-day children's event in the park that Catherine was attending as research for a piece she had been commissioned to write on sponsored children's activities. Paddington was parked beside her in another brand-new state-of-the-art buggy.

'Great,' Claire said, as she unwrapped her sandwich on her knee. 'It went really well.'

Catherine turned to look at her closely. 'Really?' she said, her eyes lighting up, and Claire knew that her smile spoke volumes. 'So, is he as nice as he seems on Twitter?'

'Yeah, he's lovely. And it's official – I have a book deal.'

'Oh my God, next time we *have* to have champagne. Anyway, congratulations!' Catherine picked up her bottle of mineral water from the grass and bumped it against Claire's.

'Thanks.' Claire took a bite of her sandwich.

'And was there flirting?'

Claire smiled and nodded as she chewed. When she had swallowed, she said, 'There might even have been some kissing.'

Catherine's eyes widened. 'Wow, get you!'

'We met up again on Sunday and hung out until it was time for him to go. It was really nice.'

'So you managed to pull off the sassy thing, then?'

'A bit. Yvonne gave me lots of flirting tips, but I didn't use them much. Mostly I was just myself – or maybe a slightly pimped-up version of myself.'

'Well, it obviously worked.'

'Yeah. He... he kind of asked me up to his room when we went back to his hotel for a drink.'

'The cheeky bugger!'

'He said he doesn't usually move that fast,' Claire said defensively, 'but he felt like we'd already known each other a long time. It was like that for me too.'

'So, did you go?'

'No. I was tempted, but it would have been kind of obvious that I didn't have a clue what I was doing. My cover would have been blown.'

'Mm, I see what you mean. That's a pity. You finally meet a man you like and he's off-limits.'

'Only temporarily, I hope. I really do like him. And I think he likes me too. He asked me over to London for a weekend.'

'To stay with him?'

Claire nodded. 'I'm going to try to get over while Mum's still in the nursing home.'

'So, what are you going to do? I mean, you can't keep fending him off for ever.'

'I wouldn't want to. But I told him I have a five-date rule.'

'A five-date rule,' Catherine mused. 'I didn't know people really did that.'

'Apparently they do. So I can date him for a while, get to know him better, without sex being an issue. And in the meantime I'm going to get some practice.'

Catherine almost choked on her sandwich. 'Practice?' she croaked when she had recovered. 'Please tell me you're not going to start trawling bars and picking up strange men.'

Claire shook her head. 'I already have someone lined up to practice on.

He's a friend of Yvonne's. I met him at a party last week. So it's all perfectly safe and above board.'

'Blimey! Does this guy know he's a sort of coach, training you up for the big occasion?'

'Oh, yeah. I was completely upfront with him about it. He knows the whole story and he's fine with it. He's a total man-whore – shags anything that moves, I gather. He's broke, so I'm paying him to... teach me.'

Catherine looked at her in slack-jawed silence. 'Let me get this straight,' she said finally. 'You – Claire Kennedy – are going to pay a guy to have sex with you. When you bust out of that shell, you don't do it by halves, do you?'

'Oh, believe me, this isn't easy for me,' Claire said, with a shaky smile. 'I'm not looking forward to it, but it's a means to an end.' She was dreading it, in fact. It would be beyond awkward, but she would try not to think about it too much, and once she'd got through it, she'd never have to see Luca again. She could put the whole episode behind her and forget about it.

'We're starting tomorrow night,' she said, feeling the stirring of nerves in her stomach at the thought of it.

'Well, good luck!'

Just then, Claire's phone pinged with a message. She pulled it out of her bag, feeling a little glow of pleasure when she saw it was from Mark:

> What are you wearing?

She smiled to herself as she texted back:

> A lot of green and a little mayonnaise. Lunch in the park = challenging!

His reply came back a moment later:

> I bet you look adorable in it. Just wanted to let you know your offer letter is being drawn up. Everyone here very excited about publishing Scenes. Must dash. x

'Sorry,' she said to Catherine as she typed a quick reply:

> Yay! Excited too. x

'That's okay,' Catherine said. 'Was that him?'

'Yes. They're getting my official offer ready,' Claire said, as she put her phone back into her bag. Mark's text had come at just the right time, reminding her why she was putting herself through the ordeal with Luca. It would be worth it if she could be with Mark in the end.

The puppet show ended to a round of applause and the crowd began to disperse, children leaping from their seats and tearing towards the playground while harried mothers were still gathering up all their paraphernalia.

'Doesn't Paddy want a go on the swings?' Claire asked, nodding towards the buggy.

'No, he's a bit tired. It's been a long day. I'll bring him home for a nap soon.' She drained her mineral water and screwed the lid back on, dropping the empty bottle into a plastic bag. 'Those kids are all hyped up on sugar,' she said, nodding to the children charging towards the playground while their mothers trotted after them, juggling change bags and juice cups while trying to maneuver empty pushchairs across the grass. 'The evil geniuses behind this event were handing out free fizzy drinks all day. I didn't let Paddy have any.'

'You're such a good mother.'

'Well, I'm lucky that Paddy doesn't put up any resistance. If he was constantly wheedling me like that lot, I'd probably have him on a drip of the stuff.'

'Is that another freebie?' Claire nodded to the buggy.

'Yeah.' Catherine looked down at the buggy with its space-age design. 'Bit wanky, isn't it? But apparently it's the must-have item for the toddler-about-town, these days.'

Claire scrunched up her sandwich wrapping. 'I'd better get back,' she said, dropping it into the plastic bag that Catherine held out for her.

They gathered up their things, and strolled towards the gate.

'Do you want one of these?' Catherine asked her, nodding down at Paddington.

'A teddy bear? I have one at home somewhere.'

Catherine smiled. 'No, a child.'

'Oh.' They paused by a bin near the exit and Catherine threw in the bag with their rubbish.

'Yeah,' Claire said thoughtfully, as they continued walking. 'I guess. I mean, not right now. But I've always seen myself having children eventually. You?'

'No, I don't think so. I'm undecided, but Hazel is a definite no, so...'

'What if you were with someone who definitely wanted them?'

'Then I guess I'd go along with it. I don't really have strong feelings either way. And I'd already have all the equipment. My kid would never be short of a designer change bag or a state-of-the-art car seat.'

'Yes, shame to let all that free stuff go to waste.'

'Well, I'll pass it along to you if you decide to go down that road. In the meantime, it keeps my eBay account nicely ticking along.'

They stopped on the path outside the gate before going their separate ways.

'Well, good luck tomorrow night,' Catherine said. 'Don't do anything I wouldn't—' She stopped abruptly and laughed. 'No, that would defeat the whole purpose, wouldn't it?'

'It kind of would.'

'And we already know you won't be good, so I'll just say be careful. And have fun.'

'Thanks. I'll try.'

* * *

On Thursday, Luca kept an eye on the clock as he worked. He knew how easy it was for him to lose all track of time when he really got stuck into working on a piece. But Claire was coming over tonight, so at five on the dot he downed tools and busied himself trying to make his shithole of a flat a bit more cheery and welcoming. It seemed the least he could do when she was paying him so much money. His place had never bothered him before, but the contrast with the comfort of her home could hardly have been starker. When he had washed up, he cleaned the table and did a quick run-around with the vacuum cleaner that was stashed in a cupboard by the door. He couldn't remember if he'd ever used it before.

Then he turned his attention to the bedroom. He turned on the light and stood in the doorway, surveying it objectively. Lit by a bare bulb in the centre of the room – he'd never even bothered to get a shade for it – it didn't look fit for a dog to sleep in. Maybe he should have taken her up on her offer to go to a hotel, he thought, as he began to strip the bed. But he felt bad enough about taking her money as it was. He didn't want her to go to any extra expense.

He felt like a shit for agreeing to be paid to have sex with her, especially when he would gladly have done it for free. It wasn't as if the arrangement didn't suit him. It would be nice to enjoy regular sex without the hassle of her getting clingy or trying to make him into her idea of the perfect boyfriend. But he could see there was no way she would have accepted a freebie. It would be worse, he reasoned, if she'd blown wads of cash for an hour or two with an escort. It showed how desperate she was that she had even considered it. He didn't like to think of her throwing herself on the mercy of some rent boy. Claire was a decent person. She deserved better. At least he could console himself with the thought that he was saving her a lot of money, and probably a world of trauma, by agreeing to her arrangement. He would look after her properly and make sure she got value for her money.

When he had changed the bedding and plumped the pillows as much as they would plump – there wasn't a lot of life left in them – he switched off the ceiling light, turned on the bedside lamp and stood back to survey his handiwork. It still didn't look cosy, but it was a bit of an improvement.

Then he showered, scrubbing his hands and arms to remove all traces of paint, and changed into clean clothes. He stuffed some condoms into the drawer of the nightstand and opened a bottle of wine to let it breathe. Then he closed the windows, cranked up the heating and waited for her to arrive.

Claire turned up almost on the dot of seven. As he had expected, she appeared nervous. 'So, boning for beginners,' he said, smiling and rubbing his hands together as he let her in. 'Ready to begin?'

'Um... yeah.' She bit her lip. Maybe that hadn't been quite the way to put her at ease, he thought.

'Sorry. Have a seat.' He motioned to the sofa, hoping she would sit on the cushion that still had some padding left. 'Would you like a glass of wine?'

'Yes, please.' She sat on the wrong side, almost sinking through to the floor. She tried to extricate herself surreptitiously, coming to perch on the edge.

'Why don't you sit on that side?' he said, pointing. 'It's more comfortable.'

She scooched over and he handed her a drink, sitting beside her.

'Cheers!' He clinked his glass against hers. 'Here's to sex education!'

'Cheers,' she mumbled, then took a huge slug of wine.

Infuriatingly, Luca's neighbours chose that moment to start a domestic. There was a lot of shouting and screaming, followed by several loud thumps, and the sound of something heavy hitting the wall. 'Sorry,' he said, rolling his eyes and getting up. He went over to the iPod dock and switched it on, turning the volume up loud. Adele's voice filled the room. He had cued it up earlier, guessing Claire would be the sort of girl who liked Adele. Most girls he knew did. Noticing that her glass was already half empty, he picked up the bottle of wine and topped it up.

'Are you trying to get me drunk?' she asked, as he sat back down beside her.

'No, definitely not. I don't want you drunk at all. In fact, I think you should slow down,' he said, nodding towards her glass, which she was raising reflexively to her lips. 'I just want you to relax.'

She lowered her glass without taking a sip. 'Sorry. I'm a bit nervous.'

'I know. But don't be.' He reached out and ran one finger down her bare arm. 'There's nothing to be nervous about. We'll take it slow. And, remember, you're calling all the shots here. You don't have to do anything you don't want to do.'

'I know. It's just— it's a bit weird, you know, doing it in cold blood like this. I mean, you didn't have to do this, with the wine and everything. I'm a sure thing, you know?' She laughed shakily.

'So you thought we'd just go straight to the bedroom and get down to it?'

She shrugged. 'I guess. I don't know. I mean, it's not as if I've ever done anything like this before.'

'Well, I thought we should talk a bit first – about what we're doing here. For example, I don't know how much experience you've had. If any,' he added, shooting her a wary look.

'You mean... sex?'

'Yes. When you say you've never done anything like this before... you have had sex before? You're not a virgin?'

'No.'

'Good.' Luca was relieved that this wasn't going to be her first time.

'I've had sex before, but I wasn't sure—' She broke off, blushing. 'I wasn't sure what was going on.'

Luca chuckled. 'You weren't sure what was going on?'

'Oh, shut up!' she huffed. 'This is hard enough without you laughing at me.'

'Sorry. So you know how it all works?'

'Yes, but I just...' She was struggling to explain. Eventually she let out a heavy sigh and said, 'I just didn't get it.'

'You didn't get what all the fuss was about?' He nodded understandingly.

'No, that's not what I mean – or not just that. I mean, no, it didn't rock my world or anything. But also I didn't understand what was going on. I didn't know if I was doing it right, and I couldn't tell if it was going well or not. I mean, he was there, whacking away—'

'Whacking away?' He laughed. He couldn't help it.

'Yes, whacking away. And he just kept on and on for absolutely ages, and I didn't know what he was waiting for, you know?'

Luca struggled to keep a straight face. 'Well, he was probably waiting for you.'

'Yeah, but that's what I didn't know. I didn't know if he was waiting for me to... you know...'

'Come.'

'Yes. I mean, maybe he thought if he kept at it long enough, I'd have an orgasm. But I was just getting bored.'

'God, I'm almost starting to feel sorry for this guy,' Luca said.

Claire sighed. 'I kind of felt sorry for him myself.'

'I said *almost*,' he said sternly, frowning at her. 'He should have taken care of you.'

'Well, anyway, I thought if he was just holding out for my sake, maybe I should fake something. But I wasn't sure how to go about it.'

'No,' Luca said firmly. 'You should never fake it. Jesus, if he thought what he was doing was getting you off, he'd just keep doing the same thing every time and it'd never get any better.'

'Well, I just wanted it to end. But I didn't know how to... bring it to a conclusion.'

'You could have told him to stop.' Luca frowned.

'It would have seemed rude to do that. I didn't want to hurt his feelings. It's not like he was forcing me or anything. I was into it – at the start. I wanted it to happen. I just thought it would be... better. More fun, you know?'

'This was your first time?'

'Yes.' She nodded.

'Well, it's usually not great the first time.'

'But it was the same every time. Not that I've had sex very often.'

'How often?'

'Um... three times,' she said, looking away.

'*Three times?* You're twenty-eight and you've only had sex three times?'

'Well, three and a half, really.'

'Three and a half?' Luca chuckled. 'We'll come back to that later. But you say you didn't know how to fake an orgasm?'

'Not really. Obviously I've seen it in movies, but it always seems a bit over the top – like that scene in *When Harry Met Sally* where she keeps shouting, "Yes," and banging the table. I'd have felt really stupid doing that. I'm not much of an actress.'

'You probably weren't on a table anyway.'

'No.' To his relief Claire laughed.

'So does that mean you've never had an orgasm?' Luca asked.

'Yes. No. I mean, yes, I have, but—'

'You're not sure?'

'No, I definitely have, but not—' She stopped, going bright red. 'I've never had one when, um... when there was someone else in the room,' she mumbled.

'Oh,' he said, a wide grin breaking across his face. 'Well, we can definitely work with that. I don't suppose you'd...'

'What?'

'Let me watch.'

'You mean...?' Her eyes widened in shock.

'Mm, that's what I thought,' he said, with a gentle smile. 'It's okay,' he said, putting his hands on her shoulders and easing them down from around her ears. 'I figured you'd be too shy for that at this stage. We can work up to it.' As he spoke he stroked her cheek with the back of his hand, his fingers trailing down her throat to the neck of her shirt. 'I'd love to watch you get yourself off,' he said, smiling at the blush that crept up her neck into her face. He popped open the top button of her shirt, never taking his eyes from hers, and she held his gaze as he opened the next two buttons, his hand splaying out across her clavicle, stroking across the top of her chest. Her breathing became deep and ragged.

'You're so gorgeous,' he whispered, leaning in to kiss her. He kissed her mouth, her ears, her neck, while his hand stroked down her side, brushing against the side of her breast and down her leg.

'You don't have to say stuff like that to me,' she said gruffly. 'Like I said, I'm a sure thing.'

'But it's true.' He smiled at her, before kissing her again on the mouth, parting her lips with his tongue. Claire clung to him, and he felt her finally relax, her body loosening as she started to kiss him back.

'Will we move to the bedroom?' he asked, when eventually he pulled back.

Claire nodded mutely.

He took her hand and led her in, then turned on the little bedside lamp. He drew the curtains, then turned to face Claire. 'Sorry it's not more...' He trailed off, shrugging apologetically.

'It's fine.' Claire gulped, her eyes huge as she looked at the bed.

'Is it warm enough?' Luca asked. He had had the heater on most of the day – he'd decided it was an allowable expense when he was being paid so much.

'Yes, it's fine. Well, I suppose I should...' She kicked off her shoes, and began undoing her shirt briskly, as if she was getting changed for swimming.

'Stop,' Luca said, crossing the room and stilling her hand. 'Let me do that.'

He bent his head, slowly undoing the rest of the buttons.

'A couple of ground rules before we start,' he said, as he peeled the shirt from her shoulders slowly, his hands stroking down her arms as he slid it off. 'One,' he said, eyeballing her, 'no faking anything. Okay?'

She nodded.

'I'll know if you do,' he warned.

'I won't,' she said breathily. 'Promise.'

'Good,' he said, sliding her bra straps off her shoulders and reaching around for the clasp at her back. He unclipped it, pulling it off her and tossed it aside. 'And two,' he said, dropping his eyes to her naked breasts, his knuckles brushing over her nipples, 'you'll stop me if you get bored.'

Claire just whimpered in response as he bent to kiss her neck, his hands stroking her bare skin, but he was pretty sure he could take that as a yes.

* * *

Claire was already more aroused than she'd ever felt in her life as Luca laid her on the bed and stretched out beside her, his hands roving over her bare flesh as they kissed and kissed. She'd forgotten how fantastic kissing was. How could she have gone so long without it, she wondered, as Luca stroked, licked and sucked every inch of bare skin he had revealed. She couldn't take her eyes off him, cradling his head as he took her hardened nipples into his mouth, overcome with amazement that he would do this. The shock of his tongue trailing across her belly made her quiver and she trembled in need as it dipped into her navel, his fingers moving to the fastening of her jeans. He slid the zip down slowly, his tongue following the zipper to trail wetly along the exposed flesh. He peeled off her jeans and tossed them aside, then hooked his fingers into the sides of her knickers, sliding them slowly down her legs, his eyes hooded as he gazed at her. She was very conscious of the fact that he was still fully clothed and she was now completely naked. She felt exposed and sat up, reaching for his belt buckle.

'Don't,' he whispered, removing her hand and nudging her to lie down.

'What should I—'

'Just relax,' he murmured, his hands stroking leisurely up her thighs, his eyes dark as he fixed his gaze on her face. 'Let's just concentrate on you for now.' Claire gasped as one hand moved between her legs and she felt his finger stroke along her heated flesh.

'Mm,' he groaned softly, 'you're so wet.' He bent his head to nuzzle the soft skin of her inner thighs.

His fingers stroking her were heaven, but as his mouth blazed a trail along her thigh and she realised what he intended to do, she shot upright.

'No!' she yelped, grabbing his head and yanking it up.

'What's wrong?' He frowned. 'Don't you like it?'

'Um... yes, I'm sure I would – but you don't have to do that.' Surely she wasn't paying him enough for that! 'I'm sure it's not very nice – I mean you wouldn't want to...'

'You're wrong,' he said. 'I do want to do this.' He caught her eye and then, when he was sure she was watching, very slowly and purposefully bent his head to give her a long lick. 'And it's *very* nice,' he said, grinning up at her.

She looked at him uncertainly.

'Relax, please,' he said, stroking her shoulders and easing her back onto the bed. 'I love doing this, honestly.'

Oh well, to each his own, she thought, lying back and trying to relax as he bent her legs up so her feet were flat on the bed. He grabbed a pillow from beside her. 'Lift up for me,' he murmured.

'What? Why?'

'I want to put this under you, so I can get at you better.'

'Oh.' She lifted her hips, wondering why she found the idea of being 'got at' so hot.

He slid the pillow under her bum and settled himself between her legs. 'God, I love my new job,' he said, as he spread her open with his fingers and bent his head to her soft, aching flesh.

She was never going to be able to relax like this, Claire thought. She felt too exposed, too self-conscious. How could she possibly forget herself when—

Oh, sweet Jesus! All coherent thought vanished and she was lost in the magic of his mouth and fingers as he sucked, licked and stroked her with an enthusiasm and relentlessness that was almost too much to bear.

'Let go! Let go!' he panted urgently, some time later.

'I am,' she whimpered, her head thrashing reflexively on the pillow. How could he think she was holding back? She was just a mindless ball of nerve endings and want.

'My hair!' he gasped. 'Let go of my hair!'

'Oh shit! Sorry.' She released her death grip, fisting the sheets in her hands instead as he nibbled her clit, her body bowing off the bed as her orgasm took hold and she came with a helpless moan. He continued to stroke and suck mercilessly, making her come again and again, wave after wave of pleasure coursing through her, each one more intense than the last. At last he let up, wrapping his arms around her and holding her tight as her body trembled in the aftermath of orgasm. When she shivered, he released her to pull the duvet over them both, then took her into his arms again. When she finally stilled, he drew back and stared down at her, stroking damp tendrils of hair away from her face. He smiled at her, looking very pleased with himself – as well he might.

'So,' he said, with a smirk, 'do you need me to talk you through what happened there?'

'No.' She smiled. 'I think that was all pretty clear.'

'Good. There'll be a test later.'

'Written?'

He shook his head. 'Oral.' He grinned, and she giggled.

She smiled into his chest. She reckoned that was a test she could ace. All she had to do was lie there while he did amazing things to her. She felt boneless in his arms as he stroked her hair.

'Well, that was a first.' She sighed, nuzzling into his chest. 'Luca?'

'Mm?'

'It's much better with someone else in the room.'

Claire couldn't remember when she'd felt so complete, so sated and content. But as she came back down to earth and reality took hold, she started to wonder what happened now. She began to feel awkward. They hadn't discussed time, but presumably she wasn't supposed to stay the night. He was already giving her far more time than she was paying for. She wished she could fall asleep in his arms, but she didn't know how long it was okay for her to stay now that the 'lesson' was over. Maybe they should have arranged an alarm or something so she would know when her time was up.

Luca didn't seem to be in any hurry to move either. But as he pulled her close again, she was startled to feel the hardness of his erection against her. Her eyes flew up to his. 'Oh, but you haven't – I mean, should I…' She was such an idiot. She'd been so caught up in her own pleasure, she'd completely forgotten about him. And he hadn't so much as unbuttoned his shirt the whole time. Shit! She began to reach for his zipper, but once again he grabbed her hand, holding it away.

'No, you don't have to do anything. I told you this time was all about you, remember?'

'But I didn't do anything,' she said, feeling mortified. 'I just lay there.'

'Stop it,' he said sternly. 'First of all, you didn't just lie there. And, anyway, there's more to this than just learning techniques. You need to learn about your own body, your own sexuality – find out what excites you, what gets you off. How can you expect to have good sex if you don't even know what you want? I think we've found one thing you like,' he said, grinning down at her.

'Yeah, it was okay.' She shrugged.

He laughed. 'Anyway, you're paying me,' he continued. 'You don't have to reciprocate every time as well. You're upholding your end of the bargain and I'm upholding mine.'

'Okay. But I don't mind – just because I'm paying you it doesn't mean it can't be fun for you as well.'

No sooner were the words out of her mouth than she realised what an idiotic thing that was to say. There was probably no way this was going to be fun for him. He was just doing a job: the sooner it was over and she was out of here, the happier he'd be. She bit her lip, cringing with embarrassment and wishing she could take the words back. It was obvious he didn't find her remotely desirable. He didn't even want her to touch his dick.

'Well,' she said abruptly, pushing away from him and sitting up. 'I'd better go.' She made an effort to sound bright and nonchalant, turning away and pretending to look around for her clothes while she blinked tears from her eyes. She was being ridiculous. This wasn't a rejection. They had a business arrangement, not a real relationship. She had to remember that.

'There's no rush,' he said. She felt him sit up beside her, but she didn't turn around. 'Is there?'

'Um, I have to... I'm meeting someone,' she said, her eyes raking the floor for her clothes. Her heart sank as she realised they were all on his side of the room. Damn! She pulled the duvet around herself, suddenly feeling very naked. 'And I'm sure you have things to do too.'

'No, not really.' He yawned. 'You're welcome to stay as long as you like.'

'Oh.' She wished she'd known that earlier. She could have lain in his arms for longer, but it would seem silly now to get back into bed – besides, she'd already said she had somewhere else to be.

'Are you okay?' he asked, and she felt his warm hand on her shoulder.

'Yes, I'm fine,' she said, half turning to him and giving him a shaky smile. 'Could you, um... give me my bra and... stuff.'

'Sure.' The bed sagged as he got up and she heard him moving around the room. The next thing she knew he was standing in front of her and she was eyeballing his crotch. 'Here you go,' he said, holding out her clothes to her.

'Thanks,' she mumbled, grabbing them from his hand, still not looking up. God, this was mortifying. Why had she ever thought it would work? She didn't even know how to get out of bed and get dressed – it was hopeless! She stared at the clothes in her hand, still holding the duvet to her as she pondered how she could get dressed and out of there. Maybe she could shimmy them on under the bedclothes? Or make a quick dart for the bathroom? She really hadn't thought this through at all.

'You sure you're okay?' Luca asked, hunching down in front of her so he could look up into her face. 'Do you want to take a shower or anything?'

'No, I'll... I'll have one at home.'

He grabbed the duvet where she held it against her chest. 'You do realise I've seen you naked already?' he said, with a smile.

'Yes, I know. I just—'

'You have nothing to be embarrassed about,' he said, one finger gently stroking her cheek. 'You have a gorgeous body.'

'Thanks,' she said flatly. The empty compliment made her feel even more foolish.

'I mean it,' he said sternly, as if he had read her thoughts. 'Maybe one day you'll let me paint you and you can see yourself as I see you.'

'Look, you don't have to say things like that to me just because I'm paying you,' she said, irked that he thought she needed his cheesy lines. God, he must find her so pathetic! 'Your job is to have sex with me, not to romance me.'

He sighed exasperatedly, releasing the duvet and standing up. He stepped away from her and leant back against the wall, his arms folded. 'My job, as I understand it, is to turn you into a sex goddess.' She looked up at him, startled by his anger. 'But you're never going to be a sensual, sexy woman if you don't *feel* it, if you don't believe in yourself as a desirable person. Do you think this is sexy,' he said, waving at her, 'cowering there like a wounded dog, trying to figure out how to get dressed under the bedclothes?'

Her eyes widened.

'Yes, I know what you were thinking. Do you think the girl who writes your blog would be shrinking under the duvet like a fucking outraged Victorian virgin?'

She flinched at the harshness of his words. 'N-no.' She was horrified to find tears welling up in her eyes. 'I know I'm not sexy, but that's why I need you to—'

'But you *are*!' He groaned in frustration, pulling at his hair. 'That's what I keep trying to tell you. But I need you to meet me halfway.' He sighed heavily, leaning his head against the wall. 'We need to rethink this whole thing.'

She gasped. Was he dumping her already? Even though she was paying him? It was almost funny – she was so crap in bed, she couldn't even get a guy to screw her for money. She couldn't speak. It was taking all her concentration willing herself not to cry.

'It's not going to work if you're just coming over here for lessons in techniques,' Luca continued. 'We need to have a more... holistic approach.'

'What do you mean?'

'I can teach you how to give a blowjob or whatever, but that's not going to turn you into the person you want to be. The technical stuff is only a tiny part of it. It's mostly about turning you into a sexually confident woman, making you feel like the desirable person you really are. And to do that we're going to have to ramp it up.'

'So... how exactly do we do that?' she asked, relieved that he didn't appear to be quitting after all.

'I think you should plan to stay over on nights when we have a lesson – at least some of the time. You can't run off like a scalded cat the minute it's over. Okay?'

'Okay.' She nodded.

'I'll let you off the hook for tonight, but next time, plan to be here for the night. Pack a bag. You can leave some stuff here, if you want. It'll be more intensive, too, so better value for money – more bang for your buck, as it were,' he said, with a lopsided smile. 'We need to spend more time together before and after because it's not all about the act itself. You need to own your sexuality. That way you can get used to undressing in front of me and being naked around me. We can shower together – maybe have sex in the shower...'

Her breath hitched at the thought of having sex with him in the shower.

'Unless you'd like to start now?' He raised an eyebrow and smiled crookedly at her.

'Um...' She was really tempted, but she didn't want him to know she had been lying. 'I really am meeting someone.'

'Okay. But you're on board with the plan?'

'Yes. But... should I pay you more? I mean, if I'm going to be staying over...'

'No. You're already paying me more than enough for something I'd do for free anyway. I don't want you to pay me more, but I want you to put more effort into it.'

God, she hadn't had a 'must try harder' lecture since she was at school. (Actually, she'd never had a lecture like this at school – she'd always been a diligent pupil.)

'I tried,' she protested, waving in the general direction of his groin, 'but you wouldn't let me.'

'I'm not talking about touching my dick or getting me off,' he snapped. 'I want you to try harder to have a bit of courage, to have more faith in yourself. Okay?'

'Okay.'

'Now, do you want me to give you some privacy while you get dressed?' The look he gave her was a challenge.

She swallowed hard. 'N-no.' Taking a deep breath, she dropped the duvet and stood up. 'I'll get dressed in the bathroom,' she said, standing before him naked and forcing herself to hold his gaze with a huge effort of will.

She was rewarded with a pleased smile – he looked almost proud of her. It made it easier for her that he didn't drop his eyes from hers, and she was grateful.

'You know where it is,' he said, and she walked at a normal pace from the room. It wasn't much, but at least she didn't break into a run. It was a start.

13

Slave To Love

Mr Bossy is a dominant, and though I don't think of myself as a submissive, I do have a strong desire to submit when I'm with him. There's something about him that makes me want to obey; to serve and please him. I crave his praise. When he tells me I'm a 'good girl', the words alone are almost enough to make me come.

So yesterday we're out in his car, tootling along in the fast lane, surrounded by other Sunday drivers, when he asks me to take off my knickers. Well, he doesn't ask really – it's more of an order than a request. So I do as I'm told, eager to please. I'm totally his bitch, and I don't even care. I'm already excited as I wriggle them off under my skirt and toss them into the footwell.

'Show me,' he says. 'Lift up your skirt.'

I look around, not sure I can do it. We're on a busy road – there are cars whizzing by on both sides.

'No one can see,' he says, understanding my anxiety, and I realise it's true. Other drivers can only see my top half. No one will know if I'm naked from the waist down. 'Show me,' he coaxes again, in that commanding voice of his.

So I grab the hem of my skirt and pull it up slowly, teasing him, finally bunching it up around my waist and turning in the seat to give him a full visual. He takes his eyes off the road for a second to glance over at me, and his little gasp is gratifying.

'Spread your legs,' he says, and I scooch down a little in my seat and spread myself open. I tell you, I'm like a little puppy that's aced obedience school around this guy. If he told me to roll over and play dead, I'd probably do it.

He takes one hand off the wheel and reaches over to grope me a little. 'You're so wet already,' he says, as he strokes me. 'Does this game excite you?'

'Yes,' I whisper. My voice is shaky as his fingers work me and I feel myself getting wetter.

'Good girl,' he says, as he withdraws his fingers. He sticks them in his mouth, sucking absentmindedly. 'Do you need to come?' he asks, as he places his hand back on the wheel, and I feel bereft.

'Yes,' I gasp. I sound like I'm choking.

'I'd like to do that for you, but I have to concentrate on the road,' he says, giving me a wicked smile. 'Put your feet up on the dash and touch yourself.'

I kick off my shoes and plant my feet as instructed.

'Good girl,' he coos, as I stroke myself, and I can feel myself getting closer at the sound of his voice. 'You're always such a good girl for me. I want you to make yourself come now. And let me hear you.'

I'm just climaxing, my body bucking off the seat, straining against the seatbelt, when we pull up at a set of traffic lights. A young guy in a black BMW pulls up beside us and glances over. I don't know if he guesses what's going on, but he grins and winks at me. I turn to Mr Bossy in panic, and he reaches out and strokes my hair, soothing me as I come down from a juddering orgasm. I'm whimpering as little aftershocks ripple through me.

'Ssh, it's okay,' he says, and tells me I'm a good girl again. 'You did great,' he says. 'I'm very pleased with you.' I don't even care then that a total stranger has just seen my sex face.

When the lights change and we pull away, I reach down for my knickers.

'Don't,' he says, and I straighten up again. 'Leave them off. I think you deserve a reward for being such a good girl. When I find some place to pull in, we'll stop and you can have my cock. Would you like that?'

I know – it sounds like a dad offering to stop for ice-cream as a treat for his little girl. But I nod eagerly, like a child gagging for that ice-cream, because I really would like that very much, and he knows it. I love having his big, thick cock in my mouth. I love how helpless and vulnerable I can make him with my hands and mouth, how powerful it makes me feel, even when he grabs my hair and controls my movements. And I love it in my cunt, moving inside me, filling me up until I don't know where he ends and I begin.

We pull into a lay-by, and he cuts the engine, turning to me as he unclicks his seatbelt. I don't know if he wants me to undo mine, so I wait. He smiles and I know he's pleased that I'm waiting for his instructions. He leans over and kisses my forehead, then my mouth as he releases my seatbelt himself.

'I'd like you to take your top off,' he says, as he pulls back, looking into my eyes. This isn't a command, it's a request. Sometimes he does this. I think he's making allowances for the fact that I'm new to all this, and I'm not as into it as most of the submissives he's been with. I'm touched that he's so considerate and patient with me, and it just makes me more eager to please him. Still, I waver, glancing towards the window. He sees my slight hesitation, but he's not displeased. This is a request, not an order.

'Please. I won't let anyone see you,' he says.

So I say yes, his favourite word, and pull my top off over my head.

'Thank you,' he says, kissing me on the forehead again.

I know my trust means a lot to him, and I feel good, knowing I've pleased him.

'Is it warm enough?' he asks, stroking my arm as I unhook my bra.

'Yes.' I smile, touched by his consideration. It's cold outside, but he's cranked up the heating and it's cosy and warm inside his car. I toss my bra onto the floor.

'Such a beautiful girl,' he says, pulling me into his lap. His hands run up and down my naked torso, over my bare breasts, and they feel amazing on my skin. He leans down and suckles my breasts, first one, then the other, taking my nipples into his mouth. Then he undoes his fly and bunches my skirt up around my waist and we fuck right there in the lay-by.

He pulls out at the last minute and comes over my breasts. When we have both recovered, he rubs his spunk all over my chest, massaging it into my skin with slow, firm movements. As his palms pass over my nipples, they harden and excitement spikes again deep inside me. He smiles, and I think he knows that he's getting me worked up again, but he just continues methodically massaging his cum into my breasts and belly.

'There,' he says, with a smile of satisfaction when he's done and I'm coated in a fine layer of his jizz, drying on my skin. He taps my waist to indicate that I can get off him, and I'm disappointed because I'm ready to go again. 'You can put your top back on,' he says, as I slide across to the passenger seat. 'But I'll keep those.' He nods to my knickers on the floor. 'Put them in the glove compartment for me.'

I do as I'm told and he drives me back to my place.

'Thank you for a lovely day,' he says, when he's parked outside my building.

'Thank you.' I smile. I'm hoping he'll come inside. I want more.

'I won't come in,' he says, answering my unspoken question. 'I have an early flight in the morning.'

I'm disappointed, but I console myself with the thought that I can have a wank as soon as I get in. I'm eager to get out of the car now.

'Don't have a shower tonight,' he says. 'I want you to go to bed covered in my cum. I want the smell of me all around you, so you think of me all the time.'

No problemo, I think – all the better for getting myself off to thoughts of him.

'And don't touch yourself,' he says then, as if he's read my mind. 'Don't let anyone else touch you either. Your next orgasm will come from me. Is that clear?'

I nod, dismayed. He's going away on business tomorrow and he'll be gone for a week. My only hope is that he'll call for phone sex and let me come then. Otherwise, I'm looking at a whole week without an orgasm. Still, I know I'll do it. The desire to please him is overwhelming.

'Yes,' I say.

He gives a little groan of satisfaction. 'You're such a good girl,' he says. 'You please me very much.' Then he leans over and kisses me again, his hand cupping my breast. His thumb flicks over the nipple, deliberately teasing, and I jump, already desperate to come again.

I don't get much sleep that night. Every time I turn in the bed I smell his musky scent all around me. It's agony not touching myself, and I wonder how I'm going to hold out for a whole week. But I do. Because I'm such a good girl for him.

Holy shit! Luca thought, closing the laptop and trying to ignore the semi he had got while he read. It was a good thing he'd decided to check out Claire's blog, he thought, struggling to reconcile what he'd just read with the Claire he knew. He couldn't believe she'd written that stuff – she had trouble even saying 'fuck'. At least now he knew what they were up against. If this was who Claire's publisher dude thought he was dealing with, it was no wonder she was worried about living up to his expectations. He'd probably dump her as soon as she refused to have a three-way or to let him tie her up. Or, worse, she might feel pressured into doing stuff she wasn't comfortable with to keep up the pretence.

It just reinforced what he had said to her yesterday. He could teach her techniques, give her experience, show her how to please a guy, and help her discover what she liked, so she could ask for what she wanted in bed. But, more than anything, they needed to work on building up her confidence so she could handle herself in any situation. She needed a bit of this NiceGirl's ballsy attitude. But the fact that she had written this stuff gave him hope. It must be in there somewhere – it was just a matter of drawing it out.

*** * * ***

On Friday evening, Claire raced home from work and packed her overnight bag. She had the whole weekend off work, and was going to spend it with Luca. It was worse than packing for a holiday. She didn't want to freak him out by bringing too much, but there was a certain amount of stuff she needed. Going through her clothes last night, she had realised she was ashamed of her underwear, and had dashed around at lunchtime buying new bras and knickers – not overtly sexy, but pretty and feminine. She made sure to cut all the tags off before packing them in her case. She didn't want Luca to know she had bought them specially for him. She toyed with the idea of buying new nightwear too. She usually slept in a ratty old oversized T-shirt or pyjamas that were built more for comfort than to get a man's pulses racing. But in the end she decided nightclothes wouldn't be required when she was staying with Luca, so she decided not to bother bringing any.

After work she went to Marks & Spencer and bought thick peppered steaks, huge baking potatoes, fat brown mushrooms, crème fraîche and chives, bags of salad, punnets of raspberries, thick double cream and a couple of bottles of red wine. She was on a mission. She suspected Luca didn't usually eat very well, and she wanted to cook him a really good dinner tonight. He had done something so nice for her yesterday, and it seemed only right to return the favour.

She got a bit carried away once she started food shopping, picking up blueberries, Greek yoghurt, eggs, sourdough bread, orange juice and coffee for the morning. She felt a little frisson of pleasure as it dawned on her that she was shopping for a lovers' tryst – a seduction dinner and a morning-after breakfast. She was finally taking part in life, instead of sitting on the sidelines watching it pass her by.

She took a taxi to Luca's and arrived laden with shopping bags and her wheelie case, hoping it didn't look too much like she was moving in. Luca grinned at her as he opened the door.

'Ready for your sleepover?' he asked, grabbing her case and waving her inside.

'I brought some stuff for dinner,' she said, holding her shopping bags aloft as she followed him up the stairs. 'I don't know if you had any plans…'

'I hadn't thought about it, really,' he said absently. 'I figured we'd just get a takeaway or something.'

'Well, I thought I could cook,' Claire said. 'I brought lots of food.'

'I'll leave this here for now,' Luca said, leaning her case against the couch when they got into the flat. He led her through to the kitchen and took one of the bags from Claire. 'Steak, cream, raspberries, wine,' he said, as he unloaded it onto the counter. 'Are you trying to seduce me?' He grinned at her.

'If you'd rather get a takeaway…' She hoped he didn't think she was acting like a girlfriend – buying groceries, offering to cook for him.

'God, no. This looks amazing! I can't remember when I last had steak. You can come and stay anytime. But you know I'm a sure thing, right? You don't have to spend your money on me.'

For a second the unspoken words hung in the air between them – *more than you're already spending.*

'Well, I have to eat too,' Claire said.

'Okay,' he said breezily. 'Let's get the oven on. I take it you were planning to bake these?' he said, holding up the potatoes.

She nodded, grateful that he wasn't going to make an issue of it. Luca turned on the oven and popped the potatoes in, and they stashed the rest of the food in the fridge.

'They're going to need a head-start,' Claire said, waving at the oven. 'Maybe we could discuss our arrangement while we're waiting. We still haven't hammered out the details properly.'

'Or we could have a quickie?' Luca said, wiggling his eyebrows suggestively.

Claire smiled. But she wanted to get some things straight before going any further. She needed to know exactly where she stood with Luca so there would be no more uncertainty. 'Let's discuss our arrangement – like what times I come here, and how long I can stay.' She didn't want a repeat of yesterday's awkwardness.

'We can play it by ear,' Luca said.

'I don't want to intrude on your life.'

'I'll let you know if you're in the way,' Luca replied drily.

'As long as you promise to tell me the minute you feel I'm crowding you. I don't want you to be afraid of hurting my feelings.'

'No need to worry about me being too much of a gentleman.'

'Okay. Now, about the timeframe – I know you said you'd give me as much time as I needed, but this can't go on indefinitely.'

'Right. And this Mark dude won't wait around for ever. Presumably you're putting off sleeping with him until you feel you've achieved the desired sexbomb status?'

'Until I feel I'm ready, yes,' she said primly. 'I don't want him to be disappointed.'

'So basically your deadline is before Mark's balls turn blue.' He chuckled.

'Well, he lives in London, so that's not so much of an issue – at least for now. Plus I told him I have a five-date rule so—'

'A what?'

'A five-date rule. You know, I won't sleep with a guy until we've been on five dates.'

'Seriously? Girls have those?'

'Apparently, yes. Yvonne told me about it. Lots of girls have them. Sometimes they're three-date rules.'

'Huh! No one's ever used that on me,' he said smugly.

Claire ignored him. 'Anyway, that gives me more time, but I'd like to get as much done as possible in the next couple of weeks. I'll have more free time while my mother's still in the nursing home.'

'Okay, then. You can come over as many nights as you want to for the next two weeks – as long as you check with me first.'

'You're sure that's not too much? I'd pay you more.'

Luca shook his head. 'No need for that. Consider it a fixed-price job. Five hundred to turn you into a sexpot or your money back.'

It didn't seem fair when she would be taking up so much of his time, but Claire could tell he wouldn't budge on this. Maybe she could find other ways to pay him extra – she could buy him groceries, give him presents... 'Okay,' she agreed. 'Now, one last thing – I made a list,' she said, bending to fish it out of her bag.

'A list?'

'Of things I want to learn.' She had typed it on the computer and printed it out. She unfolded the sheet of A4 paper and smoothed it out.

'Okay, let's see,' Luca said, taking it from her. To her mortification, he began reading the list out loud. 'Basic sex, hand job, blowjob, positions, e.g. woman on top, doggy style, sixty-nine... How much of this stuff have you done before?'

'I've had sex – I told you that. But I don't think I was doing it right.'

'Okay.' Luca's lips twitched as he placed a tick beside 'basic sex'. 'Hand job?'

'Um... same thing. I tried it, but it didn't work.'

'It didn't *work*? What exactly happened?'

'I tried to do it, but I wasn't any good at it. The guy... he kind of gave out to me.'

'What? You were giving him a hand job and he *gave out* to you?'

'Yeah,' she said, in a small voice. 'I think I was doing it too lightly. He kept telling me I didn't have to be so gentle, but I was scared of hurting him. Plus, I don't have great upper body strength. My arm was aching and he just kept complaining, so... well, I just gave up. He was really pissing me off. I mean, I was doing my best. He didn't have to be so critical.' Her cheeks flushed. She could still feel the burning shame. It had been so humiliating.

'Arsehole!'

'Well, I suppose it's like you said – if he'd faked it and pretended he was enjoying it, I'd have just kept doing the same thing.'

'He didn't have to fake it. He could have just shown you what to do, given you a bit of encouragement.'

'Anyway, I just left – got out of bed there and then and never saw him again.'

'Serves him right.'

'I don't think he'd have been crying after me, considering,' she said. 'He was probably happier on his own.'

'Wankers usually are.'

'I'm not telling you this to make you feel sorry for me, by the way. You have to tell me if I'm not doing something right. I want to learn.'

'I'll be firm but fair.' He grinned. 'Was that the half?'

'Sorry?'

'You said you'd had sex three and a half times.'

'Oh, yeah. That was the half.'

'What about positions? What have you done?'

'Just missionary.'

'Blowjob?'

She shook her head.

'Well, we can start off with this fundamental stuff, and later on, when you've got to grips with the basics, we can move on to more kinky things, like on your blog.'

'You've been reading my blog?' she asked, disconcerted.

'Yeah, of course. I needed to get an idea of what we were working towards.'

'Oh!' It felt like he had been reading her diary, discovering her deepest, darkest secrets and fantasies – which was ridiculous, since the blog was public. But that was different. Luca knew her. He knew she had written that stuff, and she felt exposed.

'Hey, don't look so scared,' he said, smiling. 'I thought it was great. Some of that stuff was shit hot!'

'But none of it's real,' she said.

'I know that.'

Oh well, at least now he knew what a gulf there was between the person she wanted to be and the reality. 'I know it's a hell of a leap...' she began, hoping he wouldn't be scared off by the enormity of the task ahead of them.

'I love that you have such a kinky imagination. It makes me think my job is going to be very easy.'

Claire was encouraged by that.

'Okay, if that's it, why don't you unpack your bag and then we'll finish getting dinner?' he said. 'I've cleared some space in the top drawer in my bedroom if you want to leave some stuff here. And I've emptied a shelf in the bathroom too.'

'Thanks, Luca,' she said, touched that he was going out of his way to make an awkward situation as easy as he could for her.

When she had unpacked her things, Claire joined Luca in the kitchen. He splashed wine into short tumblers and they drank while they worked. He sliced onions and mushrooms, while Claire crushed garlic and chopped chives to mix with the crème fraîche. Then she melted a thick slab of butter with olive oil, the steaks hissing as she slid them into the pan and the delicious aroma of searing meat filling the air. She was surprised by how relaxed she felt with Luca, chatting companionably in the kitchen as they cooked together. She had been increasingly nervous about tonight the closer it got, but now that she was here, she was fine – more than fine. She was enjoying herself.

When it was ready, they took their plates through to the living room and ate at the little folding table, their knees almost touching underneath it.

Luca cut into his steak enthusiastically. 'This is fantastic!' he said, raising his glass to her. 'Thank you.'

'You're welcome,' she said, clinking her glass against his.

'I think you're trying to feed me up,' he said, with a smile.

She was enjoying it too. The steak was juicy and tender, the potatoes soft and fluffy, topped with fat dollops of the crème fraîche and chives.

Later they ate bowls of raspberries with thick cream, sitting on the sofa.

'Are you trying to stupefy me with food and drink so I won't be able to do anything?' Luca asked her, his dark eyes twinkling.

'No, of course not. I'm here to learn.'

'Good,' he said sternly. 'Glad to hear it.'

He put his bowl on the coffee table, and Claire moved to pick it up, but he grabbed her wrist, pulling her back onto the sofa. 'Leave it,' he said softly, gazing at her intently now. His thumb stroked gently over her wrist. Then he kissed her, and his mouth tasted of wine and raspberries. 'Let's go to bed,' he murmured, pulling back.

Claire glanced at her watch. 'It's only nine.'

He cocked his head to one side and looked at her in silence, a small smile playing around his mouth.

'Oh! Yes, of course.' That was what she was here for, after all.

'Unless you'd rather watch television or something.'

'No.' She shook her head.

'Good,' Luca said, standing and pulling her up with him. 'Because I don't have a television.'

In the bedroom Luca began kissing her. He took his time awakening all her senses, just kissing and touching her until every nerve ending in her body was tingling and she was weak with desire. Their kisses became more heated until she was so worked up that she was acting purely on instinct, clawing mindlessly at his clothes, frantic to feel his bare skin against hers, her hips rocking into his, desperate for more. She tugged at the hem of his T-shirt, and he lifted his arms so she could pull it off over his head, and then she ran her hands over his chest, loving the feel of his firm, warm flesh. Lost in a fog of lust, she was hardly aware of her clothes coming off until Luca pulled away from her to remove his jeans and she realised she was only wearing her knickers. Then he pulled off his boxers and stood before her naked, and Claire just stared, her eyes raking over his taut, muscular body, taking it all in. She knew she was gawping, but Luca didn't seem to mind. Why would he, when he was so... beautiful?

'Can I?' she asked, reaching a hand tentatively towards his cock, hard and straining against his stomach.

'I'm all yours.' He spread his arms wide, and Claire couldn't believe her luck that she had free rein with his amazing body to practice on.

She wrapped her hand lightly around his cock, and felt it twitch and grow beneath her fingers. Luca sucked in a breath, his teeth clamping down on his lower lip.

'Sorry,' she gasped, pulling her hand away.

'Okay, teachable moment.' He smiled, grabbing her hand and wrapping it around his shaft again, firmer this time, his hand warm over hers as he held it there. 'Don't apologise for getting a guy hard. That's generally considered a *good* thing.'

Claire felt strangely proud that she had done this to him, and grateful that he hadn't made her feel weird and clueless for not knowing how to touch him.

She was glad they were both naked this time when they lay down on the bed and Luca pulled her close. His bare skin felt so amazing against the length of her naked body, her nipples hardening where they rubbed against his chest, the hardness of his erection digging into her stomach.

They made love slowly, and there was none of the awkwardness or uncertainty of Claire's previous experiences. Luca showed her what to do when she hesitated, sometimes taking her hand and guiding her, patiently teaching her how to touch him. He told her what felt good, and his whispered words of praise and groans of pleasure spurred her on, giving her confidence, making her feel powerful and in control. She understood exactly what they were striving for, both intent on their own pleasure and each other's, and they worked together to make it happen – Luca changing angles as he moved inside her; Claire thrusting her hips upwards to increase friction, seeking her own pleasure; Luca reaching between them to stroke her clit so she came around his dick before he finally lost it, and collapsed on top of her with a helpless groan.

* * *

Claire woke the next morning and glanced at the clock – eight fifteen. It was only half an hour since she had last woken up. She had had a restless night. Luca was a messy sleeper, and he had sprawled over her side of the bed, constantly throwing a leg or an arm across her in his sleep. Now she was trapped beneath him, one heavy arm flung across her, pinning her to the bed, his legs entangled with hers. Her limbs were getting numb, and she was aching to move, but she didn't want to wake him. She had tried gently rolling him off her in the night, but it was like trying to lift a fridge. Sleeping with someone else wasn't as easy as it sounded.

She was relieved when he opened his eyes, looking at her dazedly, but then he just sighed and nestled closer into her, his eyes drooping closed. He was asleep again in seconds. She lay there for what felt like hours waiting for him to wake up again, but finally she could bear it no longer. She really needed to pee, and she was getting restless, lying there under Luca. She slid out from underneath him and darted for the bathroom.

She wasn't sure what to do with herself when she had finished. She didn't think she'd sleep any more if she went back to bed and, anyway, she didn't want to risk getting trapped under Luca again. She'd been hoping he'd make good on his promise of showering together this morning. She'd been thinking about that since she'd first woken up. But it didn't look like he was going to be awake anytime soon, and in the meantime, she would have to get dressed. She hadn't brought a dressing gown and it was too cold to hang around naked, waiting for him to get up. She toyed with the idea of throwing on one of his shirts, but she didn't know how he'd feel about that. It might seem like something a girlfriend would do.

Her rumbling stomach settled the matter. She decided to shower and get dressed. Hopefully Luca would be awake by then and they could have breakfast together. Maybe they could do shower sex tomorrow. As she stood under the spray, Claire thought back to last night. Luca was a fantastic teacher. He was so patient and gentle, and she was so lucky to have found him. She had thought it was unbelievably big-headed of him at the time, but maybe it was a good thing he'd warned her off falling for him. It would be all too easy to think you were in love with someone who could make you feel that amazing. Of course, she had Mark to think of, so there should be no danger of that. She towelled herself dry, then threw on her clothes and went into the kitchen. She flicked the switch on the kettle and glanced at her watch. It was nearly ten. She'd have a cup of tea and wait for breakfast until Luca was up so they could have it together. Surely he couldn't sleep much longer. She was just pouring boiling water over a teabag when she heard noise at the door and froze. She knew Luca had some pretty ropey neighbours, and she hoped it wasn't someone trying to break in.

But then the door opened easily, and it was obvious that whoever it was had a key.

'Luca!' a light female voice called, and then a very petite girl with an elfin face and huge brown eyes was standing in the doorway pulling a little wheelie case after her. 'Oh!' She stopped in her tracks, clearly surprised to find Claire there.

Not as surprised as Claire was to see her. *Shit!* Fuck Luca! She had been adamant that she didn't want to intrude on his personal life, determined to avoid a situation like this, but he had insisted there were no girlfriends she needed to be aware of. So why was she now confronted with this girl who had a *key*, who looked for all the world like she *lived* here, and who was clearly shocked to find Claire in Luca's kitchen first thing in the morning, her hair still wet from the shower. She looked at the girl's case, so like the one she had brought last night. Was this the day shift arriving? Had he cleared a drawer for her too? Whatever – Claire didn't want to know. She just wanted to get out of there as fast as possible.

'Um... I was just going,' she said, dropping the spoon with a clatter and racing past the girl into the living room.

'Don't go on my account,' the girl said, following her. 'Where's Luca?'

'He's still asleep,' Claire said, grabbing her bag. She pulled on her coat hurriedly while the girl stood watching her with a bemused smile. Then she raced for the door.

'Bye!' the girl called after her, laughter in her voice. 'Lovely meeting you!'

* * *

Luca was disappointed when he woke up to find that Claire wasn't in the bed. He'd enjoyed the best sleep he'd had in ages, and he felt refreshed and ready for more. He wouldn't mind spending the rest of the morning in bed with Claire, tutoring her. He sat up and heard noises coming from the kitchen. Now that he was awake, he realised he was hungry... and Claire had brought all that food. Maybe they could have a big breakfast first and then he'd lure her back to bed for the rest of the day. Or maybe they could have a quickie and then breakfast...

He swung out of bed and headed for the kitchen, planning to surprise her. She'd probably be shocked at first, and a bit embarrassed about seeing him naked in broad daylight, but he'd win her round, he thought, grinning to himself. He loved overcoming her inhibitions. He padded through the living room and stood naked in the doorway of the kitchen, to find—

'Jesus! Ali!' He crouched, covering his dick with his hands. 'Fuck!'

'Luca!' His sister turned her back quickly, shielding her eyes with her hand. 'Please put that away.' She giggled.

'What are you doing here?' Luca called over his shoulder angrily, as he retreated to his bedroom. He quickly pulled on a T-shirt and a pair of jeans, then stomped back to the kitchen. There was no sign of Claire anywhere. 'Was there a girl here when you arrived?' he asked, scowling at her.

'Don't worry,' she said, turning to him. 'I think I scared her off. The coast is clear.'

'Scared her off?' Luca frowned. 'Fuck! What did you say to her?'

'Nothing really, I don't think.' Ali smiled at him innocently. 'She was out of here so fast, I barely had time to say "bye".'

'When was this?' Luca looked towards the door, wondering if he could still catch Claire. It was her Saturday off, and he'd told her he could devote the whole weekend to her. He didn't want her to think he was reneging on the deal. Besides, he'd been looking forward to spending all day in bed with her. It was nice to be able to relax and cuddle between bouts of fucking, without having to worry that she'd get the wrong idea and start thinking it meant something.

'About ten minutes ago.'

Luca picked his mobile up from the counter and punched in Claire's number. 'Seriously, Ali, you can't just barge in here whenever you feel like it,' he said, as Claire's phone went to voicemail. 'Hi, Claire, sorry you had to run into my *sister* this morning. She has serious boundary issues.' He sighed. 'See you later, yeah? Call me.' He hung up and tossed the phone onto the table.

Ali was staring at him, her mouth open. 'Okay, who are you and what have you done with my brother?' she asked.

'It's not what you think.' Luca sighed again. 'Anyway, you haven't answered my question. What are you doing here?'

'Well, that's a lovely welcome home,' Ali said archly. 'I just got back from London this morning. I told the taxi to drop me here because I'd missed you, and I thought we could spend the day together. I was going to take you out for breakfast.'

Luca smiled, softening a little. He could never be cross with Ali for long. 'Okay. Or we could have breakfast here, if you like. There's loads of food.'

'There is?' Ali pulled open the fridge. 'Wow, there really is! Seriously, what's got into you? You're letting girls stay overnight, you're buying food…' A smile spread across her face.

'Not girls,' Luca said crossly. 'A girl.'

'Weirder still.' She pursed her lips and narrowed her eyes, scrutinising his face. 'We're going to talk about this over breakfast,' she said. 'But first I need to pee.'

She dashed off to the bathroom and Luca started taking things out of the fridge. Minutes later, Ali reappeared. 'You have conditioner in your bathroom,' she said gleefully, as she came back into the kitchen. '*Girly* conditioner. And moisturiser.' She grinned slyly at him. 'Luca Ffrench-Carroll, do you have a *girlfriend*?'

14

Claire listened to Luca's voicemail, wishing she could rewind and start the morning again. She felt such an idiot now for running off like that, mortified that Luca might see it as the behaviour of a jealous girlfriend. It was true she had been angry at being confronted by another woman in his flat, but only because she hadn't wanted to be put in an awkward situation. If only she'd stuck around for a few minutes instead of high-tailing it out of the door, she'd have found out that the girl was his *sister*. It made sense, now that she thought about it. She had the same colouring as Luca – the same olive skin, dark hair and brown eyes. She hadn't even known that he *had* a sister. He never mentioned his family – not that they spent a lot of their time talking. It occurred to her that she knew very little about him. It would have been nice to stay and meet his sister – and then she could have spent the rest of the day in bed with him having amazing sex. She felt a pang of regret, longing to turn around and go back. But now she was reluctant to face him, embarrassed about the way she had left. She called Luca back and told him she had things to do today but she would see him that evening.

It was a beautiful day, unusually warm for May, and as she walked into town, the pavement cafés were already full of people sitting outside, enjoying the sunshine. It lifted her spirits. The weather seemed to put everyone in a good mood, and the city felt like a happier, friendlier place. She found it endearing the way Irish people got completely overexcited at the first hint of sun, immediately donning summer clothes and sunglasses, heading to the beach and dining *al fresco*. She loved days like this when the world seemed full of promise. She just wished she had someone to share it with. If she hadn't been such an eejit, she could have been sharing it with Luca and his sister. Still, she wasn't going to let that get her down and spoil the day.

Determined to make the most of it, she decided to treat herself to breakfast in her favourite café. She walked to Dame Street, and read her book while lingering over a delicious full Irish in the Queen of Tarts. But though breakfast alone with a good book was usually her idea of bliss, today she struggled to feel content. She was usually happy in her own company, but now she felt unsettled and restless. Maybe it was because of the weather or perhaps because her mother had been away from home for the past couple of weeks and she had had enough of the solitude, but she craved companionship.

When she got home, she decided to ring Mark to cheer herself up. She dialled his number, buoyed at the prospect of having someone to talk to, even if it was at a distance.

'Claire, hi!' He sounded gratifyingly pleased to hear from her and his friendly voice cheered her up. 'Great to hear from you. How are you?'

'I'm good.' She smiled into the phone. *Better now*. 'How are you?'

'Still getting the run-around from Millie,' he said, with a sigh, 'but otherwise I'm fine.'

'Oh no! What's Millie up to?'

'She left me – for the bloke across the road.'

'Ouch! That's a bit close to home.'

'Tell me about it – she didn't even have the decency to try to hide it. Every day she'd be there, flaunting herself in his front window, where she knew I'd see her.'

'Well, you're better off without her.'

'Oh, she's home again now. Came slinking back last night with her tail between her legs.' He sighed. 'That's not true, actually – her tail was in the air. She's shameless.'

'And you took her back?'

'What can I say? I'm putty in her paws.'

Claire laughed.

'So, what are you up to today? Are you getting this lovely weather over there?'

'Yes, it's gorgeous. I'm going to visit my mother this morning. Maybe I'll meet up with a friend later on, and do something.'

'How is your mother?'

'She's good, doing well. How about you? What are you doing?'

'I'm meeting the guys for a run on the Heath – I'm just waiting for them now. And later a bunch of us are going for brunch – a new place by the canal in Little Venice.'

'That sounds lovely,' Claire said wistfully, suddenly feeling very distant from Mark – he had a whole life she knew nothing about, a life she wasn't part of. She didn't know who his friends were; she couldn't picture him with them. He seemed so remote from her.

'It's a perfect day for it,' Mark broke into her thoughts. 'I wish you could come.'

'Me too.' She sighed.

'Or that I could be there with you. We could go to the Iveagh Gardens.'

She smiled, thinking of their kiss.

'Any chance of you getting over next weekend? I'm dying to see you.'

Claire thought. She knew her mother wouldn't mind. She was safe and cared-for in the nursing home and would have plenty of visitors at the weekend. She would drum it into her brothers that they had to visit too. 'Yeah, that should be doable,' she said. 'I'll look into flights and stuff and get back to you. Okay?'

'Great! Well, the guys are here. I'd better go.'

'Okay. Have fun.'

'Looking forward to seeing you again.'

'Yeah, me too. Bye.' Claire hung up, cheered by the thought of next weekend, but she quickly became deflated again. It was nice to have something to look forward to, but that didn't solve her need for company right now. In a way, talking to Mark had only made her feel more isolated, and a bit sad. Determined not to let it get her down, she rang a couple of friends to see if anyone wanted to meet up later. But Jane, an old school friend, was too busy ferrying her son around all day to parties and sports, and Catherine was on her way to a wedding in Wicklow. Oh well, she would visit her mother, then spend the afternoon reading in the garden before heading back to Luca's. There were a lot worse ways to spend a day.

She was dressed too warmly for the weather, so she swapped her boots for flat pumps and changed into cropped jeans and a short-sleeved top before going to the nursing home. She grabbed a light summer jacket from the wardrobe and was on the way out to the car when she got a call on her mobile. It was one of the care staff from the home, requesting her to see the manager when she was next visiting. She explained that she was on her way and said she would speak to Mrs Byrne when she got there.

Damn, she thought, as she tossed her mobile onto the passenger seat and put on her seatbelt. She could have done without that today. She didn't like Theresa Byrne and hated having to deal with her. She was a tough woman, who tried hard to come across as caring and maternal, but underneath the phony façade she was a hard-hearted bully. Claire found her intimidating. She was hopeless at dealing with people like that and always let them get the better of her. Still, she shouldn't let herself get wound up about it – it was probably just some administrative formality she needed to see her about.

When she arrived at the home, one of the nursing staff showed her to Theresa's office. She was sitting behind her desk – a plump, middle-aged woman with iron-grey hair cut in a rigid bob that was a monument to hairspray. Claire had never seen it move.

'Ah, Claire.' She looked up. 'Thank you for coming. Have you been in with Mum?'

'No, I'm on my way now. I called here first. You wanted to see me?'

'Yes. Sit down.' She waved Claire to the seat in front of her desk, then leant forward confidentially. 'Are you aware that we had an *incident* last night?'

Claire's stomach turned over. She knew Theresa meant her mother – she was a big fan of the royal 'we' – and her mother's 'incidents' usually involved ambulances, paramedics, heart-stopping races to hospital and teams of doctors working to bring her back to life. Why hadn't anyone called her? Jesus, had they called the house and she wasn't there? But they had her mobile number.

'Nothing to worry about,' Theresa reassured her, clasping her hands together on the desk, as if in prayer.

'Not a medical emergency?'

'Oh no! Nothing like that. Although we did end up having to call an ambulance for poor June…'

Claire wondered why she was being told about June, whoever she was.

'I'm sorry if I gave you a fright, dear,' Theresa said.

Claire nodded, disliking the woman more than ever.

'Let me explain.' Theresa drew a deep breath and assumed a solemn expression. 'As you know, residents aren't supposed to have alcohol in their rooms.'

Claire had an awful feeling she knew where this was going, but she was so giddy with relief that nothing serious had happened to her mother that she didn't really care.

'It's for their own good. The rules are there for everyone. Of course, we let them have a little drink on special occasions, but it's all properly regulated. We have a duty of care to our residents...'

Claire sat back and let Theresa's words wash over her. Apparently her mother's friends had been smuggling in drink for her and she had been holding raucous parties in her room, her fellow residents crowding in, getting drunk and disorderly, then staggering back to their own rooms trying to support each other when they could barely support themselves with their Zimmer frames and walking sticks. Last night, one of Espie's friends, June, had fallen and broken her wrist. According to Theresa, June was being very stoical about it and was standing up for 'Mum', but her family had taken a dim view and were threatening to sue the home and go to the papers with their story.

'Mum's a bit of a live wire, isn't she?' Theresa said, creasing her face into a facsimile of a sympathetic smile.

Well, *my* mum is, Claire thought. I don't know about yours. The way Theresa referred to her mother as 'Mum' made her skin crawl.

'And that's lovely,' Theresa hurried on. 'It's great that she's still so full of life. She's a real character and very popular with the other residents. But I'm afraid she's a bit of a disruptive influence on some of our old people.'

Oh God, Claire thought, resisting the urge to giggle, was her mother getting *expelled* from a nursing home?

'She's only here for convalescent care so—'

'Please don't kick her out,' Claire interrupted, hating that she was reduced to begging. 'We really need this. I work full-time, and need her to be a bit more mobile before she comes home.'

'Don't worry,' Theresa said, waving her hand in a calming gesture. 'We're not asking her to leave. If she was one of our permanent residents, we'd have to look at the situation very carefully. The welfare of our old people is paramount. However, as it's only for another couple of weeks, I'm sure we can manage. But maybe you could have a little word with Mum? We really can't afford a repeat of last night. Do you think you could get her to stick to the rules for the rest of her stay?'

'Yes, I'm sure I can,' Claire said, relieved. 'Thank you.' She had never imagined she would feel such abject gratitude to Theresa Byrne.

'No problem.' Theresa's smile was genuine this time, so delighted was she to have the upper hand. 'Maybe you could talk to her friends too. People mean well, but...' She paused. 'Does Mum have a problem?' she asked, almost in a whisper.

'Sorry?'

'Mum – does she have a little problem?'

'Well,' Claire said, feeling confused, 'she has a weak heart... and severe arthritis. You know that. I'd say she has a lot of problems.'

'A drink problem?' Theresa mouthed the words, raising her eyebrows.

'No!'

'No shame in it, you know,' Theresa prodded.

'I know, but she doesn't have a drink problem. She enjoys a drink, like the rest of us – but it's not a problem.'

'Well, if you're sure,' Theresa said doubtfully. 'There's lots of help available, you know, if—'

'Thanks,' Claire said, standing up to go. 'I'd better go and see her now. And thanks, too, for letting her stay.' Theresa stood and they shook hands. 'I'll make sure she doesn't break the rules for the rest of her time here.'

When she had her hand on the door knob, Claire turned back to Theresa. 'Her name's Esperanza, by the way,' she said, wishing she could say it without her hands sweating and her voice shaking.

'Sorry?' Theresa frowned in confusion.

'My mum. Her name's Esperanza. Esperanza Kennedy. But everyone calls her Espie.'

* * *

It was such a lovely day that she pushed her mother outside in her wheelchair to sit on the lawn.

'I got a severe talking-to from Theresa about you,' Claire told her.

'Oh dear, am I in the doghouse?'

'She thinks you have a drink problem.' Claire grinned conspiratorially.

Her mother threw back her head and laughed her hearty laugh.

'She was being all smarmy and sympathetic. Trying to get me to shop you.'

'But you held up under questioning?'

'I did. I gave her nothing.'

'You're a good daughter. I'm glad I didn't abandon you in the forest when I was skint.'

'Me too. Although I do sometimes wonder what my life might have been like if I'd been taken in by a kindly woodcutter who raised me as his own.'

'Oh!' Espie gasped, her eyes lighting up. 'Do you think *Theresa* has a drink problem? People who have one are always trying to project it onto someone else.'

'Probably. But so what if she does? She tells me there's no shame in it.'

'That's all right, then. So, am I being expelled?'

'No, but you're on a warning. She says you're a disruptive influence on the others.'

'God, it's worse than bloody school.'

'She said someone broke their wrist last night.'

'Yes – June. I do feel bad about that. But we were just having a bit of fun. They expect you to sit around all day drinking tea and watching some orange gobshite on TV getting people to guess the price of stuff. Or else it's American chat shows with people crying because they're too fat or because they've lost a load of weight and they're so happy. And they call their diet a "journey", and talk about it like it's some kind of spiritual experience. Jesus wept! And, after all that excitement, we're supposed to be tucked up in our beds at eight, fast asleep, just when there might be something on telly that you'd actually be interested in watching. We may be old, but we're still people!'

'I know, but, Mum, you have to behave for the rest of your time here. You really need to be a bit better before you come home. I can't take more time off work and—'

'I know, I know,' her mother said, in a conciliatory tone. 'I'll be good. I'll be a model old lady for the rest of my stay, promise.'

'Sorry. I know it's horrible, but it's not for much longer.'

'It's fine. Don't mind me – I'm just having a rant. It'll do you good anyway to have a break from worrying about me. I know it's a strain on you.'

'Anyway – good party?'

'Excellent party. There are some really interesting people in here. I've made some terrific friends.'

Claire wasn't surprised. Her mother made new friends wherever she went. She had a talent for it. 'Mum, I was thinking of going over to London next weekend.'

'Oh, you should!' Espie said immediately. 'Is there anything particular on?'

'No, I just want to visit a... friend.'

'One of your internet friends?'

'Yeah,' Claire said, jumping on the explanation gratefully. Anyway, it was true – she did know Mark from the internet.

'It's a great idea. Oh, there's June now,' Espie said, beckoning to a tall, solidly built old lady with her arm in a sling.

'Sorry I can't shake,' June said, when her mother had introduced them.

'How's the wrist?' Espie asked her.

'Ah, it's fine. Hurts a bit, but it was well worth it,' June said staunchly. 'I haven't had so much fun since my son and his wife dumped me in this kip two years ago.'

'Speaking of your son, is he going to sue?'

June snorted. 'No fear of him. Once he realised he couldn't very well sue this place for negligence and still leave me here to rot, he backed down pretty quickly.'

'Well, there'll be no more booze parties in my room, I'm afraid. Theresa had a word with Claire, and apparently I'm leading you all astray. But there's nothing to say we can't have a tea party, is there?'

'Nothing at all. And we don't need booze to enjoy ourselves.'

'Exactly. The company's the main thing. So, my room after dinner?'

'I'll be there.' June smiled.

* * *

When she left the nursing home, Claire didn't feel like going home to read in the garden. She wanted to be with people, feeling an overwhelming need to laugh and chat and let off steam. Her brother Ronan lived nearby, so on an impulse she decided to drop in on him and Liz. They would probably be spending a day like this in the garden, and she envisaged them all sitting there, drinking cold white wine and chatting while the children ran around, periodically being dragged into games of hide-and-seek or chase. She hadn't seen her nephews, Adam and Ben, in a while, and she loved spending time with them. Cheered by the image, she hopped into her car and drove the short distance to Ronan's house.

There was no response at first when she rang the doorbell, and she assumed it was because they were in the garden. The car was in the drive, so she knew they were at home. She was just pulling her mobile from her bag to let them know she was outside, when she heard the thundering of feet in the hall, and six-year-old Adam flung open the door.

'Claire!' he exclaimed, a big grin lighting up his face. 'Yay!'

'Hi, Adam.' She bent down to hug him. It had been a good idea to come, she thought. Adam's welcome was just what she needed today.

'Everyone's in the garden,' he said, running down the hallway ahead of her to the back of the house. 'Claire's here!' he yelled, bursting outside through the kitchen door.

Claire's blood froze as she followed him – because when Adam had said 'everyone' was there, he'd meant everyone. Everyone except her. Ronan, Neil, Liz and Michelle were sitting around the garden table with the remnants of what looked like a very boozy lunch, while their children played football together on the grass. It was very much the idyllic scene she had pictured in her head – but without her.

The children were happy to see her, Adam and Ben and their cousins Holly and Cian all rushing up to greet her enthusiastically and imploring her to join in their game, unaware of any undercurrent. But her brothers and their wives were awkward and embarrassed, and when she caught Michelle making a 'yikes' face at Liz, she just wanted to vaporise. Damn, she thought, trying not to cry, why had she come?

'Claire!' Liz said, recovering first. 'This is a nice surprise. Sit and have a drink.'

'No, I won't stay,' she said, struggling to keep her voice even. 'I was just passing and I thought I'd pop in and say hi.'

'Come on,' Ronan said, standing and pulling out a chair for her. 'Have a drink. Were you in with Mum?'

'Yes.' She walked slowly towards the table. If she ran off now, she would look pathetic. 'I won't have any wine, thanks,' she said to Liz, who was passing her a glass. 'I have the car.'

'You could have a half-glass? Or a spritzer?'

'I'll just have some mineral water,' she said, spotting a bottle.

Michelle poured her a glass and passed it to her.

'Have you eaten?' Liz asked, surveying the table. 'There's not much left but—'

'I'm fine, thanks. I'm not hungry.' She buried her face in her glass, gulping water to stop herself crying. Her throat ached. Why couldn't they have invited her? She could have done with this today. She felt so unwanted, like an outsider in her own family.

'We decided to do this at the last minute,' Liz said, as if sensing how she felt. 'It was such a gorgeous day. You have to strike while the iron's hot in this country, don't you?'

'We'd have asked you if we'd planned it,' Ronan said.

'It's fine,' she said, dredging up a smile. The last thing she wanted was to let them see how hurt she was. 'I was kind of busy today anyway.'

'Besides, she probably wouldn't have wanted to come,' Michelle said to Ronan, as if Claire wasn't there. 'I remember when I was single, the last thing I wanted to do was hang out with a bunch of couples.'

Jesus! Claire couldn't believe she was playing the couples card. Was Michelle actually suggesting that she needed a *date* to spend time with her own family?

'How is Espie?' Michelle asked.

'She's fine – in great form.' Claire wasn't about to enlighten Michelle on her mother's misdemeanors. They didn't get on, and the whole incident would probably end up as an anecdote in Michelle's column – spun so that it would read as yet one more example of what Michelle had to put up with as a long-suffering daughter-in-law.

'God, I haven't been in to see her at all yet,' Neil said. 'It's so busy at work. I suppose we might as well wait until she's home now,' he said to Michelle.

'Well, she's there for two more weeks,' Claire said.

'I want to go and see Granny!' Holly yelled, as she ran past, chasing a ball.

'We're going in tomorrow, aren't we?' Ronan consulted Liz, who nodded.

'We should all go, and give Claire a break,' Michelle said, smiling kindly at Claire. 'You've been visiting every day, haven't you?'

'Yeah, but I don't mind.' She wanted to tell Michelle that spending time with her mother wasn't an irksome chore on a par with grocery shopping or doing the ironing, but she gritted her teeth and said nothing.

'Well, you can have a day off tomorrow,' Michelle said. 'We'll take over and you can have a nice rest.'

Claire was relieved when the children started importuning her to play with them again, happy to let them pull her away to bounce with them on the trampoline.

* * *

She felt weary and ground down by the time she got to Luca's. His friendly face and sweet, welcoming smile were balm to her battered soul, and she was sorry she hadn't come back earlier. In fact, she was sorry she'd ever left his bed that morning. Now that she was there, she was desperate for him to put his arms around her, aching for him to hold her and kiss her. The longing to feel close to someone had become almost a physical pain.

'Have you eaten?' he asked, when they got inside. 'Do you want to—'

She shook her head. 'I'm not hungry. Could we just…' She nodded to the bedroom.

'Get right down to it? Sure.'

'It's just I haven't had any time with you today so…' She would scream if he didn't put his arms around her in the next ten seconds, but she couldn't exactly tell him that. 'Do you mind?'

'No, of course not.' He frowned at her in concern. 'Are you okay?'

'Yeah, I'm fine.' She had forgotten how intensely Luca looked at you – like he could see right into you. She was unable to hold his gaze. 'I just don't want to waste any more time.'

He continued to study her face for another minute, and she could only hope she didn't look as close to the edge as she felt. 'Okay, no problem,' he said finally. Then he sauntered into the bedroom, and Claire followed him.

She expected him to pull her into his arms as soon as they went in, but to her consternation, he sat on the edge of the bed, leaving her standing by the window.

He leant back on his hands and gazed up at her. 'Take your clothes off,' he said.

'What?' she breathed, her voice barely audible.

'Your clothes,' he said, his eyes glittering. 'Take them off.'

She drew a breath to protest, but checked herself when she saw the implacable glint in his eyes and understood. This was a lesson. It was what she was here for, after all, wasn't it? Blushing furiously, she grabbed her top by the hem and pulled it over her head. She willed him to close the distance between them and do the rest for her.

'Go on.'

'Sorry?'

'Keep going,' he said, nodding at her bra.

Oh, shit. He wasn't going to meet her halfway. She really couldn't cope with this, today of all days. She felt dangerously close to tears. 'I can't,' she said.

'You can't? How do you get undressed at night when I'm not there?'

She threw him an angry look. 'You know what I mean. I can't just stand here and strip in cold blood while you watch.' She sighed, hanging her head. 'I'm shy. What's wrong with that? Why does everyone have to be sassy and—'

'There's nothing wrong with it,' he interrupted her. 'I happen to find it really sweet – and quite a turn-on, actually. I like shy girls.' He grinned. 'It's so much fun overcoming their inhibitions.'

'Well, then—'

He sat up, eyeballing her. 'But what *I* like doesn't matter, does it? What turns *me* on is neither here nor there. It's not me you're trying to impress.'

'Oh. I suppose not.'

'No. So...' He looked at her expectantly.

Claire sighed. She would just have to get this over with – the quicker the better, like ripping off a plaster. It would be worth it to be wrapped in Luca's arms again. And the sooner she got naked, the sooner she'd be there. She yanked open the button of her jeans and started hurriedly pulling down the zip as she kicked off her shoes.

'Claire?'

'Yes?' She stopped.

'It's not against the clock, sweetheart.' He leant back again. 'Do it slowly. And start with your bra.'

Reluctantly she reached around and unclasped her bra. Even though she kept her gaze on the floor, she could feel his eyes burning into her.

'Hey!' he said softly. 'Look at me.'

She forced herself to meet his eyes, trying not to squirm as she slid the straps down her arms and pulled off her bra, fighting the urge to cover herself with her hands. His eyes dropped to her breasts, lingering there before returning to her face. 'And try not to look like you're being tortured.'

She glanced away again as she felt tears stinging the backs of her eyes. She couldn't let him see. But this *was* torture. She felt so humiliated, and he was so cold and distant. Surely being with someone like this shouldn't feel so *lonely*.

'You have nothing to be ashamed of,' he was saying gently. 'You have a beautiful body. You're a gorgeous, sexy woman and it makes me hard to look at you.'

She pulled the zip of her jeans down slowly. She knew he meant to encourage her, and she tried to take in what he was saying, but she felt so out of it. She hung her head, letting her hair fall forward to hide her face as she felt a tear escape and slide down her cheek.

'Claire?'

Not thinking, she looked up instinctively at the sound of her name.

'Jesus, are you *crying*?' Luca was clearly horrified. In an instant he was off the bed and pulling her into his arms.

She couldn't help the sob that escaped her then, and could no longer hold back the tears as Luca led her to the bed and pulled her into his lap.

'God, I'm so sorry,' he said, 'I'm such an arsehole.' He stroked her back soothingly as she cried.

Claire curled into him, burying her head in his neck. It was a relief to let go.

'Ssh,' Luca whispered, while his warm hand rubbed up and down her spine comfortingly.

'I'm sorry, I'm being stupid,' she said finally, brushing away her tears.

'No, you're not. I fucked up. You should have stopped me. Why didn't you say something? I didn't know I was upsetting you that much.'

'It wasn't your fault.' She sniffed. 'I just had kind of a lousy day and—'

'And my prickish ways were the last straw? I'm sorry – I shouldn't have pushed you like that.'

'No, you were right. That's what I'm paying you for. I told you not to go easy on me.' She gave a rueful laugh. 'Well, that wasn't very sexy, was it – bursting into tears in the middle of a striptease? Maybe we should start again from the top.' She wiped her eyes. 'I'll try again,' she said, pushing him away so she could get up.

'No!' His arms tightened around her. 'Hey, we're not turning you into a *machine* here. You don't have to be up for sex all the time.' He stroked her hair away from her face, brushed away the last of the tears. 'I'm sure even Hugh Hefner has his days when he's not in the mood.'

'Really?' she asked sceptically.

'Okay, maybe not Hugh Hefner,' he smiled, 'but normal people.'

This was the best she'd felt all day, Claire realised, all the stress and misery melting away as she laid her head on Luca's shoulder while his hand ran soothingly over the bare skin of her back.

'Um, Claire?' he said eventually.

'Mm?'

'Maybe you should put your top back on.'

'Oh.' She lifted her head.

'It really is making me hard looking at you,' he said, with an apologetic wince, glancing down at her naked breasts crushed against him. 'And I can't not look. I'm a guy – I'm genetically programmed to look at tits if they're on show.'

'Okay.' She scrambled off him reluctantly and crossed the room to pick up her top, putting it on with her back to him. When she turned around, he had moved and was reclining on the bed, propped up against the headboard. She faltered, unnerved at finding herself across the room from him again and wondering how she was going to get back into his arms. But he made it easy for her, holding them open wide. When she dived onto the bed, he brought her close into the warmth of his body.

'Better?' he asked, smiling at her.

She nodded.

'Do you want to tell me about your lousy day?'

'Maybe later.'

He sighed, pulling her into his side and stroking her arm. 'We're going to have to work on your communication skills.'

'What do you mean?'

'You have a hard time saying what you want. You need to work on being more vocal, telling me what you need, so I don't fuck up like I did just now.'

'I told you, it's not your fault.'

'I should have picked up on the signals. I thought there was something off when you came in. But it's not always easy to tell what you want. For instance, right now I don't know if you want me here or if you'd rather be left alone.'

'No, I want you here,' she said, wrapping her arms tighter around him. 'If you don't mind, that is.' It suddenly occurred to her that maybe he'd like a night off. He could have easy, uncomplicated sex with a normal girl who wouldn't freak out about taking her clothes off in front of him. 'I mean, it's Saturday night. You'd usually be out, wouldn't you?'

'Yeah, out on the prowl,' he said, making wolfish eyes at her.

'Well, if you want to do that, I could go.'

'I don't need to go out picking up women when I've got you,' he said, giving her a squeeze. 'I told you – I like sex, I don't want a girlfriend. This arrangement suits me just fine.'

She smiled, nestling closer, hugely relieved that he wasn't going to ditch her. How strange that Luca should be the first person not to let her down today. She'd never expected him to be so *nice* when they'd started this – so kind.

'You probably think you're transparent, but you're not,' he said. 'And you can't always expect a guy to read your mind. You need to be able to say what you want. Like tonight, you didn't want sex and that's cool. But you weren't able to communicate that to me. If I'd known, I'd never have—'

'But I did.'

'Did what, sweetheart?'

'I did... want sex,' she said, in a small voice. 'Just not – not like that. Before, you always—'

'I took your clothes off. I initiated everything.'

'Yeah.'

'I thought we could move forward. But it was too soon. I shouldn't have rushed you. You weren't ready, and I'm sorry.'

She sighed contentedly, revelling in the comfort of his arms around her, the warmth of his body next to hers.

'So you wanted to have sex tonight?'

'Yes. But I wanted you to...'

'Tell me,' he urged.

'I like it when you take my clothes off,' she murmured, looking up at him from under her lashes.

'And I *love* doing it,' he said, with a grin. 'So you wanted me to undress you. What else?'

'I wanted you to kiss me.'

He bent down and gave her a soft, wet kiss, sucking her bottom lip into his mouth. 'What else?'

'Well... I wanted to have sex.'

'How exactly?'

She frowned at him in confusion.

'Tell me what you want me to do.'

She blushed, reaching for words that wouldn't come. She shook her head defeatedly.

'Okay,' he said, smiling down at her, 'You're feeling fragile tonight, so I'm not going to make you say anything. You can just nod, okay? Or shake your head.'

'Okay.' She nodded.

'Do you want me to go down on you?' he asked, his eyes on hers.

Claire buried her face in his chest and nodded furiously.

'You want me to make you come with my tongue? And my fingers?'

She nodded again.

'Anything else?'

'Yes,' she whispered. 'This.' She reached down and put a hand over his erection.

'You want me inside you?' he asked, his voice husky.

She lifted her head and nodded, looking at him.

He smiled at her. 'There, that wasn't so hard, was it?' He kissed her forehead. 'And the best thing about vocalising is that it's so rewarding.' A warm hand slid up under her top to cup her breast as he leant in to kiss her again. 'Ask and you shall receive.'

15

'So, you have a sister,' Claire said the next morning, as they lay wrapped around each other in bed. She had slept late and woken slowly, still feeling wonderfully languorous and heavy-limbed after hours of delicious sex last night. She was glad she could stay put this morning and enjoy a lazy Sunday morning with Luca.

'Yeah, Ali.' Luca smiled. 'Sorry about that. I gave her a key once after she'd been waiting outside here and some local thugs were giving her hassle. But I've told her to try ringing the bell first in future.'

'Is she older or younger?'

'Younger.'

'You're very alike,' she said, propping her chin on his chest and looking into his sparkly brown eyes.

'Only superficially,' he said, one finger lazily stroking her arm. 'She's not really my sister. We're both adopted.'

'She's from Romania too?'

'Yeah. Same orphanage.'

'Did you know her there?'

'Yeah.' Something flickered in his eyes. 'She's the reason I got adopted, really.'

She waited for him to elaborate, but he said nothing. His eyes were evasive, following his stroking finger, and his normally open face seemed shuttered. 'How so?' she asked.

'Jacqueline wanted Ali, Ali wanted me. So she took us as a job lot.'

'Who's Jacqueline?'

'The woman who adopted us.'

'So... your mother?'

The stroking finger stilled and he was silent for a moment. 'Yeah,' he said eventually, and there was a hard edge to his voice. 'I suppose you could call her that.'

She felt a chill at his tone. She was curious as to what would make him talk so coldly about his adoptive mother. It didn't seem like him – not that she knew him very well. But there was such warmth and affection in his voice when he spoke of his sister that it was obvious he adored her. And she knew herself how sweet he could be. She wondered what his mother could have done to alienate him, but as it was clearly a touchy subject, she decided to leave it alone.

'My mother wrote a book about it,' he said, linking his hands behind his head. 'Why don't you read it if you want all the gory details?'

Claire felt rebuked. She was sorry she'd said anything. A minute ago she'd felt so close to him, and now he was angry and aloof. 'Sorry,' she said, lifting her head and lying back against the pillows so she wasn't touching him. 'I don't mean to be nosey. It just seems weird to be... like this and not really know anything about you.' She didn't want him to think it was just morbid curiosity.

'No biggie,' he said, but there was still an angry set to his mouth. His eyes flicked to her. 'Sorry I snapped at you.'

He dropped his arms to the sheet and she curled into him again, laying her head on his shoulder.

'Ali had got attached to me in the orphanage,' he said quietly. 'I guess I used to look out for her – picked her up when she cried, gave her food when the bigger kids stole hers.'

Claire wondered if anyone had looked out for him, but she could guess. She remembered the horrific images on television of naked, emaciated children strapped to beds or caged like animals, the crying babies who had never been picked up. Her mother had sobbed watching the news reports, and had galvanised the whole neighbourhood to start fundraising.

'Do you remember the orphanage?' she asked tentatively, nervous of pissing him off again. She knew it would be a painful subject and he might not want to talk about it.

'I remember some things. I was seven when I was adopted, so I was older than most. I remember having cold baths and being hit a lot by the staff. I remember lots of children running around naked and screaming. And being hungry – I remember that.'

She wrapped her arms around him, holding him tightly. She couldn't bear to think of Luca as a frightened child, cold and hungry with no one to love him. 'Sorry. I shouldn't have asked,' she said.

'It's fine. Ali doesn't remember any of it, thank God. But I remember her.' She felt him shudder against her.

'How old was Ali?'

'She was three when we were adopted.' He smiled. 'She went apeshit when they tried to take her away and she realised I wasn't going with them.'

'So they took you too.'

'Yeah. And here I am,' he said, with an air of finality, drawing a line under the subject.

Claire was grateful when her stomach let out a long, rumbling groan, helping to dispel the gloomy atmosphere that had descended and bringing them back to the mundane.

Luca laughed. 'Someone wants breakfast,' he said, giving her a squeeze.

'I actually haven't eaten anything since breakfast yesterday,' she said. 'I was running around all day, and then when I got here...'

'You were in too much of a hurry to get me into bed to bother with food,' Luca finished, grinning.

'Yeah, pretty much.' She giggled.

'Okay, let's have breakfast, and you can tell me all about your lousy day. And then we're going to work on dirtying up that beautiful mouth of yours.'

Claire looked at him quizzically.

'Dirty talk,' he explained, releasing her to throw back the duvet. 'We're going to work on your communication skills, remember?'

Claire scrambled out of bed and grabbed her clothes.

'Don't bother getting dressed,' Luca said, pulling on a pair of boxers and a T shirt. 'Here, you can put this on.' He grabbed a shirt from the back of a chair and threw it to her.

Get me, Claire thought happily, as they sat at the little table eating scrambled eggs and toast – both of them half dressed because they were going straight back to bed as soon as they were done. She knew there was nothing unusual about the scene for a lot of people, but she had never had this before, and it felt almost surreal, like she was in a movie. As they ate, Claire told him about her day yesterday.

'I like your mother.' Luca laughed when she told him about the 'incident' at the nursing home.

'You *would* like her,' Claire said. 'And she'd like you. You should meet her.' As soon as the words were out of her mouth, she wished she could take them back. She was under strict instructions not to think of Luca as a boyfriend, and here she was suggesting he meet her *mother*? *Brilliant, Claire – just brilliant.* 'So what did you do yesterday after I left?'

'Hung out with Ali for a bit, and after she left I did some work.' He nodded across the room where a huge canvas stood on an easel. Several smaller ones were stacked against the wall.

'Can I look?' Claire asked.

'Knock yourself out.'

She picked up the last piece of her toast and went over to the canvas on the easel. The paint was still shiny and wet.

'Wow!' she breathed. She couldn't claim to know much about art, but she felt the emotional punch of the piece, and she liked it immediately. She looked through the canvases by the wall, struck by the raw energy and power of the paintings. She recognised Luca's sister in a couple of portraits, and there were a few nudes among the smaller canvases. They were very sensual, erotic paintings, and she wondered who the women were as her eyes lingered on them. What it would be like to have Luca paint *her*?

When they had cleared away the breakfast things, they returned to the bedroom.

'So, communication skills,' Luca said, sitting on the bed. 'You're going to work on talking dirty – telling me what you want, in precise detail.' He grinned. 'But we'll get on to that. First, we have to get you expressing how you feel – preferably not through the medium of tears.' He frowned. 'So – say what you'd have liked to say to me yesterday.'

She stood opposite him. 'What do you mean?'

'When you were uncomfortable with what was happening. You should have told me to stop. You should have told me to fuck off and leave you alone.'

'But I know you didn't mean to upset me. Like you said, you couldn't be expected to read my mind.'

'Exactly – which is why I need you to tell me what you were thinking. So say it.' He looked at her expectantly. '"Fuck off, Luca" – go on.'

'No. It was just a misunderstanding. I know you wouldn't have—'

'Come on,' he interrupted impatiently. 'We're not moving on until you get past this.'

'But you were just trying to move things forward, for my sake. It wasn't your fault—'

'Claire,' he said, in a warning tone. 'This is the most important thing I'll ever teach you. Just say it.'

She looked at him helplessly. 'Don't I call the shots? It's my dime, remember?'

'I don't care. I'm going on strike.'

'But why would I tell you to fuck off when I know you're just trying to do what I want? That's not fair.'

'Claire. This is important. I don't want you going along with something just because you're not able to say how you feel. Not with me nor with anyone else.'

Still she said nothing.

'Okay,' he huffed. 'I've changed my mind. We'll do something else this afternoon instead.'

Claire breathed a sigh of relief.

'We'll have a do-over of yesterday's lesson. You strip, I'll watch.' He folded his arms, and regarded her with a stony expression.

Claire froze. She couldn't believe he was doing this to her when he'd been so apologetic about yesterday.

'I'm waiting,' he said, his gaze fixed on her. When she didn't move, he rolled his eyes impatiently. 'I know I said to go slow, but some time this century would be good. Come on, get on with it. Take your top off.'

She was starting to hate Luca. Her hands were clammy and tears burnt the backs of her eyes.

'And no crying, please,' he drawled. 'Because being made to feel like a sex pest is the biggest boner-killer there is.'

'No. I don't want to,' she said.

'Sorry, can't hear you.'

She took a deep breath, trying to make her voice stronger. 'I said I don't want to.'

'Still can't hear you.'

He was really pissing her off now. 'Fuck you!' she spat.

'That's better. Now try saying it like you mean it. Not whispering would help.'

'Fuck off, Luca!' she said, louder this time.

He sat forward, his face softening. 'Good. Louder! "Fuck off, Luca!"' he shouted.

'Fuck off, Luca,' she yelled back.

'Fuck off, Luca,' he roared, waving his arms like he was conducting an orchestra.

'Fuck off, Luca!'

He looked happier by the second as they shouted the call and response at each other, the volume of Claire's shouts increasing until finally she screamed at the top of her lungs, 'FUCK OFF, LUCA!'

'Yes!' He punched the air with both fists and beamed up at her, and Claire burst out laughing because he looked so damned happy that she was screaming obscenities at him. And then he joined in and they were laughing with each other. She threw herself at him and he caught her in his arms.

'Okay,' he said. 'Now we can get to the fun stuff. Unless you meant it? If you really want me to fuck off—'

'No.' She shook her head. 'I don't.'

'Sorry. I had to do that. I just need to know that you won't let me do something you don't want because you're afraid to say no.'

'I know.'

'Because you're quite shy, and that's great, but—'

'Luca.' She stopped him with a finger to his lips. 'I get it.'

'Okay.' He kissed the finger. 'Good.'

'Thank you,' she said, because she knew he was just looking out for her. Besides, all the shouting had felt good – freeing. She had enjoyed it.

'I like this shirt on you,' he said, touching the collar. 'It looks way better on you than it does on me. But I still want to get it off you.' He began undoing the buttons slowly and then he pushed it off her shoulders, but she didn't mind that she was sitting naked in his lap. She was getting used to him looking at her, and she liked the way his eyes darkened and his breathing changed, enjoying the power her body had over him.

'Let me know what you want – what you need,' he said, as his hands caressed her breasts. 'Tell me if what I'm doing feels good.'

'Can't you tell?'

'Well, yeah. But that's not the point. Dirty talk is sexy. It's a turn-on.' He smiled. 'You know it is.'

'Why do you say that?'

'I know it turns you on when I say things to you. I can feel it.'

She blushed. That was true. She found it really hot when he said things like 'You're so wet' and she could tell from the way he said it that he liked it. It excited her when he told her what he wanted to do to her, or praised what she was doing to him and told her how good it felt. She couldn't deny it. 'I don't know what to say.'

'You could tell me what you want me to do to you.'

'Um... have sex? I want you to have sex with me.'

He laughed. 'Oh, stop it, you're driving me crazy.'

'Sorry.' She bit her lip. 'I want you to kiss me.'

'Where?'

'Everywhere.'

'Be specific,' he coaxed. 'Tell me exactly what you want – where you want me to put my hands or my dick.'

'I want you to put your dick in my vagina,' she said.

'Okay, maybe we should start with something simpler. You could pay me a compliment. Tell me something you like about me – about how I look.' He pulled back and spread his arms wide, putting himself on display for her perusal.

She hesitated.

'It doesn't have to be true.' He smiled crookedly.

'You have the most gorgeous smile,' she said. 'And your eyes are... beautiful.'

'Thanks.' He grinned. 'But that wasn't quite what I had in mind.'

'I meant that,' she said, offended. 'You really do. And you have lovely hair.' She ran a hand through his curls. 'You're very handsome.'

'Thank you,' he said more gently. 'But I was thinking of something sexual

– something about my body.' His eyes dropped meaningfully to his crotch and she gasped.

'You want me to – to compliment you on your—' She couldn't even say the word, waving vaguely in the direction of his groin.

He looked at her, his head cocked to one side, waiting. When she said nothing, his fingers moved to the waistband of his boxers. 'Maybe you need a reminder.'

'No!' She put up a hand to stop him. She racked her brain. What was there to say about it? It was a penis. Though there was one thing… She cleared her throat. 'You, um… you have a very big thing,' she mumbled, her eyes sliding away.

He threw his head back and guffawed. 'A very big thing? That's nice to hear – and accurate,' he said, sobering up. 'But *thing*? Come on, Claire. Use your words.'

'You have a large penis,' she said, with a mischievous smile, deliberately refusing to use the words he wanted just to wind him up.

His lips twitched. 'Say something about how it looks when I'm aroused.'

'Um… it's hard? And it goes a bit longer.'

He chuckled, aware that she was just teasing him now. 'It goes a bit longer?' He tossed her onto the bed and started tickling her sides. 'What else?'

'It increases in circumference as well as in length,' she yelped, as he hit a particularly ticklish spot.

'Oh, baby, you're making me so hot with your talk of my dimensions. I love the way your breathing goes all funny when I kiss you here.' He kissed the side of her neck.

'I like when you touch my nipples and they go pointy,' she squealed.

'They expand and increase in volume.' He let her go and they collapsed, laughing, beside each other.

When his laughter subsided, Luca smiled at her fondly. 'What am I going to do with you?' he said.

'Well… you could have sex with me?'

'Oh, go on, then,' he said, heaving an exaggerated sigh. 'You've won me over with your dirty mouth.'

Later, when it came to the crucial moment, Luca handed her the condom. 'Have you ever done this?'

'Put on a condom? No. Not really.'

'Well, now's your chance.'

'You want me to put it on?'

'It's something you should know if you want to come across as experienced. It's pretty basic stuff.'

'Okay.' She pulled open the packet and took out the condom.

'Okay, that's the tip,' he said, pointing to the top. 'Make sure you—'

'Actually, it's not strictly true that I've never done this,' she said. 'Just not on an actual person.'

'Don't tell me – a banana?'

She nodded. 'A banana and a YouTube video.' She had been practising for this very moment, so at least there would be one thing she could do.

'Well, now's your chance to try it out on a live human being.'

She grabbed his shaft firmly, placed the condom on the top and slid it down, pleased at how smoothly it went on. 'I did it!' She grinned up at him, proud of her success. 'That was easy. It worked just like on a banana!'

'Very good. Next time I'll show you how to do it with your mouth.'

'Oh!' Her smile vanished. Just when she'd thought something was simple.

Luca laughed. 'Don't look so scared. It's not hard. Unlike me.'

* * *

'Are you okay?' he asked her afterwards, as she lay in his arms.

'Yeah... I'm fine.'

'You don't sound too sure.'

'No, I am. It's just...'

'Come on – out with it. If you have any questions, now is the time to ask them. We may not be covering this again.'

Claire took a deep breath. 'It's just that I didn't... you know...' She flapped her hand, trying to find the word.

'Come?' Luca asked, surprised.

'Yeah.'

Luca frowned. 'Are you telling me you've started faking on me? I told you—'

'No, no.' She shook her head frantically. 'I wasn't faking. That's not what I meant. I did have an orgasm. I always do when you...'

'When I finger you?'

'Um... yeah.'

'And when I go down on you.'

'Yes. But I didn't come when we were... when you were inside me. Not until you did... other stuff. I never have,' she admitted, a little frown creasing her brow.

'Is that what's worrying you? That you don't come when we're fucking?'

'Yeah.' She sighed in frustration. She felt like she was flunking class.

'That's perfectly normal,' he said.

'It is?'

'Yeah. Lots of women have a hard time coming from penetrative sex alone. Some never do. There are still lots of different positions we can try. But don't worry about it. You have a good time, right?'

'Yes, I have a brilliant time!'

'Well, that's all that matters. Try not to be so focused on it – just enjoy what we're doing and maybe it'll happen in time.'

'And if it doesn't?'

'It's no biggie. There's no right or wrong way to have sex. It's just a matter of trying different things and finding what does it for you. Then you can ask for whatever you need in the future.'

She didn't think she'd ever be good at asking for what she wanted during sex. 'Maybe you could give me a note?' she said hopefully.

'A crib sheet to hand to future boyfriends? Don't worry, we're going to do a *lot* more vocal work. You won't need a note by the time you graduate from this bed.'

'So, about these different positions,' Claire said some time later, when they were ready to go again.

'Maybe you should go on top this time,' Luca said, lifting her onto him. 'That way, you're in control.'

She straddled him and he guided her down onto his shaft. 'Just move at your own pace,' he said, gripping her waist. 'Do whatever feels good to you. Just concentrate on getting yourself off and do whatever you need. Don't think about me at all.'

Claire hesitated as she began to move. 'Isn't that rude?' she asked. She'd always been given to understand that being selfish in bed was a bad thing.

'Claire, it's sex. You're allowed to be rude. Rude goes with the territory.'

16

Absolute Beginners

Recently I've been told that my sexual confidence can come across as intimidating. That makes me kind of sad. It's not my intention in this blog to make anyone feel inadequate, so I want to take some time out to assure my more inexperienced readers that I wasn't always the smooth operator you see before you now. It took me a while to get into sex. It took even longer to turn me into the cock-hungry shag-monster I am today. My first couple of times were probably as messy and unsatisfying as they are for most people. Sex was embarrassing, bewildering and a lot less fun than dinner and a movie. If it was a choice between sex and a pizza, I'd have gone for the pizza every time.

It wasn't until I met the Artist that I discovered how much fun two people could have rubbing their bits against each other. I wasn't a virgin when I met the Artist, but I might as well have been. He was the first guy to go down on me. His was the first cock I deep-throated, the first spunk I chugged down. He gave me the first orgasm I ever had that wasn't a selfie.

He's come back into my life recently, and we're boning for old times' sake. Hence the trip down Memory Lane. It's reminded me of just how clueless I once was, and what a difference a good teacher can make. So if you're still struggling with what all the fuss is about, rest assured, no one is born this way. I was once like you – probably worse. In fact, I'd almost given up on sex. But I'm so glad I didn't.

So stick with it. It gets better. Don't feel you have to know everything right from the off. Experiment, try different things, and don't be afraid to ask questions. Learning is fun. Don't worry about getting laughed at – no guy will dare laugh when you've got his dick in your mouth or his balls in your hand.

Like everything else, practice makes perfect – and if at first you don't succeed, try, try and try again. I promise you it will be worth it.

(On the other hand, maybe you just prefer pizza. And that's fine too.)

'Good weekend?' Yvonne asked Claire the next day. They were having lunch in the back room of Bookends. Yvonne was eating a tiny pot of fromage frais while thumbing idly through a thick glossy magazine.

'Yes, lovely weekend.' Claire couldn't help grinning as she unwrapped a sandwich from the deli across the road.

Yvonne glanced up. 'Well, look at you, all sexed up!' She beamed, abandoning her magazine to focus on Claire.

'What? What makes you think I'm—'

'You have that glow,' Yvonne said. 'And I have excellent sex radar. I can always tell who's doing it and who's not. And *you*,' she said, pointing a finger at Claire, 'are doing it. Right?'

'Well...' Claire tried, but she couldn't wipe the smug smile off her face. She *was* all sexed up. There was no use denying it. She had gone from being practically a virgin to a total sex maniac in just over a week.

'So you couldn't hold out for five dates, after all,' Yvonne said, folding her arms on the table. 'I told you that was harsh.'

'Oh, um... no. This was... someone else.' She felt like a bit of a tart admitting it.

'Wow! You may be slow to get started, but once you get going, you don't hang around, do you? Where did you meet this guy?'

'At a bar. I was with a friend.'

'And you didn't make him wait. You're obviously more into him than London guy.'

'It's not like that. This guy is more just a sort of... I mean he's not boyfriend material or anything.'

Yvonne's eyes lit up. 'So you've got yourself a fuck buddy!' she said delightedly.

'I suppose you could call him that.' It seemed a pretty accurate description of her relationship with Luca – or as close as she could get without going into some very long, and mortifying, explanations.

'And you'll be seeing him again?'

'Oh, definitely.'

'Good. Because this,' Yvonne said, waving a finger around in front of Claire's face, 'is a really good look on you.'

Claire wished she could tell Yvonne that it was Luca because then she could ask her about him. She had thought about looking up his mother's book on the computer this morning when she came in, but realised she didn't even know his last name. She had tried to think of casual ways to bring him up in conversation but had drawn a blank. She knew Yvonne wouldn't mind – in fact, she'd probably be delighted since she'd suggested it herself. But she doubted Luca would be pleased if he heard she was telling his friends that they were 'together' or that they were 'fuck buddies'.

'I'm thinking of getting vajazzled,' Yvonne said thoughtfully. She had returned to her magazine. 'What do you think?' She turned the magazine around and slid it across the table to Claire.

'Oh!' Claire found herself staring at a page full of photos of women's bejewelled and sparkly nether regions under the cheery headline:

Bling up your Vajayjay!

'That butterfly is pretty, isn't it?' Yvonne said, pointing to one of the pictures. 'I might go for something like that. It's Ivan's birthday next week, so I might do it to surprise him.'

'But you'd have to get someone to do it,' Claire said, horrified at the thought of having a stranger get that up close and personal with her 'vajayjay'. 'It'd be so embarrassing.'

'No worse than having a wax.'

'Well, there's waxing and waxing.' Claire had never even had the nerve for a Brazilian.

These vajazzled girls were all completely bald. She wondered if that had become the norm. 'Have you ever had a Brazilian?' she asked Yvonne.

'I used to have them all the time,' Yvonne said. 'But now I always have a Hollywood.'

'You mean – everything off?'

'Yes, completely bare. I swear, once you get it, you never go back. It feels amazing!'

'Do you think anyone still just... leaves it?'

'Full bush, you mean?' Yvonne said. 'Eew, gross!' Her lip curled. 'I doubt anyone has that any more – except maybe oldsters who don't know any better.'

Claire blushed. 'Yeah, I was just wondering.'

'But everything goes in cycles,' Yvonne said quickly. 'I'm sure that will come back. Or you could be rocking a retro look.'

Of course Claire knew that radical waxing was very popular now, but she'd had no idea how ubiquitous it was. It had never occurred to her that her bog-standard bikini wax might be way behind the times. After all, it wasn't as if she saw a lot of naked women. But Luca did. Damn it, why hadn't he said anything? Maybe he didn't want to hurt her feelings. She hoped he didn't find it repulsive. He didn't seem to but, then, she was paying him. People put up with all sorts of things they didn't like for money. She would just have to ask him about it later – she might as well. He had already seen her in all her natural glory, so it was too late to make a good first impression on him.

'You can keep that, if you like.' Yvonne nodded at the magazine as she got up. 'I've finished with it.'

'Thanks.'

Claire spent the rest of her lunch break thumbing through the magazine. She automatically sought out the inevitable sex tips and read them with interest:

Five Ways to Drive Him Wild in Bed

and:

Bondage for Beginners!

She had read a lot of these over the years while researching her blog, but she had never had the opportunity to put them into practice. Maybe she could try some of them with Luca.

After work, she spent some time with her mother, but several of her mum's friends arrived while she was there, so she didn't stay long. Then she headed over to Luca's, picking up a pizza for them on the way. Later, when they were relaxing on the sofa with a glass of wine, she steeled herself to broach the subject.

'Luca, can I ask you something?'

'Shoot.'

'You know my— my, um... fanny?'

He smirked. 'Yes, I am intimately acquainted with your fanny.'

'Well, were you surprised when you first saw it?'

'Surprised?' He frowned at her, his lips twitching in amusement. Then he rubbed his chin, as if considering her question carefully. 'No, I can't honestly say I was surprised. I knew you were a girl, so I kind of guessed you'd have one.'

'But were you surprised about... what it looked like?'

He laughed then, a deep, throaty sound. 'No,' he said. 'I'd seen one before – more than one, actually.'

Claire frowned. This was embarrassing enough without him laughing at her.

'Sorry,' he said. 'Was it supposed to be a surprise?'

'I know you've seen them before. But had you seen one – you know, like mine?'

'They all look pretty much the same, you know, give or take.' He leant his forehead on hers, grinning at her, his eyes dancing with merriment. 'Oh, baby, all this talk of your twat is making me horny as hell. Let's go to bed.'

She huffed, pushing him away. 'But was there anything that you thought was... unusual about it?' she persisted.

He frowned, looking at her quizzically. 'No.'

'It seemed normal to you?'

'Is that what you're worried about? Yes, it's perfectly normal,' he said, leaning in to kiss her. 'But maybe I should take another look.' He popped the button on her jeans as he spoke. His fingers began tugging down the zip and she slapped them away.

'You have nothing to worry about,' he said. 'It's beautiful. I'd like to paint it. If I was a poet, I'd write it an ode.'

'And you don't think it's too...'

'What?'

She took a deep breath. 'Hairy,' she mumbled, looking down at her hands.

'Ah, so that's what all this is about. Finally!'

'So?'

'No. It's not too hairy.'

'Is it unusual, though? I mean you've been with a lot of girls. Do most of them—'

'Yeah, a lot of them have barely anything. I don't get it myself.'

'You don't mind... a full bush?'

'No, I think it's sexy, actually. It's womanly – as opposed to girly. I don't understand the obsession with making grown women look like pre-pubescent girls or sexless dolls.'

She should have known a bit of body hair wouldn't faze Luca. But maybe he wasn't the best person to ask. He was very earthy – which made him a great teacher: he was so matter-of-fact about sex and bodies, and she knew she could discuss anything with him. But it also meant he didn't have a problem with things that other people might find off-putting. Plus, he was an artist – he saw beauty in all sorts of things that most people wouldn't find beautiful at all.

'Is it unusual, though? I just don't know what a guy would expect.'

'What this Mark dude will expect, you mean?'

'Yeah. He might not like it.'

'He should feel privileged if you let him anywhere near it.'

'But the girl on my blog would probably be more up-to-date on stuff like this. If that's what everyone's doing nowadays...'

Luca shrugged. 'You should do what you want. It's your body. If you're comfortable with it, he should be too.'

'Hmm, maybe,' she said, chewing her lip.

'Let me show you something.' He took her hand and pulled her up off the sofa, leading her towards the corner of the room he used as his studio.

'What is it?' she asked warily. 'I'm not going to strip off and let you paint me.'

'It's not that. I want to show you how beautiful a natural woman can be.'

'Oh.' She tried to ignore the stab of jealousy she felt. In the studio she glanced around at the canvases stacked against the walls and on benches, and wondered if this 'natural woman' had been a girlfriend or just a model. But instead of reaching for one of the canvases, he went to a shelf in a corner of the room and took down a large book. He flipped through the pages, then laid it down on the worktop.

'Look.' He pointed to the page.

Claire came to stand beside him, looking down at the painting in the book – the torso of a naked woman lying on a bed with her legs spread. It was such a graphic close-up of the genital area that she couldn't help feeling shocked. 'It's very... powerful,' she said, trying to be grown-up about it and not show her revulsion. But she knew her lip was curling like Yvonne's had earlier over the idea of a full bush. Maybe she *should* go for a Brazilian...

'It's Courbet, *L'Origine du Monde*. Don't you think it's beautiful?' Luca was gazing at it lovingly.

'Um... no, not really. It's a big hairy snatch. I mean, I'm sure it's very good, but I wouldn't want it hanging on my wall or anything.'

Luca laughed. 'You're such a philistine!' he said, bumping shoulders with her. 'I think it's amazing.'

He was definitely the wrong person to ask, she thought. She'd start looking into waxing options tomorrow.

'Okay, look at this one,' he said flipping to another page, a painting of a naked woman reclining on a couch. 'It's Goya. *La Maja Desnuda*. This was the first depiction of pubic hair in Western art. It's a very sexy painting, isn't it?'

Claire had to admit it was. 'It's beautiful.'

'Pubic hair was never shown in classical art. You've probably heard that story about Ruskin discovering his wife had pubic hair on the night of their wedding, and freaking out because he thought there was something wrong with her.'

Claire nodded.

'It's probably not true, but the sad thing is it may be. He might never have seen a real woman naked, and in the paintings and sculptures he'd have known, they'd have been hairless.'

'Those Old Masters have a lot to answer for.'

'And now internet porn is doing the same thing – all those hairless bodies. There are probably some young guys growing up now who think that's normal.'

'That's the problem, though,' she said, turning to face him. 'Maybe Mark's one of them. I mean, not that he's never seen pubic hair, but maybe it's not what he's used to.'

Luca sighed. 'Like I say, do what you want. But will you promise me one thing?' he asked, running a hand through his curls.

'What?'

'If you do decide to hack it all off, you'll let me paint you first.'

His eyes were alive with excitement and she swallowed hard. She glanced back at the book. She couldn't see herself posing like that, her twat on display for all the world to see. But he seemed so eager.

'I don't know. How long would it take?' She would feel so ridiculous lying around naked for hours, flaunting her body like she thought she was all that.

'A few days maybe. It would just be me,' he said persuasively, tucking a lock of hair behind her ear.

'But what about afterwards, when it was finished?'

'I wouldn't sell it. I wouldn't even show it to anyone else, if you don't want me to.'

'Days?' She frowned. She didn't like the idea of lying around naked for days with him staring at her. He'd seen her naked plenty of times, of course, but this would be different. His gaze would be so intensely focused on her. She didn't know if she could handle that.

'I could do it from photographs, if that would be easier for you. I'd just have to take a few snaps. I could make the painting from those.'

'Is it just as good using photographs?'

'Well, I'd rather have the real thing, but...'

He obviously really wanted this, and he'd been so nice to her. It seemed like the least she could do. Besides, it would be good practice for her – she had to get used to being looked at naked. 'Okay,' she whispered.

'You'll do it? You'll pose for me?' His eyes lit up, and she couldn't help smiling back at him.

'Yeah, if you want me to that much.'

'Thank you.' He pulled her into his arms and kissed her, his fingers going to the buttons of her shirt as he kissed his way down her neck.

'You want to start right now?' she asked, pulling back. She wasn't sure she was ready just yet.

'Right now, I want to fuck you. I wasn't joking about all that twat talk turning me on. Besides, I want to paint you afterwards, when you're all glowing and voluptuous with that just-fucked look.'

'Oh!'

He took her hand and led her to the bedroom, and they spent the next couple of hours working on Claire's post-coital glow.

'This is how I want to paint you,' Luca said some time later, propped up on one elbow beside her in bed. 'Just like this.' His thumb stroked over her swollen lips and then his hand moved down to cup her breast, his eyes following wherever he touched. 'You're so beautiful – all full and sated, and alive.'

Maybe it wouldn't be so hard posing naked for him, Claire thought. Because the way Luca looked at her made her feel so sexy and beautiful, like she really was all that.

17

On Friday, Claire left work early and went straight to the airport. It had been a busy week in the shop, and she had hardly had time to think about her actual visit, she'd just looked forward to relaxing on the flight. But on the plane it hit her that she hardly knew Mark, and she could be letting herself in for a very awkward weekend.

So she was feeling nervous as she made her way into the arrivals hall, searching the crowds around the barrier for Mark. Then she spotted him waving at her, and was instantly reassured by the sight of his friendly face. She made her way quickly to him, and it seemed like the most natural thing in the world when he pulled her into his arms and kissed her. It was a gentle, tentative kiss – less than lovers but more than friends.

'It's really good to see you,' he said, smiling down at her.

'It's good to see you too.'

He took her bag and led her to his car, swinging her case into the boot. Her flight had got in just after eight, but the evenings were lengthening, and the sun was setting as they drove towards London.

'So, I thought we'd stay in tonight,' he said. 'I figured you'd probably be tired after your journey.'

'I am tired,' Claire said, stifling a yawn, as if by the power of suggestion. 'Why is travelling always so exhausting, even if it's only a really short trip?'

'Tomorrow night I've booked us a table for dinner at a little bistro in the village. I hope that's okay.'

'It sounds lovely.'

He asked after her mother and work, and they chatted easily for the rest of the journey. Mark's place was a large garden flat in a period building just outside Highgate village.

'This is lovely,' she said, as he led her into a bright, modern living room with wooden floors. She had expected his flat to be very sleek and minimalist, but it was much more homely and cosy than she had imagined, and felt comfortably messy and lived-in. There were books piled everywhere, and floor-to-ceiling shelves lined the walls in the living room.

'Come on, and I'll show you around,' he said, dropping her bag on the floor.

He took her on a quick tour of the flat, the kitchen living up to some of her bachelor-pad expectations, with lots of chrome appliances, high-tech gadgets and granite worktops. 'I knew you were coming so I baked a cake,' he said, pointing to a sponge that was sitting on a rack on the worktop.

'You really baked? For me?' Claire asked, touched by the sweetness of the gesture.

'Sure. It's lemon drizzle – my specialty.'

'Oh, that's my favourite! My mum makes it a lot.'

'I have a lot to live up to, then. Are you hungry, or have you eaten?'

'No, I haven't and I'm starving.'

'I thought I'd make you my world-famous nachos tonight. Is that okay?'

'Perfect.' She smiled. 'It's not fair, you know all my weaknesses.' Their Twitter conversations revolved around food almost as much as books.

'I do,' he said, with an evil grin. 'I'll take all the unfair advantages I can get.'

'Are your nachos really world-famous, though?'

He shrugged. 'Well, Twitter covers the world, so I'd say yes.'

Claire smiled.

'Now I'll show you the rest,' Mark said, and led her into the hallway.

After showing her the bathroom and his bedroom, he showed her into a second, smaller bedroom across the hall from his. 'This is you. There's an en-suite shower, or you can use the main bathroom. I've left you some towels. If you need anything else, just let me know.'

'Thank you.' Claire smiled at him. 'This is lovely.' She was so glad she had established the five-date rule, that she could get to know Mark without feeling anxious about having to fend him off and make excuses for not wanting to sleep with him.

'Well, I'll leave you to settle in, and I'll make the nachos. When you've got yourself sorted out, come and join me.'

Claire quickly unpacked a few things from her case, washed her face and put on some mascara and lipstick. When she went back to the living room, Mark was in the kitchen area. A bottle of red wine was open on the counter. He poured a couple of glasses and handed one to her.

'Have a seat,' he said, gesturing to the sofa. 'This'll be ready in a couple of minutes.'

'Thanks.'

The coffee table in front of the sofa was set with knives, forks, plates and napkins, and there were dishes of salsa, sour cream and guacamole. Moments later, Mark joined her, placing a large plate of nachos on the table.

'Dig in,' he said, handing her a plate.

'Oh my God, these are amazing,' Claire said. 'They deserve their reputation.'

'They live up to expectations?' Mark smiled.

'Definitely. If I wasn't here incognito, I'd tweet about them right now.'

'Speaking of incognito,' he said, wiping his hands. He picked up a hard-back book from the side table beside him and handed it to her.

She wiped her hands on a napkin before taking it from him. She gasped in pleasure, recognising the title. The author was Mark's latest signing, and Claire was friendly with her on Twitter. 'Thank you! I can't wait to read it,' she said, turning it over in her hands. 'It sounds great.'

'I hope you'll love it.'

'How did the launch go on Wednesday?'

'Really well. It was fun. I got it signed for you,' he said, nodding to the book.

'Oh!' Claire opened the book to the title page and saw that it was signed to @NiceGirl:

whoever you may be.

'I said I could get it to you.'

'Thanks.'

'I'm dying to know what you think of it. Let me know when you've read it.'

'I will.' It pleased Claire that Mark valued her opinion. They had become friendly on Twitter through chatting about books. The first time Mark had tweeted her it was because she had been raving about the book she was reading, and it turned out to be one he'd just published. Over time, they'd found they had very similar taste, and when they did disagree on something, Mark was always keen to hear her views.

She put the book on the arm of the sofa, and helped herself to more nachos, loading them up with sour cream, salsa and guacamole.

'How's your writing going?' Mark asked. 'How's the novel coming along?'

'Very slowly. I don't have a lot of time, what with work and looking after my mum, and the blog is very time-consuming. But I've almost finished the first draft.'

'Don't forget to send it to me whenever you're ready.'

The prospect of Mark reading her novel was exciting and also terrifying. She admired his taste and his opinion meant a lot to her. She'd hate it if he didn't rate something she'd written.

'I will.' She took a gulp of her wine. 'I just hope you like it.'

'I can't imagine not liking something you'd written.'

'Well, it's very different from the blog, obviously.' If not quite as different as he thought. They were both fiction.

Mark forked the last of the nachos onto his plate. 'What are you reading at the moment?' he asked.

The talk turned to books, and the time flew by as they discussed what they'd read recently and writers they knew on Twitter or through work. Mark shared some gossip about writers he'd met, and Claire told him about the ones who had held events in the shop, who was rude and obnoxious, who had turned out to be unexpectedly sweet and unassuming. Suddenly it was after midnight and she found she was exhausted.

'I'm going to have to call it a night,' she said, yawning.

'God, sorry – I didn't notice the time.'

'I didn't either,' she said. She had been so caught up in their conversation, she hadn't noticed it getting late, or how tired she was.

'Well, goodnight,' he said, as he got up. He pulled her into his arms and kissed her slowly and lingeringly. 'Help yourself to anything you need. I'll see you in the morning.'

* * *

The next morning at breakfast, Mark announced that he was going to take her to 'the most romantic place in London', so she was more than a little alarmed when they turned up at the gates of Highgate Cemetery.

'Seriously, this is where we're going? A cemetery?'

'I know – such a clichéd second date.' Mark smiled.

'Is there something I should know about you?'

'Wait and see.' He took her hand. 'Unfortunately, we can't just wander around on our own. You have to join a guided tour. Apart from that, the west cemetery really is the most romantic place I know in London.'

'I knew you were too good to be true.'

But it turned out he was right, and Claire found herself completely enchanted as they walked along the twisting wooded paths among ivy-clad monuments and ancient crumbling tombstones watched over by winged angels. Despite the presence of the tour group, the atmosphere was tranquil and ethereal, and it was like being transported back in time as they explored the dank catacombs and gazed in awe at colossal ornate mausoleums.

'Okay, you were right,' Claire whispered to Mark, as they walked along. 'This is incredibly romantic.'

'You like it?'

'I love it! It's so beautiful.' She thought it was one of the most extraordinary places she'd ever been to, and she only wished they could have stayed longer. She could happily have spent several hours wandering around on her own.

They picked up bread and cheese at a deli on the way home, and had lunch in the garden as it was a warm, sunny day. The errant Millie finally turned up, stalking imperiously across the grass to Claire and circling around her chair before trotting over to Mark and springing into his lap, where she curled up.

'I think you've been maligning her,' Claire said, nodding to the ginger tabby that was nuzzling Mark's hand as he petted her. 'She seems quite devoted.'

'She's just marking her territory because you're here,' Mark said, stroking Millie's ears. 'Bloody cat in the manger. Aren't you?' But his features softened as he looked down at her adoringly.

Claire rubbed her arms as the sky clouded over and the air turned chilly.

'Let's have coffee and cake inside,' Mark said, standing and starting to clear the table, 'and we can discuss the book.'

'I'll just ring my mother first,' Claire said.

Claire went to her bedroom to make the call while Mark loaded the dishwasher. When she came back into the living room, he was sitting at the table waiting for her with the promised coffee and cake, and a large pile of manuscripts in front of him. When she joined him at the table, she was alarmed to see it was printouts of her blog. She had to will herself not to blush as he calmly leafed through some of her raunchiest posts, discussing the different ways the book might be organised, chronologically or according to topic.

'This cake is delicious. I'm impressed.' A man who baked was a definite plus, Claire thought – and she was glad of the sugar to calm her nerves. She had to remind herself she was supposed to be the ballsy girl who had done all this stuff, and force herself to act casually.

'I thought maybe it could be arranged episodically,' Mark said, 'but obviously with regular characters and a constant theme running through it – a bit like *Sex and the City*. The book, not the show.'

'Right.'

'So I think maybe you need to write some extra material to give it more cohesion. I also think it needs some sort of conclusion. Maybe you should end up with one of these guys.'

'Who would you suggest?'

'You know, I always kind of thought you'd end up with Mr Bossy.'

'Really?' She gulped.

'He seemed like the one you were always drawn back to. But that was before I met you, of course. Now that I know you, he doesn't really seem your type.'

'I could still write it that way – it doesn't have to be true.' It could be fun to do, she thought. She had always enjoyed writing about Mr Bossy.

'Or how about Mr Strange? You had something pretty solid going with him.'

'Uh-uh.' She shook her head. 'The clue is in his name.'

'Can I ask you something?' he said, his tone wary.

'Yeah.'

'This guy you've been writing about recently – the Artist. Is he real?'

'Oh.' Claire thought quickly. But she had no reason to lie. It was almost a relief that there was something in her blog that was at least partly true, and it wasn't as if Mark expected her to be celibate – quite the opposite. 'Yes, he's real,' she said.

'And he's around at the moment?'

'Um... yeah, that part is true. I've been... seeing him lately.' She blushed.

'Well... maybe you'll end up with him.'

'Oh no,' she said quickly. 'He's not boyfriend material.'

'Right.' Something like relief passed across Mark's face. 'Well, you could always meet someone new,' he said, looking at her meaningfully.

'Do you have anyone particular in mind?'

He smiled. 'Call him Mr Right.'

'And what would Mr Right be like?' she asked.

'Oh, I don't know. Decent guy, likes cats. Makes a mean lemon drizzle cake, world-famous nachos...'

She laughed. 'It would be a good way of wrapping up the blog, I guess. Because I wouldn't want to tell everyone what Mr Right and I were doing. It'd be private.'

'Do you plan to stop writing the blog?'

'I think it's run its course. I'm almost out of stuff to write about. Maybe it's time to give NiceGirl her happy-ever-after and let her walk off into the sunset.'

'Well, you might want to consider the timing of that. Publication is scheduled for next spring...'

Next spring sounded so far away. Claire wondered what her life would be like then. Would she be with Mark? Could he really be her Mr Right?

Claire had tried to sex up her wardrobe a bit for her visit, but she was glad she hadn't strayed too far out of her comfort zone as she dressed for dinner that night. She was nervous enough as it was. She felt like she was going on a first date. But her little lace shift dress was a happy compromise – sexy, but not so blatant that it made her uncomfortable.

The restaurant was a cosy little neighbourhood bistro, where Mark was obviously well-known, and she relaxed as they chatted over the delicious food and wine. She wondered what date they were on now as she sipped coffee. This definitely felt like a date, but she wasn't sure if last night counted – or did the whole weekend count as one? It was on the tip of her tongue to ask Mark, but then she remembered what Yvonne had said: 'We have all the power.' It was her rule, so it was up to her to decide what counted. She didn't want things to move too fast – she still had a lot to learn.

'Well, this definitely feels like a date,' she said lightly. 'But I don't think I can count the cemetery – lovely as it was.'

Mark smiled. 'What about last night?'

'A night in?' She wrinkled her nose. 'That's what old married couples do, so I don't think I can count it.'

'Even a night in with world-famous nachos?'

'Even then. Sorry.'

'Damn,' he said, but he didn't seem put out.

Claire suddenly felt like she really did have all the power, and it felt nice.

Mark took her hand as they walked the short distance back to his flat.

'Nightcap?' he offered, when they were inside.

'Yes, please.'

He poured them both some Amaretto and they sat side by side on the sofa.

'Well, here's to second dates,' he said, clinking his glass with hers, but instead of drinking, he leant in and kissed her.

At least kissing was something she knew how to do, so Claire put her free arm around his neck and kissed him back enthusiastically. His lips felt warm and soft, and he was a good kisser. His eyes were dark as he pulled away. They both took a sip of their drinks, then simultaneously placed their glasses on the coffee table and started kissing again, sweet, almond-flavoured kisses.

She recognised the almost imperceptible shift, like a gear change, when Mark's breathing deepened and things became more heated. This was the point where Luca would start pulling at her clothes, when his hands would become urgent on her body, and she would get impatient for the feel of his skin against hers. Her hand reached out instinctively to unbutton Mark's shirt, but she stopped herself, instead placing it firmly on his chest and moving away.

Mark sighed as he sat back and picked up his drink again. He smiled at her lazily, his eyes on her lips, then tossed back the rest of his Amaretto. 'Time for bed, I think,' he said ruefully, and just for a moment Claire wished she was going with him. But it was too soon. Instead, she went to bed alone, slightly frustrated and feeling guilty for wishing Luca was there to finish what Mark had started.

18

On Monday Claire was meeting Catherine for a drink after work. She was just arriving at the Temple Bar pub when Catherine came up the street pushing Paddington in yet another new buggy.

'Hi.' Catherine greeted Claire with a quick kiss on the cheek. 'Just let me get rid of this thing before we go in.' She lifted Paddington out of the buggy and hunkered down to stuff him into a large holdall she had in the bottom, zipping it up.

'Will he be all right in there?' Claire asked.

'Oh, he'll be fine,' Catherine said, as she straightened. 'He's used to it. I get funny looks if I bring him into a bar.'

'Well, it's handy you can stuff him into a bag without anyone calling Social Services.'

'I know. I'm blessed,' she said distractedly, as she struggled with the buggy, pulling levers and kicking it as she tried to get it to fold.

'Oh, sod this,' she said, lifting it and whacking it down on the pavement in frustration. She looked around them at the crowd milling through the busy street. Then her eyes lit on a woman slumped against the side of a building, sitting on a blanket, begging from passers-by.

'Do you think she'd like a state-of-the-art pushchair?' she asked Claire. Without waiting for an answer, she ran across to the woman, pushing it in front of her. Claire watched as they spoke. There was a lot of gesticulating, and it looked like they were having an argument. Finally, Catherine bent down and put something in the woman's hand, then left the buggy with her and came back to Claire.

'Well, it was a hard sell, but I managed to get rid of it,' she said. 'She only wanted a fiver to take it off my hands.' She picked up the holdall. 'Right, shall we go?'

'You gave her money as well?' Claire asked. 'That buggy must be worth a couple of hundred euro.'

'Try five,' Catherine said, opening the door of the bar. 'I'm just glad to be rid of it. I never want to see another buggy as long as I live.'

They fought their way through the after-work crowd to the depths of the pub. There were no empty seats, but they found two stools at the bar and were served quickly by a young girl with an Australian accent.

'I shouldn't even be having this,' Catherine said, as the girl put their gin and tonics in front of them.

'Oh? Why not?' Claire asked.

'I have news,' Catherine said, with a secretive smile. Then she placed a hand over her stomach.

The Australian girl threw her a dirty look before walking away.

'Oh my God!' Claire gasped. 'You're pregnant!'

'Yup.'

'How far along are you?'

'Oh, only three or four weeks. I haven't decided exactly yet, but very early days – too soon to announce it on my blog or anything. But I can tell you.'

'Well, congratulations!'

'Thanks!'

They clinked glasses.

'So, tell all,' Catherine said, leaning forward avidly. 'How did your weekend with Mark go?'

'It was lovely.' Claire smiled. 'I had a really nice time. His place is really nice. He made me his world-famous nachos, took me to Highgate Cemetery and baked lemon drizzle cake. He's so thoughtful. And I met his cat, Millie. We discussed ideas for the book. Oh, and he wants to read my novel as soon as it's ready.'

'That's great! And was there more kissing?'

'Yes.' Claire smiled bashfully. 'There was. Quite a lot of kissing.' There had been more kissing on Sunday when he'd brought her to the airport. She couldn't help smiling when she thought of it.

'Anything else?'

'No, just kissing. I'm not ready to go any further than that yet. So it's great that I came up with the five-date rule. I can relax and just enjoy being with him for now.'

'Yeah, that was a stroke of genius,' Catherine said, poking her ice with a swizzle stick. 'And you have the distance thing, so that slows things down a bit too.'

'And five dates is just a minimum. It's not a guarantee or anything.'

'So are you two dates down now? Or is it three because you were with him two nights at the weekend?'

'No, it's two. I only counted Saturday night as a date.'

'So, how's it going with the other guy? Are you making progress?'

'I'm starting to get the hang of the basics, but I still have a lot to learn.'

'But isn't it a bit...'

'What?'

'Well... awkward. Embarrassing. Having sex with him like that – in cold blood, as it were.'

'I would have thought so, but it's not really. It doesn't feel like that – cold, I mean. Luca makes it easy. He's really nice.'

'Cute?'

'Very. Gorgeous, actually.'

'Well, that helps. And you like him?'

'Yeah. He's surprisingly sweet.'

'Do you *like* like him?'

'Oh no!' Claire frowned. 'It's not like that. I mean I love, you know... being with him.'

'Shagging him?'

'Yeah.' Claire smiled. 'To put it bluntly. And we're having all this... *sex*,' she said, her mouth automatically widening in a grin at the thought of all that sex. 'So I can't help feeling close to him in a way. But Luca and I – we're chalk and cheese.'

'What does he do?'

'He's an artist – a painter. We have nothing in common, really. I mean, I don't know if he reads, and I know nothing about art.'

'I bet you know what you like.'

Claire laughed. 'Yeah. And his paintings are amazing.'

'Maybe you have more in common than you think.'

'Well, let's see.' Claire tilted her head to the side. 'We both eat food – and breathe air.'

'You're both creative.'

'I suppose.' Claire had never thought of it like that. But to her, Luca's single-minded commitment to his art only made them seem more dissimilar. She admired his dedication, his willingness to make sacrifices to devote himself to his painting, but she didn't really understand it. She didn't think she could ever be like that. She liked her creature comforts too much.

'Anyway, I don't think it's all that important to have stuff in common. I have bugger-all in common with Hazel, really. Look at the child thing, for instance. She doesn't want any. I already have one phantom child and another on the way.'

'Well, you're both women. That's quite big.'

'There is that.'

'I do like Luca, but I just don't think of him that way. He's far too wild for me. And it's an artificial situation. We'd never have got together organically.'

In the normal course of events, her and Luca's paths would never have crossed again after that one night in Ivan's bar. They wouldn't have gravitated towards each other. Even if she'd slept with him when she'd brought him back to her house, it would have been a one-off. If it hadn't been for her bizarre proposition, they would never have got to know each other properly. She would have made assumptions about him that weren't true. Maybe he'd have made assumptions of his own about her. The thought that they would have remained strangers to each other seemed odd now, and made her feel sad. She liked Luca, and she was glad she had got to know him. But they still weren't a natural fit. They didn't belong together – not like her and Mark.

'Anyway, like I told you, Luca isn't interested in relationships. Total man-whore, remember? He likes to spread the love.'

When they had almost finished their drinks, Catherine asked Claire if she had time for another.

'Better not,' Claire said, glancing at her watch. 'I want to pop in to see Mum, and then I'm going over to Luca's for the night.'

'Another lesson?'

'Yep.'

'Probably just as well.' Catherine sighed. 'I need to get this piece on buggies finished – the deadline's the day after tomorrow.' She drained her drink, and they stood to go. 'A fantasist's work is never done.'

* * *

Claire's days followed the same routine for the rest of the week. She would visit her mother on the way home from work, then go straight to Luca's, where they would have dinner together and chat about their day, then spend the rest of the night having sex. She usually spoke to Mark or emailed him at some stage in the day, and it was like having a boyfriend, only he was split in two: there was Mark, whom she talked to, flirted with and was slowly falling for, and Luca, who took care of her physical needs. It was a strange set-up, and it would be nice when she could be with Mark and have the whole package in one person. But in the meantime she was enjoying herself, happier and more satisfied with her life than she'd been in a long time. She loved having sex with Luca, and she loved the emotional connection she had with Mark and their long chatty phone calls when they would talk about everything and nothing, from what they had for lunch to political and religious beliefs. Most often, the talk turned to books.

'Favourite childhood book?' he asked her one night.

'*Heidi*! No... maybe *The Secret Garden*. Or *Anne of Green Gables*... *Ballet Shoes*... Oh God, this is hard. There are too many good ones.'

'Well, you said *Heidi* first.'

'Okay, I'll go with *Heidi*.'

'Favourite detective?'

'That's easy. Lord Peter Wimsey.'

'Good choice!'

'You?'

'Hm... I'll have to say Miss Marple. A virago in tweed.'

'Edgy!'

'I'm so uncool. Romantic hero?'

'Mr Darcy. I'm such a cliché. Romantic heroine?'

'I feel I should say Dorothea Brooke but—'

'Too earnest. And completely deluded. She'd never have you – you're far too suitable.'

'Yeah. Bridget Jones would be more of a laugh. Or Elizabeth Bennet.'

'Or anyone, really.' Claire laughed.

* * *

Friday had been a beautiful day, and when she arrived at Luca's place that evening, the front door was open and a couple of girls were sitting out on the steps, enjoying the last of the evening sunshine. Claire was in high spirits as she went in and raced up the stairs to Luca's door. It was Friday night, the start of the weekend, and she had a day off tomorrow. She was in a celebratory mood. Her mother would be coming home on Sunday, and she wanted to make the most of every second of the last weekend she could spend almost entirely with Luca. She had bought cava and smoked salmon, crispy bread and lots of deli luxuries for an indulgent picnic-style dinner. She had been thinking maybe they could eat it in bed, grazing leisurely between vigorous bouts of sex.

'Claire, hi!' Luca opened the door and she swept past him into the living room. 'I was trying to call you. You didn't get my text?'

'Oh! No, I mustn't have heard it when I was out in the traffic,' she said, fishing her mobile out of her bag. Sure enough, there was a missed call from Luca and a message alert.

'It's just this friend of mine is playing at The Grand Social with her band tonight, and I said I'd go. I'm sorry. I'd completely forgotten about it until she texted me about an hour ago. She gave me the tickets way back.'

'Oh. Okay,' she said, trying to school her features and not look too disappointed. After all, Luca had been spending all his free time with her. It was only fair that he should have a night off. It wasn't his fault she'd built tonight up in her head and had been so looking forward to it. She just wished she'd seen his message and saved herself the trouble of coming over here.

'So we don't have time for dinner,' he said, eyeing her shopping bags. 'Sorry.'

'That's fine,' she said, desperately trying to affect nonchalance.

'You don't mind?' He gazed at her anxiously.

'No, of course not. You go – we'll still have tomorrow. That's if you're free.'

It was ridiculous how deflated she felt. She would have to rein that in. He wasn't her boyfriend – he didn't owe her anything. It was probably a good thing this had happened – it was a timely reminder of what their relationship really was. He had been very generous with his time and she had let herself get carried away, expecting him to be available to her whenever she liked. But he had his own life. 'Just let me stash this food in the fridge and I'll go.'

'Oh. No.' He frowned. 'I want you to come with me.'

'You do?' She couldn't help the goofy grin that spread across her face.

'Yeah – I mean, if you'd like to. If you'd rather not… I know it's not really your scene but—'

'No, I'd love to.' She was excited anew at the prospect of going out with Luca – and it was ages since she'd been to a gig. It would be fun.

'They're really good, the band,' he said. 'I'd say you'll enjoy it. And we can use it as one of your lessons too – kill two birds with one stone.'

'How?'

'Doing it in public.' He grinned. 'It's in your blog, remember? Your alter ego is quite the exhibitionist. That time you gave Mr Bossy a blowjob in a crowded restaurant was seriously hot! Or the time you had sex at the football match. I had to run to the bathroom with that one.'

She laughed. 'I wish I'd seen your text earlier, though. I'm not exactly dressed for a gig,' she said, holding her arms out. She was still in the fitted white shirt, denim skirt and flat pumps she had worn to work.

'You look great. And you're wearing a skirt – that's the important thing.'

'Huh?'

'If we're going to be doing it in public, easy access is essential.'

'Oh.'

Luca laughed. 'Hey, don't look so worried. It'll be fun.'

'I'm not sure I'm ready for doing it in public,' she said nervously, though she felt a thrill of anticipation.

'You know you don't have to do anything you don't want to do. Don't you?' He grabbed her hand, interlacing his fingers with hers, and looked at her so sternly that Claire knew he wanted an answer.

'Yes, absolutely. But I'd like to try.' She couldn't deny the idea excited her.

'Okay. But if you want to call it off at any time—'

'I'll just tell you to fuck off.'

'That's my girl.' Luca laughed. 'Emma's band is great. We'll have a good time either way.'

The downstairs bar was heaving when they arrived, a Friday-night cocktail of heat, light and noise as the hipster crowd laughed and roared over the crash of glass and a thumping bass soundtrack. Claire held on tightly to Luca's hand as he pulled her through the throng to the upstairs venue. The room was packed and stuffy, a crush of bodies standing, drinks in hand, in front of a small stage where the band were setting up under a banner bearing the name 'The Legendary Fall'. Luca seemed to know a lot of people and he was stopped several times as they wove towards the bar by friends greeting him with hugs and claps on the back. He was obviously very popular and everyone seemed happy to see him. There was a lot of 'Where have you been hiding?' and 'Haven't seen you in ages' while eyes slid curiously in Claire's direction. Luca didn't let go of her hand, introducing her to everyone he met and exchanging a few words with them. She couldn't help noticing the admiring, hungry looks he got from a lot of the girls, or the inquisitive, assessing way their eyes raked over her, blatantly checking her out. It gave her a shallow feeling of pride at being with him that she liked more than she should have.

They got a couple of beers, then took up position close to the stage, Luca standing behind Claire with his arms wrapped around her, occasionally bending to nuzzle her neck, for all the world like an adoring boyfriend who couldn't keep his hands off her. Claire tried to relax, but she kept wondering if he was going to jump her right there in front of everyone. She half expected to feel him pulling her skirt up from behind, and it put her on edge, even though she reminded herself that she could just tell him to stop.

Once the band started, however, she forgot her nerves, forgot about her sex lesson and just enjoyed the music. There were six band members packed onto the tiny stage, three guys and three girls. The singer was a tall, striking girl with long, flaming red hair and a powerful voice, her clothes an eclectic cross between Goth and fairytale princess. Luca pointed out his friend, Emma, a gorgeous, raven-haired girl who swayed sinuously around the stage as she played the violin, oozing sensuality. Claire was envious – she was so sexy and graceful. She wondered if she and Luca had ever been more than friends.

Claire loved the music, and she found herself having fun, dancing with the crowd, or swaying in Luca's arms during the slower songs. She felt light and carefree and *young*. It was good to be out on Friday night with people her own age for a change. The room was alive with youthful vibrancy; the very air seemed charged with energy and possibility. She felt more herself than she had in a long time – or maybe like a new version of herself that she'd never been before. Whatever it was, she liked it.

'Do you want another drink?' Luca asked her, when the singer announced that they'd be taking a short break after the next song.

'Yes, please.'

'I'll beat the rush to the bar,' he said, releasing her as the intro played. 'Won't be long.'

* * *

On his way to the bar, Luca glanced back at Claire and stopped in his tracks, turning to watch her for a while as she moved to the music. She looked so happy and carefree – and hot. She had no idea how sexy she was – which made her even sexier. And he wasn't the only one who saw it, he thought angrily, as he watched a guy beside her leering at her in a way that infuriated him. He was tempted to go back and tell him to take his eyes off her and get lost, but Claire wasn't aware of the guy's staring and it would only make her self-conscious if he drew attention to it. She was enjoying herself, and he didn't want to spoil her fun, so he told himself not to come over all caveman and continued to the bar. He kept an eye on her, though, glancing over regularly as he waited impatiently to be served. When the band left the stage and the lights came up, he was annoyed to see the guy turn to Claire and start chatting her up, leaning in far closer than was necessary to talk into her ear. She was responding to him with a polite smile, but she was darting anxious glances towards the bar. Luca knew she was looking for him and tried to catch her eye. She didn't see him, but he caught the desperate plea for help on her face before her eyes slid away again.

Fuck off, arsehole, he thought, grabbing the two bottles of beer off the counter as soon as they were served and pushing through the crowd to Claire. He hated guys like that. Couldn't he see that she just wanted to be rid of him? He obviously wasn't fluent in body language or else he was choosing to ignore hers because every time he leant closer she compensated by leaning away, until she was almost doing a limbo in the middle of the room. The guy glanced round as Luca approached with a scowl, trying to quell him. To his satisfaction it appeared to work, because the man said something to Claire, smiling regretfully before he quickly disappeared.

'Hi.' Claire smiled as he reached her, and he could see the relief in her face.

'Was that guy bothering you?' he asked, handing her a beer.

'He was just being friendly, really.'

Luca rolled his eyes. 'Yeah, right.' He took a slug of his beer. 'So, having fun?'

'Yes,' she said. 'The band's great – I love their music. Thanks for bringing me.'

'Thank you for coming.' He put an arm around her and pulled her to him, planting a kiss on her mouth. 'Sorry, I just have to go for a slash. Do you mind?' he asked, handing her his beer to hold.

'No, of course not.'

'I won't be long. Don't talk to any strange men.' He grinned, then zipped off towards the exit.

* * *

Claire turned back to the stage, doing her best to look aloof and unapproachable, while she willed the band to come back on or Luca to return. She didn't want that guy to see her on her own and come back. Though she didn't admit it to Luca, he'd been a bit of a creep and wouldn't take no for an answer, even when she'd said she was waiting for her boyfriend who was just up at the bar.

'So, you're here with Luca?'

Claire turned to see a pretty blonde standing beside her. She had seemed vaguely familiar earlier when Luca had introduced her as Aisling, and now Claire recognised her as the girl who had been sitting in his lap the night they had first met.

'Er... yeah.'

Aisling nodded, her expression openly assessing. 'Welcome to the club,' she said, with a sly smile, raising her cocktail glass in salute.

'Sorry?'

Aisling grinned, and took a gulp of her drink, obviously enjoying Claire's discomfiture. 'It's not a very exclusive club,' she said, 'but congrats anyway on becoming our newest member.' She clinked her glass against one of the bottles Claire was holding.

'I have no idea what you're talking about,' Claire said stiffly, even though she knew damn well this was Aisling's unsubtle way of telling her that she shouldn't think she was anything special because she was with Luca.

'Oh, I think you do,' Aisling said. 'Well, have fun – while it lasts.' She drifted away, leaving Claire reeling.

'Claire?' A female voice behind her called her name and she turned to see Yvonne arm in arm with Ivan, both of them clutching bottles of beer.

'It *is* you!' Yvonne said.

'Oh my God! Yvonne! Hi!' Claire's eyes darted to the exit in panic, hoping now that Luca wouldn't come back too soon.

Yvonne gave her a one-armed hug. 'You remember Ivan?'

'Yes. Hi, Ivan,' she said, as he bent to kiss her cheek.

'Lovely to meet you again, Claire.'

'I'm surprised to see you here!' Yvonne said. 'I didn't think this would be your kind of thing.'

'Yeah, I, um... I came with a friend.' She waved the two bottles of beer.

'Are you enjoying the band?' Ivan asked.

'They're good, aren't they?' Yvonne said. 'Justine – the girl who plays the keyboards – is Ivan's sister.'

'Yeah, they're great! I'm really enjoying it,' Claire said, desperately hoping they would go before Luca came back. 'This is a nice place. I've never been here before.'

'So, who are you here with?' Yvonne asked.

'Oh, just... just a friend.' Claire was relieved when she saw the band coming back onstage out of the corner of her eye.

Yvonne's eyes lit up. 'Is it that guy we were talking about the other day?' When Ivan turned away for a moment, she mouthed, 'Fuck buddy,' at Claire, her eyebrows raised.

Over Yvonne's shoulder, Claire saw Luca making his way through the crowd towards them. She tried to signal to him with her eyes that he should stay away, but either he didn't pick up on it or he chose to ignore her because he strode right up to her.

'Oh, hi, Yvonne,' he said casually. 'Ivan.'

'Luca!' Yvonne exclaimed. 'Wow, everyone's here tonight. We just bumped into Claire – you remember Claire? – and now—' She stopped abruptly as Luca slid an arm casually around Claire's waist and pulled her into his side, while he took his beer from her. 'Oh!' She smiled as her eyes darted from one of them to the other. '*Oh,*' she said, eyeballing Claire.

Claire was relieved when the light dimmed, hiding her blushes and taking Yvonne's focus off her.

'Our friends are over there,' Ivan said, waving to the other side of the room. 'We'd better go back and join them.'

'We might see you later, yeah?' Yvonne said, as the band started playing.

'What was that about?' Luca chuckled, pulling Claire in front of him and propping his head on her shoulder.

'I'll tell you later.'

As the gig drew to a close, Claire wondered if Luca had forgotten about her lesson. Not that she minded – she was having so much fun. In fact, she was glad he seemed to have forgotten it so she could just relax and enjoy herself. When the applause faded and the lights came up, everyone milled around for a while, dazed and blinking in the harsh light, ears still ringing. Emma came over to them with the rest of the band, Yvonne and Ivan.

'Are you guys coming down to the bar?' Emma asked Luca.

'I don't think so,' Luca said, looking at Claire questioningly. 'We have that thing, remember?' he said to her.

'Oh, yeah.'

'Well, some of us are going on to the Arch Club in a bit,' Emma said. 'Maybe we'll see you there.'

'Okay,' Luca said. He took Claire's hand and they said their goodbyes.

'We're going home after a drink here,' Yvonne said. 'But I'll see *you* on Monday,' she added to Claire, in a way that left her in no doubt she'd be getting the third degree.

'We could have done the *thing* in the bar back there,' Claire said, when they got outside.

'Uh-uh. There's public and public, and I know way too many people back there. We wouldn't get a minute's peace. We need to be in public but incognito. We'll go on ahead to the Arch Club.'

* * *

Luca led her out onto the quays and across the Halfpenny Bridge, up through Merchant's Arch into the cobbled streets of Temple Bar. The streets were still crowded with people spilling out of bars and clubs.

He took her through a courtyard and down a set of steps to a small, intimate club. Red plush sofas were arranged around low wooden tables, the lighting was subdued, and soft piano music poured from the speakers. He sat down on a sofa in a quiet corner of the bar, pulling Claire down beside him.

A waitress came to take their order, and they asked for a glass of red wine each.

'So what was that all about with Yvonne? Why was she acting so weird?' Luca asked, while they waited for their drinks.

'Oh, she thinks you're my fuck buddy now. Sorry.'

Luca laughed. 'Why would she think that?'

'She knows I've been seeing someone. I didn't tell her or anything. She figured it out.'

'Did she do her sex-radar thing on you?'

'Yeah, she did!' Claire said, sounding surprised that he knew about it.

'She's a bit spooky, the way she can do that.'

'I didn't call you a fuck buddy, by the way. She said that – though I didn't really contradict her.'

Luca shrugged. 'It's a pretty accurate description, I suppose.'

'So... you don't mind? That she knows we... see each other?' Claire asked.

'No. Why would I? She knows I'm not saving myself for marriage. As long as we don't have to go on double dates with her and Ivan.'

The girl came back with their drinks and Claire tried to pay, but Luca wouldn't let her.

He turned to her as the waitress left. 'Hello, gorgeous.' He stroked her cheek with a finger. 'Alone at last.'

She smiled back nervously. Then she took a big gulp of her wine. When she had put the glass back on the table, he leant in to kiss her, trailing his fingers down her arm as he did so, allowing his thumb to brush her breast in passing. She was trembling already as he opened her mouth with his and their tongues tangled together, her fingers clutching his hair. Her breathing became deep and rasping as he slid a hand up under her shirt and pulled down the cup of her bra, his thumb teasing her nipple into a hard point. God, she was so responsive! He sucked at her neck as his hand moved to circle her knee. Then he slid it higher, under her skirt, stroking the achingly soft skin of her thighs. He pushed her legs a little further apart and pulled her knickers aside, his fingers stroking along the soft folds of her flesh.

'You're so wet!' He sighed into her mouth, groaning deep in his throat as he slid a finger inside her, pumping it in and out while his thumb stroked her clit. He felt the heat and tension building inside her, her fingers digging into his shoulders as she clung to him. She opened her eyes as she kissed him, and he saw the desire mixed with panic as her muscles began to clench around his fingers.

'It's okay,' he whispered, angling his body so she was completely shielded from view. 'Let go. No one can see you.' He worked his fingers faster, and her mouth opened in a silent scream, her fists clenching on his shoulders, bunching up the material of his shirt as he felt her spasm around his fingers. He continued to stroke her, and she gave a helpless little whimper, barely audible, as he made her come again. She held his gaze the whole time, and he thought it was the hottest thing he'd ever seen. He wanted her so badly right now, longing to drag her off to the toilets and bury himself inside her. When he pulled his fingers out of her, she threw her arms around him, clinging to him fiercely and burying her head in his neck. He pulled her tightly to his body, stroking her back soothingly as she came down from her orgasm, still hot and trembling, until she went limp in his arms.

'Okay?' he asked. He pushed damp tendrils of hair off her face and kissed her softly – her forehead, her hot, flushed cheeks.

She gave him a slow, lazy smile. 'That is so going in my blog.'

Shortly afterwards, Emma and the band arrived. As they drew up chairs to join Claire and Luca at their table, Claire excused herself to go to the loo.

'I'll save your seat,' Luca said, placing a hand on the sofa beside him as she squeezed past him. He shifted uncomfortably, wishing he could follow her and fuck her up against the wall. Shit, the image of her legs wrapped around him while she bounced up and down on his dick just made him harder.

'Hi!' Aisling threw herself down on the sofa beside him, sitting on his hand.

'That seat's taken,' he said, pulling his hand from under her.

'It is now,' she said, plonking her glass down on the table in front of her and not budging.

'Seriously, Aisling. Just piss off.' Jesus, he thought, with mounting irritation, didn't she ever get the message? He'd thought the fact that he was with Claire would act as a deterrent, but he should have known better. She was like a fucking Exocet missile with her radar locked on his dick.

'Don't be so mean, Luca,' Aisling pouted. 'I haven't seen you in ages. I miss you.' She put a warm hand on his leg, inching it higher up his thigh. 'Well, hello!' She grinned, her eyes dropping to his crotch. 'You may pretend to be all cool, but I can tell you're pleased to see me really.'

'That's not for you,' he snapped, slapping her hand away.

But she slid her hand back onto him under the table.

'Poor Luca,' she purred. 'Did your little girlfriend get you all worked up, then leave you hanging?'

'She's not my girlfriend.'

'Really?' Aisling raised her eyebrows. 'That's not what she told the guy who was trying to chat her up at the gig.'

'What?' Luca was momentarily too distracted by what she'd said to pay attention to her roving hands. 'Well... I'm sure she only said that to get rid of him.' That *was* the only reason, wasn't it? Claire wasn't starting to get possessive, was she?

'Well, if you're sure.' Aisling shrugged.

'We're just hooking up. She knows that,' Luca said, trying to sound more certain than he felt.

'I could take care of it for you,' Aisling murmured, stroking his dick over his jeans. 'Must be a bit uncomfortable.' Her fingers moved to his zipper and she began tugging it down slowly.

'For fuck's sake, Aisling—' Just then he heard a gasp and looked up. His eyes locked with Claire's as she stood frozen, halfway across the room.

* * *

Claire's heart sank when she came out of the loo and saw the awful Aisling sitting beside Luca on the sofa. Damn! She'd hoped she'd seen the last of her tonight. But then, as she got closer to the table and realised what was going on, she stopped in her tracks. She didn't know where to look or what to do.

'Claire!' At that moment, Luca's eyes flew up and met hers, and he simultaneously batted Aisling's hand away.

She withdrew it slowly, smiling smugly as she looked up at Claire.

Claire forced herself to walk back to the table.

'Sorry – am I in your seat?' Aisling said, but she made no move to get up.

Claire picked up her drink and drained it. 'Don't worry about it,' she said, slamming her glass back on the table and throwing a furious look at Luca. 'I was just leaving.'

'Claire!'

She ignored Luca and raced outside. She didn't look back, but she knew he was following her. She stood at the edge of the pavement and stuck her hand out, desperately hoping she would get a taxi before he caught up with her. No such luck.

'Claire!'

She turned to face him, fizzing with rage.

'What the fuck was that about?' he panted.

'*What?*' She gave an incredulous laugh. '*You're* asking *me* what that was about? That girl had her hand on your dick.'

His eyes narrowed. 'So? You don't own it, Claire.'

'Have you slept with her?'

'We've hooked up a few times, yeah.'

'How many others of those girls you introduced me to tonight have you slept with?'

'For fuck's sake, what's it to you? You're not my girlfriend.'

'Yes, I *know* I'm not your girlfriend, Luca. We all know that, don't we? I mean, God forbid anyone should admit they have feelings for you!'

'Then why did you tell that bloke at the gig that you were?'

She huffed, aghast. 'Is *that* what this is about? Because he was being a pest and I wanted to get rid of him, okay?'

'That's all?'

'Yes, that's all!'

'So why are you acting all jealous, then?'

'I'm not jealous! I'm *humiliated*. She thought you were with me,' she said, waving her hand back at the bar, 'but you were letting her feel you up right in front of everyone. In front of *me*.'

'Well, I don't see what you have to be so high and mighty about,' Luca shouted. 'You're only using me to practice your moves so you can fuck Mr Perfect in London.'

'And I'm paying you for the privilege. You could at least show a little respect.'

'Jesus! You're not paying me enough to put up with this bullshit.'

'Oh, really?' Her mouth curled in a sneer. 'How much would I have to pay you to act like a decent human being?'

'Gee, I don't know, Claire. There probably isn't enough money in the world to turn me into a "decent human being".'

'And what if I wasn't using you for my own ends? What then, huh? If I was one of those girls, like Aisling? It wouldn't be any different, would it? I'd still be expected to know my place, not to expect anything from you. What would I be getting out of it, then?'

'A bloody great fuck! What more do you want?'

'A lot more,' she said quietly, all the fight going out of her. 'A whole lot more. Most people do, Luca.'

They faced each other in hostile silence, out of breath after their shouting match. Then Claire saw a taxi with its light on and hailed it. When it stopped, she got in and didn't look back.

19

The next morning, Claire stood on the step outside Luca's house and pressed his bell. She had tussled with herself about what she should do ever since she'd woken in her own bed, vaguely aware that she wasn't supposed to be there. Rage had boiled up inside her as she recalled their fight last night and the way Luca had behaved. But she felt bad about some of the things she'd said to him. She wondered if they had burnt their boats. Were they finished, or should one of them apologise? And if so, should it be her – or him?

Part of her would have been happy never to see Luca again. He was the very antithesis of Mark, the opposite of what she wanted in a man. But she still needed him, so regardless of who was most in the wrong, she decided she would be the one to make the first move towards trying to patch things up between them. She'd come over rather than trying to call him, sure that he would simply ignore her if she tried to contact him by phone. Only after she had rung the bell did it occur to her that Aisling might be with him, but it was too late to run away.

Luca's silent scowl when he answered the door wasn't encouraging, but at least he let her in, and she rehearsed what to say as they climbed the stairs in silence.

'I'm sorry—' they said simultaneously, as soon as he had closed the door behind them, which made them laugh, dispelling some of the tension.

'Okay, I'll go first,' Claire said. Luca waved her to the sofa and sat beside her. She was relieved to see there was no sign of Aisling.

'I'm sorry if I acted like a jealous girlfriend,' she said. 'Maybe I *have* let myself get more attached to you than I should. It's hard not to when you're giving me orgasms all the time and making me feel amazing. But I know it doesn't mean anything, and you don't have to worry about me going bunny-boiler on you, honestly. And I didn't mean what I said – I think you're a really decent person, and you've been very generous and sweet to me. So please don't quit on me, because I still need you. If you want more money—'

'I don't,' Luca interrupted. 'Look, I'm sorry too. You were right – I acted like a dick, and I'm sorry you felt humiliated. I just – I felt like you were getting possessive and I freaked out. I know I'm supposed to want more, but I just don't.'

Claire shook her head. 'I know that, and it's a pity because you have so much more to give. But I'm not trying to change you. I meant what I said about wanting more...' Luca opened his mouth to say something, but she held up a hand to silence him '...but I'm not looking for that from you, honestly,' she raced on. 'Mark wants the same things I want, and he's the reason I'm here in the first place.' She took a deep breath. 'So – do you think we could continue?'

He smiled. 'Actually, I'm relieved you said that because I seem to remember giving you a money-back guarantee.'

'So you did.'

'We can get back to it right now, if you like,' he said, taking her hand.

'Good. Because there's something I want to try.'

* * *

'Ow! Claire, what are you doing?'

'Don't you like it?' she puffed, frowning in concentration as she alternated twisting her hands in opposite directions on his shaft and slapping it back and forth vigorously. They were both naked, Claire kneeling up beside him, while Luca lay prone on the bed.

'No, it hurts!'

'Really?' she asked uncertainly, reducing the slaps to light flicks.

'Ouch! Yes, get off me!' He pushed her hands away, shunting away from her in the bed. He collapsed back against the pillows, his breathing ragged.

'Sorry.' She caught her lip between her teeth. 'I must be doing it wrong.'

'I don't think there's a right way to do that. What the hell were you trying to do?'

'I saw it in a magazine. I wanted to surprise you.' It was number one of the 'Five Ways to Drive Him Wild in Bed' in the article she'd read. She had studied it diligently and thought she'd grasped it. She'd thought she could make faster progress if she used her initiative and learnt things for herself as well as what Luca taught her. She'd hoped he'd be pleased.

'Well, you surprised me all right,' he said, his breathing calming.

'Sorry. It was supposed to be a turn-on.'

'Jesus! Where do they come up with this stuff?'

'Sorry.' She winced. 'Does it still hurt?'

'I'll be okay.'

'I probably wasn't doing it right. It's quite complicated – like trying to rub your head and pat your stomach at the same time. But I thought I'd got the hang of it.'

'Don't tell me you practised on a banana?'

'Well...' Claire gave him a guilty smile.

'Claire,' he said patiently, 'you do know the crucial difference between a banana and a dick that's attached to an actual live human being?'

'Um,' she twisted her mouth, as if trying to come up with the answer, 'you can't eat the dick?'

Luca grinned. 'Well... okay, you're right – there's no difference.'

'So, was there anything you liked about it? The banana had no complaints.'

'I liked you taking the initiative. And you looked cute with your little frown, you were concentrating so hard,' he said, touching the space between her eyebrows. 'And I liked the way your tits jiggled while you were doing it.'

'Like this?' She shimmied her chest so that her breasts wobbled.

'Yeah.' He grinned appreciatively. 'But seriously, Claire, you don't have to do these outlandish things to get a guy excited. You can pretty much just sit there, like that,' he said, waving at her naked body. 'That'll do it every time. We're about as complicated as door knobs.'

She flopped down on the pillows beside him and he put an arm around her. 'I just thought maybe I should have some sexy tricks up my sleeve, to seem more sophisticated.'

'Forget about having tricks up your sleeve. Just don't wear sleeves – or anything else. That's as sophisticated as it needs to get, honestly.'

Claire laughed.

'But it's good that you're being proactive, coming up with new ideas,' he said. 'Maybe just run them by me first, okay?'

'Okay.'

'So, was there anything else you wanted to try?'

'Well, I read loads of sex tips, but most of them sounded a bit tricky – like that one. And a lot of them were just weird – like hiding in the bathroom, jumping out at you when you come out of the shower and swatting your legs with a hairbrush.'

'Jesus, are these sex tips from the Spanish Inquisition?'

'I think they could be, actually. There was one about dripping hot candle wax on you.'

'Let's not do that.'

'Or putting a doughnut on your willy and eating it off.'

'Gives a whole new meaning to "put a ring on it",' Luca said, and Claire laughed.

'And rubbing food on you, then licking it off – that one cropped up again and again, just with different food.'

'A classic. We could try that, if you like.'

Claire nodded eagerly. She didn't want all her hours of study to go to waste. 'They usually suggest whipped cream or chocolate sauce.'

'I don't have any chocolate sauce or whipped cream,' Luca said apologetically.

'How about ice-cream, then? It's good because the cold stimulates the senses too.'

'Sorry, I don't have any ice-cream either.'

'Well, what do you have?'

Luca thought. 'How about cornflakes?'

'But I couldn't pour milk on you. It wouldn't stick.'

'No, you'd have to eat them dry.'

Claire thought about shaking cornflakes onto his naked body and eating them off it. 'Cornflakes aren't very sexy, are they?' she said.

'No. Frosties, now – that's a sexy cereal.'

'It needs to be something you can lick. Foods that melt at body temperature are sexy – like chocolate or ice-cream.'

'How about butter? That melts at body temperature.'

'Eew, no. I couldn't eat butter on its own. I'd be sick.'

'Maybe you could make yourself a few sandwiches. Have a buffet off me.'

Claire laughed. 'Okay, let's forget the whole eating-food-off-you scenario.'

'Oh! I might have some Nutella.'

'I hate Nutella.'

'You could go out to the shops and get something,' Luca suggested.

'Nah. The moment has passed.'

'Well, if you want to try it some other time, let me know and I'll have something in.'

'Okay.' She nuzzled into his neck. 'All that talk of food has made me hungry.'

'Do you want to get up and have breakfast?'

'Not yet. Let's stay here for a while.' She was very aware that this was the last chance she'd have this weekend to spend time with Luca, and she wanted to make the most of every minute.

'When's your mother getting out?'

'She's being "released", as she calls it, tomorrow morning.'

'Well, you can stay here tonight, then.'

'No.' She shook her head. 'I really need to go home and get the house ready – clean up a bit, do some shopping. I haven't spent much time there the past few weeks. I'll have to leave around lunchtime. Why don't we hang on and go out for a big brunch later? My treat.'

'Sounds good.'

'And in the meantime I'll just have to find something else to nibble on.' She raised herself up on an elbow and started kissing his neck and shoulder.

'Hey, that was pretty good sexy-talk.' He pushed his hand into her hair.

'Thanks. How's your dick now?'

'It'll live.'

'Aw, poor thing.' She began kissing her way down his chest. 'Would it help if I kissed it better?'

'It couldn't hurt.'

She was just swirling her tongue around the tip when they were interrupted by the door buzzer. They ignored it at first, but it just got more and more insistent.

'Bloody hell!' Luca grumbled, gently extricating himself from Claire and getting out of bed. 'This had better be good.'

He stormed into the living room naked and Claire heard him speaking into the intercom.

'It's my sister,' he told her, as he came back into the bedroom and pulled on his jeans and a T-shirt. 'You'd better get dressed. She won't go away – she's kind of an unstoppable force.'

As he stalked off to let her in, Claire got out of bed and scrabbled for her clothes. She was just buttoning her shirt when she heard Luca letting himself back into the flat. She froze, not sure if he would want her to meet his sister or if she should hide in the bedroom until she was gone.

'Claire!' he called from the other room, resolving her dilemma. She smoothed her hair and went into the living room where Luca was standing with the petite, dark-haired girl she had bumped into the other morning. She was dressed casually, but expensively, and she was immaculately groomed.

'This is my sister, Ali,' Luca said. 'Ali, this is Claire.'

'Hi, Claire. We sort of met before.' Ali smiled wryly. She gave Claire the once-over as they shook hands, and threw Luca a jaundiced look that spoke volumes. It obviously wasn't the first time she'd encountered a strange half-dressed woman in his flat.

'Yes, well... sorry I had to run off that time,' Claire said. 'It's nice to meet you properly.'

'Well, I'd ask what you two are up to, but I'm afraid you'd tell me,' Ali said. 'I was going to see if you wanted feeding,' she said to Luca, 'but I can see you're busy.'

'Oh, we'd fin— I mean, I was just leaving anyway,' Claire said hastily. She was gutted that her last day with Luca would be cut short, but she didn't want to get in the way.

'No, you weren't,' Luca said shortly. 'We were going to go out for brunch,' he said to Ali.

'We?' Ali's eyebrows shot up and she turned to her brother.

'Yes, we.' He shot her a warning look. 'You're welcome to join us, if you promise not to be a brat. If that's okay with you, Claire?' he asked.

'Yes, come!' Part of her didn't want to share Luca with anyone for her last precious hours, but it was better than nothing. Besides, she was intrigued to learn more about his family.

'Oh, this is brilliant!' Ali said, looking from one of them to the other. She turned the full beam of her dazzling smile on her brother. 'You have a girlfriend! I knew it!'

'Oh, I— we're not—' Claire began.

'I'm so glad!' Ali interrupted. 'You must come to my birthday party,' she said to Claire.

'That's very kind of you but—'

'You have to bring her,' Ali said to Luca, cutting off Claire once again. 'I'm sure Mum and Dad would love to meet her.' Claire was almost afraid to look at Luca, sure he would be freaking out, but he just smiled at his sister helplessly.

'We'll have a proper chat then, get to know each other properly,' Ali said to Claire. 'It's next month – did he tell you? The fifteenth of June. We'll use the sunroom, but if the weather's good we can be out in the garden. Anyway, I've got to go, but I'll see you then.'

'Aren't you going to come to brunch with us?' Claire asked.

'No,' she said, aiming a sly smile at her brother. 'I know where I'm not wanted.'

'Oh, of course you—'

'It was *really* nice to meet you again, Claire. Don't forget – fifteenth of June,' she babbled, as she made her way to the door. 'Dressy, but not too dressy,' she said, turning in the doorway. 'You don't want to upstage the birthday girl. And don't worry about a present. Just get me something small and very expensive. Only kidding!' She giggled. 'Well, bye.' And then she was gone.

'So that was your sister,' Claire said to Luca.

'Yeah.' He sighed. 'That was Ali.'

'I'm sorry I didn't get a chance to say that I couldn't go to her party. I couldn't really get a word in.'

Luca gave her a wary look. 'You don't want to come to her party?'

'Oh, it's not that I don't want to – I mean she seems lovely, and I'm sure it'll be fun, but—'

'She *is* lovely. It *will* be fun.'

'But she only wants me to come because she thinks I'm your girlfriend. I'm sorry I didn't get a chance to set her straight about that but...' She waved her hand helplessly in the direction of the door.

'She invited *you*. You should come.'

'But she thinks we're... together. And I'm sure you have someone else you'd rather bring.' She had no desire to be subjected to an evening playing the fifth wheel, watching Luca with some other girl while she stood on the sidelines. Just thinking about it made her want to cry.

'No.'

'Sorry?'

'No, I don't have anyone else I'd rather bring.' Luca looked right into her eyes then and her breath hitched.

'But... everyone will think we're together.'

Luca shrugged. 'So? We know what we are to each other. What does it matter what anyone else thinks?'

Did she know what they were to each other? Did Luca really know what he was to her? Despite what she had said to him that morning, she wasn't at all sure she knew herself.

'Look, you know you're not my girlfriend. I don't give a toss if anyone else thinks you are.'

'But your mum and dad—'

'Will be very impressed. Come on, you can make me look good for once.'

She smiled. 'You really want me to come?'

'Yes, I really do. What do you want – a gilt-edged invitation? Actually, there probably is a gilt-edged invitation somewhere. So...?'

'So...' She hesitated.

'Please, I really want you to come. If you agree, I'll do whatever you want in there for the rest of the morning,' he said, waving to the bedroom.

'You don't have to.'

'Come on, I want to. It's not like it isn't one of my favourite things too.'

'Wait – you don't even know what I'll pick yet.'

'Yeah, I do.' He smiled. 'I know all your favourite things.'

'Yes, you do,' she whispered. Their eyes met and for a moment they just stared at each other. 'Okay, I'll come,' she said finally.

'Oh yes, you will – I'll make sure of that.'

20

Claire returned home later that afternoon, feeling wonderfully relaxed and refreshed. After a glorious morning in bed with Luca (they had returned to his room as soon as Ali had left), she had taken him out for a massive brunch. She had worked up a hell of an appetite, and she didn't know if it was the sharpness of her hunger or because all her senses were heightened after sex but food had never tasted so good. Luca had surprised her by sitting beside her on the cushioned banquette instead of taking the seat opposite, and she had spent a large part of the meal eating one-handed as he held her other under the table. It confused her that he would do something that felt so romantic and lover-like when he had warned her not to think of him in that way. But then she reminded herself that he was just a very tactile person and it didn't mean anything. He had gone back to his sexy, easy-going self once she had convinced him that she wasn't going to read anything into it. So she just relaxed and enjoyed it for what it was, taking pleasure in the warmth of his hand on her leg, allowing herself to lay her head on his shoulder and indulge in the closeness for a little while. It felt like the end of a lovely holiday, and she was sad that she wouldn't be spending the night with him. He had become such a permanent fixture in her life over the last couple of weeks, and even though she knew she would see him again in a few days, she couldn't help feeling a bit wobbly when it came time for her to leave.

'What are you going to do for the rest of the weekend?' she asked, as they stood outside the restaurant.

'I won't know what to do with myself without you coming round, taking your clothes off and luring me into bed all the time.'

'I'm sure you'll think of something.'

'I suppose I could do some work.'

'Well, have fun, whatever you do.'

'You too. Thanks for brunch,' he said, before giving her a lingering goodbye kiss. And then he was gone, disappearing into the crowd.

Claire spent the rest of the day shopping, cleaning and cooking, and went to bed alone that night, missing Luca dreadfully and trying not to fret about what he might be doing – or who with.

* * *

The next morning she went to collect her mother, laden with boxes of chocolates, cards and flowers for the staff, on Espie's instructions. When they had distributed the gifts and said their goodbyes, Claire wheeled her mother out to the car and helped her in.

'I thought we might invite everyone over for dinner this evening,' Espie said, as Claire pulled out of the car park.

Claire's heart sank. She had been looking forward to a quiet few days with nothing to do, no visits to make and just the two of them for dinner. 'Everyone?' she asked.

'The whole family,' Espie said eagerly. 'You don't mind, do you?'

'No, of course not. It'd be nice.' She knew her mother was probably dying to have a get-together and let her hair down after weeks at the mercy of institutional regimes. She had been forced to relinquish control of so much lately. It had been heartbreaking to watch her power and autonomy being steadily eroded, her vivacious spirit constantly thwarted by a body that wouldn't cooperate. When she and her brothers were children, their house had been the one where everyone congregated, and their friends had always been welcome to stay for dinner at a moment's notice. Espie was a brilliant and enthusiastic cook, and no one had ever left their house hungry. Having the family over for dinner wasn't a lot to ask, and at least it was within Claire's power to make it happen.

'So, what'll we have?' Espie said. 'I could murder a nice roast with all the trimmings. I haven't had a proper roast in ages.'

'I'll do one, if that's what you fancy,' Claire said, suppressing a weary sigh. The whole family coming for a roast dinner – that would mean she'd have to go shopping again as soon as she had her mother settled in at home, then spend the rest of the day peeling, chopping and cooking. Still, she couldn't begrudge her mother a welcome-home dinner. It seemed the least she could do.

She wasn't feeling quite so sanguine about it later that morning as she peeled and sliced her way through mountains of vegetables. She tried to practice mindfulness meditation, making an effort to be in the moment, just chopping the vegetables, but she couldn't help feeling a bit aggrieved that she was going to all this trouble for her brothers and their wives, when she already knew they would take it for granted. They didn't appreciate the work that went into entertaining because they never did it themselves. She could count on the fingers of one hand the number of times she had been invited to either of their houses for dinner. She sighed as she prepared the sauce for the cauliflower cheese that her mother always insisted on because it was Neil's favourite. It was her favourite, too, but she wished that, just once, someone would make it for *her* instead of the other way around.

She really was her mother's daughter, she thought, as she surveyed the table groaning with food. There was enough to feed an army. She had made apple tart last night for her and her mum, and before that there would be roast beef, cauliflower cheese, carrots, peas, roast potatoes, Yorkshire puddings and gravy.

Luca could do with a feed like this, she thought, and wished she was cooking for him instead of her ungrateful family. At least he would appreciate it. And then she thought, Why not? There was no reason she couldn't invite him. After all, it was her home and she was the one doing all the work. Besides, her mother would be delighted. Much as she loved having the family and old friends around, nothing gave her more pleasure than meeting new people. Claire knew that anyone she wanted to invite would be welcome – and she was sure her mother would like Luca. Of course, he might not want to come. But she could ask him.

She wiped her hands on a tea towel and was on her way to the sitting room to run it by her mother when the doorbell rang. She thought she could hear children's voices outside, but it was only twelve thirty, and she had told everyone dinner would be at six.

So she was surprised when she opened the door to find Michelle, Neil, Holly and Cian standing in the porch. Holly and Cian zipped past her into the house with excited cries of 'Nana! Nana!'

'Go easy,' Michelle called after them. 'Nana's a bit weak at the moment.' She and Neil stepped inside as a bewildered Claire stood back.

'These are for Espie,' Michelle said, handing Claire a huge bouquet.

'Thanks. Um... Mum's in there,' she said, gesturing to the sitting room. 'You're very early. Dinner won't be ready until—'

'Oh, we're not staying,' Michelle explained. 'We're off to the garden centre for the afternoon, but we thought we'd drop the kids off here so they can spend some time with their granny.'

'They hate being dragged around the garden centre with us,' Neil said. 'It's so boring for them.'

'Mum's still a bit tired,' Claire protested, 'and she's supposed to be taking it easy. And I'll be busy making dinner.'

Michelle gave a brittle laugh. 'Welcome to my world,' she said. 'When you're a mum, you have to get used to doing twenty different things at once. And I'm sure Espie would like to spend some time with them,' she added reprovingly. 'She hasn't seen them in ages.'

And whose fault is that? Claire wanted to shout. But she gritted her teeth and said nothing.

'We'll just pop in and say hello,' Michelle said, 'and then we'll be off.'

Claire followed them into the sitting room. Her mother was sitting in an armchair with one leg elevated, and Holly and Cian were quizzing her about her false hip while trying to climb on top of her.

'Can we see it?'

'No, it's on the inside.'

'Does it make you go really fast?'

Espie laughed. 'No, it makes me go slower at the moment.'

'That's no use!'

'You're very early,' Espie said to Neil and Michelle, as they came in. 'Have you come to help Claire? That's very nice of you.'

Claire hid a smirk. Her mother knew damn well that it would never have occurred to either of them to help out.

'Oh, er... no. We're off to the garden centre,' Michelle said.

'We'll be back in time for dinner,' Neil added helpfully.

'Well, that's the main thing,' Espie said. 'As long as you're here to help eat it, it makes it all worthwhile.'

Michelle looked confused, as she often did around Espie. She was always off balance with Espie's acerbic humor, and never seemed quite sure whether she should take offence or not. 'We thought we'd drop the kids in with you for the afternoon, we knew you'd love to see them,' she said. 'They were dying to see you.'

'And I was dying to see them too,' Espie said, smiling at her grandchildren.

'Mum,' Claire interrupted, 'I was thinking of asking a – a friend over for dinner as well. Is that okay?'

'Oh.' Michelle turned to her, frowning. 'I thought it would be nice just to have the family today.'

'Of course, love,' her mother said breezily. 'Have anyone you want – you don't have to ask.'

'You don't want to overdo things, Espie,' Michelle said. 'You're only just out of the hospital.'

'Claire's the one doing all the work,' Espie said, fixing Michelle with a beady eye, 'so if anyone's going to be overdoing things, it'll be her. I'll be sitting here like Lady Muck, getting waited on hand and foot, like the rest of you.'

'But it can be very tiring, having a big crowd around you – family's different, isn't it?' Michelle said. 'You don't have to make an effort.'

'You know I love having a big crowd in the house,' Espie said, adding predictably, 'the more, the merrier.'

Michelle gave Claire a sour look, clearly intended to make her feel she was being very selfish and thoughtless inviting a friend to join them for the dinner she had spent all day preparing. 'Well, I'll leave you to it,' Michelle said.

'Yes, I've no doubt you will,' Espie said cheerily.

Michelle's smile wavered uncertainly. 'Be good for Nana,' she said to the children.

'Don't worry, I'm more than a match for these two,' Espie said.

'It's great to have you home,' Michelle said, stooping to give her mother-in-law a kiss on the cheek before they left. 'Take care. See you all later.'

* * *

Bloody hypocrite, Claire thought, watching Michelle leave. She'd hardly seen Espie for years before they'd had the children. She had deliberately cut her mother-in-law out of her life, having decided she was a 'toxic' person who was a drain on her positive energy. Claire knew this because Michelle had written about it in her column, casting herself as the martyred victim of a nasty, interfering mother-in-law.

This was based on a couple of incidents that had caused Michelle great offence. First, Espie had organised a surprise party for Neil's thirtieth birthday. Even though she had planned nothing to mark the occasion, Michelle claimed that Espie had stolen her thunder and was trying to usurp her rightful position as the number-one woman in Neil's life. She was particularly needled that the party was a raucous, roaring success. Neil had made the mistake of telling her he'd had the time of his life, and everyone was talking about it for months afterwards, praising Espie's warmth and hospitality.

Second, Espie had visited Michelle on the day she'd given birth to Holly, eager to see her first grandchild – when, as Michelle told her readers, she had made it quite clear that the only visitors she wanted in the first few days were Neil and her own mother; she had told everyone else that, if they wanted to do something, they could stock up her freezer with food or do a bit of cleaning in preparation for her going home, instead of crowding into her hospital room and cluttering it with flowers and baby gifts.

Not long after she had taken Holly home, though, Michelle had changed her tune and decided Espie wasn't so toxic, after all – not if it meant free babysitting on tap so she could enjoy child-free nights out and weekends away, and the 'me time' that was so precious to her as a new mother. But she had still acted like she was doing it for the sake of family harmony, at great personal cost to herself. Claire sometimes wondered how much of her own bullshit Michelle actually believed.

Back in the kitchen, Claire rang Luca, desperately hoping now that he would come. Would he think she was being clingy, trying to see him again already? Maybe it would be a good thing if she couldn't get him, she thought, as his phone rang and rang. She was about to hang up when he answered.

'Hey, sweetheart. What's up?'

'Hi.' She felt a burst of happiness in her chest at the endearment – even though she knew he didn't mean anything by it. 'I was just wondering if you'd like to come for dinner.'

'Still on a mission to feed me up?' He chuckled.

'I mean, you're probably doing something else, but I just thought I'd ask. There's all this food—'

'No, that'd be great. Thanks.'

'My whole family will be here,' she said warningly, 'so…'

'Don't worry, I won't try to jump you in the middle of dinner.'

She laughed. 'I was just warning you. In case you want to back out.'

'I don't.'

'So, you'll come? To dinner, I mean.'

'Yes, I'll come to dinner.'

'Great. We're eating at about six.'

'Cool. See you then.'

* * *

Ronan and Liz arrived at five thirty, with Ben and Adam. A tall, slender and very pretty woman, Liz was loud, overbearing and bossy. But she was well-meaning and, unlike Michelle, there was no spite in her. A problem-solver by nature, she was always cheerfully doling out unasked-for advice, suggesting places Claire might find a boyfriend or telling Espie about alternative therapies and diets she might try. Ronan was so gentle and easy-going, he was completely overshadowed by his strident wife and rowdy sons.

Michelle and Neil returned shortly afterwards and Claire gave them all drinks in the sitting room while she put the finishing touches to dinner. She had just called everyone into the kitchen when the doorbell rang.

'Who's that?' Liz asked, as they took their places at the table. 'I thought we were all here.'

'Claire asked a friend to dinner. Very unfair, I think, on Espie's first day home,' Michelle said, in a stage whisper, as Claire went to answer the door.

'Hi.' Luca bent and gave her a swift kiss on the lips. 'Am I late?' he asked, handing her a bottle of wine.

'Oh, you shouldn't have bothered – but thanks,' she said, taking it from him. 'No, you're just in time.'

She stepped back to let him pass, and found Holly standing behind her in the hall with a sly grin on her face. She skipped ahead, as Claire led Luca into the kitchen. Michelle was making a great show of being helpful, pouring wine and fussing over Espie, while Liz barked orders at her family.

Everyone looked up as Claire and Luca came in. 'Everyone, this is Luca,' Claire said, then went around the table, introducing everyone in turn.

'Well, Claire's kept you very quiet, Luca,' Liz roared, as he took a seat beside Claire. 'I hope we don't scare you off. Are you sure it's wise throwing him in at the deep end like this?' she said to Claire.

'Sorry?'

'I mean, we didn't even know you had a boyfriend, and now it's meet the whole family time.'

'Oh, I don't – I mean, he's not—'

'At least, *I* didn't know,' Liz continued. 'Did anyone else?' Everyone shook their heads. 'You should have said something. I can stop trying to think of people to fix you up with now. Thank God!' She laughed. 'Because, honestly, I was running out of ideas. Ronan, you can tell that guy at work to stand down.'

'He's not my boyfriend,' Claire said hastily, glancing at Luca. This had been a bad idea. She hoped he wouldn't freak out. 'We're just friends. But don't get that guy at work to stand up again,' she whispered to Ronan, who smiled at her sympathetically.

'But I saw you kissing in the hall,' Holly said, with a cheeky smile.

Claire blushed. 'It wasn't that kind of kissing.'

'Don't be a tattle-tale, Holly,' Espie said, as everyone settled and began helping themselves. 'So, tell us all about yourself, Luca.'

'What would you like to know?'

'Well, what do you do? Let's start with that.'

'I'm an artist – a painter.'

'I love doing painting!' Holly said. 'I didn't know that could be a job.'

'So you make a living out of painting?' Espie said. 'How marvellous!'

'Well, not much of a living.'

'Still, to be able to do something you love – I think that's wonderful.'

'So, how do you two know each other?' Liz asked. 'Cut up Ben's meat for him, Ronan.'

'Oh, we met at, um... night classes,' Claire blurted out.

'Night classes?' Liz hooted. 'I didn't think anyone actually met at night classes.'

'I didn't know you were taking night classes,' Espie said to Claire. 'You've been holding out on me.' She gave Claire a sly smile.

'I only started going while you were in hospital.'

'So what was the class?' Michelle asked.

'Um... art,' Claire said.

'Oh, so you were the teacher?' Liz asked Luca.

'Yeah,' he answered, flashing a little smile at Claire.

'I didn't know you could paint.' Ronan looked at Claire in surprise.

'Well, I can't, really. That's why I'm going to classes.'

'And what I teach Claire is more sort of... performance art,' Luca said.

'You can teach that?'

'I've never taught it before, but I'm giving it a go.'

'Anyway, I'm not very good,' Claire mumbled, hoping they would drop the subject.

'Claire's too hard on herself,' Luca told everyone. 'She's actually shown great aptitude.'

'I try hard,' Claire said, 'but it's more effort than talent.'

'Well, you know what they say,' Michelle piped up. 'It's 90 per cent perspiration and 10 per cent inspiration.'

Luca laughed. 'Yeah, that's certainly true. Claire puts a lot of sweat into it. But you've started coming up with lots of inspiration lately too,' he said to her.

'Maybe you could show us some of your stuff later,' Liz said. 'Give us a performance.'

'Yeah!' Holly clapped her hands.

'Oh no!' Claire yelped. 'Um... I don't think that's a good idea.'

Luca laughed. 'Claire's still very shy about her talent,' he said. 'She doesn't show her stuff to many people.'

'She can't be *that* shy about it,' Michelle scoffed. 'What about the rest of the class?'

'Oh, I was giving Claire private tuition,' Luca said, throwing Claire an intimate look.

'Claire's very private about her writing too,' Michelle said to Luca. 'Did you know she writes?'

'Yes. I've read some of her stuff. It's really good.'

Michelle looked at him aghast. 'Well, you're privileged! She never lets anyone see her writing. I'm a writer too, and I keep trying to persuade her to join a group with me, but so far the most I've seen of her writing is on Christmas and birthday cards.'

'You and Michelle should help each other,' Neil said bossily to Claire. 'What's the point in writing if you never let anyone read it?'

'I will eventually – when I feel it's good enough.'

'You have to get it out there some time, Claire,' Michelle said. 'Get some feedback. Connect with people in the industry who can help you.'

'And Michelle is really good at networking,' Neil said. 'She's made lots of useful contacts.'

'Claire will take the publishing world by storm when she's good and ready, won't you?' Espie said, smiling at Claire.

'Well, you can't just sit back and hope someone's going to break into your computer and discover you,' Michelle said. 'You have to get out there and chase it.'

Imagine her face if I told her I already have a book deal, Claire thought.

'Are *you* published?' Luca asked Michelle.

'No, not yet. But I feel I'm getting close. I really believe it's only a matter of time.'

'Perseverance is the thing,' Neil chimed in, playing his part in a well-oiled conversation. 'Look at how many rejections J. K. Rowling got before she was published.'

'Did you see that "Scenes of a Sexual Nature" blogger got a book deal?' Michelle said to Claire, her lip curled in a sneer. 'Bloody typical!'

'Um… yes, I did see that,' Claire said faintly. She'd known Michelle would be enraged by the news.

Luca looked at Claire, eyebrows raised, and she shook her head almost imperceptibly at him. 'Who's that?' he asked Michelle innocently.

'She's this awful little tart who writes an S-E-X blog,' she said, glancing at the children as she spelt out the word.

'That spells sex!' Holly informed her younger brother and cousins.

'It's absolutely filthy.' Michelle sniffed. 'That sort of thing sells, I suppose. But I think there'll always be room for genuine talent that doesn't pander to the lowest common denominator. That's what I pin my hopes on anyway. And you should too,' she said kindly to Claire.

'Oh, I like that blog,' Claire said. 'I think she's a very good writer.'

'You read that trash?'

'It's not trash.'

'Well, she may be a good writer, but there's no way she'd get that kind of attention if she was writing about anything else.'

'People are interested in sex, that's true.' Claire shrugged. More interested than they are in you banging on about the bloody school run, she thought.

'And have you seen the way she flirts with Mark Bell on Twitter? I don't think it's only her writing that got her that deal.'

Claire frowned, but said nothing. She hoped other people wouldn't think that.

'This cauliflower cheese is fantastic,' Neil said, helping himself to more. 'Just like Mum used to make.'

'Claire's a great cook,' Espie said, smiling at her daughter.

'I often wish I had the time to cook more,' Michelle said. 'But I'm far too busy for making elaborate dinners. I'm chauffeuring the kids around all week, making lunches, cleaning up after them, getting the homework done and a million other things. By the time the weekend comes around, I'm too knackered for anything other than a pizza delivery. Honestly, no one has any idea the amount of work us mums do.'

'I can't begin to imagine,' Espie said drily.

Michelle had the grace to blush. 'I don't know how you coped with three, Espie – and all on your own!'

'Well, we didn't make such a song and dance about parenting in my day. We just got on with it. It probably helped that we didn't have to alert the media every time our child had a poo or did something cute.'

Claire wrapped her mouth around a forkful of food to hide her smile. But Luca laughed, earning a scowl from Michelle.

'Well, things were simpler, then, I suppose,' Michelle said. 'You didn't have the same pressures. The world was a lot safer too – you could let your children run wild and not worry about where they were or who they were with.'

'Yes, that's what I did,' Espie said to Luca, with a twinkle in her eye. 'Let my children run around like wild animals while I lay around drinking gin and smoking joints. Those were the days!'

'And look how well we all turned out,' Ronan said, and Claire smiled. He always tried to be the peacemaker.

Her mother was very taken with Luca, as Claire had known she would be. She had some of her old spark about her as she talked, enlivened and invigorated by the novelty of him. She was clearly enchanted by his roguish charm and his laid-back friendly manner, but Claire was shocked to hear her inviting him to their Friday-night card game.

'You probably have better things to do on a Friday night than play cards with a bunch of old fogeys,' she said, 'but Claire will be here. And there'll be cake.'

She was even more surprised to hear Luca accept.

'You don't have to come on Friday,' she told him later, as she saw him out.

'I want to,' he said. 'I like your mum.'

'She likes you.'

'Well, I'll talk to you during the week, yeah? Phone sex?'

'Oh, phone sex!' She'd forgotten about that.

'If you want to,' he said, watching her face.

'I suppose we should. I mean, Mark lives in London, so...' Not only did Mark live in London but he often went away on business trips. He probably *would* expect them to have phone sex at some point, particularly when she'd made out she was such a fan.

'And you've made it sound pretty hot in your blog.'

'How about tomorrow night, say around eight? *Holby City*'s on, so Mum will be occupied for an hour then.'

'Eight it is. Don't forget your vibrator.'

'My... Oh! I hadn't thought about that. I figured I'd just use my...' She raised a hand.

'Well, it's up to you. I just assumed, since you used one in your blog—'

'Mm.' She chewed her lip. 'The thing is, I don't have one.'

'You've never used one?'

'No. I should probably get one, shouldn't I?'

'I think you should. Even if you don't get it for the phone sex, you should probably get some experience at using one.'

'Okay. I'll buy one for tomorrow night.'

'Talk to you then.'

* * *

'Oh, I *like* Luca,' her mother said later, when everyone had gone and it was just the two of them. 'I like him very much.'

'He's lovely, isn't he?'

'And so good-looking. You've obviously been holding out on me big-time, my girl. So tell all.'

'There's nothing to tell, Mum. We really are just friends.'

'Well, that's a pity.'

Claire shrugged.

'It's a real shame,' Espie said, as Claire began to load the dishwasher. 'Oh, and just so you know…'

'Yes?' Claire looked up.

'I don't buy that cock-and-bull story about performance-art classes for a minute.'

21

Hanging on the Telephone

The call comes in at 3 a.m.. I've been expecting it. Mr Bossy has gone to Chicago on business, and we have a 'date' tonight – in other words, we're doing phone sex.

I've been looking forward to his call, and just hearing his voice excites me. He opens with the classic: 'What are you wearing?' Now, the thing about phone sex is you don't have to make any effort. You can lie. You can sit there in a face mask and flannel pyjamas, and say you're wearing a bustier and crotchless knickers, and your lover won't know the difference. But I think that's cheating – and, besides, this is for me, too, so I want to feel sexy. I've set a mood. I've taken a long, luxurious bath. The bedroom is lit by candles, music is playing softly and I've been sipping a glass of champagne while I wait for his call. I had a Hollywood wax today, and got my hair done, just as if I was going on a real date. And when he asks what I'm wearing I'm telling the truth when I describe the black chiffon baby-doll he likes so much with the matching G string. I chose it deliberately so he can picture me clearly. He's seen me in it many times and knows just how much cleavage it shows, and that he can see my body through the sheer material.

When I ask, he tells me he's wearing silk pyjama bottoms. I smile, knowing he's worn them to please me because I like to watch him undress. I tell him I wish he was here to touch me, and he says I'll have to stand in for him, please myself the way he would if he were here.

'Lie back on the bed,' he says, 'and take off your knickers.'

I do as he tells me, wriggling out of the G-string while holding the phone to my ear with my shoulder.

'Spread your legs,' he says, and I do. Since I can't give him an actual visual, I do the next best thing. I tell him that I got waxed today and I am completely bare. I describe how soft and smooth my skin feels, and he groans into the phone.

'Oh, baby, I wish I could see you right now. Touch yourself for me.'

I start to stroke myself. 'Are you wet?' he asks, and his voice is thick and hoarse.

'Yes,' I whisper. 'I'm so wet.'

'I'm so hard for you, baby.'

'Show me,' I say. I hear rustling and I know he's pulling off his pyjama bottoms. I can imagine his cock – I know how hard and thick his erection is. I can see him in his Chicago hotel room, naked and beautiful, and the longing is almost unbearable. 'I want you so much,' I whimper.

'Ssh, baby, I know. I want you too.' I take off the baby-doll on his instructions, and we're naked together, separated by an ocean. He tells me what he would do if he were here, how he would touch me, and I touch myself the same way. I hold the vibrator close to the phone when I switch it on, knowing it's a turn-on for him.

'Let me hear you,' he says, when I come, and I'm loud, gasping and screaming into the phone. A moment later he comes and I hear his groan across the miles, feel it deep inside me. I lie back on the bed, panting as the little aftershocks course through me. For a moment we lie there in silence, listening to each other breathe.

'So, how was your day?' he asks eventually, and we start a low, murmured conversation that soothes me.

'Sleep now,' he says at last, in that masterful way of his. 'I'll call you tomorrow – same time, same place.'

'I'll be here,' I say.

I can't wait…

'So, *Luca*'s your fuck buddy!' Yvonne didn't waste much time before cutting to the chase the next day. 'When did this happen?'

'Just in the last few weeks.'

'And you've been seeing him? Like, more than once or twice? Unbelievable!'

'Thanks a lot,' Claire said drily.

'Sorry – no offence. It's just Luca doesn't usually like to repeat himself, if you know what I mean.'

'Well, it's not serious or anything.'

'I know that,' Yvonne said. 'I mean, it's Luca.'

Her dismissive tone was getting on Claire's nerves, but she stopped herself jumping in and defending Luca because she knew Yvonne would take it the wrong way. Still, at least now that it was out in the open, she didn't have to think of an excuse to talk about him with Yvonne.

'What's his surname, by the way?' she asked.

'Why?' Yvonne narrowed her eyes suspiciously. 'What do you want it for?'

'What do you think I want it for?' Claire laughed. 'Identity theft? It's not top secret, is it?'

'Why don't you ask him?'

'I will. I just keep forgetting.' And it wasn't really the sort of thing you could ask someone mid-shag. It seemed a bit late at that stage to be worrying that you hadn't been properly introduced. She'd have to pay more attention to the signatures on his paintings the next time she was in his flat.

'Okay, I'll tell you,' Yvonne said. 'But I'd better not find you doodling it in your copybook and trying it out with your own name.'

'Promise,' Claire said, rolling her eyes.

'It's Ffrench-Carroll.'

'Hmm,' Claire smiled, cocking her head thoughtfully. 'Claire Ffrench-Carroll. That has a nice ring to it, doesn't it?'

'Don't make me regret telling you.'

'Mrs Ffrench-Carroll. Luca and Claire Ffrench-Carroll. Where's my copybook? I feel a doodle coming on.'

'Seriously, Claire—'

'You're too easy.' Claire grinned. 'He mentioned that his mother had written a book, and I thought I might check it out. That's all, okay? Nothing sinister.'

'Oh! Yeah, she wrote a book about Luca,' Yvonne said, grimacing as if she'd detected a bad smell.

'It's about adopting Luca and his sister, isn't it?'

'Well, that comes into it. But it's mainly about how she wasn't able to bond with Luca and never felt any connection with him.'

'Oh God.'

'It was a big bestseller at the time, apparently. I vaguely remember my mum talking about it. It was quite controversial. She got a lot of praise for being so open and honest about her feelings. But some people thought she shouldn't have written it – including Luca. It's a very touchy subject with him.'

'I'm not surprised. That's horrible.'

'I know. It must be awful to have your mother telling the whole world that she doesn't love you.'

'What's it called?'

'*The Stolen Child*. And her name is Jacqueline Ffrench, if you want to look it up. The Carroll bit is his dad.'

'This came for you,' Tom said, emerging from the back room and handing Claire a large parcel.

'Oh, thanks,' she said, taking it from him. It felt like books, but she couldn't imagine who would be sending her books when she worked in a bookshop. Curious, she opened it carefully. She gasped as she lifted out a beautiful, cloth-bound limited edition set of Dorothy L. Sayers's mysteries in an illustrated slip cover. She didn't have to open the card inside to know who they were from. The card simply read:

Thought of you and found these. Mark x

* * *

At ten minutes to eight that evening, Claire sat on the end of her bed trying to relax. But it had been rather stressful getting ready for tonight, and instead of feeling sexy, she just felt frazzled. She had gone for a bikini wax at lunchtime, deciding she should make an effort. Reading over one of her blog posts about phone sex, it seemed unfair, disrespectful, even, not to go to the same trouble for Luca as she had for the fictional Mr Bossy. But it was a lot easier to write about this stuff than it was to achieve it in reality. She had barely had time to squeeze in the salon visit at lunchtime and hadn't been able to grab a sandwich.

Then she'd had the ordeal of vibrator shopping after work. It had taken her ages to get up the nerve to go into the shop, and all her dithering meant that she had got home late. The weather had turned unseasonably cold, and fighting her way home against a vicious wind had only added to her weariness. She cooked and ate dinner with her mother, and had only just finished clearing up in time for *Holby City*. It was a solitary pleasure for Espie, so Claire didn't have to make any excuses for holing up in her room. But she had no time for a long, leisurely bath or even a quick shower before it was time to sit on the bed and wait for Luca's call. She poured herself a glass of wine and brought it up to her room, hoping it would help her relax and get in the mood.

She was sure her mother wouldn't budge for the next hour, but she took the precaution of locking her bedroom door anyway. Then she took a big gulp of wine, set the glass on top of the dresser, and set about finding something to wear. As she frantically opened drawers, rooting through piles of M&S cotton knickers and black woolly tights, she felt hot and bothered, but not in a remotely sexy way. Unfortunately, her underwear collection bore absolutely no resemblance to her alter ego's. There were no see-through baby-dolls or lacy G-strings. There was nothing here that would give any self-respecting bloke so much as a semi. She wished she could just get into her pyjamas. But she wanted to do this properly.

Deciding that bra and pants was the best she could do, she quickly stripped and put on her nicest set. It was more pretty than sexy, but it would have to do. Besides, it's what underneath that counts, she told herself, and at least she'd had the bikini wax. She had even let the beautician go higher than usual though she hadn't had the nerve for a full Brazilian. She sprayed some perfume between her breasts and sat on the edge of the bed with her mobile beside her. She was just pulling her new vibrator out of its bag when the phone rang, but instead of Luca, the caller display showed that it was Mark. She had planned to call him later to thank him for his present when she wasn't feeling so flustered.

'Hi, Mark!' She tried to inject some calm into her voice. 'Thank you so much for the books. I love them!'

'Ah, they arrived. Good.'

'Yeah, I was going to call you later. I—' She was interrupted by the beep of call waiting. 'Sorry, there's another call. Do you mind?'

'I won't keep you. I just wanted to tell you that I'm planning a trip to Dublin next Saturday – if that's okay with you. I mean, will you be free?'

'Yes, great!'

'Good. I'll book the flight, then. I can only get over for the one night, but it's better than nothing. Anyway, I'll let you go and call you back tomorrow when I've arranged it.'

'Okay, bye! And thank you so much again.'

She hung up and pressed the button to answer the other call.

'Hi,' Luca said.

'Hi,' she said breathlessly, holding the mobile to her ear as she slid the vibrator out of the box. Now that she was on the phone to Luca, she realised she wasn't sure about the etiquette of phone sex. Was it okay to have some general chit-chat first, or would that kill the mood? Were they supposed to get straight on with it? If only Mr Bossy were at the other end of the line – he would know what to do. 'How are you?'

'Fine. Are you okay? You sound a bit...'

'I just had kind of a stressful day.'

'Do you want to do this? We could leave it till another time...'

'No, it's fine.' She took a deep breath and let it out. 'I'm ready now.'

'So... what are you wearing?'

'Bra and pants. It's just an M&S set. I couldn't find anything sexy. But it's matching and it's very nice – pink and lacy, and the pants are boy shorts.'

'Right.' She heard him chuckle deeply. 'How much was it?'

'Oh, I can't remember. I bought it a while ago, but I haven't worn it often, so—' She broke off, realising too late that he was making fun of her. 'Sorry – too much information.'

'It's fine. But we definitely need to do some more work on your chat.'

'Not to mention my wardrobe. So, um... what are you wearing?'

'Black silky jocks and nothing else.'

'Really?' That didn't sound like Luca.

'No.' She heard the smile in his voice. 'Really, you don't want to know.'

'No, tell me.'

'A fleece.'

She giggled. 'Really? Anything else, or just the fleece?'

'Combats, boots. It's bloody freezing in here.'

'Sorry. It *was* really cold today.'

'Anyway, I've brought the blow-heater into the bedroom, so it should heat up soon. I'll strip off then.'

'You don't have to. We can just pretend.'

'No, I will. We should do this properly.'

'Okay. But those blow-heaters are very expensive to run – they use an awful lot of electricity.'

'Oh, baby, you're driving me crazy,' he said flatly. 'It makes me so hard when you talk about my electricity bill.'

'Sorry. Okay, let's start again.' She took a deep breath and lay back on the bed. 'I'm wearing a lacy bra and a thong,' she said, trying to make her voice low and sultry.

There was a moment's silence, then 'Claire?'

'Mm?'

'Are you doing a funny voice?'

'Oh! No!' She blushed. So much for sounding sexy!

'So you're lying down on the bed? I wish I was there with you.'

'Me too.' She sighed.

'Take off your bra and touch yourself the way I would.'

She set the phone down on the bed and removed her bra. Then she picked it up again and distractedly pawed her breasts, pinching her nipples while simultaneously smoothing out the instruction sheet from the vibrator on the bed beside her.

'Talk to me,' Luca said. 'Tell me what you're doing.'

'I'm touching my, um... myself. I'm pinching my nipples.'

'Are they hard?'

'Hm? Oh yes – very hard.'

'I'm getting hard thinking about it,' he said. 'I wish I was there to suck them into my mouth.'

'Are you, erm... doing stuff?'

'Yeah, I'm stroking my dick, and—' He burst out laughing. 'It's going a bit longer.' He giggled.

Claire laughed. 'Oh, I wish I was there. I love it when it goes longer and fatter.'

'Hey, are you calling my thing fat?'

'In a good way.'

'What are you – what—' Luca was struggling to speak, but kept collapsing into laughter.

'Have you taken the fleece off, then?' Claire asked, which just made him laugh harder.

'I'm pretty sure that's a line that should never come up in phone sex. I'm unzipping my fleece,' he said in a husky voice. 'And now I'm taking off my – my scarf,' he wheezed.

Claire was laughing so much that tears were rolling down her face. 'I can imagine you unwinding it sexily from around your neck.'

'Okay, maybe we should start again,' Luca said finally, sobering up. 'Let's both get naked.'

'Okay.' Claire wiped her eyes and wriggled out of her knickers. 'Oh, by the way, I got waxed today.'

'Completely?' Luca asked hoarsely.

'No, but a bit more extreme than usual. The girl I go to is always trying to get me to have a Brazilian or even a Hollywood. But I think she was happy that I let her—'

'Claire,' Luca said, in a chiding tone.

'Oh, sorry. It's sort of a landing strip, and my legs are all smooth and silky.'

'Mm, I wish I was there to taste you,' he said, his voice thickening. 'I'd lick you until you came in my mouth.'

She felt the rush of moisture between her legs at his words. 'You're making me so wet,' she said. At least it was true and she didn't feel so stupid saying it.

'It's making me hard imagining you lying there, naked and spread out. Open your legs and touch yourself.'

Claire did as he asked, her breathing deepening with her mounting excitement.

'Taste yourself, like I would if I was there.'

'Um... what? I'm not that flexible.'

'Lick your fingers.'

'Oh... yeah, okay.' She stuck the thumb of her other hand in her mouth, making loud sucking noises into the phone.

'I know how good you taste,' Luca said. 'Tell me.'

'Oh, er... yum!'

Luca chuckled softly. 'Claire...'

'It's delicious. Mm. Finger-licking good.'

'You're not doing it, are you?'

'No,' she admitted. 'Sorry, but that's just gross.'

'It is not gross.' He sighed. 'Okay, why don't we play with your vibrator? Did you get one?'

'Oh yes.' She sat up and grabbed the vibrator with its instructions. Step one was putting in the batteries. Batteries! She shunted to the end of the bed, picked them up and tore at the packaging. Of course, it was practically impenetrable. 'Just hang on a minute,' she said to Luca, placing the phone on the bed so she could use both hands. 'Okay, I'm back,' she said, balancing the phone against her shoulder while she studied the instructions.

'What are you doing?' Luca asked.

'Trying to figure out how to put the batteries in this thing.'

'You don't have any batteries in it?'

'I didn't have time. I only got it this evening on the way home from work, and then I had to cook dinner and...' Once again, she'd strayed into the mundane and was killing the mood. 'Sorry.'

'It's okay. What's it like – the vibrator?'

'Oh, it's... very life-like, I suppose – except it's purple.'

'Purple?'

'Yeah. There was a choice of purple or pink. Maybe the pink would have been more realistic, though it was hot pink, so not really. Anyway, I didn't have much time to decide – I had to get home and, besides, there was this creepy guy in the shop and I just wanted to get out of there.'

'Was that your first time in a sex shop?'

'Yeah. I've looked at stuff online, doing research for the blog, but I've never actually gone into a shop before. The assistant was very nice, though. If it hadn't been for the creepy guy I might have hung around longer.'

'I hope he wasn't hassling you.'

'He was just listening in when she was telling me about the vibrators. Then she turned one of them on to show me!' Claire had been mortified when she had switched it on to demonstrate and the head had started wiggling around.

'Maybe we should go to one together some day,' he said. 'You could have a proper look around.'

'Oh, that would be good. Thank you.'

'No problem. So – where were we?'

'I was just reading the instructions for putting in the batteries.'

'Why don't we leave the vibrator for now? You can play with it later when you've got more time. It's probably best if you get to know it on your own first anyway.'

'Okay, you're right. I'll just use my hand.' Claire lay down and they began again.

She started to forget herself and get into it, losing some of her self-consciousness as she got more turned on. She began to relax as Luca murmured in her ear, telling her how hard he was and what he wanted to do to her, getting her to touch herself and describing how it felt when he was doing those things to her.

'Are you close?' he asked, as her breathing became jagged.

'Yes,' she gasped into the phone. 'So close. I'm—'

There was a tap on the door, and she froze.

'Claire?' Her mother called. 'I'm just making a cup of tea. Would you like one?'

'Shit! Hang on,' she hissed into the phone, before tossing it away from her as if it was scorching hot. She struggled off the bed, grabbing her dressing-gown and pulled it on. Then she opened the door, hoping she didn't look too flushed. 'Sorry,' she said. 'I was just... waxing my legs.'

'Sorry to interrupt.'

'It's okay. I was just finished.' Ha! If only...

'So, cup of tea?'

'I don't think—'

'Only I didn't tell you earlier, but I made paradise slices this afternoon – your favourite.'

'Lovely!' She smiled, wanting to cry. But she couldn't say no when her mother had made such an effort to do something nice for her. 'I just have to put my stuff away, and then I'll be down.'

'Right, so. We can have them while we're watching *Come Dine With Me* – I recorded it earlier.'

'Great.' Claire glanced at the clock as she closed the door. It was just after nine. She hadn't realised it had got so late. They shouldn't have wasted so much time chatting about rubbish – well, *she* shouldn't have. She knew she had only herself to blame – Luca had tried to keep them focused.

'Sorry,' she said, picking up the phone. 'Time's up. That was my mum.'

'Don't you have time just to finish off? It'll probably only take another couple of minutes.'

'I can't. I have to go downstairs and eat paradise slices and watch *Come Dine With Me* with her.'

'Oh, okay.'

'Are you going to, um... finish off on your own?'

'Yeah,' he said. 'But I'll be thinking of you.'

'Good. Thanks,' she said, then laughed – fancy thanking someone for using you as inspiration for a wank.

'Um, Claire? About that. Before you go...'

'Yes?'

'Would you send me a photo?'

'A photo of me? Naked?'

'Yeah. With your new hairdo.'

'Oh... I—'

'It's okay,' he interrupted. 'If you don't want to, that's fine. I'll be thinking of you anyway.'

'No, it's okay,' she said, wanting to be brave. She needed to get over her inhibitions, and this would be a good start. 'I'll do it. Just give me a minute.'

She shrugged off her robe and stood in front of the mirror, since that was the only way she could get herself in the frame. She wasn't very good at self-shots and it took a couple of goes before she got a photo she was happy with.

'Okay,' she said, picking up the phone again. 'It's not great, but I'll send it to you now.'

'Thanks, sweetheart.'

When they had said their goodbyes and hung up, Claire texted the picture to Luca. Then she got into her pyjamas to go down and watch TV with her mother. She was just about to go when her mobile chimed with a message alert. It was a text from Luca:

> Beautiful picture, thank you. Can't wait to see you in the flesh. X

Claire smiled and tossed the phone back on the bed. She spied the vibrator again. She'd have a play with it tonight in bed, try to get to grips with it. She hoped it was as quiet as the sales assistant had promised.

22

In 1990 Jacqueline Ffrench travelled to Romania, moved by the reports about the horrors of Romanian orphanages that emerged after the fall of Ceaușescu's regime in 1989.

She left with a truckload of clothes and toys, and a desire to help. She returned home with a family – her three-year-old daughter, Alina, and seven-year-old son, Luca.

But back home in Ireland, while she quickly bonded with the little girl, her adoptive son felt like a stranger to her. As she went through the motions of mothering the little boy, she struggled to give him what he needed most – the love and affection that had been missing his whole life. In this brutally honest account, the author writes movingly about her failure to connect with her son and confronts the heartbreaking truth that love doesn't come to command, and sometimes good intentions aren't enough.

Claire's finger hovered over the 'Buy Now' button. She felt guilty, as if she was prying into Luca's private life – which was ridiculous, since the book was available to anyone who cared to read it. But that did nothing to ease her conscience. The idea of strangers poring over the detritus of his miserable childhood sickened her, and she experienced a rush of hatred towards the woman she had never met. How could she have done that to him? Wasn't it bad enough that she didn't love him, without publicly humiliating and betraying him by using their relationship as material? Had she never thought what effect it might have on him? She stared hard at the author photo, as if she could find some answers there, but all she saw was an attractive blonde woman with a pleasant smile.

She took a deep breath and clicked to order the book, then went downstairs to help her mother get ready for tonight. Yvonne would have a conniption if she could see her now, preparing to spend Friday night playing cards with a bunch of pensioners – and, even worse, looking forward to it. But her mother's friends were fun, and Claire enjoyed their regular Friday-evening gatherings more than she'd ever enjoyed noisy bars or nightclubs. Sometimes she was secretly glad that all her friends were coupled up and she had no one trying to drag her out on the pull at weekends. Of course, she did yearn for a boyfriend sometimes, but she wasn't prepared to endure the bar scene to find one. Anyway, she had Luca now. Okay, he wasn't her boyfriend, but they were good friends and they were having regular sex, so it was close enough. She was looking forward to seeing him tonight, though she was still half expecting him not to turn up. He might find he had something better to do when the time came.

In the kitchen her mother was sitting at the table spooning tomato sauce onto pizza bases. A couple of lemon drizzle cakes fresh from the oven were cooling on racks on the worktop.

'You've been busy,' Claire said, bending over the cakes and inhaling deeply. 'They smell amazing.' She went to the fridge and took out the pizza toppings she had prepared when she'd got in from work.

'Mum,' she said, as she joined her mother at the table and began assembling pizzas, 'do you remember a book that was out a while back by a woman called Jacqueline Ffrench about a child she adopted from Romania and couldn't bond with?'

'Oh yes,' Espie responded immediately. 'It caused a bit of a stir, and it was a big hit. I always felt so sorry for that little boy.' She shook her head sadly. 'I remember seeing her on *The Late Late Show*, and everyone saying how brave she was to write that book, like she'd done something marvellous. But I thought it was cruel. No mother should do that to her child.' She spooned a dollop of sauce into the centre of a pizza base and circled her spoon, working it outwards. 'She actually said at one point that she wished she could give him back.'

'Christ!'

'I know – like a pair of shoes that you'd return to the shop. And people were telling her she was great to admit her feelings.' Espie sighed. 'I wonder what happened to that boy.' She slid the pizza across to Claire so that she could load it with toppings. 'Why do you ask?'

'I've met him,' Claire said quietly, as she sprinkled on grated cheese. She looked up at her mother. 'So have you.'

Espie frowned questioningly at her. Then her eyes widened. 'Luca?' she gasped, a hand flying to her mouth.

Claire nodded.

'Oh my God! Poor Luca – and he's such a pet.'

'Don't say anything to him,' Claire said. 'I don't think he likes to talk about it.'

'I'm sure he doesn't. When I think of what happened to all those children,' Espie said, tears welling in her eyes. 'I'll never forget seeing those orphanages on TV – all those babies with no one to love them. How could people treat children like that?'

'I don't know,' Claire said sadly.

'And then, after all that, to end up with a mother who just wanted rid of him!' She sighed. 'Do you know how he gets on with his family now?'

'He has a sister he seems really close to. She was adopted at the same time. But I get the impression there's no love lost between him and his mother.'

'I'm not surprised.'

'I'll probably have to meet her tomorrow at Ali's party. I don't know how I'm going to be civil to her.'

Espie looked at Claire thoughtfully. 'You're very fond of him, aren't you?'

'Yeah.' Claire smiled. 'I am.'

'He's welcome to spend the night here, if you want him to, Claire. You do know that, don't you?'

'I know, Mum. But it's not like that.'

'You don't have to worry about my heart. I won't expire from the shock of it. Or cast you out for bringing shame on our house.'

Claire smiled. 'I know. But we're just friends, honestly.'

'Seems an awful waste to me.'

'Actually, there's someone else – well, potentially. He lives in London. I'm going over for a weekend soon – if that's all right with you.'

'Of course. I'll be fine. Where did you meet this one? Another "evening class"?'

'I know him online, from Twitter and stuff. And he was in Dublin a couple of weeks ago and we met up.'

'Truly, you are the darkest of horses,' Espie said, looking at her quizzically. 'Not a man in sight, and then, the minute I turn my back, they're swarming out of the woodwork. Maybe I should go into hospital more often.'

'Please, don't. If that's what it takes, I'd rather join a nunnery.'

'You'd make a lovely nun.' Her mother smiled mischievously.

'I'd lead a life of quiet contemplation and find solace in my books.'

'And reflect on your sins,' Espie said, passing the last pizza to Claire for topping. 'You'd better get started on doing some sinning first or you'll have nothing to reflect on and you'll be bored out of your tree.' She began to get up as the doorbell rang.

'I'll go,' Claire said, waving her mother back down.

'Hiya.' Luca grinned as she opened the door.

'You came!' She beamed.

'I told you I would, didn't I?' He stepped into the hall and gave her a peck on the cheek.

'I just thought you might change your mind.'

'Why would you think that?'

'Well, it's not exactly cool, spending Friday night hanging out with my mum and her friends.'

'Cool?' Luca rolled his eyes. 'I'm not sixteen,' he said, as he followed her into the kitchen.

'Luca! It's lovely to see you again, darling.'

The doorbell rang again. Espie picked up her crutches and went to answer it, waving away Claire's protests. She came back with Jim just as Claire was sliding the pizzas into the oven. A big bear of a man with a long grey ponytail, he was carrying a large pipes bag on one shoulder and a twelve-pack of beer in his arms. Jim was an old boyfriend of Espie's, but they were still very fond of each other. He had been around for as long as Claire could remember and she often wondered why they had split up. They would have made such a great couple.

'Claire!' Jim set the beer down on the table, shrugged the instrument bag onto the floor, and enveloped her in a hug. 'And who have we here?' he said, turning to Luca.

'This is Claire's friend, Luca,' Espie said.

'Very pleased to meet you, Luca,' he said, shaking his hand firmly. 'Do you play?'

'Play?'

'An instrument,' Espie explained. 'I forgot to ask you. We usually have a bit of music after cards.'

'Oh no. I'm not really musical at all.'

'You sing maybe?' Jim asked eagerly.

'Not really. Just in the shower, and Claire will tell you it's nothing to write home about,' he said, smiling at her.

Espie gave Claire a sharp look. 'Luca's an artist,' she told Jim, as proudly as if he was her own son.

'An artist?' Jim was clearly impressed. 'Well, isn't that wonderful?'

Claire broke open the beer carton and started putting bottles into the fridge. 'I'm just going to finish setting up inside,' she said, when she was done.

'I'll help,' Luca said, following her out of the kitchen.

'Why did you say that about the shower?' Claire hissed, as soon as they were out of earshot. She started laying out plates on the large round table. 'Here, put these around,' she said, handing Luca a packet of napkins.

'Sorry. I didn't realise it was a secret.'

'That we're sleeping together? Yeah, it kind of is.'

'Why? Are you ashamed of me?'

'No, of course not! But that doesn't mean it's something I want to discuss with my mum.'

'Your mum's cool. I'm sure she wouldn't mind.'

'Oh, she wouldn't. She was saying it was okay for you to spend the night here.'

'Really?' Luca paused in what he was doing and raised his eyebrows. 'So I have your mother's permission to have my wicked way with you under her roof?' he asked, with a crooked smile.

'But I said we were just friends, and I told her about Mark, and then you come in and say that—'

'Sorry.'

She sighed. 'It's all right.'

'We could be friends with benefits.'

'I suppose.' She knew her mother wouldn't bat an eyelid, and it would be handy if Luca could stay here sometimes. She took a handful of glasses from the sideboard and began putting them around. 'You don't have to stay for the music, by the way, if you don't want to.'

'I'd like to.'

'They're pretty good. Jim plays the uilleann pipes, and Mum plays the bodhrán. But feel free to leave any time, if you get bored.'

'So, what about you? Do you play any instrument?'

'Not really,' she said, blushing. 'I mean I do kind of join in the sessions sometimes, but it's not exactly an instrument...'

'Do you sing?'

'No.'

'What, then?'

'It's kind of embarrassing,' she said, wincing.

Luca grinned. 'Is it a comb and paper?'

'No! Though that's not far off.'

'Go on... tell me.'

'Spoons,' she mumbled. 'I play the spoons.'

Luca threw back his head and laughed. 'You play the spoons? Seriously?'

'Hey!' she said, punching his shoulder playfully. 'Jim taught me when I was a kid.'

'So is it just the spoons, or do you play any other kitchen implements? Garlic press? Cheese grater?'

'Okay, it's not a sexy instrument, I'll give you that.'

'It's not an instrument. It's cutlery.'

'Well, it's more than you can play.'

The doorbell was ringing as she finished setting the table. Espie led everyone into the sitting room and introduced them to Luca.

Lily was a stooped, white-haired lady with a kind, wrinkled face. 'Luca, I'll try to remember that,' she said, as she shook his hand. 'My memory's not what it used to be. Lady Gaga, that's me.'

It was a joke she had made many times before, but Espie, Claire and Jim laughed anyway.

Mary was next, a stout woman with a shock of wiry grey hair and a permanently harried expression, carrying a violin case. 'Lovely to meet you, Luca,' she said, as she took his hand in her gnarled, twisted fingers. 'I brought the fiddle,' she said, to Espie and Jim, 'but I don't know if I'll be able to play. The arthritis has been very bad this past week. But I'll give it a go and see how I get on.'

Espie's neighbours, Nancy and Michael, were carrying guitars. They had lived across the road from Espie since they had moved to Dublin from Cork almost twenty years ago.

Everyone dumped instrument cases and greeted each other before taking their places at the large round table. They were a motley collection of people, brought together at various stages by Espie, but they had forged strong friendships over the years, and Claire was touched by their joy in each other's company.

'So, we have new blood,' Jim said, rubbing his hands as he sat beside Luca.

'Do you know how to play forty-five, Luca?' Espie asked him.

'Haven't a clue.'

'Ah, not just new blood,' Jim said. 'Prey!'

'Don't worry, I won't let them fleece you,' Espie said.

'We only play for small change,' Claire said to Luca, as she sat beside him.

As the evening wore on, Claire kept them supplied with a steady supply of food and booze. It was good to see her mother enjoying herself, and she was glad that Luca seemed happy too. He was a big hit with the ladies, who fussed over him, plying him with pizza and cake, and telling him how handsome he was.

'It's good to have another man to swell the ranks,' Michael told him. 'We're sorely outnumbered, aren't we, Jim?'

'Aye. We're a dying breed,' Jim agreed.

'Well, women live longer,' Espie said, 'because we're tougher and lead exemplary lives. Speaking of which, you must come for my birthday next month, Luca. We're having a bit of a party.'

'Great! I'd love to.'

'I'll be sixty-nine, but I'm celebrating anyway.'

'So, where are you from, Luca?' Jim asked, during a lull, while they waited for Lily to play a card.

'I grew up here, in Dublin. I was adopted from Romania.'

'Romania? Were you in one of those awful orphanages?' Nancy asked, with a pitying expression.

'Yeah. I was in a couple, actually.'

Claire shot him an apologetic look and he gave her a little shrug, seemingly not bothered.

'Ah, that's terrible,' Jim said, clapping him on the shoulder. 'I'm sorry for that.'

'Have another piece of cake,' Mary said, sliding the plate across to him. 'Sure there isn't a pick on you.'

'They were desperate places, weren't they?' Michael shook his head sadly.

'It was no Disneyland,' Luca said.

'Shooting was too good for that bastard Ceaușescu and his wife,' Espie said.

'But you're here now,' Jim said consolingly, putting a hand over Luca's on the table. 'That's the main thing.'

'And you've got a great girl there,' Michael added, giving Claire a wink.

Claire squirmed, but Luca grinned as he took another huge slice of cake.

'It's still your turn, Lily,' Espie said, nudging her.

'What's trumps again?'

'Diamonds,' everyone chorused patiently.

* * *

'Do you have any songs of your people, Luca?' Michael asked later, as they all set up to play.

'He's from Dalkey,' Claire said.

'Sorry. I haven't been in Romania since I was seven. Anyway, I'm not a singer.'

'He only sings for Claire's benefit, apparently,' Espie said archly.

'Actually, do you have any paper?' Luca asked Claire.

'Sure.' She went across the hall to the room she used as a study and grabbed a sheaf of A4.

'Thanks,' he said, when she handed it to him, and produced a pencil from a pocket. 'Do you guys mind if I sketch you?' he asked, raising the pencil and paper.

'No, not at all,' Espie said, and everyone agreed.

Luca's fingers flew over the paper as they began to play, and Claire watched him, fascinated not only by his skill but by the way he seemed to capture the very essence of each person with just a few strokes. Soon the table was covered with sketches. 'They're really good,' he said, nodding at the shambolic group of musicians.

'They are.' They were all playing well, and Nancy and Jim, who took turns singing, both had beautiful voices.

The only discordant note was the violin, which constantly jarred on the ear as Mary kept hitting wrong notes. 'Sorry, that was brutal, wasn't it?' she said, when they had finished the first song. 'I can't seem to get my hands to do what I want them to do.'

'It was grand, Mary!' Jim said. 'We all know what you meant.'

'Maybe I should stop playing,' she fretted. 'I don't want to spoil it for everyone.'

'Don't be daft,' Espie said. 'It wouldn't be the same without you.'

'Oh well, if you're sure…' Newly emboldened, Mary scraped away for the rest of the evening, missing more notes than she hit, but clearly having a whale of a time.

* * *

'I take it all back,' Luca said later, when they were alone in the kitchen. 'Spoons is a very sexy instrument.' He pulled her into his arms and kissed her, one hand sliding up underneath her shirt to caress the bare skin of her back. 'I've missed you,' he said. 'It seems like ages since you've been in my bed.'

'I've missed you too.'

He bent to kiss her again, and Claire clung to him, kissing him back, her breathing becoming ragged.

'I won't be able to see you next week either,' she said. 'There's a book launch at the shop on Thursday, Mark's coming over on Saturday, and I don't want to leave Mum on her own too often.'

'Mark's coming over?' He frowned, releasing her.

'Just for the night.'

'But you're still sticking to your five-date rule?'

'Yeah. I still need more practice.'

'Okay. Good. Don't let him rush you into anything.'

'I won't,' she said, laughing at his grumpy expression and his over-protective attitude. If she didn't know better, she'd almost have thought he was jealous.

'Ready, Luca?' Jim said, appearing in the doorway. He had offered Luca a lift home.

'I'll see you the Saturday after next, then,' he said, as Claire saw them to the door. 'You're still coming to Ali's party with me?'

'Definitely. I'll pick you up.'

23

It's Different for Girls

The trouble with threesomes is that everyone wants the same thing, so no one gets what they want: paradoxical, but true. Try this – picture a threesome. What do you see? (I'll come back to you at the end of class.)

I've always found the idea of a threesome very exciting. In fact, it's a favourite fantasy of mine, and recently I found out that Mr Strange feels the same way. So, happy days, right? We both want the same thing. But what I see when I fantasise about a threesome is me and two members of the opposite sex, and I suspect it's the same for most people. So, probably not happy days.

Still, when Mr Strange started making noises about a threesome, I decided to give him the benefit of the doubt and asked exactly how he saw that panning out – just in case he'd surprise me, just on the off-chance that he'd be the tenth dentist – the one who recommends the regular toothpaste. Who would be the players in this three-way, I asked him.

Reader, I was not surprised. Sure enough – 'The two of us and another woman, of course,' he answered, quick as you like. Almost as if he'd given this some consideration. I got the feeling he thought I was worried that I wouldn't be one of the number. 'Of course you'd be there, babe,' he told me reassuringly. 'It wouldn't be the same without you.' Sweet.

I asked him to tell me about his fantasy threesome and he described it in detail – how I might be sucking his cock while this other girl sat on his face; how he would fuck me while she fingered his arse; how I and this player-to-be-named-later would team up to give him a blowjob, touching each other and putting on a show for him. It was a very erotic fantasy, and he got hard talking about it. He touched me as he spoke, and we both got very turned on.

It was such an exciting fantasy for him that I wanted him to have it. I told him I would do it – but only if he could reciprocate.

'What do you mean, "reciprocate"?' he asked. He already wanted to say yes to whatever I wanted, I could tell – he was so eager to make this happen. I wondered if he already had another girl picked out – if the player-to-be-named-later had in fact been named already.

So I told him I would do his fantasy threesome with him if he would do mine. I started describing it to him in detail, like he had – how he might hold me from behind, fondling my breasts while he watched the other guy go down on me—

I didn't get any further. 'Hang on,' he said. 'You think about having a threesome with two guys?'

'Yeah – of course,' I told him. 'Same as you. I fantasise about being double-teamed by two members of the opposite sex.'

While his mouth was flapping open, I continued to tell him my fantasy – how he would whisper things in my ear as he held me, dirty things that would make me wet. The guy with his mouth on me would tell Strange how turned on I was. When my body started to thrash and convulse with orgasm, Strange would restrain me, pushing me back to the bed and holding me down, so I couldn't escape the biting pleasure, and I would cry out at the intensity of it. He would hush me, whispering soothing things in my ear while I came and came. And then I would have their cocks in me – first one and then the other, in my cunt, in my mouth.

I told him the whole fantasy with many variations. It made me very wet telling it, and I could tell he was excited too, by the thought of me with two guys – watching me get fucked, seeing me suck someone else off. He kissed me and touched me as I spoke, and we ended up fucking for a very long time. When I came and my body bowed off the bed, he pushed me back down and held me there, as if remembering something I had said.

'That was very hot, listening to your fantasy,' he said later.

'So, do you still want to do a threesome?' I asked.

'Us and another woman? Hell, yeah.'

'But not us and another man? You just said it was hot. It obviously turned you on.'

'Yeah, listening to you talking about it. But I couldn't do it. I just couldn't be with a guy.'

'Why not?'

'Because I'm not gay!' he finally shouted, as if it was obvious.

'But neither am I, Strange.'

Neither am I.

He tried to tell me that it was different for girls. He said women's bodies are softer, more beautiful, more desirable. They just are, according to him – it's not subjective. He started talking about girls' boarding schools, pillow fights…

'That's a male fantasy,' I told him. 'I've never been to boarding school.'

I tried to convince him that I didn't want to be with a woman any more than he wanted to be with a man, but he didn't get it. I blame porn. I blame Madonna and Britney. And Katie Perry. No wonder men think straight women should be up for a little girl-on-girl action. All it takes is daring, or a bit of persuasion, and next thing you know, there you are, kissing a girl and liking it.

So I don't think Strange and I will be having a threesome any time soon. Because we both want the same thing: to be double-teamed by two members of the opposite sex.

(So, what did you see? You and two members of the opposite sex, right? Well, a girl can dream.)

On Thursday evening, Bookends was packed for the launch of Rosy Sinnott's debut novel. Tom and Claire were kept busy manning the till and bagging books, while Yvonne poured wine and sparkling water.

'Have you read it?' Tom asked Claire, nodding to the stacks of Rosy's book that were piled up beside the till.

'Yes – I thought it was brilliant. You?'

'Same.' Rosy's novel was already being called the literary debut of the year, receiving rave reviews in the press.

'Ooh, I need one of those,' Rosy said, approaching the counter and pointing to the tray of drinks.

'Help yourself,' Yvonne said, and Rosy took a glass of white wine.

'Well done, Rosy,' Tom said to her. 'You've got a great turnout. I loved the book.'

'Oh, thank you, Tom. That means a lot.'

'Congratulations,' Claire said to her, as Tom turned away to serve a customer. 'I hope it's a great success.'

'Thanks. This is so exciting,' she said, looking around at the guests, the big displays of her book, and the posters of the cover. 'Nerve-racking, but exciting.'

'I'm really pleased for you, Rosy. The book is brilliant – you deserve it.'

'I still can't believe it! It's just so amazing to see my name on a real book.' She took a slug of her wine. 'I really hope you'll be next, Claire.'

'Me too,' Claire said, with a wistful smile. Rosy knew she was a writer. Their paths had crossed several times at writing and publishing events.

'Excuse me.' Rosy's editor approached, touching Rosy's elbow. 'Sorry to interrupt,' she said to Claire, 'but I think we should start the speeches now, okay?'

'Sure,' Rosy said, putting down her glass. 'We'll talk later,' she said to Claire, as her editor led her to the lectern they had set up in a corner of the shop.

Claire had always felt a twinge of envy at events like this, and now, even though she had a publishing deal, she still felt a little jealous of Rosy as her editor made a glowing speech about the book. She wondered if she would ever have a night like this, and imagined Mark making a speech about her, telling everyone what a wonderful writer she was, what a great book she had written. As thrilled as she was that he was publishing the blog book, it would be amazing to have a book published that she could actually put her name to – one she could tell her family and friends about, something that would make her mother proud.

She needed to make more time to work on her novel. She had been neglecting it lately, preoccupied with looking after her mother, seeing Luca and writing her blog. But she wanted to get it into shape so she could let Mark read it. It was another reason why it was the right time to wind up the blog – it would free her to work on her novel. Because this was what she wanted, she thought, as Rosy was introduced and took the microphone. She wanted to be standing where Rosy was some day, and she had to do everything in her power to make that happen.

* * *

On Saturday Claire got ready to go out for her third date with Mark. He had flown into Dublin in the afternoon and she was meeting him for dinner at a restaurant close to the Merrion Hotel, where he was staying. It was a pity that he didn't have more time, but he had just managed to squeeze in a quick visit between a friend's stag in London last night and travelling to Edinburgh tomorrow for a christening. She was flattered that he had made such an effort just to spend a few hours with her.

'You look lovely,' her mother said, when she came downstairs.

'Thanks.' She had bought a new dress especially for the occasion. 'I won't be late,' she said.

'Be as late as you like,' Espie said. 'Don't worry, I won't be waiting up for you.' She was sitting at the kitchen table, but Claire noticed that she sounded breathless, and there was a slight tremor in her voice as she spoke.

'Mum, are you okay?' Claire asked, crossing to her and peering into her face.

'I'm fine,' Espie said, but there was a definite wheeze in her voice that struck fear into Claire's heart.

'You don't sound too good.' She sat at the table, putting a hand over her mother's. 'Maybe I shouldn't go out.'

'Don't be daft. I just overdid it a bit today.' Nancy and Michael had taken her to the Japanese Gardens in Kildare. 'It's probably all the fresh air, making me tired. I'll take it easy for the night and I'll be fine.'

'I can easily cancel. Mark won't mind.'

'After coming all the way over from London just to see you? You are *not* cancelling on him.'

Claire thought. Maybe she could ask someone to come over. Neil and Michelle never went out on a Saturday. Maybe one of them could—

'And before you even think it,' Espie said, 'you are not setting Michelle on me. I'll be grand. If the worst comes to the worst, I have the panic button.' She pointed to the medical-emergency necklace she always wore.

'Call me before it comes to that.'

'I will. But I'm feeling better already,' she said, and her voice did sound stronger. 'Go on, you're not getting out of your date that easily, my girl.'

'Okay. But promise you'll call me if you feel at all wobbly.'

'I promise.' Espie patted her hand. 'Now go – enjoy yourself, and stay out as late as you want to. Don't come home at all, if you like.'

'Mum! I *will* be home.'

* * *

'It's so lovely to see you,' Claire said to Mark, as they were seated in the restaurant. 'I can't believe you came over just for one night.'

'You're worth it.' His eyes glittered as he gazed at her. 'You look gorgeous.'

'Thanks.' Claire blushed. 'So do you,' she said shyly. If she wasn't worried about her mother, she would have gone to his hotel room with him tonight if he'd asked her. She wanted badly to kiss him, and she could have made out with him without worrying that he would expect sex. It probably wasn't helping that she hadn't seen Luca all week. Maybe in future she should have a session with him to take the edge off before going out with Mark – like eating before going to a party.

But, as it was, she would be going straight home. She was finding it hard to relax. She had placed her phone on the table. She didn't normally do that as she considered it rude, but she didn't want to risk missing a call from her mother.

'I read your latest blog post,' Mark was saying. Claire detected a slight hesitancy in his tone that made her wary.

'Oh?'

'Yeah. I must admit, I was kind of...'

'You didn't like it?' she asked anxiously.

'No, I enjoyed it. I was just a bit... disappointed, I suppose.'

'Disappointed?' Oh, crap! Did he like threesomes? Had he thought she'd be up for that? It wouldn't really be surprising, considering some of the things she'd written about. Thank goodness she hadn't said she was into them. 'You – you like threesomes?' she asked, trying hard to sound blasé about it.

'No!' he gasped, laughing. 'Christ, no – not at all. I mean, not that I've ever—'

'Yeah, me either.' Then she remembered she had written about having enjoyed group sex, and she blushed.

'So, was it the writing?' she asked. She was so relieved that it wasn't the threesome thing that she didn't even mind. 'We wouldn't have to include that one in the book.'

'No, the writing was fine – I really liked it. I was just...' He hesitated. Then he sighed and said, 'It's silly, but – I just thought I might get a mention.'

'Oh!' It had never occurred to her that he would expect her to write about him, but of course it made sense. He thought she was writing about real people all the time.

'Sorry, I know it's stupid.' He shifted awkwardly, glancing away. 'I mean, we haven't even got to the fifth date yet.'

'Well, you know all the people I write about on my blog aren't necessarily real.'

'I know, but... the Artist is real, and I know you're seeing him at the moment. So I thought...'

'Oh.' The realisation that he was jealous took Claire by surprise. It had never occurred to her that he might be. 'It's different with you—' She stopped, not sure how to explain why it was different. She couldn't tell him he was the only real person she'd ever be writing about – apart from Luca. But she wanted him to understand because she couldn't see herself ever writing about him, even after they'd started sleeping together.

'How so?' he asked.

'Well... for one thing, because you know about the blog,' she said, finding her excuse. 'Those other guys didn't, so I knew they wouldn't read it – or if they did by some chance come across it, they wouldn't know it was me writing it. I'm not anonymous with you, and I'd feel weird writing about you when I know you're going to be reading it.'

'I can understand that,' he said. Then he tilted his head to the side, considering. 'I tend to forget how different you are from your alter ego.'

Not for the first time, she hoped he didn't find her a disappointment compared to the ballsy NiceGirl. 'It's easier to be upfront online,' she said. 'Especially when no one knows who you are.'

'You said "for one thing". Was there another?'

Claire took a deep breath. It was time to be honest with him – at least partly. 'Well, because I feel like we – what we have – it's different from anything I've had before. I think it could be... more. I mean, I'd like it to be more.' She held her breath as she waited for his reaction, afraid she might have blown it.

'I'd like that too,' he said easily, and Claire exhaled. She should have known Mark wouldn't be scared off. She had been spending too much time around Luca. She was starting to expect all men to be commitment-phobes.

Their eyes locked and his expression changed to something more intense.

He was the first to look away. 'About that,' he said, fiddling with his coffee spoon. 'I'm not seeing anyone else, and if we're going to do this...'

'Oh! Yes.' Claire blushed. 'I see what you mean.'

'I know it's difficult in a long-distance relationship, and maybe I'm not as evolved as I should be but, like I said, I'm not good at sharing.'

'No, I feel the same. I wouldn't want to see anyone else either. I mean, I'm not really seeing anyone now—'

'Except the Artist?'

'Well, yes. But that's – it's a limited-time thing. It'll be over soon.'

'Really?' He seemed pleased.

'Yes. It'll definitely be finished by the time we have our fifth date.'

Claire had tried to ignore her phone over dinner and give her full attention to Mark, but she jumped now when she heard her ringtone. She was relieved to realise it was coming from the next table. But it put her on edge, and she glanced anxiously at her phone throughout the rest of the meal. The problem was, she knew her mother didn't want to be a burden and 'put a stop to her gallop', as she would have said, so she didn't really trust her to call, except in the most dire circumstances, and she was worried she would leave it too late.

'Is everything okay?' Mark asked, as their plates were cleared away. 'You seem a bit agitated.'

'Sorry. It's just – I'm worried about Mum. She seemed a bit under the weather this evening. Actually, I was going to cancel—'

'God, you should have said.'

'She insisted she was fine and I should go out, but... Sorry, do you mind if we cut this short? I can't relax.'

'No, of course not.' Mark was already signalling to a waiter for the bill.

'I feel awful,' Claire said apologetically, though at the same time she was relieved. 'When you've come all this way and you're just here for one night...'

'It's fine, honestly.' Mark placed a wad of notes in the leather folder and told the waiter to keep the change. Then they got up to go.

'You can come back with me for coffee, if you like,' Claire told him, as they left the restaurant.

'I can?'

'My mother will be there, obviously.'

'Well, as long as she wouldn't mind…'

'No! Not at all – she'd love it. I just thought I should warn you…'

'No hanky-panky?'

Claire laughed. 'That wasn't what I meant. I just don't want you to feel like I'm bringing you home to meet my mother. We just happen to live together.'

'I'd love to meet your mother,' Mark said. 'And I'd like to have more time with you.'

Claire briefed him in the taxi. 'My mother doesn't know anything about my blog or the book deal. As far as she's concerned, you're someone I met on the internet – which is true, if you think about it.'

'Okay.'

'And don't let her know we came back because I was worried.'

'No, of course not.'

Claire touched his hand. 'Thank you for doing this.'

'No problem.' He gripped her fingers and she smiled at him gratefully.

* * *

The lights were still on downstairs when they arrived at the house. 'You're home early,' her mother called from the living room, over the sound of the TV, as they stepped into the hall.

'Hi.' Claire stuck her head around the door. 'We decided to come back here for coffee.'

'Oh!' Espie sat up, turning off the TV with the remote.

'Mum, this is Mark,' she said, as he followed her into the room. 'Mark, this is my mum.'

'Hello,' he said, shaking her hand. 'Pleased to meet you, Mrs Kennedy.'

'Call me Espie.' She smiled at him. 'Sit down,' she said, patting the sofa beside her.

'Espie – that's a nice name,' Mark said, as he sank into the sofa. 'Very unusual.'

'It's short for Esperanza.'

'Oh, like Oscar Wilde's mother? Wasn't that her name?'

'Close,' Espie said. 'She was Speranza. But that was just her pen name.'

'Oh yes.'

'It's lovely to meet you, Mark, but I hope you didn't come home early on my account,' she said, narrowing her eyes at Claire suspiciously.

'No, we just thought it would be nice to have coffee here,' Claire said innocently. 'I'll put the kettle on.'

'Well, don't count me in,' Espie said, getting up. 'I'm going to bed.'

'Are you sure?'

'Yes, I was about to go anyway when you came in. Night, love,' she said to Claire. 'Bye, Mark. I'm sure we'll meet again some time.'

'Yes, I hope so. Goodnight.'

'So – coffee?' Claire said to Mark, when they were alone. 'Or would you like another glass of wine?'

He leant back against the sofa, looking at her speculatively. 'Come here,' he said, patting the sofa beside him. His eyes were hooded and heavy.

Claire sat beside him and he put an arm around her. 'I'm glad your mother's okay,' he said.

'Sorry we had to leave early.'

'That's okay.'

He nuzzled her face, and then they were kissing – long, slow kisses at first, but then it became urgent and grabby and they were lying face to face on the sofa making out like teenagers while Claire's mother slept upstairs.

'Claire,' Mark panted into her mouth, as she pulled his shirt out of his waistband, 'can I ask you something?'

'Mm.' Her fingers wriggled underneath to touch hard, warm flesh.

'Do you ever break the rules?' He lifted her leg to hitch it across his, and Claire gasped as she felt his erection against her.

'Sometimes.' She wanted nothing more right now than to forget about the five-date rule and have Mark inside her, right here on the living-room sofa. But she wasn't ready for that yet. 'But never my own rules,' she said.

Mark stilled, leaning his forehead against hers, his breath hot on her face.

'I think I'd better get a cab, then.' His weight lifted off her and he sat up, running a hand through his hair.

Claire struggled upright beside him, adjusting her clothing. 'I'll call one for you.'

They kissed at the door when the taxi arrived, then Claire went up the stairs to bed. She couldn't wait for the fifth date. But in the meantime, she thought, opening the drawer in her nightstand, this would be a good time to get in some practice with her vibrator.

24

'Ooh, you look very fancy, Luca,' Jula said, as he emerged from the house the following Saturday. It had been a beautiful day, and Jula and Danuta, the thin, almost translucently pale Polish girls who shared the basement flat, were sitting on the front steps enjoying the last of the evening sunshine and sharing a bottle of wine.

'Where are you going? Big date?'

'Party.' He sat down on the step above them, placing his gift-wrapped parcel beside him. 'It's my sister's birthday.' He tilted his face towards the sun and closed his eyes, trying to relax. There was still warmth in the evening air.

'You want a glass of wine?' Danuta asked. He opened his eyes to find her waving the bottle at him.

'No, thanks,' he said, glancing at his watch. 'Claire will be picking me up in a few minutes.' It was still only seven fifteen, but he had been ready far too early, and he had become increasingly twitchy and anxious as he waited for her. When he couldn't handle any more antsy pacing around his flat, he'd decided to come down and wait outside.

'Ah, your girlfriend?' Jula smiled. 'She's pretty.'

Luca smiled. 'Yeah, she is pretty. But she's not my girlfriend.'

Jula and Danuta shared knowing smiles, but said nothing, and went back to their conversation.

Luca checked his watch again, but only a minute had passed. It was ridiculous how nervous he felt, but he really didn't want to go to his parents' house. He wouldn't do it for anyone but Ali. Still, for her sake, he would grit his teeth and endure it. He would even try to be pleasant and play the part of the loving and beloved son. As if he knew fuck all about that!

At least Claire would be with him, he thought. It wouldn't be so bad with her there. In a way, he was almost looking forward to it. He liked the idea of his mother seeing him with Claire, this lovely, kind, decent girl who cared about him – even if it was just as a friend, and her heart belonged to Mr Perfect. Childishly, he thought he could prove Jacqueline wrong, demonstrate to her that he *was* lovable, with Claire as his evidence. He knew it was twisted, but he wanted to point up his mother's inadequacies by flaunting Claire in front of her, so that she would finally realise that 'It's not you, it's me.'

Claire pulled up almost on the dot of seven thirty.

'Goodnight, girls,' Luca said to his neighbours, grabbing his parcel as he jumped up. He bounded over to the car. 'Hello, gorgeous.' He smiled at Claire as he slid in beside her.

'Hi.' She turned to him. 'You look lovely.'

'So do you.' He leant in and kissed her cheek. She smelt amazing. 'I wish we could blow out this party and just drive off somewhere together,' he said, on an impulse.

'You couldn't do that to Ali. She'd be so disappointed.'

'I know. I wouldn't. But I'm really glad you're coming.'

'Well, I'm the one with the car and the beer money,' she quipped. Then she blushed. 'Sorry, that sounded awful. I didn't mean—'

'I know.' He wasn't offended. He knew she'd only said it because she couldn't take a compliment and laughing it off was a reflex with her. 'Anyway, it's free booze. But I don't think I could face it on my own,' he said seriously, taking her hand. 'So thank you.' He kissed her knuckles.

'You're welcome,' she said, and he was glad that for once she had simply accepted that he was happy to have her with him.

'Okay,' she said, starting the engine. 'I think I know my way to Dalkey village, but you'll have to give me directions from there.'

* * *

Claire usually avoided routes she didn't know well, and she hadn't driven to Dalkey very often. It wasn't helping her concentration that Luca was fidgety and restless, constantly shifting around in his seat, tapping his fingers on the dash or jiggling his legs. She tried to ignore him and focus on where she was going.

'It's so beautiful out here,' she said, as they drove along the coast road, glancing at the perfect blue sea dotted with coloured sails. Summer had arrived at the beginning of June and seemed set to stay, with unbroken sunshine and soaring temperatures. Everywhere people were out enjoying the weather, playing games, strolling along with ice-creams, or sitting outside bars and restaurants under bright awnings, their high-spirited chatter and laughter drifting through the car window.

'Mm,' Luca agreed distractedly, seeming oblivious to his surroundings. 'We're almost there. Turn right here.' He pointed to a narrow road climbing away from the seafront and directed her along a hilly, twisting road lined with massive gated houses. 'This is it,' he said, indicating a set of wrought-iron gates standing open to the left. The tree-lined gravel drive sloped towards the sea, turned right and opened out onto a paved area to the side of a tall double-fronted house.

'Wow!' Claire breathed, as she parked beside a black BMW. She couldn't believe this was where Luca had grown up. 'This is an amazing house,' she said, peeping at him warily. He had gone very quiet.

He shrugged in reply and removed his seatbelt, but made no move to open his door. His agitation seemed to have been replaced by gloom, and she sensed he was reluctant to get out. She touched his leg, giving him a reassuring smile.

'Right, let's get this over with,' he said, opening his door.

As Claire stepped out onto the drive, the sound of the waves on one side mingled with the buzz of the party on the other. The location was stunning. The house clung to the cliff, nothing between it and the broad sweep of Killiney Bay, breathtakingly beautiful panoramic views spreading out in every direction. She went to the low stone wall at the edge of the garden and looked down to the beach at the bottom of the cliff, where foamy white waves crashed against the rocks. She turned back to the house, which was fronted by a terraced garden dotted with tiled benches, flowerbeds and quirky sculptures, and planted with an abundance of shrubs. Lanterns hung in the trees, and the deck around a large sunroom was strung with fairy lights.

Luca grabbed her hand, holding it so tightly it was almost painful as he led her towards the house.

'Luca and Claire are here,' Ali called over her shoulder, as she came barrelling down the steps that led to the front door. She threw her arms around Luca, and the tension seemed to leave his body, his grip on Claire's hand relaxing.

'Happy birthday, Ali,' he said, kissing her cheek.

Ali released him and hugged Claire. 'Thank you so much for coming. It's lovely to have you here – both of you.'

'Thanks for inviting me,' Claire said. 'Happy birthday!'

'Come and meet Mum and Dad,' Ali said, leading the way to the house.

Luca's hand tightened around Claire's again as they followed Ali up the steps to the open front door. They stepped into a high-ceilinged hall with a wooden floor. A large vase of tall white lilies on an elegant side table perfumed the air. Claire recognised the slim blonde woman who came to meet them from her author photo.

'Why don't you do the introductions?' Ali said to Luca. 'I have to check on the caterers.' She skipped off through a side door.

'Claire, this is my – this is Jacqueline,' Luca said, as he drew her forward. Claire noticed Jacqueline's hastily disguised wince at his use of her name. 'Jacqueline, this is Claire.'

'It's lovely to meet you, Claire.' Jacqueline smiled as she extended her hand.

'Nice to meet you too,' Claire said stiffly, as they shook. She felt Jacqueline scrutinising her closely, as if she was trying to figure something out.

'I wish I could say I've heard a lot about you,' she said, 'but I'm afraid it's not true.'

'There's not much to tell,' Claire said, blushing. 'We're not really—'

'We haven't been together very long,' Luca interrupted, putting an arm around her waist and pulling her into his side.

Claire smiled helplessly, feeling wrong-footed.

'This is my husband, Jonathan,' Jacqueline said, as a tall, lean man joined them in the hall. Grey-haired and handsome, he was considerably older than his wife. 'Jonathan, this is Luca's... friend, Claire.'

'Pleased to meet you,' he said, as he shook her hand, eyeing her as curiously as his wife had done. 'Hey, Luca,' he said, pulling him into a hug.

'Why don't you take Claire upstairs, Luca, and show her where everything is?' Jacqueline said. 'We're putting jackets in your old bedroom. Then come down and join everyone in the sunroom.'

* * *

Upstairs, Luca showed Claire into his room. While she ducked into the ensuite to fix her hair and makeup, he went to the window and stared out at the sea. He wished he could have brought Claire here and shown her all this as something that was a part of him, somewhere he belonged – the beautiful house, his clever, talented family and the lovely life they led. But it was nothing to do with him. He felt as much a guest as she was – just as welcome, just as superfluous, every bit as much of an outsider. It highlighted how little he had to offer on his own account, and it struck him how bare and bleak his life must seem to her, how rich hers was by comparison – not just materially, but in people who cared about her and would always be there for her.

He was beginning to regret insisting she come. He didn't like who he was around Jacqueline and he didn't want Claire to see him like that – so cold and churlish, so ungrateful to the woman who had rescued him. He knew he owed her everything, and he had tried to make allowances and forgive her – not for not loving him, that wasn't her fault: there hadn't been much to love in the cold, scarred, battle-wounded boy she had brought home and, anyway, love wasn't a decision you could make. But he did blame her for writing that book. It wasn't because it came as a surprise to him that he was unloved, but until then it had been their secret, and keeping it was something they had done together. They'd worked as a team, the magician and her little accomplice – some sleight of hand here, a bit of misdirection there, and, ta-da! No one was the wiser. Until the day she broke faith with him and let everyone see behind the curtain, exposing him as the graceless impostor he really was.

'This is an amazing house,' Claire said, as she emerged from the bathroom. 'Your parents must be loaded.'

'They're pretty well-off. Jonathan's a surgeon, and Jacqueline's a very successful journalist. So…'

'Wow.' She was looking troubled, probably wondering why his parents didn't help him out when they were so wealthy.

'And what about Ali?'

'Ali has her trust fund. She has plenty of money of her own.'

'Oh!'

'They did the same for me,' he told her. 'I got money when I was twenty-one, same as Ali.'

'What happened to it?'

He affected nonchalance. 'I burnt through it pretty quickly. I spent most of it on drugs and generally getting wrecked.'

He waited for her reaction, but she didn't say anything. She didn't seem shocked or disapproving, just looked at him calmly, accepting what he was saying without comment or judgement.

'They were pretty decent about it,' he continued. 'Obviously they couldn't keep giving me money to squander on drugs so they cut me off, but they paid to send me to a pretty high-end rehab. And they made it clear I was welcome to move back here once I'd sorted myself out.'

'But you didn't?'

'No. I'd leeched off them long enough. Rehab was all about standing on your own two feet. I thought I should try that for a while.'

'Good for you!'

It killed him that she actually looked proud of him. 'Well, I'm not making much of a go of it.' He gave a self-deprecating laugh. 'I'm not exactly the poster child for turning your life around. You've seen where I live.'

'But you're standing on your own two feet. You're not relying on anyone else for handouts when you could easily have moved back here and continued to take money from your parents. And you've got off drugs and stayed clean. I think that's pretty admirable.'

'Less admirable than not getting fucked up in the first place.'

'I'm not so sure.'

He smiled. He knew he didn't deserve her faith in him, but it felt good having it. 'Come on,' he said, taking her hand. 'We should find Ali and give her her presents.'

* * *

Downstairs, Luca led Claire into the large sunroom. Decorated in creams and greens, filled with plants and overlooking the sea on three sides, it felt like an extension of the garden. The walls were strung with fairy lights, and a long table in the centre of the room was set for dinner, with little vases of flowers dotted along the centre, the coloured glasses and floral tablecloth giving it a light, summery feel. The doors were thrown open, and guests were milling around on the deck overlooking the garden.

'This is gorgeous!' Claire gasped.

'Where have you two been?' Ali rushed up to them. 'I probably shouldn't ask,' she continued, without waiting for an answer. 'Come and have a drink.' She linked Claire's arm and led them to a table covered with ice buckets containing champagne, where Jacqueline and Jonathan were distributing drinks.

Jonathan picked up a bottle as they approached and poured a glass, handing it to Claire.

'Oh, thanks, but I'm driving,' she said. 'You have this.' She passed it to Luca, and Jacqueline frowned as he took it from her. 'I'll just have a mineral water, please.'

'Oh no!' Ali exclaimed. 'You should have come in a taxi. Everyone should have champagne for my birthday.' She pouted prettily.

'You could have one glass,' Jonathan said. 'You're allowed one, and it'll be well out of your system by the time you leave anyway.'

'And we'll be eating too,' Jacqueline added.

'Okay, thanks.' Claire smiled. Jonathan poured another glass and handed it to her.

'You should stay the night,' Ali said. 'Then you could drink as much as you like.'

'Yes, why don't you?' Jacqueline said. 'Luca's room is ready.'

'I don't mind not drinking,' Claire said, glancing at Luca. She wasn't sure how he would feel about staying over. She knew it was upsetting for him being there, and she didn't want to make it any worse.

'You need to get back early in the morning, don't you?' he said to her.

'Yes!' she said, glad he had given her an indication of what he wanted to do.

'Well, she can drive home in the morning from here, can't she?' Ali said. 'We're not in Outer Mongolia.'

'Might as well be for all he visits,' Jacqueline muttered, under her breath.

'I really should get home tonight,' Claire said apologetically, to Ali.

'So, how did you two meet?' Jacqueline asked.

'Claire works with Yvonne Redmond,' Luca said. 'We met through her.'

'Oh, and where do you work?'

'In a bookshop,' Claire said.

'Which one?' Jonathan asked.

'Bookends. Do you know it?'

'Yes, it's a great shop.'

'How long have you been there?' Jacqueline asked.

'Um... almost four years now.'

'And Ali tells us you live in Ranelagh?'

'Yes. I live in the house I grew up in – with my mother.'

'With your mother?'

'Yes, she's – well, she's a bit incapacitated, and she has a heart condition, so she needs someone there.'

Claire was starting to feel uncomfortable under Jacqueline's intense scrutiny and incessant questioning.

'Have you always lived at home, then?'

'No, I went to university in Edinburgh.'

'And what did you study?'

'English literature.' This was beginning to feel like a job interview.

'You'll have to forgive Mum,' Ali said, smiling indulgently at her mother. 'She doesn't usually give people the third degree, but it's the first time Luca's brought a girlfriend home.'

'Oh, I'm not—'

'Yes, you're a first,' Luca said, smiling fondly at her as he put an arm around her waist. She didn't understand why, but for some reason Luca obviously wanted his mother to think they were a couple. So she put an arm around him and smiled back at him, gratified when she felt him relax beside her.

'Yes, well, I must admit I was quite surprised when Ali told me Luca was bringing someone,' Jacqueline said to Claire. 'I'm sorry if I'm being rude—'

'It's fine,' Claire hastened to assure her.

'But it's really lovely to have you here, Claire,' she said, once more giving

Claire that look, as if she was a complicated puzzle. 'I must say, you're not at all what I expected.'

'Oh.' Claire tried not to let her expression falter, but she felt hurt by Jacqueline's remark, taking it to mean she found her a disappointment.

'Stop that,' Luca whispered to her, frowning at her sternly, as if he knew what she was thinking. 'She means she thinks you're too good for me,' he said, in a louder voice. 'Don't you, Jacqueline?'

'No, of course not,' Jacqueline snapped. 'Please don't do this today, Luca.'

'What did you expect?' he asked his mother, his lip curling in a sneer. 'Some skank or junkie? Someone more suitable for a scumbag like me?'

'Of course not!'

'Luca, please,' Ali whispered, her eyes darting between her mother and brother.

'Sorry, Ali.'

Claire felt his body slump against her, the fight seeming to go out of him. He took a swig of champagne.

'You're drinking,' Jacqueline said tightly, her eyes frosty as they focused on his glass.

'Jesus!' Luca swore under his breath. 'Yeah, I'm drinking. So what? So are you.'

'Yes, but I'm not—'

'Neither am I!' he roared.

'You have a problem, Luca,' Jacqueline hissed. 'And the sooner you face up to it, the better. You can't drink in moderation, so—'

'That's not true,' Claire said. 'I've never seen Luca drunk.' Now that she thought about it, she'd never seen him drink more than a beer or two, or a couple of glasses of wine at the most. 'I've never seen him even slightly tipsy.'

'Well, lucky you. I hope you never have to. But he's put us through hell—'

'I think you've got that the wrong way around,' Claire said quietly.

'I beg your pardon?' Jacqueline said haughtily. 'I don't know what he's told you but—'

'He didn't have to tell me anything,' Claire said, wishing her voice wasn't trembling. 'It's all in the public domain. You put it there.'

'Oh God!' Jacqueline rolled her eyes. 'Not the book again!'

'Leave it, Claire,' Luca said quietly to her. 'It doesn't matter.'

'Of course it *matters*!' She turned to Jacqueline. 'Luca is one of the kindest, sweetest, most lovable people I've ever met, and if you can't see that, then it's your loss.' Not sure what to do after delivering her speech, she put down her glass, turned on her heel and made for the door.

'Claire!' she heard Luca call after her, as she bolted outside and down the steps into the garden.

She ran to the wall that edged the cliff, shaking and on the verge of tears. Oh God, what had got into her? She hated rows and she was useless at confrontation. She couldn't believe she'd spoken to Luca's mother like that – and in the middle of Ali's party. It was a horrible thing to do, she thought, as she swiped away tears with the back of her hand. How could she face any of them again? She just wanted to run away. Maybe she could hide in her car until it was time to leave. She felt she should go back and apologise, but she hadn't really said anything she was sorry for. She'd said that Luca was sweet and lovable, and she wouldn't take that back. She'd said he didn't drink much, which was true. Oh, yeah – and she'd accused his mother of putting him through hell. That was rude, but she still wasn't sure she regretted it. However, she should at least apologise to Ali for causing a scene at her party. She genuinely felt bad about that.

'Claire!' She turned to see Luca hurtling down the steps towards her.

'God, I'm so sorry,' she said, when he reached her.

'Hey, it's okay,' he said, pulling her into his arms. 'Don't be upset. I shouldn't have brought you here. I'm sorry.' He took her to one of the seats and sat her down beside him.

'What must Ali think of me, behaving like that at her party? I have to apologise to her.'

'Don't worry about it. She's used to me and Jacqueline kicking off.'

'That's different – you're family. You're allowed. It just got to me, the things she was saying about you. It's not fair.'

'But it's true what she said. Except the bit about not being able to control my drinking. Jacqueline has very black-and-white ideas about drug use. She doesn't understand that I can drink normally. But I can.'

'I know.'

'I'm not going to turn into some Dr Jekyll type after a couple of drinks. Or do I mean Mr Hyde? Anyway, whichever was the scary one.'

'Mr Hyde.'

'Right. I was never a very committed druggie in the first place, and I don't have a drink problem. But the rest...' He sighed. 'Jacqueline knows me a lot better than you do. It was sweet of you to say those things about me, but they're not true. I'm not a very nice person. And I did put them through hell. I was out of control when I was younger – doing drugs, always getting into fights...'

'It's understandable you were a bit messed up.'

'Because I decided to be. I did it deliberately to get back at her. I went looking for trouble, and if I couldn't find it, I made it. I wanted to make her life a misery.'

'I still don't think that means you were bad – just unhappy and troubled. And, anyway, you've changed now.'

'Maybe,' he said. 'Anyway, just forget about it and come back inside. We still haven't given Ali her presents.'

'I don't think I can face any of them again – especially not Ali. I could really use a drink, though.'

'Wait here, then. I'll get you one.'

She watched as he bounded up the steps to the deck. He passed Ali on the way and spoke to her, waving in Claire's direction before continuing into the house. Ali came over to her, carrying a bottle of champagne as well as her own glass.

'Are you okay?' she asked, sitting down beside Claire and setting the bottle on the ground.

'I'm so sorry, Ali. I don't know what got into me.'

Ali held up a hand, stopping her. 'Don't worry about it. Believe me, I'm used to a bit of drama whenever Mum and Luca have to share the same space. To be honest, I think it's lovely that he has someone on his side. I'm always caught in the middle between him and Mum, and then I feel bad that I don't stick up for him more.' She smiled and took a sip of champagne. 'He really doesn't have a drink problem. She's wrong about that.'

'I know.'

'I'm glad he's got you, Claire. I don't think I've ever seen him so happy.'

'Oh, but we're not—'

'Yeah, yeah – whatever. I don't know why you're both so keen to keep it a big secret.' She gasped, clutching Claire's arm. 'You're not married, are you?'

Claire laughed. 'No!' She debated whether she should tell Ali that there was someone else, but Mark wasn't her boyfriend – at least, not yet. Besides, she'd upset Ali enough for one night.

'Phew! Thank goodness for that. I might have had to challenge you to a duel or something if I found out you were messing my brother around.'

Luca returned with a couple of glasses and Ali's present, and sat down on Claire's other side. 'All okay now?' he asked, handing Claire a glass and picking up the bottle of champagne.

Claire nodded.

'Why don't you stay the night?' Ali said to Claire. 'Then you could relax and have a proper drink.'

'We could leave first thing in the morning,' Luca added.

'I doubt your mother would want me spending the night here after that performance.'

'You're *my* guest,' Ali said. 'I'm inviting you to stay. Anyway, she's seen a lot worse than that, hasn't she, Luca?'

Luca laughed. 'Much worse.'

It would be nice to be able to relax and enjoy a good drink, Claire thought – and she wasn't looking forward to the drive home in the dark.

'If you don't mind...' she said to Luca.

'No. Whatever you want.'

'Okay, then. Thanks.' She smiled at Ali. Then she fished in her bag and pulled out a small gift-wrapped parcel and a card. 'Happy birthday,' she said, handing them to Ali.

Luca handed his over too and Ali immediately began ripping them open.

'Oh, I love it!' she exclaimed, when she uncovered the blue sea-glass pendant Claire had given her. 'Thank you.' She hugged her.

She was even more enraptured by Luca's painting. 'You know that's my absolute favourite and I've hankered after it for ages.'

'I know. I've seen you eyeing it up every time you're over. I'm surprised you didn't just ask me for it.'

'Because I knew you'd give it to me, and I didn't want you to lose out on a sale. I was planning to save up to buy it, but I was afraid you'd sell it to someone else before I got the chance. Thank you so much.' She hugged him tightly. Then she stood up. 'Right. I'd better go and mingle – and collect more booty. See you guys later. The food will be served shortly.'

'Do you really not mind staying over?' Claire asked Luca, once she was gone.

'No, I really don't. Besides, I kind of like the idea of fulfilling some of my lurid teenage fantasies by having a girl in that room.'

'Okay, then,' she said, clinking her glass against his. 'Here's to making your teenage fantasies come true.' She sipped her champagne.

'I should warn you,' Luca grinned, 'I had some pretty filthy fantasies when I was a teenager.'

'Nothing I can't handle, I'm sure.' Claire nestled into him as he put his arm around her. 'It's so beautiful here. Nothing but sea everywhere you look. It must have been amazing growing up in this place.'

'Once I got used to it, I suppose it was. It completely freaked me out at first.' Luca chuckled.

'Why?'

'I was terrified of the sea. Didn't know what to make of it, I suppose. I'd never seen it before – never even heard about it.'

'Never heard about it? You'd never seen it in a book or anything?'

'There weren't any books,' he said quietly. 'The first time I saw a book was on the plane coming over here. Jacqueline had got some for us.'

'Oh.' Claire swallowed the lump in her throat.

'The first time I was brought to the beach I went ballistic. Screamed my lungs out, and had to be taken home. It was the same with grass.'

'Grass?' She frowned.

'Yeah, I didn't know what that was either. I was afraid to walk on it.'

Claire drank some more champagne, letting her hair fall over her face to hide the tears that had welled in her eyes. She couldn't bear to think of Luca as that deprived, frightened little boy who'd never heard of the sea nor felt grass beneath his feet. It made her want to wrap her arms around him and hold him tight, as if she could absorb all the hurt. It was no wonder he was a bit screwed up – it was amazing he could function at all.

'Top-up?' he asked, holding up the bottle.

Claire realised she had drained her glass. She turned to him, holding it out.

'Claire?' His smile faded as he saw the tears in her eyes. 'Shit, I didn't mean to upset you. It was supposed to be a funny story.'

'Hilarious,' she said drily, as he filled her glass.

'Sorry.' He hugged her, kissing her forehead. 'No more stories about Little Orphan Luca.'

* * *

The food was laid out as a buffet in the sunroom, and Claire was relieved that when they had loaded their plates Luca found them seats at the opposite end of the long table from his parents. She knew she was an awful coward, but she would be happy if she never had to face Jacqueline again, and was determined to avoid her for the rest of the night – though she felt her eyes on her sometimes during the meal, watching her and Luca with that perplexed expression.

They sat near a group of Ali's friends whom Luca knew well. They were welcoming and fun, and she was glad that Luca had relaxed and seemed to be enjoying himself as they talked and laughed.

When they dimmed the lights and everyone sang 'Happy Birthday', Claire saw Luca watching Jacqueline as she carried a cake covered with candles to the table, her smiling face illuminated in their glow. Something in his expression struck her like a knife to the heart, and it hit her with devastating clarity why he was so truculent, defensive and cold with Jacqueline. It wasn't because he hated her: it was because he loved her and knew she didn't love him back. Maybe there was a bit of him that wanted to hurt her, but mostly, she thought, he just wanted to protect himself from being hurt any more than he already had been. So he pretended he didn't care, that he didn't love her any more than she loved him, that he didn't want or need anything from her. Maybe that was why he kept all women at a distance.

Later, as Bono and Andrea Corr sang 'When The Stars Go Blue', she spun in Luca's arms beneath the canopy of stars, the music drifting out across the bay, drowning the crash of the waves below. Sky and sea bled into one in the darkness, and Claire's head, on Luca's shoulder, was pleasantly fuzzy from the champagne. The party was winding down around them.

'Tired?' he asked her, when the song finished.

She lifted her head. 'I'm still up for a few teenage fantasies, if you are.'

'Hold that thought.' He clasped her hand and led her towards the house.

She followed him into his bedroom, but when he turned to her, she pushed him down onto the bed, locked the door and leant against it. Holding his gaze, she unzipped her dress all the way down the back and pushed it off, letting it slide down her legs to pool at her feet.

'What's all this?' Luca asked, his eyes dark and hungry as Claire reached around to unclip her strapless bra.

'Call it my end-of-term showcase.' She smiled, looking right at him as she removed her bra and tossed it aside, not squirming even when his eyes dropped to her chest. She was happy for him to look as she walked slowly to him in nothing but her knickers and high-heeled shoes.

'You are so getting an A,' he muttered, as she crawled over him on the bed.

25

When Luca woke early the next morning, Claire was still sleeping soundly in his arms, her head nestled into the crook of his neck. He'd missed waking up with her like this since her mother had got out of hospital and she no longer stayed over at his place: the warmth of her body snuggled against his; the softness of her skin; kissing her slowly awake in the morning and making love to her gently, languorously, when they were both barely conscious. He hadn't wanted to stay here last night – he'd wanted to get away as quickly as possible – but he was glad now that they had. It was different with her here.

He loved the way she had defended him to Jacqueline and replayed the things she had said about him over and over in his mind. He knew he shouldn't feel good about it because the row had upset her, but he couldn't help it. It meant a lot to him that she had overcome her shyness to stand up for him like that. And later, when they were alone, she had shed all her inhibitions along with her clothes and seduced him until every lonely, horny ghost of his teenage self had been well and truly laid to rest. She had been magnificent.

He was tempted to kiss her awake now, but they hadn't had much sleep last night. He should let her rest. And, much as he'd like to lie there with her until she woke up, he was gasping for something to drink. So he extricated himself gently and slid out of bed, careful not to disturb her, then pulled on last night's clothes and went downstairs.

He made coffee, took it out on the deck and sat at the table, watching as the sun rose over the bay.

'Good morning! You're up early.' His father shuffled onto the deck in his dressing-gown and slippers, coffee in hand.

'Morning. So are you,' he said, as Jonathan sat down opposite him.

'I don't sleep much, these days. One of the perks of getting older.'

'Is it a perk?'

'Well, it is today. I get to spend some time with my favourite son before everyone else is up. It's good to see you, Luca. How are you?'

'Fine.'

'It's nice to have you here.' Jonathan looked out at the horizon. 'We'd rather see you, you know,' he said tentatively, turning to Luca. 'Even if it means rows.'

'You don't have enough aggro in your lives?'

'We'd rather you came round for a fight than not at all.'

'Fun for all the family, huh?' Luca laughed and Jonathan joined in.

'Maybe that's the best we can do,' he said wryly.

'Sorry,' Luca said seriously. 'I don't want to be mean. I just think it's probably better for everyone if I stay away.'

'She does regret that bloody book, you know.'

'Really?' Luca ran his thumb around the edge of his mug. 'She's never said sorry.'

'Have you?'

Luca raised his eyebrows in acknowledgement – it was a fair point. 'She just winds me up every time. I try to be nice and not lose it but—' He broke off, sighing in frustration.

'I know you do. But she tries too. You have to give her a chance.'

'Well, she started it,' Luca said, aware of how childish he sounded. 'What did she mean by saying Claire wasn't what she expected?'

'It wasn't an insult. You have to admit, most of the girls you've been with have been a bit more... well...'

'What?' Luca knew exactly what Jonathan meant, but he couldn't imagine him actually saying it. What word would he use? Sluttish? Tarty? Jonathan was far too dignified and courteous to call a girl anything like that.

'Well, more... outgoing,' he finished awkwardly.

Luca grinned. 'Claire's very reserved.'

'She seems lovely.'

'She is.'

They sat in silence for a while, drinking their coffee as the sun rose in the sky, sending a streak of yellow across the bay.

'I'm not an alco, you know,' Luca said eventually. 'Just by the way.'

'I know you're not.'

'Then why can't she see it? Why does she have to accuse me of that in front of everyone and treat me like a lush who's fallen off the wagon? It's not fair!'

Jonathan sighed. 'Your mother has... issues about drinking. Her father was an alcoholic.'

'I know, but it's not as if we're related. She doesn't have to worry about it running in the family.'

'That's not the point. Things were very bad for her growing up. And you had the drug problem. She doesn't think there's any grey area. It scares her, that's all. You have to make allowances.'

Luca drained his mug. 'I'd better go and see if Claire's awake,' he said, getting up. As he stood, he caught a glimpse of something out of the corner of his eye. 'Oh my God, did you see that?'

'Is it a dolphin?' Jonathan jumped up, looking out to sea.

'There – look!' Luca pointed as it arced out of the water again. 'Wow, that's amazing! It's so close.'

'We've seen them a few times in the last couple of weeks.'

'I must go and get Claire.'

* * *

Claire woke up alone and wondered where Luca had got to. She hoped she hadn't slept very late. She would have liked to sneak away before everyone else was up and avoid seeing his mother again.

'You're awake!' Luca exclaimed, as he burst into the room. 'Come outside, quick – there's a dolphin.'

He threw himself onto the bed beside her, and all the urgency seemed to go out of him. He sighed happily as he studied her face. 'Good morning.' He kissed her and his mouth tasted of coffee. His tongue slipped into her mouth as he rolled on top of her, and their kisses became hot and greedy.

'I thought you wanted me to go see a dolphin,' Claire breathed, as his lips moved to her neck.

'Dolphin schmolphin,' Luca mumbled into her throat. He kicked off his shoes, then tossed back the duvet and pulled her onto his lap so she was straddling him.

Claire giggled. 'Maybe I want to see a dolphin.'

'You can see it another time. I'm sure he's not going anywhere.' His hands cupped her breasts as he thrust upwards, the seam of his jeans rubbing against her tantalisingly. 'Dad says they've been hanging around here for weeks. Ten a penny.' His eyes were hot as she ground against him greedily, seeking more friction. 'Anyway, you've seen a dolphin before, right?'

'Well... only on TV.'

'There you go. Seen one dolphin, seen them all.'

* * *

Claire had missed her chance of escaping without bumping into Jacqueline again, because by the time they finally made it downstairs, everyone was up. Ali was sitting with her father on the deck and Jacqueline was in the kitchen presiding over the grill, while the mouth-watering smell of bacon filled the air. Claire felt seedy in yesterday's clothes, and more than a little ridiculous teetering around in her fancy shoes and party dress first thing in the morning. She really hadn't thought this through at all. She wanted to get home as quickly as possible and change.

'Good morning! Will you two have bacon butties?' Jacqueline asked, as they came into the kitchen.

'Yes, please!' Luca said. 'It smells fantastic.'

'I really should be going,' Claire said, 'but thanks anyway.'

'You'll stay for some breakfast, surely?' Jacqueline said. 'It'll be ready in a few minutes.'

'Yeah, you don't have to rush off straight away,' Luca said. 'You can stay for some breakfast at least.'

She had called her mother last night and told her she was staying over. Her brothers always visited on Sunday mornings, so she didn't even have the excuse that her mother would be on her own. Anyway, she hadn't managed to avoid Jacqueline, so she might as well stay. Besides, her stomach was doing somersaults in anticipation of that bacon. 'Okay, thanks.'

'Go and join them on the deck and I'll bring it out when it's ready.'

Luca headed out, but Claire hung back, letting her hand slip from his. Now that she was faced with Jacqueline, she felt she had to say something to clear the air.

'Um, is there anything I can do to help?' she asked.

Jacqueline looked at her in surprise. 'Thanks. You could make tea. The kettle's just boiled.' She nodded to a teapot sitting in front of the kettle.

Claire's heart pounded as she drew out the tea-making, trying to summon the courage to say her piece. 'I'm sorry I was rude to you last night,' she said finally, while she poured boiling water into the pot, glad that she had something else to focus on and didn't have to look at Jacqueline as she spoke.

'But you're not sorry for what you said.' Jacqueline looked at Claire sharply, seeming almost amused.

'Well, I...' Claire felt herself going puce.

'It's okay,' Jacqueline said, with a bitter smile, turning back to her bacon. 'As you so rightly pointed out, I put our lives in the public domain, so everyone is entitled to an opinion.'

The sound of laughter drifted in from the deck.

'I really do want the best for him,' Jacqueline said, looking out through the glass. Luca was leaning on the rail, laughing as he chatted with his father and sister. 'Despite what you may think.'

'I'm sure you do.'

'There's a jug of Buck's fizz in the fridge,' Jacqueline said briskly, as she loaded a plate with butties. 'Could you bring that out as well?'

Claire tottered over to the fridge and took out the jug.

'Oh God, those shoes,' Jacqueline said, her eyes on Claire's feet. 'Be careful. Don't worry about the teapot. I'll come back for it.'

'I'll just take them off,' Claire said, bending down to remove them. 'I didn't know I'd be staying over.'

'What size are you? Maybe we could find something more comfortable for you to wear.'

'Five.'

'Oh, I'm a five. I'll have a root around after breakfast.'

'Thanks. That's very kind of you.'

Barefoot, she followed Jacqueline onto the deck and they laid everything on the table.

'Oh, poor Claire!' Ali said, when she saw her. 'You only have your party clothes. I could have lent you something to wear.'

'It's fine,' Claire said, as she sat down beside Luca and they helped themselves to bacon butties.

'Buck's fizz?' Jonathan raised his eyebrows as Jacqueline poured the cocktail into champagne glasses and began passing them around.

'Well, it is my birthday,' Ali said, taking a glass from her mother. 'That means champagne at every meal, even breakfast.'

'It was your birthday yesterday,' Luca said to her.

'But the festivities go on all week,' Ali said. 'One day isn't enough to celebrate the wonder of me!'

'Luca?' Jacqueline held out a glass to him, with a tight smile. She looked like a hostage who was trying to appear relaxed while someone held a gun to her back.

Luca held his hands up in a gesture of surrender. 'I'll just have juice.'

'Go on, take it,' Jacqueline said, and Jonathan smiled at her with something like pride.

'No, really – thanks.'

'Okay.' Jacqueline visibly relaxed as she put the glass down.

It had been a small conciliatory gesture on her part, and Claire was glad that Luca met her halfway and was making an effort not to antagonise her. 'I'll just have juice, too, please,' she said. 'I have to drive home straight after this.'

'I'll get it,' Jacqueline said, and went indoors.

Jonathan smiled at Luca, giving him a pat on the back. 'Are you two staying for lunch?' he asked.

'Oh, I have to get home,' Claire said.

'Do you *have* to go?' Ali asked her.

'You're very welcome to stay, Claire,' Jacqueline said, as she returned to the table.

'Thanks, but I really need to get into some normal clothes,' she said, gesturing to her dress. 'And I thought I might bring my mother out to Dun Laoghaire, go for a walk along the pier.'

'Would she be up to that?' Luca frowned.

'I don't plan to make her hobble down it on her crutches. She has a wheelchair. My mother had a hip replacement recently,' she explained to the others.

'Well, I'll come with you. I can push.'

'Oh no, you have to stay, Luca,' Ali pleaded. 'I hardly got to spend any time with you last night.'

'You should stay,' Claire said to him quietly.

'So, will you?' Ali said to him. 'We can go down to the beach. It'll be like old times.'

'Okay, then,' he relented, smiling indulgently at his sister.

'Good,' Jonathan said. 'We'll have a proper family Sunday lunch.'

Jonathan and Ali beamed delightedly at this idea, while Luca and Jacqueline exchanged nervous glances.

'Oh, look!' Ali squealed, pointing out to sea, where two fins arched out of the water and disappeared again. 'Dolphins!'

'See what I mean?' Luca said to Claire. 'Ten a penny. And there are two of them now.'

They all stood up to watch, leaning against the rail, shouting with laughter as both dolphins leapt right out of the water, turning perfect somersaults before diving back beneath the sparkling surface.

'It really was lovely to meet you, Claire,' Jacqueline said later, as the whole family saw her to her car.

'You must come again soon,' Jonathan added.

'And be prepared for a sleepover next time,' Ali said, hugging her goodbye.

Claire was carrying her shoes, wearing an old pair of plimsolls Jacqueline had given her. She felt a fraud, knowing it was unlikely she would ever be back there with Luca.

'I'll see you on Tuesday,' Luca said, giving her a lingering kiss on the lips as the others went back towards the house. 'And thank you for last night,' he whispered in her ear.

'What about this morning?' she asked teasingly.

'That wasn't too shabby either.' He grinned. 'But last night was… incredible.'

'Well, I couldn't have done it without you.'

Claire couldn't get the goofy grin off her face as she got into the car and pulled out of the drive – or, in fact, for the entire journey back to Ranelagh.

***

Later that afternoon, Claire drove her mother to Dun Laoghaire, and they went along the pier, Claire pushing Espie in her wheelchair. Half of Dublin seemed to be there, strolling, jogging and generally making the most of the rare heatwave. When they walked back, they queued for ice-cream at Teddy's and sat looking out to sea eating 99s, while Claire told her mother all about the party, Luca's family home and the dolphins.

'And what was the mother like?' Espie asked her, always avid for more details.

'She was... nice enough. A bit uptight – and there was a lot of tension between her and Luca. But she wasn't as cold as I'd expected. I was a bit rude to her,' she admitted.

'That's my girl!' Espie said.

'Well, I felt bad about it, but she was being mean to Luca so...'

'She had it coming, then.'

'How was everyone this morning?' Michelle, Neil and their kids had been leaving when Claire got home.

'They were grand. Holly had an awful tantrum, but I'm sure you can read all about it in Michelle's next column, so I won't spoil it for you.'

'Ooh, can't wait!' Claire laughed. 'You shouldn't have told me. I'll never sleep with the anticipation.' She scooped up the last of the ice-cream with her tongue and bit into her cone.

'Where did you sleep last night?' her mother asked slyly, giving her a sideways glance.

'I slept in a very nice bedroom with a sea view,' Claire told her primly.

'You're so cruel. I could have you up for elderly abuse, you know.'

'And I could push you off the end of the pier. Don't let my mild-mannered façade fool you.'

Espie laughed. 'I can get out of this chair. I'm only in it because I'm lazy and I like having you push me around.'

'I know – you're a complete charlatan. I don't know why I put up with you.' She finished her cone, wiping her hands on a tissue. 'Anyway, I think you'll find that not sharing the details of my private life doesn't count as abuse.'

'So there is something to share, then?' Espie's eyes twinkled.

'We really are just friends, Mum – me and Luca.'

Espie gave her a skeptical look.

'Okay, friends with benefits – but still just friends.'

'That's such a pity. Because I have my eye on this amazing hat...'

'I'm not getting married just because there's a hat you want to buy. But your birthday's coming up...'

'Oh, by the way, if Luca's coming to my party, make sure to tell him he's not to buy me a present.'

'Okay.'

'Tell him he'll be turned away if he does. I'll show him the door. Zero tolerance.'

'Okay, okay! I'll tell him.'

* * *

Claire was just about to get into bed that night when Mark rang on her mobile. It was only nine thirty, but she was exhausted after all the fresh air and lack of sleep the previous night.

'Hi. Good weekend?' he asked.

'Yeah, really nice. The weather's been amazing.'

'Same here.'

She told him about last night's party, carefully editing Luca out of the proceedings and telling him it was 'my friend Ali's birthday' – which was strictly true. Mark had gone to Brighton with 'the gang' for the weekend.

'So how's your mum?' he asked.

'She's good – doing really well.'

'Only I was wondering if you could come over next weekend, by any chance. I have to go to New York the week after that, and I'm dying to see you.'

'Oh.' Claire was taken aback, her mind flying in several directions at once. Was she ready for this? Would it mean the end of her and Luca? Was she off work next weekend? Would she sleep with Mark? Could she get a cheap flight at such short notice? How would Luca feel about it? Could her mother cope on her own for a couple of nights? 'Yeah, that should be doable,' she said finally.

'Great!'

'I'll just look into flights and stuff and get back to you. Okay?'

'Brilliant! I'm really looking forward to seeing you again.'

'Yeah. Me too.'

When they hung up, her mind was racing. She knew she could take the weekend off – Yvonne would be happy to cover for her. And her mother would be fine on her own: she had plenty of friends and neighbours around who would keep an eye on her and help her with anything she needed in terms of shopping. Maybe Jim would even stay for the weekend. So that wasn't a problem.

But what about her and Luca? It was ridiculous to think he'd even care, since he'd been coaching her for this very moment. So why was she feeling guilty?

26

Claire called round to Luca's as planned on Tuesday evening after work. She had booked a flight for Friday afternoon, and had decided to count the weekend as two dates, so Saturday would be her fifth date with Mark. Now she just had to tell Luca.

She arrived laden with carrier bags, as usual. Since her mother had come home and Claire no longer spent the night at Luca's, they had been eating takeaways or ready meals rather than waste time cooking – sometimes forgoing food altogether to spend more time in bed. But Claire still found a pretext to buy groceries, sneaking food into Luca's fridge when he wasn't looking, or pretending she had simply got carried away in the supermarket.

'No point in letting it go to waste,' she'd say, as she filled his cupboards.

'So – good news!' he said, as he let her in. 'The gallery sold one of my paintings today.'

'Oh, that's brilliant! Congratulations!'

'Thanks,' he said, taking her bags from her and starting to unpack them on the counter. 'I thought we could go out to celebrate – my treat!'

'Oh, you shouldn't spend your money on me.'

He turned to her. 'Is that your way of saying you don't want to be seen in public with me?'

'No, but... maybe it's my way of saying I don't want to waste time out in a restaurant when we could be in bed.'

'What have I created? You're insatiable.' He shook his head ruefully. 'Surely you could afford one night off.'

Not when it might be our last, she thought sadly. 'We could get a posh takeaway – compromise.'

'Have it your way,' Luca said, going back to unpacking the groceries. 'But I'm paying.'

'Okay. So how much did this painting sell for?'

'Three grand. So I'll get fifteen hundred.'

'You only get half? That's terrible.'

'That's the way it is.'

'It must be so hard to make a living at this.' No wonder he lived in a shit-hole and couldn't afford to pay his electricity bills.

'It is – almost impossible. But I'm having a solo show there in September, so who knows? Hopefully I'll sell a lot more then.'

When they had finished putting everything away, they moved to the sitting room.

'Wine?' Luca asked, picking up a bottle of red.

'Yes, please.' Claire sat on the sofa as he poured two glasses, trying to get up the nerve to tell him about Mark. She had meant to say it first thing when she arrived, but he'd had his news about the sale, so it hadn't seemed the right time – and then the moment had passed.

'How was lunch yesterday?' she asked, as Luca handed her a glass and sat beside her.

'It was fine. I behaved myself. I went on the dry to keep Jacqueline happy. We haven't turned into the Waltons, but there were no fights.'

'Have you ever tried to trace your real parents?' she asked suddenly. A shadow passed across Luca's face. 'Sorry, none of my business.'

'No, it's okay. Jacqueline tried to trace them. But they didn't keep very good records in those places. I was about nine months old when I was put in the first orphanage, but I still have no idea how I got there.'

'What about Ali?'

'They already knew who her parents were. They'd got their permission to adopt her.'

'But she didn't find out anything about yours?'

'No. She drew a complete blank. And do you know what I felt?' he said, his lip curled in disgust. 'I was *relieved*. I didn't want her to find them. I was terrified they'd send me away to live in a hut on the side of some mountain in Romania. I knew she didn't want me, but I didn't want her to find my real mother because I didn't want to be *poor*.' He looked up at her and she was appalled to see his eyes were shining with tears. She wished she'd never brought the subject up.

'You know most of the kids in those so-called orphanages weren't orphans at all?' he asked.

Claire nodded.

'I wanted to be. I wanted her to find out that my parents were dead, so there'd be no chance of her ever sending me back.' He laughed harshly. 'I told you I'm not a very nice person.'

'Jesus, Luca, you were only a *child*.'

It broke her heart to think of Luca living in terror of having what little hard-won stability he'd finally got in his life snatched away. And instead of making him feel safe, Jacqueline had fuelled his insecurity with her precious 'honesty' about her feelings. It was a bloody good thing she hadn't known about this on Saturday, Claire thought furiously – she'd have had a hard time restraining herself from punching the woman. Did Jacqueline have any idea of the torture she'd put Luca through?

'She shouldn't have made you feel that being sent away was a possibility in the first place. Did you tell her that was what you were afraid of?'

'No. I didn't want to put the idea in her head in case she hadn't already thought of it.' He took a gulp of wine. 'I've never told *anyone* that before, actually.'

'Not even Ali?' She frowned.

'God, no. Especially not Ali.'

Claire wondered why especially not her, when he was so close to her. But he got up then and went to the table, leafing through a pile of papers. Confession time was clearly over.

'So, what do you want? Pizza? Thai? Indian? There are menus here somewhere.'

She drank some wine and decided that this was as good a moment as any. She knew it was cowardly, but she didn't want to be facing him when she told him her news.

'I'm going over to stay with Mark next weekend,' she said to Luca's back.

'Oh?' He stilled, and now she wished she hadn't been so spineless because she wanted to see his face. She had no idea what he was feeling. His hands resumed their searching.

'It'll be our fifth date on the Saturday.'

'Right,' he said, turning to her slowly. 'So, this is it, then?' he asked, leaning against the table and folding his arms.

'I guess so,' she said, plucking nervously at the upholstery of the sofa. Even though he was facing her now, she still couldn't tell how he felt about it.

He came to sit beside her on the sofa again, looking at her with concern. 'Are you ready for that?'

She shrugged. 'I think so. Don't you?'

'Well, I don't think there's much more I can teach you,' he said, with a wry chuckle. 'Not after that performance on Saturday.'

She smiled.

'But don't let him pressure you. If you need more time, just tell him to back off. Take it as slow as you like. Make him go at your pace.'

'It's not that I need more time... I don't think.'

'You don't sound very sure.'

'It's just – I don't know...' She struggled to explain how she was feeling.

Luca was silent, waiting patiently for her to say what was on her mind.

'It's just that I'm fine now with *you*. I feel like I know what I'm doing. I'm confident, and I'm relaxed about being naked around you. I can take the initiative.'

'Boy, can you!'

'But that's *you*. I know you and we're friends—' She pulled herself up. 'Well, I think we're friends—'

'We are friends.'

'So I feel comfortable with you. I don't feel like I have to perform and you're judging me. I don't have to try to impress you. I can just be myself. But I'm afraid that with someone else I'll be back to square one and it'll be like starting all over again.'

'Don't worry, you'll be fine. And it won't be like starting again. It'll be like... riding a bike. Just a different bike.'

She laughed.

'And don't worry about impressing him – just be yourself.'

'But what about us?' she asked, blurting out the thing that was worrying her most.

'What about us?'

'Will I ever see you again? Will we still be friends?'

'Yeah, of course,' he said immediately, and she sagged with relief. 'I mean, if you want to be?'

'I do.' She nodded eagerly. She couldn't imagine not having him in her life now.

'Me too.' He sank back against the sofa and blew out a breath. 'So, this is it?'

'Yeah.'

'I'm going to miss this,' he said, waving his hand between the two of them.

'Me too.'

He reached for her and pulled her into his lap so she was straddling him.

'So, what do you say?' he asked mischievously, as he trailed a warm hand underneath her skirt. 'One last undress rehearsal?'

* * *

They didn't have any dinner in the end, instead spending all the time they had together making love. Claire knew she was kissing Luca more passionately, clinging to him more fiercely than ever before, sucking his cock like it was the last time – because it was. He seemed more intense, too, kissing her frantically, pushing into her faster and harder than he ever had before, touching her everywhere as if he were trying to memorise every inch of her skin. He went down on her for so long that she thought she was in danger of forgetting his face. It had been the most intense, exhilarating, satisfying sex of her life.

So why did she feel so deflated as she travelled home later that night in a taxi? What had she been expecting? Some display of jealousy? Luca begging her not to go? It wasn't as if he hadn't been clear from the start about what their relationship was – and what it wasn't. He had told her right from the beginning that she wasn't to think of him as a boyfriend, so she could hardly expect him to declaire undying love for her and beg her to stay. But, still, she couldn't help feeling rattled by how cool he had been about it all – the ease with which he could watch her move on to another man. Maybe she'd fallen a little bit for Luca's easy charm. But the kind of casual, no-strings arrangement that was all he could handle would never be enough for her. He was wrong for her and she had always known that. With Mark she could have a proper grown-up relationship and the kind of life she wanted. She was probably just feeling wobbly about taking it to the next level.

It was a pity Luca didn't want to be in a relationship because she thought he would be better at it than he gave himself credit for. But he didn't, so he would go back to his old ways, and she would go to London next weekend and sleep with Mark. There was nothing stopping her – certainly not Luca.

27

On Friday evening Mark took Claire to the same village bistro they had gone to last time. The restaurant was buzzing, and her niggling doubts melted away as they chatted over the delicious food and wine. He was wearing a casual lightweight suit and a beautiful dove-grey shirt, and she was struck anew by how handsome he was. She found herself starting to wonder what he would look like naked, and felt a little shiver of excitement at the thought of finding out tomorrow night – or maybe even tonight, if she decided to break her own rule. The idea of sleeping with him didn't faze her. She had no worries about disappointing him in bed, and she was suddenly overcome by a feeling of well-being, as if everything was as it should be. Luca was right. It would be like riding a different bike.

'When are you off to New York?' Claire asked.

'Next Friday. A friend's getting married there so a few of us are going over and staying on for a few days after.'

'That should be lovely.'

'I wish you could come. I don't suppose there's any chance...?' He looked at her hopefully. 'I know it's short notice.'

'No,' she said, with a wistful sigh. 'I wish I could.' She hadn't had a proper holiday in ages, so she could probably have afforded it. But she couldn't leave her mother just now. 'I'd love to go to New York.'

'You've never been?'

'No.'

'Oh, you have to go. Let's go together! I mean not now, obviously, but we should plan it.'

'That would be great.' Claire felt excited already at the idea of going to New York with him, even if it was just a vague, far-off prospect.

'We're invited to a dinner party with some friends tomorrow night, if you'd like to go?' he said.

'That'd be lovely.' She smiled across at him. 'I'd really like to meet your friends.' She was touched that Mark was so ready to make her part of his life.

'Emma will be there, so there'll be someone you already know.'

'Oh.' Emma was Mark's colleague – Claire knew her on Twitter as @Locksie. 'But she won't know it's me. I mean, you haven't told her, have you?'

'No! She won't have a clue. But at least you'll know who she is.'

'It'll be nice to meet her in real life, even if I can't reveal my true identity.' Claire laughed. 'God, now I know how Superman and Spiderman and that lot must feel.'

'Does that make me Lois Lane?'

'Or Mary Jane.'

Mark laughed. 'I quite like the idea of having a superhero girlfriend. What would your power be?'

'Hmm.' Claire racked her brain, but the only superpowers she could think of that NiceGirl might have were bordering on obscene, and she didn't want to go there. 'Um... being super-nice?' she said weakly.

'I can vouch for that.' Then he leant forward and whispered, 'But you're going to have to do a better job of hiding it or everyone will discover your secret.'

Between the main course and dessert, Claire went outside to phone home. 'I just want to check on my mother, make sure everything's okay,' she said to Mark.

Espie's Friday-night card party was in full swing, and she could hear lots of chatter and laughter in the background when her mother picked up.

'I'm fine,' Espie assured her. 'Nancy and Michael are just down the road, and Jim's coming over for the day tomorrow. He's going to stay the night.'

'TMI, Mum.' Claire laughed.

'In the spare room,' Espie said. 'Even if the spirit was willing, I don't think that lump of metal in my hip would be up to any high jinks at the moment.

Getting my knickers *on* is enough of a challenge. I won't be whipping them off in a hurry. Anyway, are you having a nice time?'

'Yes, lovely.' There was a burst of laughter in the background, and Claire felt a pang, almost wishing she was there. 'Sounds like you're having fun.'

'We're having a great night. Everyone else brought food, so I didn't have to lift a finger. It's a pity you're not here. They all miss you – especially Luca.'

'*Luca*'s there?'

'Jim called in to him on his way over and asked if he wanted to come. That was nice of him, wasn't it? Poor Luca, I think he's pining for you.'

'Don't be daft, Mum.' She didn't want to disillusion her mother by telling her that Luca knew she was spending the weekend with another man and didn't give a toss. Not only did he not care, he had personally coached her for the occasion. He had just stopped short of making her a packed lunch.

'He actually won a couple of tricks tonight,' her mother continued. 'It's a pity we didn't up the stakes, because I think he could do with the money. Jim's trying to teach him the spoons now – you should see him!' She giggled. 'He's all fingers and thumbs.'

'Well, tell everyone I said hi.'

'I will. Do you want to talk to Luca?'

'No. I'd better get back to Mark. Night, Mum.'

She felt unsettled as she walked back to her table. It was ridiculous! She was in a lovely restaurant with a really nice man who wanted to be with her, yet she felt almost resentful about being there with Mark instead of at home playing cards with her mother and her cronies – and Luca, who would ultimately only ever want to be friends. She didn't like to think of him being there without her, jealous of the time other people got to spend with him. At the same time, a little part of her was glad to know that he was safely holed up at her house instead of out on the prowl, picking up girls.

'Everything okay?' Mark asked, as she pulled out her chair.

'Fine.' She smiled at him as she sat down, determined to throw herself wholeheartedly into this – whatever 'this' turned out to be. At least it had potential.

* * *

They were quiet as they walked the short distance back to Mark's flat in the balmy night air, but Claire's mind was buzzing. She had to get over this pointless hankering for Luca. And she had a pretty good idea how to do it. Luca had warned her when they started not to confuse sex with romance, but she had been so inexperienced that it was probably inevitable she would develop feelings for him when they had been so intimate with each other. Once she started sleeping with Mark, she would transfer those feelings to him and everything else would fall into place. She'd forget all about this stupid fixation on Luca. Mark was everything she wanted. All she had to do was sleep with him, and she'd be fine. Maybe she'd abandon her five-date rule and let it happen tonight.

So when they were back at the flat and Mark started kissing her, she didn't hold back, happy to follow wherever this led. She wasn't going to stick to rigid rules any longer. When his kisses became more urgent, she kissed him back just as feverishly and when his hand slid up to cup her breast, she didn't push it away, but arched into it while her fingers raked through his hair. And yet, though she was making all the right moves, she felt detached somehow, like she was outside her body, watching, and this was all happening to someone else. She just couldn't get into it.

Mark must have sensed that something was off because his hand stilled, his kisses slowed and then he was peeling away from her.

'Sorry,' he said, putting some distance between them. He looked flushed and contrite. 'Am I moving too fast again?'

'No. I just – I'm just tired.' She stifled a yawn and realised she really *was* tired. That was probably all it was – her libido was at a low ebb because she was tired and a bit stressed.

They went to bed shortly after, Mark kissing her goodnight with a peck on the lips. But Claire found she couldn't sleep, all the conflicting feelings of the evening crowding in on her and making it impossible to let go. What the hell was wrong with her? She was with a lovely man who liked her, shared her interests and wanted to shag her – and if his kisses were anything to go by, it would have been brilliant. A man, moreover, who wanted a relationship, not just a string of meaningless shags. So what the fuck was she doing alone in bed, wishing she was... what? Back home, playing cards with Luca?

She sighed in frustration. With no prospect of sleep in sight, she took out her laptop and started writing a draft of a final blog post. She decided to write about Mark – almost as if by writing it, she could make it come true.

Fridays I'm In Love

Not just Fridays. But I've met someone, and he doesn't live in the same city as me, or even the same country, so we're doing the long-distance thing and mostly I just see him on weekends. It's not very long-distance – we're just a short flight away from each other – but it's fun and exciting, and it's given a whole new meaning to That Friday Feeling.

I like him an awful lot. And that's all I'm going to say on the subject. Because this one's different. So I'm closing the bedroom door, and I'm shutting down the blog. No more Ms NiceGirl. Because after all the men I've known – Mr Bossy, Mr Curious, Mr Strange, Mr Bump and Grind, Mr Ed (remember him?), Mr Handy – I've finally found the one I was looking for all along… Mr Right.

It needed work, but it was a nice idea, she thought, as she switched off the laptop and put it away. She liked to think of NiceGirl getting her happy-ever-after. And she'd get her own happy ending too. Tomorrow would be date number five. She would sleep with Mark and everything would be fine.

28

The following evening they took a taxi to Mark's friend Olivia's house in Belsize Park. Claire took his hand in the back of the cab, sighing happily as his warm fingers curled around hers. It had been such a lovely day. She had worried there might be some awkwardness after last night, but Mark was his usual friendly, relaxed self, and she felt perfectly at ease again.

It had been a beautiful summer's day, the sun hot in a cloudless blue sky, a gentle breeze taking the edge off the temperature so that the heat wasn't oppressive. They had had a blissfully lazy day in the garden, chatting, reading the papers and stroking Millie, punctuated by coffee and tea, cold white wine, croissants, salmon quiche and strawberries. Claire felt almost drowsy with pleasure, as pampered and content as Millie.

'So, this is our fifth date,' she said, as they walked up the path to his friend's house.

He stopped and turned to her. 'Is it? I wasn't sure – I mean I didn't know if you counted this weekend as one or—'

'It's definitely our fifth date,' she said. 'And, by the way, I'm not seeing the Artist any more.'

'You're not?'

'No. I broke it off with him before I came over here,' she said, with a calm smile.

He smiled back, his eyes glittering with intent. Then he took her hand and continued walking.

A very pretty girl with long, shiny dark hair answered the door. 'Mark!' she squealed, pulling him into a hug.

'Olivia, this is Claire,' Mark said, once he was released. 'Claire, Olivia.'

'Hi, Claire, it's lovely to meet you,' Olivia said, as they shook hands.

'You too.'

'Well, come in, come in.' Olivia ushered them into the hallway. 'Let me take your coats. Gosh, I love your dress.'

'Thank you,' Claire said, as she handed over her jacket.

'We're all in here.' She led them into a small dining room, where people were already seated around a large table. Banks of candles on every surface gave the room and everyone in it a soft glow.

There was a chorus of 'Mark!' as they entered, and he waved at them all in greeting.

'Everyone, this is Claire,' Olivia said, 'Mark's friend.'

Claire nodded shyly as they all said hello.

'Sit down, you two,' Olivia said, waving them to a couple of chairs beside each other. 'Claire, this is Diane, Patrick, Emma and Jamie.'

'Emma works with me,' Mark whispered to Claire, as she sat down beside Jamie. She wondered why he was whispering and he raised his eyebrows meaningfully – at which she realised this was the Emma she knew as @Locksie on Twitter and with whom she had chatted often.

'Oh!' she breathed. She wouldn't have known her from her Twitter avatar, but now that she knew it was her, she recognised the face. It felt strange not to be able to acknowledge that they knew each other – sort of.

'Andy's still to come,' Olivia was saying, 'but we're getting sloshed while we're waiting. Red or white?'

They both asked for red, and when she had filled their glasses, she sat down opposite Claire.

'I haven't seen Andy in ages,' Mark said to Olivia.

'None of us has,' she said.

'Is he bringing anyone?'

'I'm not sure. He was a bit vague. He broke up with Sam a couple of months ago, and I don't think he's seeing anyone else.'

'So, you're from Dublin, Claire?' Emma asked her.

'Yes. I'm just over for the weekend.'

'You're staying with Mark?' she asked, smiling knowingly at him.

'Um... yes.'

'Well, you're a dark horse, Mark,' Jamie said. 'You never told us you were having an international fling. All those business trips are starting to make sense now.'

'They *were* business trips,' Mark said. 'Claire and I have only just started seeing each other. And it's not a fling, by the way.'

'Ooh!' Jamie and Patrick chorused childishly.

Claire suddenly felt self-conscious, as if she was on trial with his friends and they were all sizing her up. She got the feeling these people were very important to him, and she wanted them to like her.

'Don't mind them,' Mark said to her. 'They're such children.'

'Sorry,' Emma said to Claire. 'We're being silly – too much wine and no food. Where's bloody Andy?' she shouted to the table at large.

Right on cue, the doorbell rang. 'That'll be him now,' Olivia said, getting up and leaving the room.

'Thank God for that,' Patrick said. 'At last we can eat.'

'What are we having anyway?' Diane asked. 'Does anyone know?'

'Knowing Olivia, it'll probably be some vile invention of hers.'

They were all chatting and giggling about Olivia's cooking when she came striding back into the room. Claire was surprised that she was rather stoney-faced – and was she imagining it or had she glanced warily at Mark?

'Andy's here,' she said tightly, 'and he's brought someone.' She was followed into the room by a tall, dark-haired man and a ravishingly pretty girl with thick waves of strawberry blonde hair tumbling down her back.

Everyone fell silent, and all eyes flew to Mark.

'Hi, you guys,' the blonde said, smiling. Either she was oblivious to the atmosphere in the room or she was choosing to ignore it. Patrick and Diane were obviously stunned, Jamie looked cross, and Emma appeared downright hostile as they greeted her in turn. They all kept darting furtive glances at Mark, as if they were expecting him to explode.

'Sophie.' Mark finally nodded in acknowledgement.

'And who's this?' Sophie asked, her eyes settling on Claire.

'This is Claire,' Mark introduced her. 'Claire – Sophie and Andy.'

Sophie extended a heavily braceleted hand. 'Nice to meet you, Claire.' She smiled, blatantly sizing her up. Then her eyes slid questioningly to Mark. 'Well, you haven't wasted any time,' she said, as she took the seat on Mark's other side, her dazzling smile never slipping. 'I go into rehab for five minutes and find I've been replaced.'

Her mischievous smile belied the bitterness of her words, but they hit Claire like a slap. She didn't know where to look. Was this why everyone had been acting so shiftily when Sophie arrived – because Mark was supposed to be her boyfriend and instead he'd turned up with *her*? Because he'd cheated on Sophie while she was in rehab?

Irritation crossed Mark's features. 'Sophie, you know we'd—'

'So, what's for supper, Ol?' Sophie interrupted, pouring herself a huge glass of wine. 'I'm starving!'

'Should you be doing that?' Olivia asked, frowning, as Sophie raised the glass to her lips.

'Oh, Christ, you're right!' Sophie stopped herself as she was about to take a sip. She lowered the glass. 'God, I'm such a dunce! I'll never graduate from rehab like this. Here, you have it,' she said, sliding the glass across to Andy.

Olivia smiled reluctantly. 'I'll go and get the first course.'

'What do you think it's going to be?' Sophie hissed, once Olivia was out of the room. 'Not one of her "creations", I hope.'

'So how was rehab?' Jamie asked cheerfully.

'Boring! Though I did have a little fling with a crackhead from Scotland – that was fun.'

'You're not supposed to get off with people in rehab,' Jamie said. 'Isn't that against the rules?'

Sophie shrugged. 'You have to do something to pass the time. So, Claire, where are you from?'

'Dublin.'

'Ah, lovely! I was in Dublin once. At least I think it was Dublin,' she frowned, 'but I was off my head, so who knows? I had a pint of Guinness, though, so it probably was Dublin.'

'You can get Guinness anywhere,' Patrick pointed out.

'True, but you wouldn't get me drinking it. I must have been doing the tourist thing.'

'Are you and Andy...?' Mark trailed off.

'What? Banging each other?' She glanced at Andy. 'God, no! I love Andy to bits, but we don't fancy each other at all, do we, babe?' she said to Andy, who shook his head.

'Nope, not a bit,' he said.

'Andy was very sweet,' Sophie said, 'driving down to pick me up when I was sprung from rehab, when a certain other person seems to have forgotten my existence.' Her eyes returned pointedly to Mark. 'At least some people still love me.'

'You know we all love you,' Mark said blandly.

Ouch, Claire thought. That had to sting. It was such a brutally noncommittal reply to Sophie's obvious fishing.

There was an awkward silence, broken by Olivia returning with the starters.

'What's it meant to be, Ol?' Sophie asked, prodding the food suspiciously with her fork.

'It's tilapia in a chilli sauce.'

'Tilapia is a white fish, isn't it?' Sophie frowned. 'Why is this black?'

'It has a dusting of cocoa powder,' Olivia told her cheerfully, as she finished handing plates around.

Everyone looked at her in alarm and began poking tentatively at their food.

'Well, *bon appétit*, everyone!' Olivia said, sitting down and attacking her starter enthusiastically.

Claire cut off a tiny piece of fish and put it gingerly into her mouth. It was absolutely disgusting, but she forced herself to swallow it.

Sophie had no such compunction. 'Ugh! It's chocolate fish.' She grimaced, pushing her plate away after one bite. 'That's vile, Ol!'

'Claire seems to like it, don't you, Claire?' Olivia said.

'It's, um... interesting.' Claire had managed to dig out some fish from beneath the cocoa topping and was valiantly chewing it. The rest she was trying to hack up and move around so that it would look like she'd eaten more.

'No, she doesn't,' Sophie said flatly. 'She's just being polite.'

'You don't have to eat any more of it,' Mark said to Claire. 'It's terrible.'

Thankfully, the next course of pork in vanilla sauce was marginally more successful.

'Pork and custard!' Sophie pronounced, and that was exactly what it tasted like. But at least the sauce could be avoided, and Olivia hadn't added any 'gourmet' touches to the vegetables.

'So, what's the news?' Sophie asked, as they ate. 'What did I miss while I was in rehab?'

'Mark's publishing that blog, "Scenes of a Sexual Nature",' Emma told her.

'Oh my God, really?' Sophie chuckled. 'Have you met her, then? Your precious NiceGirl?'

'Yes, I have.'

'What's she like?'

'He's not telling us anything about her,' Olivia said.

'She wants to remain anonymous.'

'I love that blog,' Sophie said. 'Do you know it, Claire?'

'Yes, I read it all the time.'

'Mark's a bit obsessed with her, aren't you, Mark? He flirts his arse off with her online. You want to watch him with that one, Claire.'

'Claire has nothing to fear from her,' Mark said, smiling secretively at Claire.

'And you really won't tell us anything about her?'

'Nope.'

'You're no fun. I bet she's a hag. That's why you won't tell us.'

'I'll tell you this much – she is definitely not a hag.'

Claire felt unnerved. She wasn't sure what was going on. Sophie certainly wasn't behaving like a woman who'd just caught her boyfriend cheating on her. And Mark wasn't acting guilty. Maybe what Sophie had said was just banter – a bit of harmless teasing between friends. But if that was so, why all the strange looks when she'd turned up?

'Is anyone up for a picnic on the Heath tomorrow?' Olivia asked later. She had produced cheese and crackers to end the meal, and everyone had fallen on them hungrily, making up for dinner. 'It's meant to be another lovely day.'

'What do you think?' Mark asked Claire.

'It's up to you…'

'We'll give you a ring in the morning and let you know,' Mark said to Olivia.

'And Andy's having a barbecue tomorrow night,' Sophie said.

'Yes, you're all invited,' Andy said.

'Claire's going home tomorrow, so we won't be around for that,' Mark said.

'Oh, that's a shame. What time is your flight?' Olivia asked Claire, as she started clearing the table.

'Eight twenty.'

'Well, *you* can still come, Mark,' Sophie said.

'I'm taking her to the airport.'

'Oh, bum!' Sophie pouted prettily.

'If you want to go, I can easily make my own way to the airport,' Claire said quietly, to Mark.

'No, I want to take you.'

'Course he does,' Sophie said gaily, leaping up to help Olivia. 'Mark is the model boyfriend at all times. I can vouch for that. If you ever need a reference, Mark, I'll be happy to provide a glowing one.'

'Thanks a lot, Sophie,' Mark said drily, as she followed Olivia from the room.

Soon after that, the party started breaking up.

'Well, I guess we should be off,' Mark said to Claire. 'I'll just find Olivia to tell her and then I'll call a taxi.'

'Okay. I'm going to the loo.'

When Claire got to the top of the stairs, she heard muffled voices coming from a door opposite. She recognised Sophie's and it sounded like she was crying.

'I mean, I've gone to all this bloody trouble to clean up my act and sort myself out, and he doesn't even *care*. He's fucking moved on!'

'But you didn't just do it for him, did you?' Olivia said softly.

'Of course I did it for him!' Sophie said, on a sob. 'He's all there is. Oh God, Ol, what am I going to do? If I can't get him back...' She sniffed.

Claire froze. She knew she shouldn't eavesdrop, but she needed to know what was going on between Sophie and Mark.

'You needed to sort yourself out anyway,' Olivia said sensibly. 'For your own sake.'

'I know. But what's the point? If I can't have him, I'd rather be back on drugs.'

'You're such a drama queen,' Olivia mocked, earning a half-laugh from Sophie. 'I wish you'd at least given me some warning you were going to turn up tonight.'

'I was afraid you'd tell me not to come.'

'I might have done,' Olivia said.

'Honestly, Ol, I didn't care about doing it for myself. The whole time I was in rehab, I just thought about *him* – how pleased he'd be. I wanted him to be proud of me.'

'He is proud of you, babe. We all are. But you may not get him back. You have to accept that.'

'I can't!' Sophie wailed.

'Sorry, Soph, but Claire seems really nice. She could be good for him.'

'Not like me, you mean. God, I've never wanted to get wasted so much!'

'I didn't mean that, but you hurt Mark a lot.'

'I know, I know,' Sophie sobbed. 'I've been a total flake and a fuck-up and I messed him around too many times. I've let everyone down so often. But if he'd just give me *one* more chance...'

Claire turned and raced downstairs, as if she was being chased. Mark was waiting for her in the hall.

'Okay?' he asked, looking at her with concern.

'Fine,' she said faintly.

'The taxi's outside.'

She felt too shaken to say anything in the cab on the way home. When Mark glanced over at her and asked if she was all right a couple of times, she just smiled and said she was fine, but the conversation she had overheard had really rattled her. Mark obviously knew that something was up – and he probably had a good idea of what it was. But it would have to wait until they got home. She needed time to gather her thoughts and calm down.

'Well, that was an interesting evening,' Mark said wryly, when they got back to his flat. 'Sorry about the food.'

'It's not your fault. It was... different.'

'So, would you like a drink? Or do you just want to go to bed?'

At the mention of bed, Claire knew she had to say something. She suddenly felt like an impostor. Everything had changed, and she couldn't go to bed with Mark now, knowing she might be sleeping with someone else's boyfriend.

'I'd like a drink,' she said, even though she'd already had more than enough. 'Some wine would be nice.'

'Coming right up,' Mark said, glancing at her warily. It was like there was a bomb in the room, and they had to be careful not to trigger it.

When they were settled on the sofa with their drinks, she took a deep breath and began, 'So – you and Sophie...'

Mark let out a long sigh of resignation or relief – perhaps both. 'What she said about me moving on while she was in rehab – it's not true,' he said. 'We'd broken up long before then.'

'So why did she say that?'

He shrugged. 'Sophie likes to make mischief. And she has a rather creative relationship with the truth. Honestly, Claire, you could ask anyone around that table tonight. They all know it wasn't true.' His eyes radiated sincerity.

Claire just nodded.

'She doesn't really mean any harm,' he said.

Claire wasn't so sure about that. She felt Sophie had been deliberately trying to unnerve her. And it had worked.

'Do you believe me?' Mark asked.

'Yes,' she said. 'It was a bit of a shock, though, hearing that out of the blue.'

'It's all in the past.'

'But she's still in your life.'

'She's a friend. You're still friends with the Artist.'

'I suppose so,' she conceded.

'More than friends,' he mumbled.

She wished she could tell him that he had no reason to be jealous, that she wasn't friends with any exes because she didn't have any exes, because she'd never had a proper relationship with anyone *ever*, least of all Luca, and that she was the only person in this room who had any possible cause to be jealous. But she couldn't say any of it.

'I've known Sophie for a really long time. I can't just cut her out of my life.'

'She doesn't seem your type,' Claire mused.

'She's not. That's why I'm not with her any more,' Mark said. 'We're not good for each other. It just took a while to figure that out.'

'I don't think Sophie's there yet.' Claire thought of what she had overheard. Sophie had sounded devastated.

'Maybe not,' Mark conceded. 'But there's nothing I can do about that. Other than not encourage her, which I don't.'

That was true. She had almost felt bad for Sophie, he had been so cold and aloof.

'I really like you, Claire,' he said pleadingly, taking her hand, his thumb stroking over her fingers.

'I really like you too.' And when he leant in for a kiss, she met him halfway. But she still couldn't shake the feeling that she was trespassing.

'Have I blown this?' he asked, pulling back, perhaps sensing her hesitance.

'It's not your fault.'

He sighed wearily. 'Bloody Sophie! I should be used to her sabotaging my life by now.'

'Sorry. I do really like you, Mark. I just can't... not tonight.'

'I know,' he said, standing and pulling her to her feet.

'I'm really sorry.'

'Don't be. There's no rush. We've got plenty of time.'

But they didn't have plenty of time, Claire thought, as she got into bed alone. She was going home tomorrow, then Mark would be in New York and it would be weeks before she could see him again. Bloody Sophie, indeed! Mark wasn't the only one whose life she was sabotaging. She tried to ignore the niggling voice in her head that said Sophie was just a convenient excuse because she didn't want to admit that her heart simply wasn't in this.

29

Luca was glad of the distraction when Ali showed up at his flat on Sunday afternoon. He didn't know what was wrong with him. He'd thought he'd be glad to have all his time to himself again – he'd been neglecting his painting lately – but he missed Claire. He wasn't used to having sex with someone he had any kind of relationship with. It was a novel experience for him and, to his surprise, he liked it. He had thought it would be boring having sex with the same person over and over again, but it added a whole other dimension that made the sex more interesting and nuanced and... *better*. And it was relaxing not having to worry about Claire getting clingy and making demands on him.

'Where's Claire?' Ali asked, wandering from room to room.

'She doesn't live here, you know.'

'Doesn't she?'

'No. So, what's up?' he asked, as he cleaned his hands on a rag.

'Nothing much,' she said, prowling around restlessly, like a caged tiger. 'I just haven't seen you in a while. I thought I'd take you out to dinner.'

'Dinner?'

'Yes.' She turned to him. 'You remember dinner? It's the meal that comes after breakfast and lunch.'

'Oh, that dinner.' He could tell she was in one of those moods where she wanted to make things up to him. He sighed. She would never be done trying to make things up to him.

'Yes, that dinner. My treat.'

'You shouldn't spend your money on me. We can have dinner here.'

'Really?' she asked, tilting her head to the side and looking at him sceptically. She skipped over to the kitchen area, opened the fridge and peered in. 'What would we have?'

'I'm pretty sure there's some cheese that's still broadly feasible.'

'You mean this?' she asked, her lip curled as she held up something green and hairy that might once have been cheese. He couldn't really tell from where he was standing. He felt bad because Claire had left it there and he'd let it rot. He didn't like her wasting her money on him.

'Okay, not cheese, then,' he conceded.

'What do you normally have for dinner? What would you have if I wasn't here?'

He really had no idea. When he was working flat out, like he was now, he often forgot to eat until he realised he was almost faint with hunger. Then he'd just grab whatever was closest to hand.

'You don't have anything, do you?' she asked crossly.

'I do sometimes,' he said defensively. 'If I think of it.'

Ali rolled her eyes. 'And what do you have then?'

'Toast.' He grinned.

Ali tutted. 'You don't eat enough. Look at you – you're skin and bone. Come on, I'm taking you out for dinner, and that's that.'

'I don't know...' He hesitated. 'I have a lot of work to do.'

'Luca,' she said sympathetically, 'you need a break.'

She was probably right. He was getting paint-blindness, and he felt dizzy and disoriented from too little sleep. Apart from the few hours he'd spent at Claire's house on Friday night, he hadn't been outside the flat in days – that couldn't be healthy. And, now that he thought about it, he *was* really hungry.

'Okay, you're on. I'll just go and clean up a bit,' he said, waving his paint-stained hands.

'Let's see what you're working on,' she said, darting over to the canvas propped up on an easel by the window. 'Luca, you shameless hussy! You're doing a rude painting of your girlfriend!'

'She's not my girlfriend. And it's not rude.' He frowned. Claire was obviously naked in the painting, but her shoulders were hunched, her arms held straight in front of her covering her breasts, and her head hung shyly, her dark curtain of hair completely shielding her body from the viewer's gaze. He had wanted to capture the private nature of her sexuality – the 'for your eyes only' aspect of it that he found so tantalising. Except it wasn't for his eyes only any more...

'Does Claire know you're putting nudie pictures of her on display?'

'I'm not. This isn't going in my show.' It begged the question why he was working on it now when he should be concentrating on pieces for his exhibition.

'So, how is Claire?' Ali asked, as he began putting away brushes and paint. He could hear the forced casualness in her tone.

'She's fine – I think.'

'Is she around? We could ask her to join us for dinner!' Ali said, as if the idea had just occurred to her. But he knew her too well. He could tell this was what she had been thinking of all along. 'Why don't you give her a call, see if she's free?'

'Can't – she's in London for the weekend.'

'Oh, pity. Well, never mind,' she said brightly. 'And put on something respectable,' she called after him, as he went to get cleaned up.

Luca started scrubbing his face and hands to remove the worst of the paint, then changed his mind. 'I'm just going to have a quick shower,' he called to Ali, as he stripped off. It would wake him up and make him feel more human.

'Okay. I'll be out here nosing through your stuff.'

When he had dried himself, he pulled on a T-shirt and a pair of black jeans that were a bit scruffy, but clean. 'I hope we're not going anywhere too poncy,' he said, as he rejoined Ali in the main room.

'No, definitely not. You need feeding up, and you don't get big enough portions in poncy restaurants. You need steak and lots of vegetables. I'm taking you to Roly's.'

'Do I look respectable enough for that?' he asked, spreading his arms.

Ali surveyed him. 'You look very rock and roll. I don't know how you manage it, but somehow you manage to make your scruff look like a deliberate fashion choice.'

'How do you know it's not deliberate?'

'I've seen behind the curtain. Come on. Let's get some potatoes into you quick.'

* * *

In the restaurant, Ali told Luca what to order, and he let her boss him around, knowing it would make her happy. When the waiter came, he followed instructions and asked for vegetable soup, followed by steak with mashed potatoes. Ali then proceeded to order every vegetable side dish on the menu.

'We don't want you getting scurvy,' she said, smiling at him over her menu as he looked at her in alarm. 'And anything we don't finish you can bring home in a doggy bag.'

'Where it will meet the same fate as that cheese,' he said, smiling fondly at her.

'How long is Claire in London for?' she asked.

'Just the weekend,' he said.

'You must miss her a lot,' Ali said, clearly fishing.

'Ali,' he said gently, 'it's not what you think – me and Claire. We're just friends.'

'Since when do you have women friends?'

'I have plenty of women friends.'

'Women friends you sleep with on a regular basis?'

'There's a first time for everything. Anyway, you don't know what we do.'

'You're not seriously trying to tell me you're not sleeping with Claire?'

'I'm trying to tell you that it's none of your business.'

'So you admit that you are!' Ali's eyes lit up with delight.

They were interrupted by the waiter arriving with their starters.

'So, are you friends with benefits? Booty-call buddies?' she asked, diving into her smoked salmon. 'How would you describe your relationship?'

'I wouldn't,' he said implacably, as he picked up his spoon and started on his soup.

'You're no fun,' she said crossly.

'But in answer to your question—'

'Yes?' Ali sat up eagerly.

'I do miss her.'

Ali grinned happily.

'As a friend,' he added. 'We're just friends, Ali.'

Ali gave him a doubtful look. 'I've seen you with her, remember? You know what I think?'

'No.'

'I think you're in love.'

'No, I'm not. Don't be stupid,' he snapped.

'Hey, don't look so scared,' she said, covering his hand with hers. 'I think she feels the same way about you.'

Luca considered telling Ali that Claire was in London with another man right now and putting paid to any romantic notions she had about them. But if she was convinced he was in love with Claire, she would only worry and feel sad for him so he said nothing. He knew how badly Ali needed him to be happy because if he wasn't, she felt it was her fault – their mother had seen to that when she had written her book.

He knew it wasn't intentional, but in describing the circumstances of their adoption – Ali's inconsolable grief at being separated from him, how she had screamed and clung to him when they had tried to take her away – Jacqueline had cast Ali as the architect of his unhappiness, burdening her with the responsibility for the course his life had taken.

'So what about you?' he asked, to change the subject, when their mains were served. 'Any special someone in your life?'

'Ugh! I'm not discussing my love life with my *brother*.'

'Ha, you can dish it out, but you can't take it.'

'Shut up and eat your vegetables.'

* * *

After spending the day with Mark's friends at the picnic, Claire was relieved to be alone with him on the drive to the airport – not that she didn't like them, but she found it a strain spending a lot of time with a group of people she didn't know and was glad when they could finally get away. Besides, she had found Sophie's constant clamouring for attention exhausting – especially when so much of it was directed at Mark. All morning she had gone out of her way to make a point of how long she had been a part of Mark's life, constantly reminiscing about places they'd been, meals they'd shared, mutual friends they'd lost touch with, and Claire had no doubt it was all aimed at unsettling her. But though she found it wearisome, she couldn't bring herself to resent Sophie – not when she remembered what she'd said last night about Mark: '*He's all there is.*' When she felt like that about him, who could blame her for putting up a fight?

'Sorry,' he said. 'That was a baptism of fire. I hope it hasn't put you off ever coming back.'

'No. I had a really nice time. Thank you.'

'Good. I know Sophie can be a pain in the arse – but she's going through a tough time at the moment.'

'I know. She seemed nice, really.'

He smiled at her. 'You're very sweet.'

Sweet. Claire felt a little knocked off balance by that. She wasn't sure it was a good thing that he found her 'sweet'. He'd said it before, and it sounded like a compliment, but she couldn't help feeling patronised. Besides, she wasn't sure 'sweet' was really his thing. It wasn't a word anyone would ever associate with Sophie, for instance, and although they weren't together any more, he obviously still liked her a lot. He might not realise it, but he lit up like a struck match whenever she was around. She seemed like a take-no-prisoners kind of girl, and Claire got the impression men found her challenging and exciting in equal measures. She was ballsy, blunt and upfront about what she wanted, and she was more like NiceGirl than Claire would ever be. Mark had told Claire the first time they'd met that she was very different from what he'd expected. Maybe he'd thought she'd be more like Sophie.

'You're very quiet,' Mark broke into her thoughts. 'You okay?'

'Yes, fine. I'm just tired.'

He went into the airport with her and waited while she checked in, then walked with her to the security area and gave her a lingering goodbye kiss.

'Thanks again,' Claire said. 'I had a lovely time.'

'I'll call you from New York. And I'll get over to Dublin as soon as I can after I get back.'

'That'd be great. Well, I'd better go.' She gave him another quick kiss before turning to go through security.

In the cab from the airport she rang Luca. She was anxious to speak to him. He'd said they'd still be friends, but she was worried they'd drift apart now they were no longer sleeping together, and she wanted to make sure that didn't happen.

'Hey, sweetheart.' She was instantly reassured by the warmth in his voice. He was her friend, she thought, and that wasn't going to change.

'Can I come round tomorrow night after work?' she asked. 'If you're not busy, that is.'

'Yeah, of course. How was your weekend?'

'Great. It was really nice. But I'll tell you about it when I see you.'

'Okay.'

'I'm in a taxi, and I'm almost home, so I'd better go. But I'll see you tomorrow.'

'Can't wait.'

* * *

The following evening Luca felt unaccountably nervous as he waited for Claire to arrive. He was looking forward to seeing her, yet there was a strange feeling of dread in his gut at the same time. What was that about?

Still, when he opened the door and found her standing on the step, laden with carrier bags as usual, those other feelings melted away and he was just happy to see her.

'Claire!' He pulled her into a hug, then ushered her in. 'You look great!'

He took some of her bags from her as they headed for the stairs. 'You'll have to stop doing this,' he said, nodding to the bags.

'It's nothing much,' she said gruffly.

In the flat, she dumped a couple of the bags by the sofa, then went to the kitchen to help Luca unpack the rest.

'Mm, airport goodies,' he said, as he unloaded smoked salmon, Toblerone, red wine and champagne. 'Are we having a celebration?'

'Well, I thought we could have a sort of graduation ceremony,' Claire said, taking out the champagne. 'I bought this on the way over, so it's already cold.'

'Great.' Luca got glasses out of the cupboard, and Claire opened the champagne with a loud pop. She poured slowly, giving the bubbles time to subside.

'Cheers!' Luca clinked his glass against hers. Then they went into the living room and sat on the sofa.

'These are for you,' she said, picking up the bags beside her and passing them to him. 'Sorry they're not wrapped.'

'What's all this?' He took them from her.

'It's just a present, for being such a good teacher.'

'Claire, you shouldn't be spending your money on me.'

'It's not much.'

He pulled two T-shirts from the first bag, unfolding them and holding them up. 'These are great – I love them.' The other bag had a large shoebox containing a pair of heavy boots. He smiled, brought back to the night he had met Claire. They were similar to the ones he had been wearing then, except these were in one piece. It was such a thoughtful present.

'Not very exciting, I'm afraid.'

'They're brilliant. Thank you.'

'I hope I got the size right,' she said.

He turned them over. 'Yep, perfect. You shouldn't have, but thank you.' He leant over and gave her a quick kiss. Her lips were cool and tasted of champagne.

'You look tired,' she said.

'Yeah, I am.' He dug the heels of his hands into his eyes.

'Not getting much sleep by the look of things.'

'No, I've been working a lot.'

'Is that all?' Was it his imagination or did she seem cheered by this?

'Yeah, that's pretty much all I've been doing lately. The painting's been going really well. I'm working on stuff for my show.'

'That's good. I heard you went to Mum's card game on Friday.'

'Yeah. I cleaned up – did she tell you? Came away with sixty cents.'

'Whoa! If you keep that up, you'll be able to give up painting and become a professional gambler.'

'I'm planning to build up to a whole euro next time.'

'Did you do anything else at the weekend?'

'Just went out for dinner with Ali yesterday. Otherwise I've been living like a hermit.' He took a gulp of champagne. 'So, tell me all about your weekend,' he said. He knew he had to ask, but he felt as if the words were being dragged from him.

'It was good. We spent a lot of time with Mark's friends, and they were all really nice. And he said maybe we could go to New York together some time.'

'And did your lessons come in handy?' Fuck! Why the hell had he asked that? Now she'd tell him, and he really didn't want to know. *Please don't go into details*. The idea of hearing about what she and Mark had got up to made him feel sick.

'Yes, they were very useful. I was a credit to my teacher. You'd have been so proud of me.'

'Great.'

'One lesson in particular,' she continued.

'Well – glad I could be of help.' He drained his glass. 'Top-up?' he asked, reaching for hers.

'No, thanks.' Her glass was still half full. Luca poured himself some more. 'I mean, before I'd probably just have gone along with having sex because I'd have been too embarrassed to say I didn't want it—'

Luca froze. 'Wait. You didn't have sex with him?'

'No.'

'You mean... on the first night?'

'All weekend. And it wasn't because I was scared or didn't think I could give him a killer blowjob. I just didn't feel right about it so...'

The relief hit him like a cartoon wrecking ball, ludicrous and shocking, and he almost laughed out loud with the surprise of it, coupled with the sudden, alarming recognition – *so that's how I feel*. Ali was right.

'That's brilliant!' He grinned. She frowned at him. 'I mean it's great that you spoke up for yourself and took control,' he amended hastily.

'Yeah, it felt good. And it's all thanks to you.' She leant over and gave him a kiss on the cheek, but as she made to pull away, he put a hand on the side of her face and kissed her properly. It felt so good to be kissing her again. To think he'd almost lost her because he'd been too stupid to recognise his own feelings. He reached to pull her closer, but Claire was pushing him away.

'I can't,' she said shakily.

'Hey, what's wrong?' he asked, smoothing a lock of hair behind her ear.

'I can't... do this. I can't be like this with you any more.'

Luca frowned, trying to digest this. 'Oh.'

'I thought we'd... I mean, I'm with Mark now. It would be cheating.'

'Right.' He sat up and edged away from her a little. 'But you said you didn't sleep with him.'

'No, I didn't – because I wasn't ready. I would have been doing it to please him, or because I felt too awkward turning him down. But I will, when the time is right – on my terms, like you taught me.'

'Oh, right. Sorry, I thought...' He shook his head. Shit! He'd finally woken up and realised how he felt about her, and it was too late. He wanted to howl at the unfairness of it.

'No, *I'm* sorry. I should have been clearer...'

'No harm done,' he said briskly. 'Probably just as well anyway.' He poured the last of the champagne into both their glasses. 'I really should get back to work.'

'Oh. I thought maybe we could have something to eat...'

She looked so disappointed, he felt like a shit, but he just wanted to get her out as quickly as possible and be on his own to try to absorb what had just happened. His head was reeling and he needed to be alone. Besides, he couldn't guarantee that he wouldn't burst into tears any second now. 'Sorry. Some other time, yeah?'

'Um... yeah, sure.' She gave him a smile and drained her glass. 'Well, I suppose I should go, then.' She stood.

'Thanks again for the presents,' Luca said, as he saw her to the door.

'It's nothing. Well, bye.' She was about to go, when she turned back in the doorway. 'Luca, we're still friends, right?' she asked, grabbing his hand.

'Yeah, of course!' He looked down at her hand in his, his thumb stroking over her fingers. 'I just – I don't know how good I'm going to be at this friends thing, okay?'

'But you'll try? I really don't want to lose you.'

He sighed heavily. 'Yeah, sure. I'll try.'

30

The next day Luca tried to throw himself into his work, but he spent most of the time standing pointlessly in front of the canvas, utterly uninspired and unable to focus. He tossed down his brush in frustration. This had felt so futile lately, like he was bashing his head on a brick wall. He knew he was good, it wasn't that. He had no insecurities about his art, no real doubts about his ability. But he also knew that talent wasn't a guarantee of success or even recognition – either critically or commercially. Sometimes it seemed completely arbitrary, and it was incredibly frustrating to see all the money and acclaim lavished on artists who weren't half as good as he was.

Maybe he should pack it in and get a real job. He'd never cared about materialistic stuff before. He had been content making art that satisfied his own creative objectives, and was prepared to live with the consequences. But the trouble with wanting Claire was that it made him want all this other stuff too. He had never been bothered about being the kind of guy who could show a girl a good time or provide her with creature comforts. Claire made him want to be that guy. He wanted to be someone she could depend on – someone who could make her life easier, instead of being another drain on her energy and resources. He wanted to be able to do nice things for her – take her to New York and buy her presents. In short, he wanted to be bloody Mark.

* * *

In the days afterwards, Claire felt adrift. Despite his assurances that they would still be friends, she felt that Luca was distancing himself from her. By the following Monday she hadn't heard from him for a week. She told herself that he was probably just concentrating on his work, but she couldn't help wondering what else he might be doing. When Yvonne talked about a party she'd gone to at the weekend, Claire asked casually who'd been there in the hope that she would mention Luca, but she didn't.

'But what's happened to you?' Yvonne asked sharply, peering into her face. 'You've lost that glow. You look all lackluster and— Oh my God! You're not doing it any more.'

'No,' Claire admitted, with a wan smile. 'I'm not.'

'But what about the guy in London?'

'Well, first we were doing the five-date rule, and then—'

'I should never have told you about that stupid rule,' Yvonne interrupted. 'It's not for everyone, you know. And it obviously doesn't agree with you. Anyway, it doesn't work for long-distance relationships – you don't see each other often enough. You could be a hundred before you'd get a shag.'

'Well, now he's in London and I'm here, and he's going to New York next week...'

'Well, hop on the minute he gets back. And in the meantime you've always got Luca.'

Claire shook her head. 'Luca and I aren't a... thing now.'

'Oh,' Yvonne said, apparently unsurprised. 'I guess having a regular fuck buddy would be too much of a commitment for him.'

Claire wanted to spring to Luca's defense, but she had a feeling Yvonne might be right.

Luca wasn't the only one Claire was fretting about. She was also anxious about what Mark did when she wasn't with him. Though they had spoken almost daily on the phone since she'd got back, it had done nothing to put her mind at rest, and when she asked him what he was doing in the evening, she was always on full alert for any mention of Sophie. She thought she trusted Mark, but she still felt insecure at the thought of him spending time around Sophie, even if it was in a group.

'So, what are you up to tonight?' she asked, when he called her on Tuesday night.

'Oh, nothing much. Just having a quiet night in with Millie. I have a lot of reading to catch up on.'

'Anything else planned for the week?'

'Well... it's Patrick's birthday on Thursday, so we're going out for that.'

Had she imagined it or was there a cautious note in his voice?

'We?'

'Yeah, everyone – the usual suspects.'

'Will Sophie be there?'

'Sophie, Olivia, Andy, Jamie – the whole gang,' he said casually – perhaps too casually?

'Well, have fun,' she said, determined not to sound needy or paranoid. 'I wish I could be there.'

'I wish you could too. Hey,' he said then, 'why don't you hop on a plane and come?'

'Nah, I can't,' Claire said, happy he'd asked. He wouldn't want her there if he had something to hide. 'Wish Patrick a happy birthday for me.'

'Will do.'

'And enjoy New York.' A thought suddenly occurred to her. 'Mark... is Sophie going to the wedding?'

The moment's silence on the line told her all she needed to know before he said, 'Er... yes, she'll be there.'

'Oh. Well... have fun.'

'Thanks,' he said, subdued. 'And when I come back I'll organise a trip over to Dublin as soon as possible.'

'Great! Looking forward to it.'

* * *

When Thursday evening rolled around, she still couldn't help feeling anxious at the thought of Mark being out with Sophie. There was no doubt in her mind that Sophie would go all out to win him back. She would just have to trust Mark not to let himself be won.

'Luca hasn't been around for ages,' her mother said to her that evening, when they were watching TV together.

'I know.'

'No chance he'll come over tomorrow, I suppose?'

'No, I— I think he's busy.'

'Aw, that's a shame. He'll be missed.' This was true. He was already a great favourite with Espie's friends, who had been asking after him last Friday, obviously disappointed he hadn't turned up.

'Ah, well,' her mother continued. 'I suppose a guy his age has better things to be doing at the weekend than hanging around with a bunch of old fogeys.'

Yeah, Claire thought sadly – like going out on the prowl.

'And so do you. You should be off out with him. You know you don't have to be here, don't you? Not that we don't love having you…'

'I know. But I wouldn't be out with Luca anyway.' She sighed. Maybe she was kidding herself that they could be friends. Thinking back, he had been humiliatingly eager to get rid of her when she had called round to his flat after coming home from London. Besides, where would she fit into his life now? If his social life centered on picking up women for casual sex, she would only cramp his style. 'Like I said, he's busy. He's doing a lot of work at the moment.'

'Well, I hope he'll still come to my birthday party next week. You'll ask him again, won't you?'

'I will,' Claire said, glad she had an excuse to ring him. If he was offhand with her, at least she could cover her embarrassment by saying her mother had insisted she call so she was only following orders.

'I miss Luca,' Espie said.

'Me too.' Claire sighed. 'Me too.'

* * *

'Hi, honey, I'm home,' Claire called, as she let herself into the house the next evening. She had spent all day at work rehearsing her phone call to Luca and was resolved to make it as soon as she had finished helping her mother get the food ready for tonight's gathering. In her more optimistic moments, she thought maybe she would even persuade him to come.

She was greeted with silence. Her mother didn't respond as she usually did, like a cheery fifties housewife, with some crack about having her martini ready or fetching her pipe and slippers. She was probably in the loo, Claire told herself, trying to shake the sense of foreboding that settled on her, but as soon as she stepped into the kitchen, she knew something was wrong. She couldn't put her finger on it, but the house felt different somehow. A thought came into her head: *There's nobody here.*

She raced to the stairs, her heart pounding as if she already knew. When she pushed open the door of her mother's room, she found her lying on the bed, her head at a slightly awkward angle, her shoes kicked off on the floor beside her.

It took a split second, and then it hit her like a series of punches to the solar plexus that kept coming, robbing her of breath, draining the strength from her muscles so she fell to the floor, every thought in her head reduced to a single word that repeated on a loop. *No.*

* * *

The next hours passed in a blur of phone calls, tears and her brothers' ashen faces as they turned up at the hospital. Later, the three of them went back to the house and Claire made tea. As she switched on the kettle, she noticed the bowl of raw cake batter on the worktop, the spoon abandoned as if mid-stir, and she realised that that was what she had seen when she came home, without registering it. On some subliminal level, she had noticed it and known that her mother was dead.

'Do you want one of us to stay the night?' Ronan asked her.

'No,' she whispered, pressing a tissue to her raw eyes. 'Thanks, but I'm fine.'

'Are you sure?' Neil asked.

'Yes. You should go home.'

They all agreed there was nothing they could do for now, so they might as well go home and try to get some sleep.

'We'll be back first thing in the morning,' Neil said, as they left.

She had never felt so alone as she did when she had closed the door behind them. Already the house felt so empty, like the heart of it was missing – the thing that had made it home. She went into the living room and flopped onto the sofa, letting the tears roll down her face, too numb even to wipe her eyes with a tissue. She didn't know how she'd ever have the energy to get up and go to bed. Maybe she should have got someone to stay, so she would be forced to behave in a more normal fashion. But suddenly she knew there was only one person she wanted now.

She had been so afraid of calling him lately, but now she grabbed her mobile from her bag and dialled Luca's number without a second thought. It didn't even occur to her to worry that it was Friday night and he might be out.

He answered quickly. 'Hi, Claire.' She tried to decide if he sounded distant or cold, but she couldn't tell.

'Hi.' She took a deep breath, meaning to break the news gently. But then she just said 'Mum died tonight,' her voice breaking on a sob, and then she was howling, unable to say any more.

'Oh no!' Luca gasped. 'Jesus, I'm so sorry.'

She gulped, trying to control her sobbing so she could speak. 'I was wondering if— if you could come over. If you can't, that's fine—'

'Yes, of course. I'll be there right away.'

'Okay.' She sniffed, tears coursing down her face. 'Thanks.'

She couldn't settle to anything as she waited for Luca to arrive. She sat, she stood, she paced. She turned on the TV and turned it off again a few minutes later when she realised she was staring unseeingly at it. She was so agitated, she felt as if she would start clawing her own skin off if he didn't turn up soon. When the bell rang, she raced to the door and threw it open, sobbing with relief when she saw Luca standing in the porch. She didn't even say hello before she threw herself at him. His arms came around her, vice-like, and he lifted her off the ground, carrying her into the house and kicking the door closed behind them. Then they just stood in the hallway, clinging to each other. Luca held her so tightly, it was as if he was trying to pull her inside his skin.

'What happened?' he asked, when her sobs finally subsided. She drew back to look at him, and his eyes were shining with tears.

'She had a heart attack. I came home from work and found her.'

'I'm so sorry,' he said. There were streaks of red paint on his face, and his hands were covered with a motley assortment of blues and yellows. He must have been working and dropped everything as soon as she called.

'Can you stay?' she asked hoarsely, her throat raw from crying.

'Whatever you want.'

'I mean, stay the night – with me. As a friend...'

'I know what you mean.' He kissed her forehead.

'Thank you.'

She took his hand and they walked upstairs to her bedroom. It seemed to take Claire for ever to get undressed and into her pyjamas. Her limbs felt leaden and uncoordinated, as if she was drunk. Luca stripped down to his boxers and climbed into bed beside her, pulling her into his arms and rubbing her back soothingly until she fell asleep.

* * *

She woke early the next morning, and left Luca to sleep while she showered and dressed. Her head was already buzzing with all the things that needed to be done that day. She didn't bother with breakfast, unable to decide whether she was hungry or not. She was having a cup of tea when her brothers and their wives arrived. Ronan and Neil were red-eyed, Michelle and Liz pale and drawn. No one looked like they'd had much sleep. Michelle gave Claire an awkward hug, which felt weird because Claire didn't think they'd ever hugged before.

Liz made tea and they all sat around the kitchen table to plan the funeral, making lists of what needed to be done. All the while, Claire kept expecting her mother to stick her head around the door and ask if they wanted a cup of tea or a piece of cake warm from the oven. She was jolted every time it hit her anew that Espie was gone.

'I suppose Jim and that lot will want to play the music,' Neil said, when they were discussing the finer points of the funeral.

'Oh, I never thought of that!' Claire said. 'But, yes, I suppose they will. It'd be nice.'

'As long as that mad old bat with the fiddle isn't involved.'

'Mary?' Claire said. 'If the others are playing, Mary has to join in. That's what Mum would have wanted.'

'I doubt it,' Neil argued. 'Mum wasn't tone deaf.'

'That's not the point. She loved Mary. She always let her play. You know Mum – she wouldn't want anyone left out.'

'Well, on your head be it.'

'Hello.' Everyone looked round as Luca came into the kitchen. There were a lot of raised eyebrows and furtive glances, all eyes shifting curiously from him to Claire.

'You remember Luca,' she said.

'Good morning,' he said to everyone, then crossed to Claire. 'You should have woken me up,' he said quietly, dropping a kiss on top of her head.

'No need. Help yourself to anything you want for breakfast.' She smiled weakly up at him.

He went over to the worktop and flicked the switch on the kettle. 'Does anyone want toast?'

'No, thanks,' Michelle said. 'We had breakfast at home.' Liz, Neil and Ronan declined too.

'Claire?' Luca looked to her. 'Toast? Scrambled eggs?'

'No, thanks. I don't want anything.'

'He's making himself at home, isn't he?' Michelle muttered, eyeing Luca suspiciously as he busied himself with the toaster.

Claire said nothing. She didn't feel like justifying his presence in the house to anyone.

'I thought I'd say a few words,' Michelle piped up. 'At the funeral – you know, a eulogy.'

'Really?' Even Neil was aghast at this announcement.

'Yeah. I'd like to talk about Espie – what sort of person she was, what she meant to us all.'

'Are you sure?' Liz asked her. 'You and Espie didn't exactly see eye to eye, did you?'

'Oh, I'm not denying we had our moments,' Michelle said, with a tinkling laugh. 'But sparks are bound to fly when two strong women are pushed together. We were very fond of each other, really.'

'You were?' Ronan frowned.

'Of course! You know, I don't think Espie really *got* me until the children were born. But she started to appreciate me after that, when she saw what a good mother I was. She was always telling me how much she admired my parenting skills. I think she was a little bit envious, if I'm honest, because she didn't think she was a great mother herself. And she often said she wished she'd kept a record of the minutiae of her kids' lives like I have in my column.'

Claire gritted her teeth and said nothing.

'I have lots of ideas already,' Michelle said.

She probably had the whole thing written in her head, Claire thought.

Maybe she even had it filed away, like a newspaper obituary, just waiting for the opportune moment to whip it out.

Luca put a mug of hot tea in front of Claire, then sat beside her with his own mug and a plate of toast topped with scrambled eggs. He pushed the plate between them, and Claire reached out automatically and took a piece. The eggs were buttery and comforting, and as soon as she started eating, she discovered she was hungry.

'This is really good, thank you,' she said softly.

Luca smiled at her in response.

'You should have said you were hungry, Claire,' Michelle said. 'I'd have got you something.'

'I didn't know I was.'

'Okay,' Liz said, looking through her list, 'so as soon as we're ready, Neil and Claire will go to the funeral director's and get the ball rolling. Ronan will talk to the priest and I'll stay here and man the phones, let everyone know, and organise the caterers.'

'Do you know where Mum's will is?' Neil asked Claire.

'I'm not sure, but it's probably in the safe.'

'There's no rush, but you should try to dig it out in the next couple of days.'

Michelle poured herself more tea. 'Of course the house will have to be sold,' she said.

Claire flinched, and Luca put an arm around her, scowling at Michelle.

'Michelle!' Neil chided, rolling his eyes in Claire's direction.

'I'm just saying! Sorry, Claire, I don't mean to sound callous, but I'm only stating facts.'

'We don't have to think about that now,' Ronan said, glaring at her.

'No, of course not. I'm just being practical. I mean, Claire knows the house is left between the three of you. I didn't mean any harm,' she said to Claire. 'You know that, don't you?'

'Yes, it's fine,' Claire said dully, clenching her fists under the table.

'Sure, you won't know yourself now you can have a bit of independence. Find yourself a nice little apartment somewhere.'

'Yeah, brilliant,' Claire whispered, wishing her mother was there to make one of her dry comebacks that would go right over Michelle's stupid head. She couldn't stop the silent tears that rolled down her cheeks.

'You could even move to London, like you always planned.'

Luca's eyes darted to Claire, and he looked surprised.

'Well,' Neil said awkwardly, 'if you're ready, we should go to the funeral director's.'

'Yeah. I'll just brush my teeth,' Claire said, anxious to be off. She had no will to fight, but she didn't want to spend another minute with Michelle.

'Anything I can do?' Luca asked, as she got up to go.

'No, there isn't – but thanks. You don't need to hang around here all day.'

'I can come back tonight, if you like – stay with you again?'

'Yes,' she breathed, in relief. 'I'd really like that.'

* * *

On her way out to the car with Neil, she checked her bag for her mobile to make sure she had it with her. She was surprised to see she'd missed a couple of calls from Mark, and there was a message from him on her voicemail.

'Hi, Claire, I know you probably don't want to speak to me right now, but please ring me back when you get this. We need to talk. Just call me back, okay?'

She frowned, perplexed. He sounded agitated. But why would he think she didn't want to speak to him? He seemed to have decided she'd been deliberately avoiding his calls. It was almost as if he knew what was going on, but he couldn't possibly. She rang him back in the car.

'Claire,' he answered immediately. 'Thank you for calling me back. Look, all that stuff on—'

'Mark,' she broke in, 'my mother died last night.'

There was a moment's silence. Then, 'Oh, Christ, I'm so sorry. That's awful.'

'Yeah. That's why I didn't answer your calls. I only got your messages just now.'

'What happened?'

She went through the story once more, reciting it by rote.

'Oh, Claire, I'm sorry. When's the funeral? I could try and get back early—'

'It's on Monday, but don't worry about coming. Really. So what was it you wanted to talk to me about?'

'Oh, don't worry. It'll keep.'

'Okay. Well... I'd better go. I've got a funeral to arrange.'

'I'm really sorry, Claire. If there's anything I can do, just let me know.'

'Thanks.'

The day passed in a blur of arrangements, phone calls, visitors and endless cups of tea as people called to offer their condolences and to sit around reminiscing about Espie. Everyone brought food, and Claire was running out of space to store it all, the fridge groaning under the weight of lasagnes, quiches and casseroles, the worktops covered with cakes of every size and variety. Each time she had to talk about her mother, Claire started crying again, and she felt completely drained and exhausted by the evening, longing for the time when everyone would be gone and she could just curl up in bed with Luca.

* * *

'Oh, it's you,' Michelle said, when she opened the door to Luca that evening, stepping back ungraciously to let him in.

Claire's other sister-in-law was in the kitchen, but everyone else seemed to have gone.

'Where's Claire?' he asked.

'She's having a lie-down,' Michelle said, and pursed her lips disapprovingly.

'Okay. I'll just... go up and see if she needs anything,' he said, heading for the stairs.

'I hate to say it,' he heard Michelle whisper loudly as he left the room, 'but I think Claire's being a bit of a drama queen.'

Luca stilled, one foot on the bottom step.

'Well, her mother has died,' Liz said.

'Yes, but she's not the only one. Neil and Ronan lost their mother too and you don't see them carrying on like that. I think she's milking it a bit, making it all about her.'

'It's not a competition for who's the most upset. Claire lived with Espie. They were very close. It's only natural—'

Luca was about to carry on upstairs when Michelle said something else that stopped him in his tracks.

'And what's the story with this Luca? Why is he suddenly around all the time? Has he moved in or what?'

'He's just being supportive to Claire. I think it's nice that she has someone.'

'She has her family. If you ask me, he thinks he's onto a good thing here. Did you see his face when I said the house would have to be sold?'

'He was just concerned about Claire. It was rather insensitive to bring that up today.'

'Well, I wouldn't trust him as far as I could throw him. I think one of us should have a word with Claire, put her on her guard.'

'Oh, come on. Claire isn't stupid.'

'But she's a bit naïve about men. She hasn't had many boyfriends. It would be easy for someone to take advantage, flatter her with some attention. Especially now when she's just suffered a loss—'

Luca didn't wait to hear any more. He felt like running away, mortified that Claire's family could think he was on the make, but he forced himself to carry on up the stairs. Surely Claire wouldn't believe that about him if they said it to her. He knocked on the door of her room before entering. She was lying under the duvet, fully dressed.

'Are you okay?' he asked softly. 'Do you want anything?'

'No, thanks,' she said, as he crossed the room and sat on the bed. 'Are Michelle and Liz still here?'

'Yeah.'

'I'm just being a wimp, hiding up here until everyone's gone. I can't take any more of Michelle being "marvellous".'

'I'll tell her to fuck off if you want.'

Claire smiled. 'Better not. She already doesn't like you. I think she suspects you're after my money.'

Luca laughed in relief. 'Yeah, I heard her talking. She's going to warn you about me.'

'Oh God – sorry. She's an awful wagon.'

'It doesn't matter. I'll let you know when the coast is clear.'

'Thanks,' Claire said, her eyes drooping closed.

'You should try to get some sleep.' Luca kissed her forehead and crept quietly out of the room.

When he went back downstairs, Claire's sisters-in-law were in the kitchen, surveying the food.

'I don't know what people are thinking,' Michelle said, standing in the open fridge doorway. 'I mean, they must know that Claire's on her own now. She'll never get through all this.'

'Well, we could divide it up for her and put it in the freezer,' Liz suggested, standing at the table, beside the cakes. 'It'd be handy for her to have some stuff ready when she comes home from work.'

'I know people mean well, but it's not thoughtful,' Michelle continued, as if Liz hadn't spoken.

'Or she might have people over,' Luca suggested.

'Who would she have over?' Michelle said dismissively. 'Well, it would be a shame to let all this go to waste. I'll take this,' she said, pulling a huge tray of lasagne out of the fridge. 'It'll save me having to cook for a couple of nights. I was up to my eyes this week already, and now with this funeral on top of everything else, I won't have a minute.'

'Maybe we should stay and eat with Claire tonight,' Liz said uncertainly.

'I think she'd rather be on her own,' Michelle said.

At least she'd got that right, Luca thought.

'I'll be here anyway,' Luca said, adding, under his breath, 'eyeing up the silverware.'

'What?' Michelle asked sharply, turning to him. 'What did you say?'

'Nothing.'

Liz smirked at him, obviously having heard, but said nothing.

'You can take these casseroles, Liz.' Michelle heaved two large dishes onto the table. 'My lot won't eat them anyway. They won't touch anything with gravy.'

'Maybe just one...'

'Take them both. They'll freeze well. And I'll take all this cake. Holly has a bake sale in school this week, so we can get rid of a lot of it that way. And the rest I'll freeze and use for school lunches.'

'We should leave something for Claire,' Liz said.

'There's still a chicken in the fridge,' Michelle said. 'It's raw, but Claire has nothing else to do now. It'll do her good to have something to occupy her – take her mind off things. She needs to keep busy.'

The doorbell rang. 'That'll be Neil and Ronan back,' Liz said, going to answer it. She returned, followed by the four children. 'Neil and Ronan are waiting in the cars, so we'll be off,' she said to Luca. Then she started barking instructions at her children. 'Take that dish, Adam. Ben, you take the other one. Hold it straight – don't let it drip on the floor.'

Luca watched as Claire's sisters-in-law and their progeny went through the kitchen like a team of worker ants, streaming in and out of the house, the children bearing dishes of food almost bigger than themselves to the cars, until the place was empty except for him and a lone chicken.

When he went to tell Claire everyone had gone and it was safe to come downstairs, he found her asleep. He was glad – she must be exhausted. He felt so helpless in the face of her grief, and he wished there was something he could do to make her feel better. He pondered this as he returned to the kitchen. Unfortunately, sex was off the table. He knew he could make her feel good that way, but even if he wasn't supposed to be keeping his hands off her, now probably wasn't the time. What else did people turn to for comfort? Food? Maybe he could make her dinner. He opened the fridge and stared into it, almost empty now except for the chicken – thank goodness her sisters-in-law had left that. Now he just had to figure out what the fuck to do with it.

He took it out and examined it, relieved to find that there were cooking instructions on the bottom. It seemed you basically just had to bung it in the oven – that should be easy enough. He rooted around and found potatoes and vegetables, and set to peeling and chopping. The vegetables, however, didn't come with instructions, and he wasn't sure what to do with them once he'd cut them into pleasingly even chunks. And there should be gravy too. He had no idea how gravy happened. He'd ask Ali, he thought, grabbing his phone. When she didn't answer her mobile, he rang home. Jacqueline answered.

'Hi. Is Ali there?'

'No, she's out. You could try her mobile.'

'I did. She's not answering it.' Luca hesitated. 'I wanted to ask her something but... I guess I can ask you instead.'

'Okay...'

'How do you make roast potatoes? Really good ones like you and Ali make.'

'Oh. You're cooking?' She sounded surprised.

'Um... yeah. I'm making dinner for Claire.'

'Sounds romantic.'

'No, it's really not. Her mother died last night.'

'Oh, I'm so sorry. Give her my condolences.'

'Yeah, I will. So... roast potatoes? And I need to know about gravy too. I mean, where does that, like, come from?'

'Okay, for really good roast potatoes, you're going to have to parboil the potatoes first...'

* * *

Luckily, Claire came downstairs just as Luca was starting to worry that the chicken would go cold. His mother had told him how to let it rest, and it was sitting on the worktop under foil.

'I fell asleep,' she said, rubbing her eyes as she came into the kitchen. 'Gosh, something smells really good.'

'I made dinner,' Luca said. 'Sit down.' He waved at the table, which was set for two. He had even lit a candle.

'Oh! Do you want me to help with anything?'

'No, thanks. Just – don't look,' Luca said, as he began hacking at the chicken with a knife. He was relieved when Claire sat down with her back to him. It might not look very pretty, he thought, as he tore at the meat, transferring huge chunks – you couldn't really call them slices – to two plates, but it smelt fucking delicious. He cut up the whole chicken and divided it equally, piling it up on the plates. It looked like an awful lot, he thought, surveying it dubiously. Maybe you weren't meant to serve the whole thing in one go. He shuffled some meat back into the dish from both plates until the portions looked more reasonable. Then he added roast potatoes, carrots, stuffing and gravy.

'It's chicken,' he said, as he plonked a plate in front of Claire.

'Thank you. This looks amazing. But you really needn't have gone to all this trouble. There's already tons of food in the house.'

'Not any more,' he said, as he poured them both wine. 'Your sisters-in-law made off with it all.'

'Oh,' Claire said. 'I might have known.' For a moment she just looked at her plate. She took up her knife and fork and began to eat slowly, carefully. And then, to Luca's horror, she began to cry silently, great fat tears rolling down her face and splashing into her gravy.

'Oh God, is it awful?' He winced apologetically. 'Sorry.'

Claire shook her head mutely.

'Really, if it's terrible, just don't eat it.'

Claire wiped her eyes with her napkin. 'It's not that…'

Luca threw down his napkin and got up, crouching beside her to put his arms around her. 'Hey, come on,' he said gently, rubbing her arms. 'It doesn't matter. It's just a stupid chicken. There are some frozen pizzas in the freezer. I just thought—'

She sniffed, shaking her head. 'It's not that, Luca, honestly. It's gorgeous.'

'Really? You're not crying because it's horrible?'

'No. I'm really not. It's perfect.'

'What is it, then?'

'It's just that it's so… beautiful.'

'Really? My cooking is so good it made you weep?'

She laughed softly, brushing away her tears. 'It's… so thoughtful. It's such a lovely thing to do. I'm touched, that's all.'

'Oh. Well, if there's nothing wrong with it, you'd better eat it before it goes cold.' He gave her a soft kiss on her forehead and got up, returning to his seat.

'Better?' he asked, as Claire resumed eating. She nodded, smiling at him.

'Oh my God, this *is* good,' Luca said. There had been a lot more bother involved in making roast potatoes than he'd anticipated, but it had paid off. They were crunchy on the outside and meltingly soft on the inside. Good enough to make angels weep, he thought – literally.

'Are you okay?' Luca asked Claire later, as they lay in bed together like the previous night.

'Mm. I just can't get to sleep.'

'Do you want to read for a while? I don't mind if you want to turn the light back on.'

'I wish I could, but I don't think I could keep my eyes open. I'm too tired to read and too awake to sleep.'

'I'll read to you, if you like.'

She turned to him. 'Would you?'

'Sure.' He shrugged.

Claire turned on the bedside light. There were a couple of books on the nightstand, but she ignored them, getting out of bed and going to the bookcase on the far wall. She wanted the comfort of something familiar – the book equivalent of a roast-chicken dinner – and she knew what she was looking for. She found it quickly and got back into bed, handing it to Luca.

'*Pride and Prejudice*?' he read the cover. 'I've never read this.' He leant back against the headboard, opening the book. 'Are you ready?'

'Ready,' she murmured, snuggling down beside him and closing her eyes.

'"It is a truth universally acknowledged",' Luca began, '"that a single man in possession of a good fortune, must be in want of a wife..."'

Claire relaxed to the deep, soothing tone of Luca's voice as he read the familiar story.

31

'I brought this over last night,' Luca said, in the morning, handing Claire a large square parcel wrapped in brown paper, 'but I wasn't sure... I was going to give it to Espie for her birthday. I thought you might like to have it.'

'I told you she said not to get her a present,' Claire said, sitting at the table to open it.

'She said not to *buy* her a present.' Luca smiled. 'And I didn't.'

'Oh.' Claire tore at the paper, guessing what it was. Her eyes welled when she uncovered the painting and recognised her mother and her friends grouped around a table playing cards. Even Luca was there at the bottom of the picture, his back to the viewer, and Claire was opposite him, her head bent as she studied her cards, frowning in concentration. But Espie was at the centre, all the light in the painting falling on her as she pulled a card from her hand, her eyes alight with triumph.

'Oh, Luca!' Tears spilt from Claire's eyes. He had captured her mother so perfectly – not just her physical likeness but her essence. It was almost as if she was alive again, here in the room with them. She flipped the canvas around, where Luca had scrawled the date and title on the back. '*The Trick*,' she read.

'Maybe I shouldn't have given it to you,' he said, his eyes full of concern. 'I didn't mean to upset you.'

'No, it's perfect.' She threw an arm around him and kissed his cheek. 'Thank you. I just wish Mum could have seen it. She would have loved it so much – once she got over being cross with you for giving her a present.' She wiped her eyes. 'I'm going to bring it to the mortuary tonight and ask them to put it on the coffin tomorrow at the funeral.'

It was another long, deadening day of arrangements, tea and visitors. Claire was so weary of the inertia, she was almost relieved when it was time to go to the mortuary that evening, finally signalling the beginning of the end.

She had questioned the wisdom of bringing the children, worried that they would be spooked by seeing the body laid out. But Michelle insisted that it would help them come to terms with their granny's death. More likely, Claire suspected, she thought it would be good material for her column.

'Is she going to be a vampire now?' Ben asked solemnly, as he gazed into the coffin.

'Some people don't become vampires,' Adam said. 'They have the true death.'

'I hope she is one,' Ben said. Then he gasped. 'She wouldn't bite us, though, would she?'

'No,' Adam said firmly. 'She'd only bite bad people, like murderers or... the government.'

Cian was sobbing uncontrollably in Michelle's arms. 'I think it's hit him that he's never going to see his nana again,' she said to Claire, over the top of his head.

'Maybe he will,' Adam said.

'That's right, Adam.' Michelle smiled down at him. 'We'll see her again in Heaven, won't we?'

'We might see her before that,' Adam said, 'if she turns into a vampire.'

Claire was touched by the number of people who came to the mortuary. She thought she would be shaking hands for the rest of her life as friends and neighbours streamed past for what felt like hours, offering their condolences. There were some unexpected faces, some Claire hadn't seen in so long it took her a moment to place them, and a few she didn't recognise at all.

Afterwards the house was thronged, and Claire was kept busy with the caterers, seeing that everyone got food and topping up glasses. She was too preoccupied with looking after the guests and chatting to people to think about getting anything for herself, until Luca thrust a plate into her hand.

'You should eat,' he said, leading her to an empty chair and handing her a glass of wine. Claire thanked him, and began mechanically forking food into her mouth, barely even tasting it.

'You're looking after Claire, are you, Luca?' Mary said, joining them. 'Good lad,' she continued, without waiting for an answer.

Jim soon joined them, followed by Lily, Nancy and Michael, forming a little huddle around Claire and Luca. It was strange to see them so subdued, but Claire was touched by their gentle concern for her, and admired the way they looked after each other in their mutual grief. And she couldn't help feeling a little childish glee that their obvious fondness for Luca and their assimilation of him into their little gang was pissing off Michelle, if the suspicious looks she was throwing in their direction were anything to go by.

Claire looked around the room, filled with chatter and laughter. There were so many friends, some of whom her mother hadn't seen in a long time. It was sad that they were here now, when it was too late.

'Mum would have loved this,' she said quietly, her eyes filling. It seemed horribly unfair that Espie was missing her own party.

Luca took her hand silently, and she interlinked her fingers with his. She was so grateful that he was here. She didn't know how she'd have coped without him in the last couple of days. It struck her how much more alone and lost she'd have felt if not for his constant reassuring presence. Everyone was being so kind, but they all left in the end and she was so glad that she wasn't alone when they were gone.

'Can you stay again tonight?' she asked him.

'Of course,' he said, squeezing her hand. 'Whatever you want.'

'Thank you.'

'Besides,' he smiled, 'there's going to be a ball at Netherfield. I don't want to miss that.'

* * *

The following day was warm and bright, and Claire was glad that the glare of the sun gave her an excuse to wear dark glasses and hide her ravaged eyes as the family left the house and got into the funeral cars. She was dimly aware of the blur of faces as they pulled up outside the church and got out, surprised and touched to see Luca's parents among the throng with Ali. He seemed as surprised to see them as she was.

The service was sad, the music unbearably moving. When her mother's friends started playing, Claire hoped Mary's tuneless scraping wouldn't reduce her to giggles. But the violin was so heartbreakingly sweet and melodious, she had to check that another musician hadn't taken over at the last minute. She broke down again at the sight of the old lady, her teeth gritted and her face set in a grimace of concentration while tears rolled down her cheeks.

'What's *he* crying for?' she heard Michelle hiss further along the pew, as Luca discreetly wiped tears from his eyes. 'And why is he in the front with Claire? Who does he think he is – chief mourner or something? He's not even family.'

None of them had had the energy to dissuade Michelle from speaking, but they had insisted that Jim should be allowed to do the main eulogy so she was cut mercifully short. Jim's speech was fittingly funny at times, evoking the spirit of the friend he had lost.

Claire broke down completely as the service ended, sobbing uncontrollably and clinging to Luca, who was practically holding her up as they followed the coffin out of the church. Outside, everyone stood chatting, and once she had recovered, Claire moved around, thanking them for coming and inviting them back to the house after the crematorium.

'Mary, your playing was beautiful,' she said, as soon as she saw the old lady.

'Ah, I couldn't let Espie down, today of all days. She was always very forgiving, but I wouldn't have been able to forgive myself if I hadn't done right by her.'

'I hope you're not in too much pain?'

'Can't feel a thing. I took an extra dose of morphine and some other stuff, just to be on the safe side. What you might call a cocktail of drugs,' she said cheerfully. 'Though I am a bit woozy now. I could do with a sit-down.'

'Why don't you get into one of the cars? We'll be going shortly.'

'I'll look after her,' Jim said, appearing and leading her away.

Tom had closed the shop for the morning so he and Yvonne could both be at the funeral. He hugged Claire and told her to take as much time off work as she needed. Yvonne's eyes kept darting to Luca. She was obviously dying to ask questions, but aware that now was not the time.

Catherine was delighted to have finally encountered the infamous Michelle first-hand. 'I wouldn't have missed your sister-in-law's eulogy for the world,' she told Claire. 'Comedy gold.'

'I know. I wish Mum could have heard it – it would have given her such a laugh.'

'I don't think I've ever heard a eulogy before that eulogised the person giving it. Pure genius!'

Ali hugged her fiercely, while Luca's parents greeted her with more restraint.

'It was good of you to come,' she said, as she shook their hands.

'I hope we'll see you at the house again soon,' Jonathan said.

'Yes, get Luca to bring you some Sunday for lunch,' Jacqueline said, her eyes drifting to Luca, who was chatting with Jim and Michael. 'We'd love to see you.'

* * *

Claire was glad it was a smaller core group of family and friends who came back to the house after the crematorium. Her energy was dwindling after the strain of the last couple of days and she just wanted to be with people who didn't require her to make any effort. Some people had come a long way, and she was glad to see her mother's old friends reunited, chatting about old times and remembering Espie, as long as she didn't have to do anything. She made sure there was plenty of food and drink, and let them get on with it. The party went on late into the evening and, much as she appreciated their support and friendship, Claire was relieved when people started to leave. She felt completely drained, tired to her bones: she wanted to get into bed and sleep for a week.

'I'd love to stay and help you with the clearing up,' Michelle said, 'but we need to get the kids to bed. It's been a very long couple of days for them.'

'That's fine.'

'But you have all the time in the world now anyway. There's no rush. You should leave it all until tomorrow.'

Claire nodded, wishing her sister-in-law would go. That was what she really needed right now – *advice* about tidying up. So helpful.

When the last guest had left, she surveyed the mess in the living room. While she was glad to be alone again, it also brought home to her how alone she was now. When the house had been full of people, she had had something else to focus on, and the business of the funeral had carried her through for the past few days. There had been so much to plan and so many people around all the time. But now it was over and there was nothing left to do, nothing else to think about. She felt overwhelmed by the emptiness of the room and hugged herself as tears sprang into her eyes.

Suddenly she felt arms wrap around her from behind and she jumped.

'Hey,' Luca said softly in her ear, pulling her closer. 'Sorry, did I give you a fright?'

'I thought everyone was gone.'

'Everyone else has. The caterers are packing up in the kitchen. They, um… they need to be paid.'

'Oh! Of course.' She wriggled out of his arms and picked up her bag from the floor, pulling out the envelope with the caterers' money. They wanted to be paid in cash and she had the exact amount ready. She went into the kitchen and found them packing up the last of the glasses.

'Thanks.' She smiled at Mike, handing him the envelope. 'You did a great job.'

'Thank you,' he said, pocketing the envelope. 'Okay, we're all done here.' He swung up the box of glasses and nodded to his partner. Luca came into the kitchen as they left.

'Thanks for sticking around,' she said to him. 'You're a good friend.' Her voice broke.

Luca rushed to her, pulling her into his arms. 'You're exhausted,' he said, brushing her hair off her face as he looked down at her. 'Why don't you go to bed and I'll start clearing up this lot?'

'You don't have to—'

He put a finger on her lips, silencing her. 'I know I don't have to. Now, go on.' He bent and kissed her forehead, and she turned to go. She was too tired and the thought of her bed was too tempting to resist. 'I'll be up shortly,' he said, as he turned to the sink, rolling up his sleeves.

'You're staying?' She turned in the doorway.

'Oh.' He frowned. 'Do you want to be alone?'

'No, I really don't. I'd like you to stay.'

She left him in the kitchen, slinging things into the sink, and dragged herself up the stairs to bed. She was half asleep already as she undressed and crawled into bed. But she was still just awake later when Luca got in and wrapped his arms around her. She turned into his body and drifted off.

32

Claire felt lost in the days following the funeral. She was beginning to regret taking the week off work, but changing her mind would require a decision that she couldn't summon the energy to make. She didn't know what to do with herself, and couldn't seem to rouse herself to do anything more energetic than lie in the garden, soaking up the sun, or slump on the sofa watching box sets of *Friends*. She had seen them a million times before, but she found the familiarity comforting. She missed her mother dreadfully, longing to be able to talk to her again, or even watch TV together in companionable silence.

She felt adrift, the focus of her life snatched away. For so long everything had revolved around looking after her mother, worrying about her, organising her, spending time with her. Now she constantly felt as if she had forgotten to do something important, and her stomach would lurch with sickening dread of the consequences. Then she would realise once again that there was nothing to be done and no one to worry about – but there was no comfort in that. It left her on edge, unable to concentrate or settle to anything.

On top of that she was exhausted, suffering from the crash that often follows a long period of tension. It wasn't just the stress of her mother's death and its aftermath. It was the accumulation of years spent in a perpetual state of suspense. Her mother's health had been so volatile that Claire had been constantly on tenterhooks for the next crisis – the breathless race to hospital, the hours spent in corridors and waiting rooms, anxiously awaiting test results or the outcome of an operation. She was physically and emotionally drained.

Everyone was telling her she should take a holiday, now that she had the chance. She hadn't had a proper one in ages, since her mother had become too incapacitated to travel. Mark would be back from New York on Friday, and he had invited her to stay with him for the weekend, but she couldn't face the upheaval of flights or the idea of having to be social and, besides, she wasn't in the mood for somewhere as busy as London. But the idea of getting away was appealing, and as the week wore on, she increasingly felt the need for a change of scene. The good weather was making her long for the seaside. The heatwave was forecast to continue for the rest of July, and she knew the perfect place where she could go to relax, and spend a restorative couple of days just eating, sleeping and lazing in the sun.

'How'd you like to come to the beach with me for the weekend?' she asked Luca, the following evening. 'Unless you have other plans, of course,' she added, suddenly remembering that he might rather stay in Dublin with the chance of getting laid than go away with her for a weekend of celibacy by the sea.

'No, I don't have plans. I'm a bit broke, though…'

'It won't cost anything. I have a place we can stay. Just don't expect anything fancy.'

'Where are we going?'

'Brittas Bay. Mum has a mobile home there – had,' she amended. 'It's mine now, I guess.'

'Cool. I'll dig out my bucket and spade.'

*   *   *

A weekend away with Claire – Luca wasn't sure what he'd let himself in for. He hadn't even had time to assimilate his feelings yet. He'd only discovered he was in love with her when her mother had died, and then he had wanted to step up and be a friend to her. Now he felt completely at sea, clueless as to how to be with her, terrified of screwing up and losing her, and just as scared of keeping her in his life but only as a friend.

He thought how arrogant he'd been when she'd first come to him, warning her not to get attached. Jesus, he should be so lucky! He'd been so sure of himself, so certain that she was the only one in danger of getting emotionally involved. What he hadn't considered was that he would also be experiencing a kind of intimacy he wasn't used to.

Claire had got under his skin – like painting, he thought, as he picked up his brush and got back to work. That had crept up on him, too, when he wasn't looking. It had started in rehab.

Art therapy had been part of the program, and he had resisted it at first, as he had resisted all help. He had refused to be moved, shoring up his defences against anything or, indeed, anyone that might touch him, determined to be cold, aloof and, above all, not to care. But he'd gone through the motions, as he had with the rest of the program, and art had got in somehow, breaking through his defences, seducing him until he found himself pouring all the emotions he had kept buried for years into his paintings.

It had scared him at first when he'd seen all that stuff spilling out of him. He'd felt raw and exposed, as if he had no skin. Every shitty thing inside him was there for all to see, in thick, vivid colour – all his cringing fear, his anger, every rotten thing at the core of him made real, given substance; and beyond that, his vulnerability, loneliness and sadness. And yet he didn't want to stop. It felt cathartic and healing, as if all the poison was being leached out of him and what was left was fresh, clean and healthy.

He could never regret rehab because it had given him one of the best things in his life. He would never regret knowing Claire either, even if they could only be friends. Maybe it was for the best that they couldn't have sex any more. He wasn't very good at forming lasting relationships with the women he slept with. They tended to end up pissed off with him.

Besides, who was to say this thing with Mark would last? Maybe if he stuck around long enough...

***

That night, Claire went online for the first time since her mother had died, catching up with NiceGirl's Twitter and Facebook friends. When she logged on to Twitter, she found herself mentioned in a tweet from Mark's friend Emma, aka @Locksie:

Locksie @PublisherMark So disappointed in you. I thought you were being true to @NiceGirl.

It was from last Friday, the day Mark had called saying they needed to talk, and she had been too busy arranging the funeral. She knew Emma was just joking – as far as she was concerned, NiceGirl and Mark had nothing more than a light-hearted online flirtation. But what did it mean? Thursday had been Patrick's birthday party. Had something happened with Sophie? She tried to follow the conversation back, but drew a blank. Some previous tweets appeared to have been deleted. Perplexed, she went into Mark's feed and scrolled back to Friday, trying to piece together conversations. There had been lots of activity with his friends, and his responses mainly consisted of him telling them nothing had happened. There was a reply to an @Soph, who had to be *the* Sophie, simply saying:

cease and desist

Frustratingly, @Soph's account was locked, so Claire sent her a follow request.

She thought she would have to wait a day or two for her request to be accepted, if Sophie accepted it at all. So she got ready for bed and tried to forget about it for now. But just as she was about to go to bed, she got a notification that she was now following @Soph. She went straight back onto Twitter, into @Soph's account and scrolled down to Friday's tweets. She had been very active that morning, throwing out lots of veiled hints that something had happened the night before:

@Soph The sweetest hangover. :)
@Soph Don't worry re that last tweet, rehab fans. Was high on life last night. Strong stuff, but not on the prohibited list.

And finally:

@Soph Hey la, hey la, my boyfriend's back.

Claire waited for the appropriate feelings of hurt and betrayal to kick in, but she felt only mild dismay. Of course, Mark was clearly denying that anything had happened, and she had more reason to trust him than Sophie. Maybe that was why all she felt was a strange sort of detached curiosity because, deep down, she suspected Sophie was just trying to stir things. Or maybe the general numbness she had been experiencing since her mother's death was deadening the impact, and it would hit her later when she was more herself.

But right now all she felt was intrigued, and she wanted to get to the bottom of what had really happened. So she sent a DM to @Locksie:

@Locksie Soz, have been away from Twitter – family crisis. What's @PublisherMark been up to? Email me gossip, please!

Then she turned off her laptop and went to bed.

* * *

The next day was sunny and warm, as promised. Claire was up early, feeling brighter now that she had something positive to focus on. She loaded the car with supplies and went to pick up Luca.

'So, Brittas Bay,' he said, as he swung in beside her, throwing his bag onto the back seat. 'I haven't been there in years. We used to go sometimes when we were kids.'

How funny, Claire thought, that they could have been there at the same time all those years ago.

'But mostly we went to beaches closer to home,' he continued.

'We pretty much lived at Brittas Bay during the school holidays,' Claire told him.

They had spent long summer holidays there as children, living a beach-based life no matter what the weather. They had been able to roam freely, making friends with other kids staying in the caravan park, playing in the dunes and swimming in the sea. Every meal was eaten outdoors. It had been an idyllic existence for a child.

In latter years, she had spent the odd weekend there with her mother, but they hadn't been for some time, first because the weather was never good enough to entice them down, and then because her mother was too incapacitated for caravan living. Claire had missed it, and she was glad to have the opportunity to use it again, possibly for the last time. She knew her mother had left the mobile home to her, but she wasn't sure she would be able to keep it on. The site was expensive, and there were service charges on top of that. If she didn't use it, she didn't think she could justify the upkeep on purely sentimental grounds. She would have loved her nephews and niece to enjoy it, but her brothers weren't keen on caravan holidays, and her sisters-in-law even less so.

She felt herself start to relax and unwind as they breezed along with the windows down, summery music blaring from the speakers. When she caught her first glimpse of the sea, the water sparkling and shimmering in the sunshine, her heart gave an instinctive leap, just like it always had when she was a child. She turned into a little side road and opened the electronic gates to the caravan park, driving down the soft grass track to their site.

'Home, sweet home,' she said, pulling up in front of a large caravan, set on a grassy area, with a picnic table beside it. The garden was neat, a pile of inflatable toys and body boards piled up in the corner beside a threadbare set of goal posts and a covered barbecue.

'Really?' Luca looked delighted.

'I told you not to expect anything fancy.'

'It's perfect!'

Claire felt better already as they got out of the car and she took a deep lungful of the sea air. She opened the door of the caravan and Luca followed her inside. He stood in the middle of the little living room, then gave a long, luxurious stretch, his T-shirt riding up to reveal the fine black hair of his happy trail against the white skin of his taut stomach. The living area was roomy enough as mobile homes went, but it suddenly felt very small with Luca in it, and Claire felt a moment of apprehension. She hoped it wouldn't be awkward spending the weekend in such close proximity while keeping their distance physically.

Luca was studying a corkboard over the little seating area, pinned with photographs and flyers for local businesses and takeaways. 'Is this you?' He was pointing to a photo.

'Yes.' Claire blushed. It featured her in a swimsuit on the beach as a gawky eight-year-old, her hair in pigtails, her legs buried in sand. 'Aw, you were cute.' He studied the other photographs. 'And then you were *seriously* cute,' he said, pointing to a photo of her as a teenager, all budding breasts and stick-thin thighs in a halter top and frayed jean shorts. 'I wish I'd bumped into you then.'

'Come on, let's get the car unpacked. And then we can hit the beach.'

They unloaded the stuff from the car, and stocked up the fridge and cupboards, finally grabbing their bags. 'You can sleep in here,' Claire told Luca, opening the door of the biggest bedroom.

'Where will you sleep?' he asked.

'Here.' She showed him the other room. There was just about space for the narrow single bed.

'Looks cosy,' he said regretfully. 'I wish I was sleeping here with you.'

She shot him a warning look.

'I know, I know.' He held up his hands defensively. 'I promised to behave myself, and I will.'

'So, lunch first?' she said. 'We can eat up here at the picnic table. For the full nostalgic experience, we should really eat on the beach, so everything gets nice and sandy, but I'm not *that* dedicated to nostalgia.'

'Great.'

'I'll put the kettle on.' She dumped her bag on the bed, slipped past him, and busied herself getting lunch ready.

They sat outside with big mugs of tea and picnicked on crusty rolls, cheese, ham, apples and grapes.

'This is so good,' Luca said, wolfing down the food hungrily.

Claire was enjoying it too. All the flavours tasted bright and alive, and she had more of an appetite than she'd had all week. 'Everything tastes so much better outdoors,' she said. 'Especially at the sea.' She breathed deeply, suffused by an enormous feeling of well-being.

'It's beautiful here.' Luca sighed, turning his face to the sun. 'So peaceful.'

She was pleased that he appreciated it as much as she did. 'Mum would be glad we're doing this,' she said. 'She loved it here.'

Later they trailed down the wooden walkway that led to the beach, cresting over the grass-covered dunes. Claire pulled off her sandals, her feet plunging into the warm, powdery sand as they stepped onto the beach. She turned and looked back at the dunes. It was hard to believe that once they had seemed so huge, and it had felt daring for her and her brothers to jump from the top into the soft sand beneath, like launching yourself off a cliff.

They spread their towels on the sand, stripped down to their togs and made for the sea.

It took Claire a while to ease herself fully into the water, gradually acclimatising to the cold, but once she did it was wonderfully invigorating, awakening all her nerve endings and bringing her senses to life. Claire looked at Luca beside her, his hair tangled and curly from the salt water. He was so beautiful she wanted to cry. Why had their lessons had to end, she wondered sadly. If only she could have had a few more weeks when he was hers to kiss and touch. Why couldn't Mark have waited just a little bit longer?

Later, as they lay on the sand, she pushed on her sunglasses, and took her book out of her bag.

'Did you bring *Pride and Prejudice*?' Luca asked, propping himself up on an elbow and holding out his hand for it.

'You don't have to read to me,' Claire said.

'Hey, I don't want you to go on without me.'

'Okay,' she said, handing him the book. She had to admit, she loved being read to – it was all the pleasure with none of the effort, like receiving oral sex. She lay down and closed her eyes, relaxing to the deep tone of Luca's voice. She found herself drifting in and out of consciousness as the words washed over her...

'"... for the young man wanted only regimentals to make him completely charming. His appearance was greatly in his favour; he had all the best part of beauty, a fine countenance, a good figure, and very pleasing penis."'

'What?' Claire reared up with a jolt and turned to Luca.

'Just checking you were still listening,' he said, with a cheeky grin.

She laughed and lay down, closing her eyes once more. 'I'm listening. And Jane Austen is spinning in her grave.'

'"... a fine countenance, a good figure, and very pleasing address,"' Luca continued. When he got to the end of the next chapter he closed the book.

'Do you think Mr Darcy is really well-hung?' he asked.

'You should so be in a book club,' Claire said drily, turning to face him. 'I have no idea! What makes you think about that?'

'Well, all the girls go nuts for him, but he seems like a bit of a git to me. He must have something going for him.'

'Well, he's loaded.'

'Yeah, I got that.'

'And he's handsome.'

'And tall.'

'Very tall. Anyway, he's not a git. He turns out to be really nice – you'll see.'

'When are we going to get to the bit where he goes skinny-dipping?'

'I thought you didn't know anything about *Pride and Prejudice*?'

'I don't. But I remember all the girls going on and on about that scene,' he said, rolling his eyes.

'That didn't happen in the book. It was just in the TV series.'

'I'm not surprised. He doesn't seem the type.' He was silent for a moment. Then he said, '*We* could go skinny-dipping.' His smile faded. 'Maybe not such a good idea,' he said. 'Sorry. This friends thing takes a bit of practice.'

'No harm done,' she said, feeling disappointed. He wasn't the only one who was having trouble drawing the boundaries between friends and lovers.

* * *

Later they barbecued steaks and ate at the picnic table as the sun sank in the sky.

'I'm going to have an early night,' Claire said, yawning as she cleared the table. It was only nine, but she was exhausted. 'I can hardly keep my eyes open. It must be all this fresh air.' She took an armload of plates into the caravan, and as she was dumping them in the sink, she heard voices outside. She went to the window and saw Luca talking to a girl as he gathered up the rest of the stuff. Tall and slender, her blonde hair was pulled into a high ponytail. She looked around the same age as Claire, but she wasn't one of the regulars she had got to know over the years they had been coming here. Luca had put down the glasses he'd been holding to talk to her. Even though she couldn't hear a word that was being said, Claire could tell the girl was flirting with him – her posture, her smile, the coy way she twirled her hair around her fingers as she talked to him. She was suddenly filled with an overwhelming urge to run out and kick sand in the girl's face. So much for feeling numb, she thought. And she'd forgotten all about being tired because she was fantasising about wrestling that girl to the ground, and she knew she'd have the strength to do it.

She was about to go outside, at least to make her presence known, when the girl nodded to Luca, turned and wandered off. He gathered the glasses up again and came back inside.

'Who was that?' Claire asked.

'Her name's Aideen,' he said, as he dumped the glasses in the sink. 'She's staying in one of the caravans with a friend. She asked if we wanted to go to the pub with them.'

'*We?*'

'Yeah. I told her I was here with a friend too.'

Claire felt knocked back. But, of course, that was all she was to him now.

'She probably thinks I'm another guy,' she said, with a hollow laugh. 'Her friend would get quite the surprise when you turned up with me.'

'Oh, I never thought of that.' Luca laughed. 'But maybe her friend's a lesbian. She might think it was her lucky night!' He turned on the tap. 'Anyway, I presumed you wouldn't want to go. I said we were going to bed early.'

'Just because I'm having an early night it doesn't mean you have to,' she said. 'If you want to go to the pub...'

'Not particularly.'

She knew she was being unfair, acting so possessively. There was nothing to stop him going to the pub with Aideen, letting her take him back to her caravan...

'Or,' she said, sliding a hand up under his T-shirt to the warm skin of his back, 'you could stay here with me. We could go skinny-dipping.'

'Claire...'

She stood on tiptoe and kissed him softly, coaxingly, and he almost responded, but then he was pushing her away gently. 'I thought you were tired,' he said.

'I'm having an adrenalin rush.' She tried to kiss him again, but he held her off.

'Claire, stop.'

'Why? I thought you wanted to go skinny-dipping.' As soon as he released her, she reached for him again. 'Or we could just stay here,' she said, toying with the drawstring of his shorts.

'Stop,' he said firmly, stilling her hand with his. He put his hands on her shoulders and looked into her eyes. 'I came here to be with you, okay? You don't have to take your clothes off to make me stay. I'm not going anywhere.'

'Sorry.' She hung her head, tears stinging her eyes. She let out a long, heaving breath. 'I'm going to bed. We can leave that till morning.' She nodded to the plates piled in the sink.

'I'll do it,' Luca said. 'See you in the morning.' He kissed her on the forehead – a brief, chaste kiss that made Claire want to scream in frustration – and turned back to the sink.

* * *

Maybe coming here hadn't been such a great idea, Luca thought, as he washed up. And to a fucking caravan, of all things! He'd find it hard to keep his distance from Claire on the Serengeti Plain, but squashed together in a caravan...

He really wanted to kiss her. He was aching to take her to bed. Turning her down just now had been one of the hardest things he'd ever had to do, especially when he could see in her face how hurt and rejected she'd felt. But she was vulnerable right now. She was sad and maybe a bit lonely, and he couldn't take advantage. Besides, she would probably regret it later. Then things would be awkward and they wouldn't be friends any more. It wasn't worth risking losing her. Sex was easy – he could get his rocks off with anyone. But he didn't have another friend like Claire.

He heard voices and laughter outside, and turned to see a group of teenagers walking past, dressed up for a night out in jeans and sparkly tops. Maybe he needed to get laid. He should go to the pub, hook up with that girl and get Claire out of his system once and for all.

* * *

In her bedroom Claire lay awake, listening to Luca moving around outside, anxiously waiting for the click of the door or the noise of the shower, any sound that would tell her he was going out. She couldn't relax until she knew if he would go to the pub or not. She turned on her laptop to check her emails. There was one from Emma in her NiceGirl account:

Hi,

    Sorry to hear about your family crisis. Hope it wasn't too serious, and that everything's okay now.

Anyway – gossip. We were all at a friend's birthday last week, including Mark's ex, Sophie. (I don't know if you follow her on Twitter – @Soph?). Anyway, she's still carrying the most ginormous torch for Mark, but he's with someone else now, and she came out all guns blazing, making it really obvious she wanted him back. And when Sophie wants something... well, let's just say she'd give the Terminator a run for his money.

Anyway, long story short, things got a bit messy and she was all over Twitter the next day hinting that something had happened between them. Mark swears it didn't. So it's all very he said/she said. Sophie can play dirty, and I'm more inclined to believe Mark.

Luckily I don't think Mark's new girlfriend is on Twitter, so she may have missed the whole thing. Mark asked us to delete all the tweets relating to it – I obviously missed one. Oops!

So, that's all the gossip. It's probably nothing, and I shouldn't even be telling you. But I guess it's okay since you don't know any of the people involved – except Mark, of course.

He tells me you're going to stop writing the blog...

The rest of the email was publishing talk.

When she had finished reading it, Claire shut down her laptop and sank back against the pillow. So something *had* happened between Mark and Sophie at Patrick's party – or maybe not. And Claire found she didn't care either way. The numbness was back. She heard Luca going into the other bedroom, the door closing behind him with a soft click. She turned off the light and settled down.

33

Claire slept late, and woke feeling relaxed and refreshed. Luca still wasn't up at noon when she sat outside with toast and coffee. She was pleased he was getting lots of sleep – he needed it. She was also glad of the quiet and solitude to mull things over in her head and sort out her feelings. She knew she should have been distraught or at least unnerved by Emma's email last night. She ought to have been fretting about what might have happened between Mark and Sophie. But instead she just felt a wonderful sense of freedom that she didn't really mind. She wasn't in love with Mark, and she knew now that sleeping with him wouldn't change that. The utter indifference she felt at the idea that he and Sophie might have got together again said it all. The feeling just wasn't there, and she could no longer fool herself that it would come in time.

Luca, on the other hand, only had to *talk* to another girl to bring out the green-eyed monster in her. It was a real shame because Mark was the one who wanted to have a real relationship with her. But there was no point in denying it any more, at least not to herself – she loved Luca, and she'd rather be his fuck buddy, if that was all that was on offer, than have something more meaningful with anyone else.

It was almost one when Luca finally emerged, yawning and blinking in the sunlight, but bright-eyed and looking rested.

'Good morning,' he said, sliding onto the bench beside her. 'Or should I say afternoon?'

'I take it you slept well?' She suddenly felt shy and awkward, hoping he wouldn't say anything about her attempt to seduce him last night.

'Yeah, brilliant. You?'

'Yes, great.' She was relieved that he was his usual friendly, easy-going self.

'I could get used to this,' he said, turning his face to the sun and closing his eyes.

'Me too. I wish—' She caught herself. She had been about to say that she wished they could stay here like this for ever, just the two of them. But she couldn't say things like that to Luca – it would scare him off.

'What?' He opened his eyes and turned to her.

'Oh, nothing. I wish I didn't have to go back to work tomorrow. There's coffee in the pot...'

They spent the afternoon on the beach, swimming, reading and lazing in the sun. Since her mother had died, Claire had found that some days were better than others, and today she was engulfed by one of those waves of sadness that left her feeling submerged and remote from the world, rendering her catatonic. Everything – the sound of the waves, the roughness of the sand against her skin, even the smell of the air – evoked other times, and she was swamped by memories of her mother, remembering all the times she had come here as a child with her brothers, and later, when it was just Espie and her, the wonderfully indulgent weekends they'd had there together. The long days playing on the beach; the nights when their caravan had become Party Central, Espie inviting all their neighbours over for barbecues that went on long into the night. They were happy memories, yet they hit her like punches, leaving her weak and aching, longing to have her mother back, just for an hour – or even five minutes...

Luca seemed to pick up on her subdued mood, and she was grateful for his sympathetic, undemanding presence beside her while she let the heat of the sun and the gentle crash of the waves soothe her.

She felt her spirits lift towards evening, and she was almost happy later as they sat side by side at the picnic table, eating pasta and garlic bread, and drinking red wine warmed by the sun. If she wasn't quite blissful, she was at least content.

'Feeling better?' Luca asked her.

'Yeah, thanks. Sorry I wasn't great company today.'

'Don't be daft.'

'So – home tomorrow.' She sighed as she poured more wine.

'Yeah, and just when the book's getting exciting,' Luca said. 'I mean, there was practically a car chase. I can't believe Lydia ran off with Wickham!'

Claire was enjoying watching him discover *Pride and Prejudice* for the first time. It was so familiar to her that it was hard to imagine anything in it coming as a surprise.

'And now she's ruined. It's a bit harsh, isn't it?'

'Yeah, poor Lydia. But that's the way it was in those days. Once a girl had sex, she was ruined for life.' *Like me*, she thought wryly. *Being with Luca has pretty much ruined me for anyone else.*

'Are you going to keep this on now?' Luca asked, waving to the caravan.

'Yes, I am.' She hadn't been sure before, but over the past couple of days she had made up her mind to keep it. She loved the freedom of it, and the peace – and with her mother gone, she could make more use of it. She would be able to come here on the spur of the moment, whenever the mood took her – just throw some stuff into the car and go. The idea was very appealing. 'It's nice to have somewhere to escape to. And when the weather's like this, it's lovely to just hop in the car and really make the most of it.'

'It's perfect. Though I think it would be great in any weather.'

'Yeah, it is. I love being at the beach at any time of year.' There was a special kind of cosiness about being snuggled up in the caravan listening to rain pelting down outside. 'I might come here to write sometimes,' she said. 'You can use it, too, if you ever want to get away, to paint or whatever.'

'Really?'

'Sure – any time. It's just sitting here. I'd like people to enjoy it. And Mum would have liked you to use it,' she said. 'She was very fond of you, you know.'

He reached out and stroked her hair. 'I was fond of her. I wish I could have known her longer.'

They were just finishing off the last of the wine when Aideen appeared along the path. Claire willed her to pass by, but she strolled up to the table, smiling broadly at Luca. She was wearing cargo shorts and a crop top, revealing an expanse of tanned stomach and a sparkly belly-button ring. Her long blonde hair was tied in a high ponytail.

'Hi, again,' she said to Luca, her smile faltering a little as her gaze moved to Claire.

'Hi.' Luca smiled back. 'Claire, this is Aideen. Aideen, Claire.'

'Hello.' Claire forced a friendly smile.

'Hi, Claire. This is the friend you're here with?' she asked Luca.

'Yep.'

'Oh, I thought... Anyway, I just came to invite you over for a drink. Um... both of you. We're down there, third on the right.' She waved in the direction she had come.

'Thanks,' Luca said.

'Just drop over whenever you like.'

'Thanks,' Claire smiled, 'but I think we're going to have an early night.' She took Luca's hand in both hers, turning it over and stroking the palm, playing with the soft pads of his fingers. 'Aren't we?'

'Um... yeah,' he said uncertainly, frowning down at their hands. 'Thanks anyway,' he looked up at Aideen and smiled.

'Okay. Some other time maybe.' She turned to go.

Luca went to withdraw his hand as she walked away, but Claire held onto it, intertwining her fingers with his.

'Claire...'

Still holding his hand, she leant in and kissed the corner of his mouth, willing him to meet her halfway. She hardly knew what she was doing, acting purely on instinct. She just knew she didn't want him to be with that girl – or any girl except her. She kissed the other side of his mouth coaxingly.

'Claire... stop.' He looked cross as he snatched his hand away. He stood abruptly, collecting the empty dishes from the table, and stomped into the caravan.

Claire gathered up the glasses and empty wine bottle and followed him. He was throwing the dishes into the sink with a clatter, his back rigid with tension as he leant on the counter. She dumped the glasses on the table and went over to him.

'Luca.' She put a hand on his shoulder and when he turned to face her, she swooped in and kissed him again. His lips were firm, and tasted fresh and briny, like the sea. But they were unyielding, and then he was pushing her away.

'Jesus, Claire, give me a break!' he yelled, as he held her at arm's length.

She flinched at the harshness of his tone.

'Sorry.' He released her and raked a hand through his hair. 'But I'm trying to be a friend here, and you're not making it easy. You said you don't want us to be... together that way any more so I've kept my distance. You wanted me to keep my hands to myself, and I have. But you can't keep doing this. I don't know what you want from me.'

'I want this,' she said, putting her hand on the back of his neck and pulling his face down.

He leant his forehead against hers, resisting the pressure of her hand urging him to go the last couple of centimeters. 'No,' he said, shaking his head. 'You don't.'

'I've changed my mind.' She kissed him again pleadingly, and she felt him start to respond, but he wrenched his lips away.

'Don't,' he breathed against her mouth. 'Look, if this is about that Aideen girl, I told you—'

'It isn't. It's about you and me.' She kissed him again, encouraged because he didn't push her away this time. She sensed him weakening. 'Please,' she whimpered, running her tongue along his bottom lip, hearing his sharp intake of breath. 'I want *you*.' She took his hand and clamped it against her breast. 'And if you want me to tell you in detail – I want you inside me, I want—'

'Christ, I want you too,' he groaned, wrapping his arms around her, and then he was kissing her back hungrily, desperately, angling his head this way and that. She felt a triumphant thrill as his tongue slid into her mouth.

He pulled back just enough to speak. 'Are you sure?' he asked, his breath hot on her lips, his dark eyes burning into hers. 'Do you really want this?'

She nodded frantically and he buried his head in her neck, placing soft open-mouthed kisses along her throat before returning to her mouth. Then he picked her up, her legs wrapped around him, and carried her to the bedroom, not breaking the kiss. They fell onto the bed in a tangle of legs and arms and tongues.

* * *

Claire woke the next morning, her limbs knotted around Luca's, the heat of his skin against hers. He was still fast asleep – not surprisingly, since they had made love half the night, first frantically, and then more slowly, Luca kissing and touching her with infinite tenderness, almost reverence. They had looked into each other's eyes the whole time, and it had felt so loving that she still felt cocooned in the warmth of the afterglow.

She propped herself up on an elbow and watched Luca sleeping. He was so beautiful. She dropped little butterfly kisses on his shoulder and neck, the corner of his mouth, half hoping he would wake up and they could do it again. He stirred, his eyelids fluttering, but then he settled again, his breathing returning to a calm, steady rhythm.

Eventually she got restless and uncomfortably hot lying tangled up with him. So she extricated herself and slid out of bed. She pulled on some clothes and tiptoed into the living area. When she had put the coffee on and heated the grill to make toast, she grabbed her laptop and sat down at the table with it while she waited for the coffee to brew. After checking her emails and having a quick look at Twitter and Facebook, she opened the word processor and pulled up the draft she had written for a possible final blog post and read over it.

Fridays I'm In Love

She felt a world away now from the person who had thought that might come true. She would have to come up with a different ending for NiceGirl. Of course, it didn't have to be true – why break the habit of a lifetime? – but this felt all wrong. Besides, it was so obviously about Mark that it would give him the wrong idea. No, NiceGirl would need a different kind of happy-ever-after. Maybe she'd leave it open-ended, with NiceGirl still searching for her Mr Right. Or maybe she had already found him, she thought, glancing towards the bedroom – albeit a reluctant Mr Right.

The coffee pot bubbled and hissed to its finale, and she had just got up to make toast when her mobile rang. She grabbed it and went outside, not wanting to wake Luca. Her heart sank a little when she saw that Mark was calling, and she hesitated a moment before picking up. She knew she needed to talk to him, to break up with him, but she didn't feel ready to have that conversation yet. She didn't have much experience with that sort of thing, and she needed more time to think about what she would say. In the end, she hesitated so long that the phone rang out, and the missed-call alert flashed up on the screen. She rang him back straight away.

'Hi, Mark,' she said, trying to inject some enthusiasm into her voice. 'Sorry, I didn't get to my phone in time just then.'

'Hi. How are you?'

'I'm okay.'

'Listen, the thing is I'm at the airport. I'm flying over to Dublin. So can I come and see you later?'

'Oh! You're coming here?'

'Yeah. Look, I think we need to talk and it's not really a conversation I want to have over the phone.' He sighed. 'Emma told me you were asking her about me and Sophie – except she didn't know it was you, of course.'

'Oh... yeah.' Claire felt guilty for going behind his back. 'Sorry about that.'

'It's okay. I mean, I wish you'd just asked me, but I can understand why you didn't.' He sighed. 'Nothing happened but... I'd really like to talk to you face to face. Can I come round? Or meet you somewhere? I'll be in Dublin in about an hour and a half.'

'The thing is I'm not at home at the moment.'

'Oh.'

'Yeah, I'm in Wicklow. I came to the beach for the weekend. With a... friend.'

'Damn.' He laughed softly. 'I thought I'd surprise you. Stupid idea. I have to get back for work stuff tomorrow, so I have an early flight in the morning.'

'Well, I'm going home today anyway – back to work tomorrow. I could meet you later.'

'Great. I'm staying at the Merrion. Ring me when you're home and we'll arrange it then.'

'Okay. Talk to you later.'

* * *

Luca woke up with a smile on his face, automatically reaching out for Claire, and was disappointed to find her not there. He sank back against the pillows, feeling rather pleased with himself as images from last night flashed through his mind. He didn't have any regrets about it and he didn't think Claire would either. There hadn't been a glimmer of hesitation or uncertainty about the way she had made love with him. He knew she had wanted him every bit as much as he wanted her, matching his passion and desire kiss for kiss and touch for touch. He'd almost told her last night – he'd almost said the words when she was lying beneath him and he was moving inside her. He'd chickened out in the end. But he would tell her later, he decided, feeling giddy and loved-up as he got out of bed, pulled on some clothes and went in search of Claire. He was in love, Mark was toast, and all was right with the world.

He heard her voice outside when he walked into the living area. Looking out of the window, he saw her talking on her mobile. She was so gorgeous. After they'd had some breakfast, he'd persuade her to come back to bed for the rest of the day. Sod the beautiful weather.

There was hot coffee in the pot and he poured himself a mug and sat at the table. As he pushed Claire's laptop aside, his fingers brushed against the mouse and the screen lit up. His eyes drifted idly over the open document that appeared, and then he froze, his mug halfway to his lips, as the words sank in. He pulled the laptop towards him and read it through again carefully, this time letting the full meaning of it hit home.

She'd got out of bed with him this morning and written *this*! God, what an idiot he'd been to think anything had changed. But what the fuck did he expect? He had only himself to blame. He knew she wanted to be with Mark – that was the beginning and end of what their whole relationship had been about. How could he have forgotten? She'd told him she just wanted to be friends. She hadn't been thinking straight last night – and he'd been thinking with his dick. She'd just wanted a warm body, and he was there when Mark wasn't. He should have stood his ground, turned her down.

But what difference would it have made? Would this be any easier if there hadn't been that last time? He was being ridiculous, he told himself, getting pissy because a gorgeous girl had fucked him senseless. He needed to get some perspective. There were worse things than being used for sex... by the girl you loved. It just didn't seem like it right now.

He jumped up guiltily as Claire came in from outside, pushing the laptop away from him.

'Hi.' She smiled as she crossed to the table. He was relieved that she didn't seem to have noticed the laptop and the screen had gone to sleep again. 'I was about to make toast when Mark rang,' she said, fiddling with the grill. 'Do you want some?'

'Yes, please.'

'So – that was Mark. He's on his way over to see me.'

'Oh.'

'Yeah. I thought we'd spend most of the day down here and go home in the evening, but I think we'd better leave this morning instead. He's only here for the day, and I've to sort out clothes for work tomorrow. Sorry. Do you mind?'

'No.' He shook his head dazedly.

'I really need to see him, especially after...' She trailed off, her eyes drifting to the bedroom.

Shit! So much for her not feeling any regret. Mr Right snapped his fingers and she went running to... what? Confess all and beg his forgiveness? Pretend it had never happened and bury her dirty little secret for ever?

'Look, I'm sorry about last night,' he said.

'You are?'

'Yeah – I mean, about crossing the friends boundary.'

'Well, it wasn't exactly your fault. I practically begged you.'

'Whatever. Anyway, no harm done, is there? I mean, you don't have to tell Mark about it.'

'No, but I—' She stopped abruptly, biting her lip. 'No, I suppose I don't,' she finished.

'You're upset, you're not yourself. I think you're allowed a mistake in the circumstances.'

'A mistake. Right.'

'I'll pack up my stuff,' he said, getting up and heading for the bedroom, 'so I'll be ready to go whenever you want.'

'There's no hurry,' she called after him. 'Come and have your toast.'

'Wouldn't want to keep Mr Fucking Right waiting,' he mumbled angrily to himself, as he balled up his clothes and stuffed them into a bag.

* * *

Claire was a bundle of nerves as she made her way to the Merrion Hotel that evening. Luca had been quiet and subdued on the drive home from Brittas, and it had put her on edge. He seemed down, and even though he was perfectly civil, she couldn't shake the feeling that he was pissed off with her. When she'd dropped him off at his door, he'd kissed her cheek and thanked her for a lovely weekend, but he still seemed distant, and she'd wondered if he was deliberately trying to keep her at arm's length. Had he guessed how she felt about him last night? Was he being aloof on purpose to remind her that it was just a casual thing and didn't mean anything? She had already decided not to mention that she was breaking up with Mark in case Luca freaked out, thinking she had read too much into last night and was doing it so she could be with him.

The whole thing was nerve-racking, and now she had the ordeal of dumping Mark to go through as well. She wished he *had* cheated with Sophie, so she would have the perfect reason to dump him – no explanations necessary.

She found Mark waiting for her in the lounge. She was struck again by how good-looking he was – and how unaffected she was by him.

'Hi.' He kissed her cheek and hugged her. 'How are you?' he asked.

'I'm okay. Good days and bad days.'

He nodded. 'I'm really sorry again about your mum.'

'Thanks,' she said, as he released her and they sat side by side on the sofa. 'And thank you for the flowers.'

A waitress came and they ordered tea. 'So,' Mark said, when it had been served, 'I take it you saw some stuff on Twitter about Patrick's party.'

'Yeah,' she said cautiously.

'I wanted to talk to you. I mean, I wasn't hiding anything. I rang you the next day, but your mother had died so...' He shrugged. 'And then it never felt like the right time to bring it up.'

'I hadn't seen any of it at that stage anyway. I hadn't been on Twitter.'

'I thought you probably hadn't. So then I thought it would all just blow over and there was no need to upset you with it.'

'You didn't think I had a right to know?'

'Know what?' he asked. 'Nothing happened. It was a lot of idle gossip.'

Claire raised a sceptical eyebrow. 'Nothing happened?'

He looked at her silently as if weighing something up. Then he seemed to come to a decision. 'Okay.' He sighed. 'Full disclosure. We kissed. But that's all, I promise. It was a mistake, and I'm sorry. Sophie and I have this... thing. I suppose it was unfinished business, but it won't happen again.'

'Sophie seemed to be reading an awful lot into a kiss.'

'That's just Sophie.'

'And what about New York?'

'Look, I won't lie – she made it clear she wants us to get back together. But nothing happened, I promise.' He took her hand. 'So, can you forgive me?' he asked, looking earnestly into her eyes.

She took a deep breath. 'I forgive you, but—'

'Thank Christ for that,' he said, putting an arm around her. 'Because I really don't want to lose you.'

She wriggled out of his embrace. 'I hadn't finished. I said I forgive you, Mark,' she said, looking down at her hands. 'But that doesn't mean I want to be with you.'

'You don't think you can trust me again,' he said. 'But Sophie and I are over, I swear.'

'I don't think you'll ever be over, not really. You love her, don't you?'

'No, I—'

'You may not want to,' she continued, as he shook his head, 'but I think you do. Whether you do something about it or not, she'll always be there, and anyone else is going to feel like second best. And no one should settle for second best.'

He looked at her in silence, his expression anguished and confused, as if he was going through some sort of internal struggle.

'Oh, fuck.' He huffed out a breath, propping his forehead on the heel of his hand. 'I do love her, don't I?' He peered up at Claire from beneath his lashes.

'Yeah, you do.' She laughed wryly. 'Tough luck!'

He smiled at her fondly. 'You don't hate me?'

'No, I don't hate you. Full disclosure – you got lucky. Because I'm in love with someone else too, as it happens.'

'Well, I hope he's a better prospect than Sophie, whoever he is.'

'Not really. He's not into anything serious.'

'God, why can't we just be in love with each other? We'd be great together,' he observed.

'I know! We're perfect on paper.'

'We're both nice, we both want commitment…'

'At least you know Sophie wants to be with you.'

'Yes, but she's such a pain in the arse.' They laughed.

'Luca's lovely. But he'd run a mile if he knew I wanted to be his girlfriend.'

'Christ! What a pair. Are you *sure* we can't make this work?' He grinned, waving his hand between them.

'Hmm, maybe I was a bit hasty,' she joked.

'Seriously, Claire,' he said, sobering up. 'I think we could have had something.'

'Yeah,' she said sadly. 'I think you're probably right.' Maybe if she hadn't known Luca, if he didn't have Sophie… She took a sip of her tea. 'Um, Mark… can I ask you something?'

'Yes?'

'Are you still going to publish my book?'

He threw back his head and laughed. 'Of course I'm still going to publish your book. And I'm still waiting to read your novel too.'

'Right. Great.'

'Well, good luck with your chap,' he said, raising his teacup to hers.

'Good luck to both of us!' She clinked her cup against his. 'I think we're going to need it.'

* * *

A week later, Claire still hadn't seen or heard from Luca, and with every day that passed she became more anxious. She didn't want to race around and tell him she had broken up with Mark in case it freaked him out. But she was terrified he'd be off banging some other girl if she left it too long.

On Monday she was only half listening to Yvonne recounting her weekend's activities as they unpacked boxes when Luca's name brought her up with a jolt.

'Sorry, what did you say?'

'I said I almost felt sorry for Luca, with that cow Aisling crawling all over him. I don't know if you remember her – she was at Ivan's bar that night.'

'She can do the splits,' Claire said, feeling queasy.

Yvonne laughed. 'Fancy you remembering that! Anyway, she's been trying to get her claws into Luca for ages, and I think she senses his weakness now and she's closing in for the kill.'

'Weakness? What weakness?'

Yvonne shrugged. 'I don't know exactly, but there's something wrong with Luca. He's off his game. He's not his usual cocky self.' She sighed. 'I know I shouldn't feel sorry for him – that boy's brought it all on himself – but I can't help it. He doesn't deserve Aisling Wilson.'

'So, did he...' Claire gulped '...did he go off with her?'

'No.' Yvonne laughed. 'He went home on his own to paint and sulk, so he lives to fight another day. You should have seen Aisling's face...'

Claire spent the rest of the day trying to come up with an excuse for calling over to Luca's after work. She knew she shouldn't need an alibi – they were supposed to be friends, and he hadn't given her any indication that he had changed his mind about that. But, nevertheless, she thought it would seem more casual if she had a reason for calling. Unfortunately he hadn't left any of his stuff in her car after their trip to Brittas – she had done a thorough search. There wasn't even anything she could pretend she *thought* was his. If only she could offer him another five hundred for an advanced course of lessons, she thought desperately.

Finally she came up with something. It was spurious at best, but it would have to do. So, after work that evening she made her way to his place. She didn't call in advance, not wanting to give him the chance to put her off.

When she got to his building, the door was open and two pale blonde girls were sunning themselves on the steps. They said 'hi' to Claire as she passed. Her heart was hammering as she climbed the stairs. Maybe she should have rung the bell, even though the front door was open. Luca might not even be in. And what if he wasn't alone? Maybe Aisling Wilson would be there, doing the splits – on his face. This was probably a really bad idea...

She tried to steady her nerves as she knocked on his door.

'Claire! Hi.' He looked surprised to see her, but she couldn't tell if he was pleased or not as he stood blinking at her in the doorway.

'Hi. Um... can I come in?'

'Yeah,' he said. He stepped back, holding the door.

She was relieved that he seemed to be alone.

'It's nice to see you.' He smiled. 'Drink?'

'Yes, please.'

'So, what brings you round?' he asked, as he handed her a glass of red wine. He waved her to the sofa and she sat. She took a sip of wine, feeling almost as nervous as the first time she had come here.

'Um... well, I was thinking about...' She wasn't sure how to start. 'Remember I said I'd pose for you... you know, naked?'

'Yeah,' he said warily, eyes narrowed.

'Well, I never did, and I thought I should arrange to... do that.'

'Right.' He looked at her quizzically, his expression torn between amusement and bewilderment.

'So, um... when would be convenient for you?'

'Look, I'm not going to hold you to that.'

'A promise is a promise,' she said.

'Well, I'm letting you off the hook.'

'Oh, okay.' She felt deflated. That hadn't got her very far! Now she needed to think of something else to say, so she could casually drop her news about Mark into the conversation. 'What have you been up to?'

'Just working mainly,' he said, waving at the easel by the window.

She stood and walked over to look at the painting.

'How about you?' he asked, as he poured himself a drink.

'Oh, just the usual – work and writing. And I've broken up with Mark,' she blurted.

'You have?' He swung round to her.

'Yeah. Well... called things off. Breaking up sounds a bit dramatic since it never really got started in the first place.'

'Who broke it off?'

'I did.' She studied his expression, but she couldn't tell what he was thinking.

'Why?'

She shrugged. 'I just didn't feel that way about him. I realised I never would.'

He frowned. 'I thought he was "the one". Mr Right.'

'What? Why would you think that?'

He sighed. 'I saw your blog post,' he admitted sheepishly. 'I didn't mean to read it, but your laptop was open the other morning and—'

'Oh!' she gasped. Oh, Christ, he'd read that the morning after they'd had sex. He probably thought she'd just written it. No wonder he'd been a bit off with her on the way home. 'But that wasn't about Mark. I mean, not really. You know my blog is a load of bullshit.'

He laughed. 'That's true. So you broke up with him on Sunday?' he asked, and finally she could read his expression: he was happy.

'Yes,' she said, smiling back at him.

'Does this mean—'

'We can be fuck buddies now!' she exclaimed.

Suddenly he became very still. '*What*?' he whispered.

'You and me, I mean. Not – not me and...' She trailed off as his face was completely transformed. She was taken aback by how angry he looked.

'*Fuck buddies*?' he snarled. 'You want me to be your *fuck buddy*?'

'Well... yeah. I thought—'

'Because that's all I'm good for, right?' He banged his glass down on the table. 'Just a meaningless fuck!'

'No, of course not! But—'

'Just while you wait for the next Mr Right to come along, of course,' he fumed. 'And then what? I'm supposed to melt into the background? Stand by and watch the girl I love walk off into the sunset with—'

'What?' Her voice came out as a stunned whisper, barely audible. 'The girl you—'

'Love. To bits,' he said, with a look of such helpless yearning Claire thought her heart might burst.

'Oh.' Tears stung the backs of her eyes.

'Yeah. So I'll pass on the whole fuck-buddy thing, if you don't mind. Look, I think you should—'

She cut him short by launching herself at him so that she knocked the breath out of him and he was forced to catch her in his arms as she wrapped her legs around his waist.

'Claire, get off me!' he said irritably, trying to detach her, but she clung on tighter.

'Oh, Luca! I love you too,' she said, kissing his face. 'So much.'

He became very still. 'What?' he breathed. He lifted her off him, planting her on the floor. 'Say that again.'

'I love you. To bits.'

'You do?' He looked at her wonderingly, and then his whole face lit up like he was having an epiphany.

'I do.' She reached up and touched the side of his face, his stubble rough against her fingers.

'How come you've never said?'

'Because I didn't want to freak you out. I knew you didn't want me ever to fall for you—'

'What on earth gave you that idea?' he said crossly.

'Er... you did. You told me I wasn't to get hung up on you, remember? It was your number-one rule.'

'Oh. Yeah.' He laughed ruefully. 'So I did. You're not the only one who's full of shit.'

'Well, I broke your stupid rule anyway.'

'Good. It *was* a stupid rule. I don't know what I was thinking.'

'Why didn't *you* say something?'

'Because you were with Mark. I thought he was what you wanted. And then I almost told you that night in the caravan,' he said. 'But the next day I saw your blog...'

'I didn't write it that morning,' she said. 'I'd written it way before that and I was just looking at it because I needed to change it.'

'Anyway, I thought Mark was The One. So I was trying to do the decent thing and walk away from the girl I love – even though it was killing me.' He shrugged. 'I was being all noble and stuff.'

She tilted her head to the side. 'Well, you can do that, if you like. Or you could be the one who gets the girl. It's up to you.'

'I've never done the decent thing in my life,' he said, pulling her into his arms. 'Why start now?'

* * *

'Mm, I've missed being here,' Claire said later, as they lay entwined in Luca's bed.

'Seriously? In this shithole?'

'No, not your flat – though I've kind of missed that too. *Here*,' she said, pressing her naked body against his and nestling into the crook of his shoulder. 'I've missed being *here*.'

Luca sighed contentedly, stroking her back. 'Claire, can I ask you something?'

'Yeah?'

'Did you really come over here tonight to arrange to pose naked for me?'

'Um... no,' she admitted.

'I thought it seemed a bit random.'

'But I will,' she said, drawing away from him. 'A promise is a promise.' She shook off the covers and stood on the bed, looking down at him. 'So,' she said spreading her arms to encompass the room, 'where do you want me?'

She didn't squirm even a little bit as Luca's eyes raked slowly over her body. Then he reached up and grabbed her wrist, yanking her back down beside him. 'Here,' he said, wrapping his arms around her. 'I want you here.'

She nuzzled his chest, smiling as he bent to kiss her. 'Here is good.'

* * *

MORE FROM CLODAGH MURPHY

The next charming, hilarious, relatable read from bestseller Clodagh Murphy is available to order now here:

https://mybook.to/ClodaghMurphyNewBackAd

ACKNOWLEDGEMENTS

Huge thanks to my brilliant editor Rachel Faulkner-Willcocks and everyone at Boldwood Books for dusting off Claire and Luca's story and giving it a new lease of life. I'm so excited to have this novel embarking on a new journey and I know it couldn't be in better hands.

Special thanks also to Conor Kostick and the Irish Writers Union for their support and advocacy, which helped to make this publication possible.

Practice Makes Perfect began life many moons ago as *Some Girls Do*, and I'm eternally grateful to everyone who championed the book the first time around or helped in some way with the writing of it. Thanks as ever to:

Property wiz Louise Clark for lending me the house in Dalkey, which not only provided the perfect bolthole for writing much of the book but also made its way into the story, sparking the inspiration for Luca's family home.

The lovely and supremely talented artist Gina McKenna Burns for letting me follow her around and pick her painterly brain.

Everyone who's spread the word and shared the love along the way, especially my friend and hugely accomplished fellow author Claire Allan who's been such a great cheerleader for this novel from the start.

Finally, to readers old and new – thank you all.

ABOUT THE AUTHOR

Clodagh Murphy is an Irish author of romantic comedy novels. After more jobs than she can remember, she's now a full-time writer, the job she's been training for all her life. She lives in Dublin with a sibling and a cat and writes in a cabin in the garden.

Download your exclusive bonus content from Clodagh Murphy here:

Visit Clodagh's website: www.clodaghmurphy.com

Follow Clodagh on social media here:

facebook.com/clodaghmurphyauthor
instagram.com/clodaghmurphybooks
bookbub.com/authors/clodagh-murphy

ALSO BY CLODAGH MURPHY

A Merry Irish Christmas

Practice Makes Perfect

Boldwood
EVER AFTER
xoxo

JOIN BOLDWOOD'S **ROMANCE COMMUNITY** FOR SWEET AND SPICY BOOK RECS WITH ALL YOUR FAVOURITE TROPES!

SIGN UP TO OUR NEWSLETTER

HTTPS://BIT.LY/BOLDWOODEVERAFTER

Boldwood

Boldwood Books is an award-winning fiction publishing company seeking out the best stories from around the world.

Find out more at www.boldwoodbooks.com

Join our reader community for brilliant books, competitions and offers!

Follow us
@BoldwoodBooks
@TheBoldBookClub

Sign up to our weekly deals newsletter

https://bit.ly/BoldwoodBNewsletter

www.ingramcontent.com/pod-product-compliance
Lightning Source LLC
Chambersburg PA
CBHW021140160426
43194CB00007B/642